Figure of Eight

by

Anna Hyndman Lahna & Graeme Milne

authorHOUSE®

AuthorHouse™ UK Ltd.
500 Avebury Boulevard
Central Milton Keynes, MK9 2BE
www.authorhouse.co.uk
Phone: 08001974150

© 2010 Anna Hyndman Lahna & Graeme Milne. All rights reserved.

No part of this book may be reproduced, stored in a retrieval system, or transmitted by any means without the written permission of the author.

First published by AuthorHouse 3/8/2010

ISBN: 978-1-4490-6638-3 (sc)

This book is printed on acid-free paper.

Thank you to our parents, families and all of you from The Old Monk, you know who you are!

CHAPTER 1

I woke up feeling blue. I knew old man Whin had gone. I must have been aware of it all night. How could I forget something so important? I'm sure my dreams had been filled with images that would haunt me for days. It still stung though, as realization dawned on me. I felt almost as raw as when I first heard. I was going to miss him. I was going to miss him a lot. We'd seen some good times, old Whin and I. I could spend hours thinking about the funny things we had seen, the laughs we'd had. There had been tears but no one wants to remember those, not on a day like today. Today was the funeral and I'd be there, of course. I had prepared myself for it and for the past week this feeling of closure drew nearer and nearer. I still felt bloody sad though. Whin would be cross with me. He understood sadness, like anyone, actually, possibly more than anyone but he only allowed himself to see the positive side. That must've been tough, considering the unfortunate things he had experienced. Today I was going to show him. I wasn't going to disappoint him. I would arrive at the church, give him the best send off I could and then join the others at The Cock Inn, for the wake.

The wake is always the best and the worst part of the day, I find. There is relief in the air, that the nasty side has been taken care of and then there's amusement at the funny anecdotes that are passed around, remembering the most hilarious highlights of the deceased's life. I usually find that younger attendees feel guilty that a good time is being had by all and that misery should prevail. The older folk are usually thinking, lucky bastard, wish it had been me! They would be those with the impaired vision, colostomy bags and appointments for double hip replacements. All deaths are sad but I suppose it depends on how the person died and more importantly what age they had reached as to the intensity of loss and pain at a funeral. Anyone who was an octogenarian or older deserves a huge round of applause, no, sod that, a bloody standing ovation for having made it. Sad to see them go but Jesus, what a fucking miracle. Younger than that but still over 50, is still a major achievement in my eyes but there's definitely a sense of failure. There's a sense of 'bugger', a bit like losing the egg and spoon race when you and your dad have been practising for weeks. Younger still but old enough to vote is a complete waste and from infancy is just desperate.

Old Whin though, he had lived a bit, that's for sure. For a smoker, eighty-seven was fantastic. To some, that's an inspiration. The number of times I'd heard that smoking and drinking must be good for you, because meat and fish are smoked to keep longer and vegetables are pickled, you'd think it were true! It was an odd motto to live by, but hey, these were the old boys at the pub, so if they thought it, who was I to argue?

Determined to compose myself before the car arrived, I searched for the time. An hour to go till it all kicked off. That's not too bad. I can cope with that. I'm used to hanging around. That's really all I ever do. Apart from that though I still seem to have people needing me. I feel I share so many secrets.

The doorbell went and suddenly it was pandemonium. The silent grief was gone and was replaced by a type of excitement. Perhaps it was the knowledge that it was the beginning of the end. Things had to be done and done properly. It felt as though everyone were terribly pleased to do these things in order to take their mind off the enormity of it all.

I travelled in the main car, of course. The journey wasn't long but it only seemed fitting that the decent thing was done. Old Whin would have laughed at the pomp and circumstance we had put on, on his behalf but underneath it all, he would have been as pleased as punch although possibly very slightly embarrassed that we had thought so much of him. It may have even brought a tear to his eye. He wasn't really a sentimental old man but he had had his moments.

The car almost floated down the road. We drove so slowly that the short walk to the church actually took 10 minutes more to drive. The flowers in the Black Maria up in front spelt out Whin in white chrysanthemums and as we drove smoothly past the Post Office, the people in the street just stared, perhaps only just discovering that the biggest character of their neighbourhood had died.

Pulling alongside the coffin-bearing hearse, the driver, clad in the typical sombre black uniform and hat, opened the door for us and respectfully kept quiet and slightly bowed his head whilst we disembarked. It wasn't warm, not like the day before he died. It was almost as if the day was grieving too. It was windy, unusually so for September. Actually it was more gusty. I would have to work hard today. All I could hear was the crunching of gravel as three other cars pulled up behind us. It all looked so very strange. Everyone looked so awkward and no one made eye contact. Nervous coughs broke the silence and the occasional rattling of coins as men dug their hands deep into their trouser pockets. What is it with men and rustling around in their pockets?!

I had never been inside this church, in fact I don't really remember being inside any church. It's just not the sort of place that I ever get taken to. This one was cold and dark, not particularly pretty, quite functional though. More of a utilitarian sort of church, I guess. The odd smell hit me as soon as I entered the building. I felt very uneasy and just wanted the day to be over. To be honest it was just the service I was dreading. Once we all got to the pub and started drinking, I would be needed and things would almost return to normal.

I heard the first sob as the coffin was brought down the aisle. I don't know who started it but after that the occupants of the first front rows seemed inconsolable. One lady, who I had not met before gave a beautiful, heartfelt message of thanks to Whin, for his love and companionship. I wondered if she had been Whin's sister. I did remember him talking about family, years before, although I wasn't really sure if he had ever been married. This eulogy was followed by an old man, who I could only assume was Whin's brother. He looked similar, although he had a lot of white facial hair and a bit of a stoop. He too gave an emotional speech and at one point had to pause, as he seemed too overwhelmed to continue. It suddenly dawned on me that I knew none of his family and only a handful of his friends. Looking around the congregation I spotted perhaps five people I recognised. Add to that the landlord at the Cock Inn and the total was a measly six! I had spent all day, every day with Whin for as long as I could remember and I felt sickened at how little I really knew about the man. At that point, ignoring the rest of the service, I made a vow that during the wake, I would listen intently to the ramblings of his nearest and dearest and glean some information. I promised to myself that I would retain all of these facts. I'm not sure why. I just felt a desperate need to hold onto something of the man that had been part of my life for so long.

The service was coming to a close and as the coffin was taken back out of the church doors, the guests followed, pew by pew. We took a short walk to the cemetery and all gathered around a big deep hole in the lawn. Although the earth was dry and hard, thoughtful gravediggers had placed wooden planks around the edge. The vicar appeared and with a black book in hand, uttered the final words as the coffin was lowered into the ground. The two speakers in the church clung to each other, their shoulders convulsing with sorrow.

I made my way over to a shaded grave. It was good to view the mourners from a distance. I felt unconnected and from here I could view the proceedings and felt I was not in the way. As I stared at the events, I saw one of the lamenters leave the graveside and trot over.

'All right Bert?' he muttered nodding his head questioningly. Bert nodded back without saying anything. Nothing needed to be said. We all felt the same, sheer sadness at losing such a good mate. I recognised the bloke sitting with us. I think he worked with Whin years back. I'm sure he had been in the Cock Inn a few times in the past. I just couldn't remember his name though.

'Going to the Cock, Dan?'

Arhh yes Dan. Danny Brayfield. It felt good to put a name to the face. This was the start of my promise to Whin. I would learn as much about each of his loved ones and thereby get to know more about him.

'Yeah, of course'. Dan looked put out that Bert should even need to ask.

'I just can't believe he's gone', Bert muttered as he bowed his head and looked forlornly at his shoes. 'It's just such a shock. I'd been talking to him only the day before he..he..' Bert broke off. It seemed ridiculous to point out the obvious. He was finding it hard to keep his emotions in check and talking really wasn't helping. Well, talking about poor old Whin wasn't helping. Perhaps a totally random and unconnected conversation would take his mind off this sad sad day.

Dan sighed deeply and said 'Aye, I know what you mean. I hadn't seen him for a bit but you just knew it would take just a pint at The Cock and it would be like time had melted'. Dan looked at Bert and immediately felt uncomfortable. He realised that Bert didn't really want to talk about it and to be honest neither did he. What can you say? It's such a personal thing, grief. Everyone has to deal with it in their own way. He pulled out his fags. On opening the new packet of B&H, he offered one to Bert.

Bert shook his head. 'Haven't smoked in years. Not good for your health apparently' he smirked. 'Here, take this'. He pulled me out of his pocket and handed me over to Dan. 'Old Whin won't need this now and I won't have a use for it. It would be good to keep it in the gang'.

Bert smiled as he looked at me. That smile could tell a few stories and I wanted to know them all. 'Blimey Old Whin's clipper'. He's had this old thing for years. Ever faithful! Cheers Bert. I shall take good care of it.'

Dan lit his cigarette and slipped me into his pocket. For a moment he held onto me, almost as if I felt like part of Whin. I was relieved.

I knew I'd be no use to Bert and admittedly I had been a bit anxious that I would be made redundant. This came as perfect news and I felt elation for the first time since Whin's death.

Dan stood smoking, silently. Both men just watched the service and the small throng of people. The sky was heavy with dark clouds and rain threatened any minute. I supposed that pretty much summed up the general mood of the day.

As Dan stubbed out his fag on the gravestone, he tried to make out the details of the faded inscription. All that was legible now was the name Heather and the year 1787. How depressing. No one living today would remember her. No one alive would have any idea what kind of person she was, what made her laugh. She may well have been a beauty with the kindest heart or just as easily been an absolutely bitch and hell to live with. Now though, she was six feet under and totally alone. How easily all our lives are forgotten. I would hate to think that one day Whin would be forgotten.

The wind picked up and both Dan and Bert pulled their inadequate jackets tighter around them, almost in perfect unison. They stood up instinctively knowing that the other just wanted to get to the pub and start drinking to the memory of their dear old friend.

The two men lumbered slowly towards a blue Mondeo, when Dan said 'Forget the hearse Bert, I'll give you a lift to the pub.'

Dan started up the engine and Bert looked around to see where his fellow mourners were. Spotting some in the distance making their way from the churchyard, he felt comforted that they weren't the first to leave. In some respects I understood how Bert felt. It just seemed plain wrong to leave Whin all alone in a dark hole. He should be going down the pub with us all. Sitting up at the bar, pint in front of him, ashtray to the side, fag in one hand and me, his faithful old clipper in the other being twiddled with!

'Yeah, sure' Bert said. 'Cheers mate'. He jumped in and let out a big sigh. It was the kind of sigh that had been brewing all day. A sigh of mixed emotions; relief, sadness and a kind of vague concern as to which of the old gang would be next.

We swung into the small car park at the rear of the Cock Inn and I caught Dan staring at me whilst Bert reversed into a slot in the corner. What was he thinking about? What were all the stories he knew that would shed more light on Whin's life?

It looked like we were the first to arrive. That was fine. I don't think any of the three of us had a problem with that. The sooner the celebrations commenced the better we would all feel. We needed to get stuck in. A few pints, a few tales of Whin and the pain would subside a little. Well, that's what we were all hoping.

Opening the familiar wooden door, we noticed that a black banner had been hung over the bar counter. In huge white letters it spelt 'We will miss you'. It was probably left over from someone leaving the neighbourhood and hosting a party at the pub. That really didn't matter, it summed it all up perfectly.

Geoff, the Landlord, came out from the kitchen into the bar and nodded at us. I assume he felt that his time would be better spent preparing his pub in readiness for the afternoon's event than attending the funeral. I could see that round the corner, near the fireplace, was a table already laden with food. Food typically associated with wakes. Uninspiring food that does its job. Egg mayonnaise triangular sandwiches, chicken drumsticks and if we were really lucky there might be a pot of potato salad, home made by Geoff's wife Pam. Each plate was covered in cling film, waiting for all the guests to arrive. It would then seem so much fresher and with no curls on the sandwiches, it wouldn't feel as though it had sat there since 7am. Of course it also served as a deterrent to the white fluffy rather smarmy pub cat called Sid. He usually twirled his way round the legs of the diners who were enjoying one of Pam's generous Sunday roasts. He would turn on the charm with anyone who had food and considering he was fairly successful, he was not a fat animal. Today though, Sid was nowhere to be seen. This was unusual in itself as he was not really an outdoor cat and much preferred the home comforts of a crackling fire and the odd stroke from the punters.

Geoff automatically drew two pints and placed them on the bar counter. He didn't need them to order, he knew exactly how the men felt and exactly what they needed. Both mourners nodded in appreciation and took sips before they even sat down. They made their way over to a table not far from the door. The wanted to show their respects for Whin but at the same time they appreciated that they were not family and didn't even really know many of the others gathered today in the church. Sitting right here was perfect.

One by one the guests arrived and after 4 or 5 had made their way in, the rain came down torrentially. The following people were soaked after running the short distance from the car park.

'Glad it held off until after the service' Dan said. 'I think we would have all felt even worse'.

'You're not wrong there', Bert agreed.

Silence fell again as both the men watched and searched for recognisable faces.

As the pub filled up, the tension lifted. The drinks were going down well and the atmosphere was improving minute by minute. It was obvious that it wasn't going to be party of the year but it felt good that people were starting to feel more like celebrating Whin's life rather than mourning his departure.

I have always felt that being alone is the best way to mourn the loss of a loved one but being together is the perfect way to celebrate their existence. I could hear the noise level increasing and intermittently a laugh could be distinguished. Whin's old stories had started then. That was good.

A younger lady, possibly in her mid forties came over to the table and kissed Bert and Dan on their cheeks before sitting herself down on the spare seat. She pulled off her black gloves slowly, removing a finger at a time. Both men seemed mesmerised by this and neither of them spoke.

'I'll have a Vodka and Diet Coke, there's a love Dan,' she said confidently.

'Right-O Fiona', Dan muttered as he stood up and headed off to the bar.

'So,' Fiona casually began whilst also folding her arms over her ample bosom. 'You ok then Bert?' she finally added.

'Not too bad. Mustn't complain.' Why do older people always say that? 'What about you?' Bert added awkwardly.

'Well it is a shock to be back here but of course I wouldn't have let the old boy down. He deserved a decent send off, did old Whin. Mind you, took me 3 hours this morning. Usually it only takes 45 minutes! The traffic was horrendous.'

It dawned on me at that point who she was. Fiona was Whin's neice. I had heard about her. She seemed a nice enough lass but her reputation was rather meaty! She talked for England, never said no to Vodka and was very rarely without male company. The male company did seem to change as often as her knickers but good on her. I knew was she worked in the banking world but that and the rumours of her exploits were all I really knew of her. I was trying to second-guess that the white haired speaker in the church was her father. I could be wrong. Whin had never really talked about his family that much. There may have been many references that I just hadn't picked up on. Now, though, I was going to listen intently and try and piece it all together.

Dan came back from the bar, armed with two more pints and a vodka for Fiona. Fiona nattered on and I could see that Bert and Dan were finding it difficult to keep up. Their eyes kept glazing over and it pretty obvious, well to me anyhow, that they were deep in thought. Thoughts a thousand miles away. Thoughts of how they had come to meet Whin. Both of the men had known him a long time but had met him in very different circumstances. I hadn't been with Whin then. I didn't know the full stories, although parts of their friendship had been reminisced over the years. It made me think about the early years with Whin and I. It was a while ago now but just thinking about it made me smile.

• •

FLASHBACK

• •

I was bought at over the counter at an everyday convenience store, you know like 7-11, something like that.

Whin lit up as soon as we left the shop and he held me in his hand for a while. It was almost as though having me there was a comfort to him. I was elated. This was going to be such an exciting adventure. I'd heard lots about what to expect but now this was real. I belonged to someone.

It was summer and very hot. All the kids were out on bikes and skates, making the most of the sun and the school holidays. The streets were packed with people and everyone seemed so happy. Maybe though it was just time making it feel that way. In contrast though, Whin seemed so down. There were no smiles from him and when passers-by greeted him, he just nodded in acknowledgement but still no smile. We made our way along the busy main road and headed towards a quieter, more suburban street. I was thinking that maybe we were going home, back to Whin's but I was wrong. We made out way to a park and sat on a bench in the shade. I was still in Whin's hand and as he chain-smoked, I tried to comprehend what on earth could possibly be the reason for such sadness. A day like today was enough to warm anyone's cockles. But with no one for him to talk to, it was unlikely I was going to get any answers just yet.

The afternoon passed slowly. The day seemed to get hotter before eventually the light began to fade gradually and the air had cooled a little. Families had packed up their belongings and made their way out of the park. Whin did not seem to be considering moving. He still sat on the bench, gazing into the distance, his mind a million miles away. Occasionally he pulled out his cigarettes and lit one. I noticed that his stout fingers were stained a deep yellow brown. They were nicotine stains so it was obvious he was a heavy smoker and today was not just a one off.

Suddenly Whin jumped up and briskly walked towards the park entrance. He stuffed me and the fags in his shirt pocket. The huge wrought iron gates were still open as we trotted out back towards the main shopping street. There were plenty of people about but gone were the children and the mums with prams.

We walked down the High Street, turned left at the traffic lights and on down the hill. Lights were coming on in the homes now so I was guessing it was about 8pm or there abouts. Ahead of us I could see a traditional pub. A quaint village style pub, you know with low ceilings, a crackling fire and huge Sunday roasts. My heart leaped as we boldly walked straight up to the wooden door and up to the bar. This was more like it, lots to see and loads to hear.

Whin sighed deeply as he sat at the bar counter. 'Pint please Geoff' he ordered as he removed his fags and me from his shirt pocket. Ah well, he was a local then. Knowing the name of the Landlord is always a giveaway.

'You alright Whin?', came Geoff's response. 'You look a bit pale'.

'Yeah, I'll get over it', replied Whin rubbing his forehead. 'Bit of a shit day Geoff, but nothing that time won't heal'.

'Want me to leave you alone?' Geoff kindly volunteered.

'No', said Whin 'but I could murder one of Pam's cheese and pickle sandwiches'.

'Coming right up' said Geoff as he leaned in slightly. 'Put a smile on your face though or Pam will be dragging it out of you'

Whin smirked slightly and brought his pint to his lips and downed about a quarter of it before resting it back on the counter. He lit up another cigarette and looked around the room. I wasn't sure what day of the week it was but if it was a weekend, it was very very quiet. There were a couple of old boys at a table, not really saying much but enjoying each other's company. Three young lads and a pretty brunette were standing at the bar. They all seemed keen on her and she looked like she was enjoying the attention. The lads were all wearing jeans, which had seen better days and my guess that each of them were in the construction industry and they had come in to down a couple of beers before heading home to their respective missus.

Geoff walked round the bar to the young lass and pulled her aside gently. From here nothing could be heard of their conversation, more's the pity, but as the girl's eyes lost their twinkle and stared firmly at the floor, it seemed to me that she was being told off. I guessed that the brunette was Geoff's daughter and when I saw her walking back sullenly behind the bar and upstairs, I realised that I had been correct.

A couple perhaps in their mid 50's were sat by the fire, which of course was not lit in this heat. I surmised that this must be a new relationship as their conversation was very animated. They were not a couple that had spent 30 years together. It was either an affair or the beginning of a blossoming relationship. Their body language was screaming 'passion' and they were still very much at that 'tactile' stage.

Whin downed some more of his pint and by the time Pam brought the sandwich over, he had drained his glass. 'Same again, poppet?' she asked.

'Cheers Pam'. Whin wasted no time in getting to grips with his huge doorstep crusty bread sandwich. He gave her a wink and tried to look as happy as he normally did.
Pam bent over the counter and said gently 'You ok darling? You seem a bit pale.' She leant her elbows on the bar and rested her head in her

hands. 'You haven't been in for a few days'. It didn't look like she was going to leave him in peace and he knew he wasn't going to get away with passing it off as a cold.

'I'm ok Pam. Honestly. I just had some bad news. It just gets to you when they are so small'.

'Oh, you poor love'. She drew another beer and handed it over to him. 'Here, have this on the house'. She continued to stand over him but decided against questioning him any further.

'Cheers', he said as he supped his free beer. 'That sandwich was great'.

'Want another one? She asked temptingly.
'No thanks Pam. That just did the trick'.

She left him to it but as she made her way back into the kitchen, she pulled Geoff aside. He started to moan about Claire, from what I could work out, that was the pretty young girl, but Pam interrupted him. She nodded towards Whin, who was concentrating on his drink and said "I'm a bit worried about him, Geoff. He seems so down. I'm not really sure what's happened but he mentioned some bad news of a little'un. See if you can't get it out of him. These things need to be talked about." She started to walk away but added 'Don't worry, I'll have a chat with Claire.

Geoff sighed and carried on filling up the box of pork scratchings for under the counter. What on earth was he meant to do? Was he a grief councillor? Mind you that seemed to be the biggest part of being a landlord. Your advice was always sought.

Whin continued with his pint and lit numerous cigarettes. I felt so sorry for the man. I could almost feel his pain. He had a kind face. I bet his eyes twinkled when they laughed and his tanned, lined face could tell a few stories. In his stockinged feet, I reckon he checked in at 5 feet 9 and although he wasn't fat, he was a chubby man. His body said chubby but his face said gaunt. That didn't seem to fit. I suppose grief does that to you. His face did look paler than his hairy arms and hands.

Geoff trotted up to him and said 'I saw Bert in here the other day' said he's moving back.' He rolled his eyes and continued 'Oh Lord, what have I done to deserve the two of you back in the bar together?' Geoff smiled, making it clear that he was overjoyed at the prospect. Two of his favourite punters back as regulars. They were mates. Now if only the others would come back, that would be hysterical!

Whin recognised Geoff's facial expressions as he was pondering the possibilities of reuniting the old gang. 'Blimey Geoff, you'll have your work cut out if you want to get everyone together again'. His brief smile answered Geoff's unasked question. He would do exactly that. He would get as many of the old mob assembled. If that's what Whin needed then that's what he would do for his old friend.

Geoff trotted off to the back of the bar, where the old-fashioned dial telephone sat. 'A couple of calls, that's all it would take', he thought. 'If I call Danny and Bert, they can contact the remaining blokes'. He smiled and lifted the receiver. Dan's number went straight to answer phone but Geoff left a message, explaining his plan and asked if he could pass it on.

Bert's number was engaged so he made a mental note to call later. Walking back to the bar, he suddenly remembered the last time all the gang had been together. A grimace tore across his face.

• •

FLASHBACK

• •

CHAPTER 2

The wake was fully underway now and all the attendees were either half cut or well on their way. I could see the likes of Bert and Dan were possibly finding this more difficult than family. They were used to sitting in this pub, drinking themselves under the table, in fact it felt just like any other day apart from the stark reminder that Whin wasn't with them. That detail tore into them at the end of each conversation. Whin had a habit of either punctuating the change of topic with a punch line or a relevant interesting fact.

I watched the pub crowd divide into three groups; there were the family most of whom had not even been that close to Whin but felt a sense of duty. Then there were the friends who had been an important part of his life, who going to miss him dearly. Then there were the regulars who were in the pub, felt a little guilty as they had known Whin by sight but his departure would have no effect on lives whatsoever.

The more the alcohol flowed, the less sense the mourners were talking. In jokes were being bantered around and half the time, I had no idea what was going on. Usually I liked nothing more than listening in to drunken recounts of bygone days but right now I was on a mission and it was all very frustrating. I was beginning to give up on the whole idea of finding out more of Whin and his life until one of the regulars pushed past a very intoxicated mourner on his way to the toilets at the back of the pub. The volume of booze had taken effect and believing his masculinity and pride were at stake, the mourner, whose face I recognised but whose name I had totally forgotten, decided to shout at the rudeness of this man. The regular, although nowhere near as inebriated as his opponent snapped his head around and told the guy to 'fuck off'. He was a rough looking man, possibly in his mid thirties. Dressed in an England t-shirt and trainers with very little hair, he looked just the sort you would avoid at all costs, in a normal sober state of mind. The mourner, however, was taking no such notice and shouted obscenities back. Brave, possibly, stupid, definitely. The younger man snarled and shouted within an inch of his face, spittle flying from his mouth. He shoved the older man hard and he fell back against the table that we were sat at. Dan, Bert and Fiona all jumped to their feet, mainly to avoid the wash of alcohol that flew onto the floor. In the midst of all the commotion, I soared across the room and hit the back wall with a thud.

The brawl was enough to bring a close to the celebrations and Geoff decided to call time. There was disappointment written over the faces of most of the customers, as they had truly believed that if an occasion like this wouldn't get Geoff to permit a lock-in then nothing would. A few looked genuinely relived. These were mostly the family members who had done their duty but were wondering how they could make their excuses and get on with their lives.

For the next thirty minutes, Geoff and Pam coaxed people to finish their drinks and leave the building. Bert and Dan were the last to leave. Frustrated that the evening had not gone as planned and had ended on a sour note, they supped their pints incredibly slowly. Pam was not taking any of their nonsense and threatened to take the glasses away so both men downed their drinks. As they were exiting, Dan realised that the lighter was missing. Me!! He tried turning back and pleading with Geoff to allow him to search for me. Geoff thought it was just another excuse to stay behind and roughly pushed him into the night. The day had been difficult enough without having to deal with drunken scraps and extended hours.

I could hear the fracas outside although the stone walls were very thick, one of the side windows had been opened just to ventilate the smoky bar. 'Damn' I thought. I just had to pray that Geoff would find me in the morning and would realise Dan had been speaking the truth and I would be handed back.

I settled down to a lonely night in the corner.

CHAPTER 3

The next thing I knew, Verity the cleaner had swiped me from the floor and popped me in her pocket in one swoop. Alarmed at first but confident that I would be handed back into the Lost Property box for Dan to claim me later, I relaxed and enjoyed the world from a different perspective.

Verity was amusing to watch. Her bright bleached hair and shameful roots along with her constant mumbling made Verity the character we all knew and loved. On many an occasion Whin had bumped into Verity, often as she was late finishing her shift at the pub whilst Whin was extremely early in arriving for his first pint. She had probably been a beauty in her day, before the stress of her unruly offspring or her errant husband had affected her skin, eyebags and physique.

I had heard a lot of the rumours about Darren, her eldest, and her most worrisome child. He seemed to have been inside more than anyone else I'd heard of and he was still only 22! Or thereabouts. This morning Verity seemed to be particularly upset about something and her mumbling almost sounded threatening. Knowing that Verity was all mouth and no trousers, I wasn't in the least bit frightened. She had something on her chest and if I listened carefully enough I just might find out what her problem was. Not that I could do anything about it but since Whin's departure, my curiosity had grown by the second. I was hungry for information, details of people's lives. I wanted to know secrets and lies and what connected people to others. I suppose the key to my gossip thirst was due to living with Whin all that time, although for the life of me I couldn't really see the connection.

Relaxed now, although listening intently, I enjoyed the next hour or so, close to Verity and her foul smelling cleaning jacket. She was very thorough and I was impressed at how she could have easily cut corners in her work but was honest enough to clear up the unseen corners of the pub, seemingly at her own expense. Her mumbling grew clearer the nearer we got to her finishing her chores. I wasn't too sure who Reg was, probably her husband, but it seemed the prodigal spouse had returned and was causing her more anxiety than when he had gone AWOL. 'That dirty bitch', I presumed was possibly the woman who had enticed Reg away. It appeared that she was having a child with Reg although Reg didn't seem too keen on this idea and had returned to his wife's bosom for protection. Verity's main problem looked as if 'that dirty bitch' was hassling her for early maintenance and she really didn't see the best way forward.

Poor love. What an awful triangle. Delighted, I'm sure by the return of her man, her usually painful existence had increased to a level where she no longer knew the best course of action. Not dissimilar an experience to possibly nearly every human on earth at some time in their life. Should she kick Reg out of the house and continue her single mother journey? This had its benefits. As hard as it would be to make ends meet and keep her sons on the straight and narrow single-handedly, at least the unexpected twists and turns of life would be kept to a minimum, save those of her boys' exploits. On the other hand, having another very large mouth to feed and the staving off of money hungry scorned ex-lovers would be a small price to pay if Reg could keep her boys out of trouble permanently. Well perhaps permanently would be asking too much but a year would be a good start.

My mind was reeling. This was just one morning in the life of Verity. I had no idea how she coped with this constant pressure. I didn't know how many other jobs she held down as well as the pub cleaning but I was pretty certain that she had very little time to herself. I began hypothesising by wondering what she did for fun. I imagined that Bingo might feature heavily in her weekly treats but other than that I felt she had tension filled days punctuated by pain and sadness.

Verity was known around the town as a slogger. She could be trusted and although sometimes she came across as a little judgemental, she was harsher on her own family than anyone else's. I wondered what time she finished her shift and when she would tell Geoff that she had found me. I was surprised to find myself saddened that I wouldn't hear the end of her dilemma. That I wouldn't be around to find out what conclusion she had reached and what the outcome would be. Still I had work to do and finding out all about Whin, was my objective and purpose. I couldn't be derailed by small time gossip.

The mumblings continued and the vacuum cleaner still hummed. It seemed to go on for an age. I was sure that this pub was immaculate by now. Eventually though Verity came to a standstill. She wasn't even out of puff! She sat on a stool at the bar and pulled out a packet of Richmonds and lit it. Exhaling and sighing at the same time, I realised that Verity dealt with the turmoil in her life by working through it. Polishing, hovering and scrubbing were her very own counselling sessions. From the bar, I looked at the woman from a new angle. I knew I shouldn't feel pity for her but it was difficult not to. She was about mid forties and looked about 60! The strains of her existence were etched quite clearly on her face. She was by no means large but her bad posture created an illusion of sagginess. The laughter lines were too deep to be considered attractive and the years of worry and sleepless nights had forced dark circles under her eyes to remain permanently. Deeply inhaling her cigarette, she studied her cheap chipped nail varnish. Almost amused at the state of them, she smiled and at that point I believed she had made a decision. Too bad I wasn't going to be around to find out. Surely now she would hand me over the Geoff, and I could just wait until Dan returned to collect me.

Verity slipped from the barstool and put the cleaning equipment back into the cupboard behind the bar. She grabbed her tatty fake leather bag and trotted towards the door. I began to panic. She had forgotten to hand me in. Suddenly she stopped and turned. She hurried back behind the bar and called up the dark stairwell to the apartment above. "Geoff, GEOFF" she repeated. "Any chance on a sub for the wages love?"

Thudding on the steps meant that Geoff had heard her plea and was coming down. "Verity, you finished already? Now what's all this about a sub?"

"Look Geoff, I have some stuff to sort out tonight and I could really do with a sub to tie me over?" She asked earnestly.

Geoff examined her face and rolled his eyes. "Go on then, but just don't make a habit of this".

To his surprise Verity leapt over and kissed him, on the lips!! "Verity!" he exclaimed. "What on earth was that for?"

"You're a star, " she grinned. She took the notes that Geoff had briefly counted from the till and stuffed them in her bag. "See you tomorrow, Geoff," she said breezily and waltzed out of the pub.

For a moment I was stunned. I was incredibly curious to know what she was up to so fleetingly I forgot that I hadn't been reported and I was on my way home with Verity instead of waiting for Dan.

Oh well, maybe tomorrow when we go back to the pub, Geoff will recognise me and will put me aside for Dan.

The bus journey was fairly unpleasant. I wasn't a good passenger on public transport. Nothing to do with being too snobbish, it was just the lurching round corners and the throbbing of the large engines made me feel very motion sick. Cars were one thing but buses were a nightmare for me. Fortunately though, the journey was reasonably short. As Verity stood to wait for the next stop, I looked out of the window. The street looked ok. The houses were modern and bland but I'd seen worse, much worse. I guessed it was on some kind of estate as the houses looked pretty identical. The England flags hanging out of windows gave me an indication of the sort of people I would be likely to meet but all the same I was quite excited. I was going to get a chance to meet the people in Verity's life that gave her so much pain. Plus hopefully I would also get to find out her decision.

The house was almost opposite the bus stop. It wasn't a proper bus stop, it didn't have a bench and a covering in case of rain. It was just a simple pole with a timetable attached half way down and a sign at the top indicating that the no.3, no.17 and no.101 stopped here. More interested in the house and its occupants, I turned my gaze towards the front door. There were no mattresses or motorbike parts in the front garden but I was still surprised to see how untidy it was. From what I had seen at the pub, I was expecting a spotless home too. Still I shouldn't be so judgemental, I was sure that the interior wouldn't let me down.

My heart sank though when we finally entered the house. Although the carpets were clean and it was obvious that great care had been taken to dust and polish what she could, the paint work was flaking and the general appearance was tatty. Verity went straight into the kitchen at the end of the hall and put the kettle on. A few dirty cups sat on the work surface but other than a few crumbs, the room was clean. I had guessed that her sons had been up and helped themselves without any consideration for her. Verity collected the cups and put them straight into the washing up bowl. Verity gazed out of the window onto the small weed ridden patio behind the house. A dilapidated shed sat at the side and a little square of lawn lay to the far end. Nothing else was in the garden save a carousel style washing line. It was obvious that apart from perhaps drying a few clothes, the garden was never used.

The kettle boiled and the noise brought Verity out of her trance. She concentrated on preparing her cup of tea and then sat in the lounge on a moss green velour sofa. There was no noise in the house so assumed that she was alone. I was wrong though. After a few minutes, I could hear footsteps on the landing and a flushing of the toilet. Crashing down the stairs came a large man wearing nothing but a pair of greyish white boxer shorts with Lover Man emblazoned all over them. Judging the man's age to be in his late forties, I assumed this was the husband causing all the trouble. Without a word, the man stumbled over to the matching armchair and collapsed. Verity jumped up almost immediately and gently asked "Cup of tea Reg?" The man grunted in response and leaned out to grab the remote control for the TV.

Verity toodled off to the kitchen to grab another clean cup. Reaching up to the cupboard she added "What do you fancy for breakfast?"

I could see Reg from my position in Verity's house-coat pocket and could see that whilst he shouted back "Usual please love", he was also picking his nose and wiping the contents on the side of the armchair. How vile! How on earth could Verity and 'that dirty bitch' be fighting over this man? How was he a prize?

I could hear Verity tutting. Perhaps she knew exactly what that disgusting man was doing. Maybe she was just thinking how arrogant he was expecting her to prepare a full fry up after the nonsense that had gone on. Verity didn't speak out aloud, no mumblings so I had no idea what was going through her mind.

In no time at all, the delicious smells from the stove meant that Reg's breakfast was ready and as Verity laid the small table in the kitchen, Reg hauled his lardy frame into the room, aware that his presence was now required. "Cheers love" Reg beamed as he rubbed his hands and sat at the two-seater table. "You not eating?" he asked. He couldn't give a monkeys whether Verity was eating or not, it just seemed the best thing to say.

Verity shook her head slowly and grimaced. All that grease and fat made her feel quite queasy. She watched her husband devour the bacon, eggs and fried bread and turned away in disgust. She opened the door onto the backyard and stood outside in the sunshine. It was cool but sunny, just how she liked it. She pulled her pack of Richmonds out and lit up. Her breakfast at 6am had consisted of a small bowl of 'No-Frills' cornflakes. She would start thinking about making herself a small marmite sandwich a bit later but the stench in the kitchen was more than she could stomach.

Even in the garden, she could hear Reg munching through his enormous fry up but she was concentrating on something else. Maybe she was making plans for the future. From what I had seen so far of Verity's life, I came to the conclusion that her best choice would be to leave the fat lardy pig in the kitchen to look after the wayward boys by himself. Lord only knows what state they would get themselves into but at least the poor woman would be free. I knew deep down it wasn't really that simple and that it was very, very rare for mothers to walk out on their children, even if they were as bad as her brood. A loud slam of the front door indicated that one of the boys had returned from a morning of crime, probably.

"Oi, keep it down", Reg bellowed from his flimsy kitchen chair. A thunderous banging up the stairs was the only response. "Bleeding kids", Reg muttered as he pushed another huge fork load of food into his greasy mouth.

Verity barely acknowledged the banter and continued puffing. She looked tense, more stressed than before. At work it was clear, she had a job to do and had something to occupy her wandering mind. Here at home, it was all just a constant reminder of how dull, dull, dull it was and how tough her meaningless existence was. Her mind seemed less clear now and she seemed to be wavering. The impact of welcoming her untrustworthy husband home seemed to sink in.

Shaking her head whilst grinding the butt out on the ground, Verity had finally come to the right conclusion. With no hesitation whatsoever she marched into the kitchen, past Reg, still shovelling food into his greedy gob and continued up the stairs to her bedroom at the front. The room was pink. Unmistakeably pink, with pink wallpaper, pink duvet cover and even a lurid pink carpet. It was almost too much to look at. It was revolting but pathetically sweet and childlike. It would appear that although the rest of her life was just grot, she tried to pretty things up in her inner sanctum. The only place where she had previously had any control over had now been infiltrated. Now off course in stark contrast to the overwhelming femininity, soiled underpants lay at the foot of the bed and a scent of fat, hairy, sweaty man still hung in the air. Her only refuge had been tarnished. It had been stolen from her. In the cold light of day it was so abhorrent to her that without any uncertainty she grabbed a cheap zip up bag and threw the numerous male belongings, which she found strew around the room. It was as if the more she stuffed the bag full, the more her spirits rose.

A perpetual heavy beat could be heard from one of the other two remaining floors and although it was giving me a headache, Verity appeared to be deaf to it. So determined to rid this filth from her life, she almost skipped out of the room which the heavy bag and floated down the stairs.

She stood in the kitchen doorway and with a hard stare and both hands on hips, she caught Reg's attention mid shovel. Steve carried on ploughing the grub in but managed to splutter "what's up babe?" whilst ketchup dribbled down his stubbly chin.

Verity stood her ground and waited until the plate was cleared. After a particularly nauseous belch, she removed the cutlery and crockery from the table and placed it in the sink. She then turned to face her unperturbed husband and said in a clear, calm voice, "I have packed your things Reg. Please collect your bag, by the door, and leave. I don't want to see you again and as I presume you will return to that dirty bitch, I will have divorce papers served to her house."

Slowly Reg turned to face the door and could see the zip up case Verity had left at the bottom of the stairs. He spun round and without warning slapped her round the face. I suspected that Verity was used to this behaviour as although I detected a flinch, she didn't fall to the ground in tears and sob in fear. She stood, with her head held high and repeated "Please go Reg".

Reg's lips curled in anger and he lurched towards her grabbing her by the neck. Intent of throttling her, his eyes seemed blank, far away. Verity's composure was almost gone and as she turned more and more purple, Reg's rage grew and grew. He spat in her face and bellowed at her. She was called every name under the sun. 'Fucking whore' seemed to be the most popular. I could only stare in morbid fascination. Here I was, watching the life being drained out of this wretched woman and I could do nothing. As Verity's defiance grew weaker, I heard a pounding down the stairs. The boy upstairs was descending. I only hoped that he would shoot straight out of the door. The packed bag must have stopped him in his tracks as I heard a faint, unsure voice call out "Mum?"

Steve seemed oblivious to this and continued with his aim. Verity must have heard and I felt her stiffen. Heavy footsteps echoed down the hallway. Suddenly a tall yet slender shape appeared at the doorway and I heard a sharp intake of breath.

"Get the fuck of my mother, you bastard" was the automatic response giving the sight in front of the poor boy's eyes. Reg flinched and came to his senses.

"Shit, shit, shit", he kept repeating. "What the fuck have I done?" He turned to face the boy and whispered "What have I done?"

Verity appeared to be lifeless but a single flicker of her right eye showed that she was possibly just unconscious. The boy, who I could only presume was Darren, stared blankly at his father then launched himself at the crouched figure. Thumping his back wildly, a tirade of obscenities flowed from the lad's mouth.

Reg pulled himself to his feet whilst deflecting most of the blows. His intentions were clear, to get the hell away from this place. Working out his best course of action, he realised that he would have to make the boy see sense. He very quietly began "Darren, listen mate, your mum is gonna be fine. Just let me take my bag and I'll disappear and I promise you that I wont come back"

This stopped Darren in his tracks. His eyes were full of tears and his face was a deep red. Pausing to think things through, he looked at his mother crumpled on the kitchen floor and murmured "Get out. Get the fuck out".

Reg didn't need to be told again and ran toward the hallway. Even though he was still only wearing his pants, he couldn't miss this opportunity to escape. Grabbing the bag, he shot out of the door and down the short front path. Turning left, he must have suddenly remembered the park at the corner of the road. At least there he could grab some clothes out of the bag.

I felt her sobbing before I heard her. The departure of Reg seemed to bring Verity back to life. Or maybe she was just being clever, feigning death or something.

"Sorry, sorry" Darren mumbled as he drew back. "Can I help you up?" he asked in a small frightened voice.

"Mmmmmm" was all that Verity could manage. It was too early for bruises to appear but from the state of her face right now, they were going to be corkers. Darren helped her up and sat her at the kitchen table. He grabbed a tea towel hanging from the stove handle and dabbed her bleeding mouth. The welts around her neck looked painful. She was holding her head in her hands and although she must have been very sore, she looked so relieved. Her decision had been made and she walked away bruised but intact and alive.

"Mum," Darren said softly. "Shall I call the Doctor?" He sat at the table on the chair opposite and gave her time to respond.

Verity shook her head slowly. She lifted her eyes and they smiled at her son. "No love, I'm ok. A couple of bruises that's all. I don't need no doctor. I could murder a cup of tea though".

Darren managed a smirk. She was ok. If her sense of humour was unbroken, then she was going to be fine. He put the kettle on and something in his demeanour told me that things were going to change and change for the better. He turned on the kitchen tap and squirted some washing up liquid into the bowl. By the look of it, it was the first time he had ever attempted housework. Even in Verity's condition, she noticed her son's attempts and tried to smile. As it was too painful, she rested her head in her hands and looked thoroughly exhausted.

The day passed slowly and instead of racing around, Verity took it easy. She didn't want the neighbours to see her face and she really didn't feel up to anything much. Darren was being a diamond. He had brought endless cups of tea and hung around in case he was needed. Even when some of his scrawny youth friends turned up, caps on, fags in mouths, he still turned them away and busied himself in the house.

Around teatime, the front door crashed open and Verity almost leapt out of her skin. Through the fug of smoke in the lounge, she could see her youngest, David, appear in the doorway. "What's wrong mum?" he asked, surprised to see her curled up on the sofa. It was such an unusual sight that it took him by surprise. Verity tried to cover her face and neck whilst replying that she just felt a little tired. Her attempt to sound calm failed miserably and Dave inched towards her suspiciously. He knew immediately that something was wrong but wasn't quite sure what he should be looking for.

"Fuckin' 'ell mum!" he shouted. "What 'appened?" He stood in disbelief staring at the mess in front of him. I could tell by his expression that he was torn between sympathy and anger. The poor lad can't have been much older than fifteen. The fact that someone could do this to his mum, totally infuriated him. Racing into the kitchen, he was shocked to see Darren armed with a tea towel. "What the fuck's being goin' on? he demanded. "You do this?' he asked as he gesticulated toward Verity.

"Piss off you nob" came the insulted response and amazingly Dave's attitude altered. I could just about see him sit at the kitchen table staring questioningly at this brother.

"Darren mate, what's been goin on" he pleaded. "Whats up with mum?" He looked like a young boy at this point. Young, frightened and very confused.

"All right Dave, it's all right". Verity had never heard Darren so protective towards his brother. Her ears pricked up as Darren continued. "Now listen, Dad just got a bit cross, that's all. Mum's fine but they just decided that they thought it might be better if Dad went and lived somewhere else. No need to get upset. Mum's just got a bit of a headache and after she's eaten a nice dinner," he said nodding towards the microwave, "she'll be fine".

Dave ran back into the lounge and hugged his mother. It was very touching to watch as the young lad buried his head in Verity's lap and sobbed. I couldn't really see David as an emotional sort but I did feel a bit choked up. Verity ran her fingers through Dave's very short hair. She found the shaved patch where a Nike tick had been etched into the back of his head, just the weekend before.

"We'll be fine, son. I just wanted Dad to go and let us be. Now the three of us can carry on but," she said determinedly "I want both you boys to promise me that all your nonsense is gonna stop. I ain't got no patience to be running around after you both and you'll send me to an early grave if you don't pack it in and behave."

Dave nodded, still cuddled up in her lap and I could hear a faint snotty mumble of agreement. Darren appeared from the kitchen and sat on the sofa arm. "S'all right Mum, we're gonna look after you now. We don't need that pig no more". He sat up and said "Right, where d'ya wanna eat your dinner?"

Verity looked up at Darren and said "Oh love. I'm not sure I can't eat right now". She looked a bit guilty but I could imagine she was probably still really sore.

"No Mum, you've gotta eat and its only chips and beans so it ain't much".

Verity nodded slowly. It had been a rough day and probably a nice dinner would help. She started to get up and Dave stopped her "Eat 'ere Mum". He said patting the sofa. "Eat on ya lap and I shall stick the TV on".

Verity slowly and painfully munched her way though a large plate of baked beans and chips. 'Bless em', she thought. The pair of them were in the lounge. David was curled up on the carpet by her feet and Darren was half lying on the sofa next to her. She had let them have a couple of beers that Steve had left behind in the fridge. It wasn't as if she didn't know they drank. 'Better they do it here where I can keep an eye on them' she thought wisely.

Drinking was one thing but smoking was another. Darren had been brave enough to admit to his mum that he smoked some time back but as a fully-fledged adult now he could pretty much do what he wanted. David though hadn't been caught and wasn't going to admit to it. As he watched his mum and brother puff away through soap series after soap series, he was desperate but he wasn't gonna leave his mum tonight. She needed protecting in case that bastard returned. Darren however, had run out of his normal brand and was tucking in to Verity's stash. "I'll get you some in the morning Mum. Promise!"

Verity winked and said "Cheers son".

The doorbell rang constantly but half the time the boys let it be. They weren't going out tonight. Each time it rang and no one answered the door, the atrocious abuse that was hurled through the letterbox increased. Verity visibly stiffened each time these unruly yobs screamed obscenities. Her nerves were on the edge and she could really do without this unsettling performance. Darren noticed his mother's jitters and grabbed his jacket and me and swept out of the door casually stating over his shoulder "Be back in a minute".

As soon as we left the relative comfort of home, Darren's behaviour changed completely. The mild tempered lad insistent on caring for his battered mother was gone and in its place was an angry and aggressive young man. Zipping up his stained green bomber jacket, we strode down the path. Darren grabbed the guy who presumably had been swearing through the letterbox. He took hold of him round the neck and then punched his ear. The shaven haired teenager was stunned. Clearly he had never seen Darren this furious. "Oi, you sick bastard, what the fuck you playing at?" he shouted at the stunned youth lying on his back, now nursing a bleeding ear. "My mum doesn't need your crap".

"Calm down Daz, I was only playing. I.I. I just wanted to get you out tonight to go up that pub and get down to b.b.business" he stammered not really understanding what the problem was.

"Get up you lazy cunt" Darren laughed. His anger had dissipated now and he was up for another beer. Dave was at home looking after mum and he felt he deserved a night out. He offered his hand to the bloke still on the floor and said "Come on Matt, you tosser".

They laughed, although I still detected an element of confusion in young Matt. We all trotted down the road, passing houses, which looked identical. 'How on earth do they remember where they lived? I mused. 'Most of the houses had had their numbers ripped off so it must be the patterns on the net curtains that tells them apart', I thought bitchily.

After a while the lads pushed open the door of a run down pub on the corner of the estate where they lived and a fairly busy main street. The pub was heaving and loud music belted out. The punters seemed oblivious to it and just shouted louder, over the top of it. Squeezing our way to the counter, Matt asked Darren what he wanted and Darren shouted back "Beer mate, cheers".

Two very dodgy blondes were working behind the bar and from the look of it, one was rather keen on Matt as she ignored the other waiting customer and singled him out. For a moment the shouting got even louder at the very injustice of it all but a big bald burly guy came from the back of the pub and started taking orders and thing calmed down a bit. The blonde purposefully stuck her large breasts out as she reached up to pick out two pint glasses and looking at Matt, the sentiment was not lost on him. Slightly blushing, Matt reluctantly averted his eyes, to count the change he dragged from his jeans pocket, and I could see he was flustered, either that or his maths skills were severely lacking. Several times he tried to add up the coins in his hand but I guessed his mind was elsewhere!

Eventually handing over the correct money, Matt winked at the blonde and grabbed his two full pints. Muscling our way over to an already crowded corner, some boys in the distance recognised my companions and I realised at that moment that their status must have been pretty high as two seats were immediately cleared for them. The lads sat and glugged half their drinks before even acknowledging their mates. Darren grabbed Matt's cigarette packet and lit up. Matt seized the pack back again along with me and stuck us in his shirt pocket. Darren seemed not to notice.

Matt spoke first and asked a spotty guy next to him where Adam was. The acne ridden boy just gazed at him blankly and shrugged but I heard someone else shout "Don't worry mate, he's here". Matt nodded his appreciation and continued drinking. I could see that Darren was eyeing up another corner but I couldn't really see the source of his interest.

"Shit, is that Billy?" Darren's eyes widened as he shoved Matt and repeated "Matt, Matt, is that Billy over there? Matt nearly spilled his drink but rather than berate Darren, he dutifully turned his head and scanned the other side of the pub.

"No, its his mate Tony", he said casually. "Relax, I'll go find Adam and we can get started". Matt downed his drink and stood to go and search the elusive Adam. I spotted the blonde before the boys did. She was supposed to be collecting glasses but the look on her face told me she was making a beeline for the boys. Matt's eyes caught hers and she smiled. Darren watched the two of them amusingly. He knew Nikki well, I could tell. I'd even bet there had been intimacy but what ever they'd had, there was nothing there now. Not even a tad of jealousy studying these two flirt.

Nikki's tight pink t-shirt was straining over her large chest. Matt was beside himself and could hardly keep his eyes of them.

"Nice tits Nik", Darren shouted, obviously eager to take the opportunity to embarrass his friend.

"Shut it you", Nikki sniggered, secretly pleased at the attention. She stood in front of Matt and coyly gazed it into his eyes. "Call me," she said quietly.

I got the impression that Matt's tongue had turned to custard, as he seemed totally incapable of speaking. He nodded and grinned inanely.

Nikki grabbed a few empties and tottered back to the bar, at least looking like she was doing her job. Matt watched her for a few minutes and then dragged his eyes away and concentrated on the matter at hand. Dropping his fag butt onto the rank carpet he made his way over to the Gents, whilst searching the bar thoroughly for Adam. Seeing him nowhere he pushed open the door to the Men's and was hit by a rancid smell. "Jesus," Matt exclaimed "It's getting worse". It was usual for pub toilets to be particularly nasty places. Although I'm sure most landlords do their best at hygiene and ordering the cleaner to do a through job, the overall result is always the same. A nasty niff and stained, slightly damp carpets, especially near the urinals. This however, was bad, really bad.

Moving through the door and into the toilet, Matt at last spied Adam. Sat on the floor, looking totally wasted, was a pale gangly youth. A tell tale corner of darkened foil was lying by his side. Matt hurried over to him, lifted him forward and tried to open his eyes. "Adam," he whispered, unsure of who else was in the room. "Adam", he repeated "You got my order?"

A slight moan escaped Adam before he slumped back against the wall. "Fuck", said Matt in annoyance. He slapped the wall and then after a slight pause, he rummaged through his pockets. He found a half filled fag packet, which he swiped and about twenty quid in change. That went straight in his jeans pocket. He frantically searched his jacket and jeans but nothing else was there except a key. "No point taking that," Matt muttered aloud, "he ain't got nothing to steal!"

Cross now, Matt made his way back to the guys in the corner. Guessing the guy had already been checked over was pretty straightforward but poor old Matt wasn't the brightest button and his version was that Adam had done a shifty. That was the story he told Darren anyway.

Darren was puzzled. It wasn't like Adam to let them down. He'd had enough for today and decided to call it quits. His need wasn't quite as urgent as Matt's so slugging the remaining dregs in his beer glass, he slapped Matt on the back and headed off back to Verity.

I was getting dizzy from all the handovers. Here I was in some den of iniquity with Lord knows who about to get into God only knew what. I longed for the security of Whin and his routine. I missed him like crazy and all the nonsense I had been caught up with since the funeral, although had admittedly it had kept my mind off my sorrow, had also brought it home to me in no uncertain terms how good Whin and I had been together, what a perfect couple we had made. I was dreading the next move but I had a feeling that it might involve a large breasted woman called Nikki.

True to form, Matt decided to wheedle his way back up to the bar and order another drink. Catching Nikki's eye, he ordered another lager and waited for her to stick her hand out for the cash. As soon as she did, Matt grabbed it and pulled her over the counter so he could make himself heard. Most of the ordering at the bar was by sign language and as plenty of the clients were regulars, the girls knew what they wanted anyway, and which drinks!

"What time do you knock off tonight?" Matt asked and continued, "Fancy a little bit of fun?"

Nikki beamed. "Thought you'd never ask, you cheeky sod!" She looked very pleased with herself. She looked up at the pub clock and said "I've got about 15 minutes left so if you wanna wait, I'll come and find you".

With a spring in his step and a wide smile, Matt trotted back over to the corner and joined the boys. For the next twenty minutes of so, the conversation was pretty dire. There was a lot of trivial talk about football. Whin had never shown any interest in the game and so I had no idea about the rules or the players. Trying to ignore them, I kept thinking about Whin and I remembered our first day.

· ·

FLASHBACK

· ·

Whin hadn't noticed Geoff's facial expression changed to that of utter misery. I could see that he was thinking about a reunion. In fact I knew what he was doing. This funeral he had attended must have been pretty bad and he was trying to take his mind off it by concentrating on something more positive and enjoyable.

I congratulated myself for my psychological skills and started paying even more attention. I had clocked the pain on Geoff's face but as I had no idea to what that referred, I decided I would focus on Whin. I might get a clearer picture that way.

"Geoff", Whin called out. "Geoff, how you gonna get everyone together then? You got all their numbers?" He asked hopefully.

"No. I haven't but I'm hoping that between Bert and Dan, we should be able to rustle up all the others." The grimace had disappeared now like he too had made a conscious decision to give attention to something a lot more pleasant.

Whin looked slightly disheartened. He knew Bert and Dan were great blokes but they were never going to set the world alight and relying on them to arrange a get-together would mean it was never going to happen. His mood darkened again and I could almost see the depression descend. I just wished I could help him and I guess I was comforting him but the amount of cigarettes he was getting through would only really assist him in getting a hacking cough.

Geoff turned to serve another customer and with the banter that took place, it seemed that he was another regular. Whin looked up as he heard Geoff bellow with laughter.

"Blimey, Tom. What a surprise. Good to see you mate". Whin's expression was sheer joy. From the conversation that followed, it appeared that Tom was a frequent guest but mostly in the afternoons and occasionally for lunch too, if he could manage it. Whin on the other hand was usually in late afternoons and evenings. Overjoyed at seeing his old friend the two of them grabbed a table and sat together.

Even through his delight, Tom could see unhappiness behind his mask. Without stopping to think about the consequences, he ploughed in and asked "You ok mate? You seem a bit down". Normally Whin would hold his private thoughts and keep his emotions in check but the strain of the day and the shock of seeing Tom after such a long time, took him by surprise and it all came gushing out.

"Oh Tom," he said shaking his weary head. "It's been a really tough day. I just can't get my head round it." Tom sat nodded his head patiently. He had a feeling this was going to take a while.

Whilst Whin hung his head trying to put things in an order that would make sense, Tom turned to put in another order with Geoff. Luckily Geoff was looking in their direction. He had a hopeful look on his face. He might have just got off the hook. It looked like Whin was going to spill the beans with Tom instead. Relief spread across his face and acknowledged the order and pulled out two fresh pint glasses.

Tom turned back and held Whin's arm. Normally it was quite taboo to hold another man or have bodily contact but on this occasion it seemed perfectly natural and acceptable. He leant in slightly and spoke quietly "Whin, it's ok. In your own time."

Whin looked up and saw the kind look in his companion's eyes. He relaxed a little. I felt his whole body loosen up and he took a long deep breath. "I'm not really sure where to start Tom. It's all so bloody complicated. There had been a threat of tears earlier but now he felt quite composed and he began.

• •

FLASHBACK

• •

CHAPTER 4

It was gone 9pm when Nikki finally sauntered over to the corner. Her tight t-shirt had a few beer stains on which bizarrely excited Matt even more. He seemed so fidgety. I really couldn't work out what was wrong with the boy. Nikki's ridiculously tight jeans showed off every curve of her shapely figure. Matt stood up as she approached. He seemed keen to leave. Outside the pub, Nikki's heels clattered on the pavement. "Where we going then?" she asked demurely. I wasn't sure that demure was really her style. Brazen was the word that came to mind. She was playing a game, I could see that but dense old Matt was blind to her ladylike charms. He seemed to be in a rush and every minute that passed, he seemed to get worse.

"Come on love, it's a surprise", he said much more confidently that he felt, I believed. We started off in a new direction and I was pleased to see that we were leaving the estate behind us. It wasn't really me. Not that I was a snob or anything but I just had a certain standard. To be honest I was terrified. I had no idea what kind of people I was hanging out with now. I couldn't predict the evening ahead let alone a whole future and it suddenly dawned on me now, how far away I was from Dan and the chance to catch up on news of Whin. How the hell was I going to get back to The Cock?

Excitedly Nikki took Matt's hand and allowed him to lead her off into the night. It was dry but any warmth of the day had vanished a while ago. Nikki though seemed totally unaware and wore nothing over her tight t-shirt. Matt grinned at her and off we went.

I grew bored of trying to second-guess which road we would turn into, which house we would arrive at. The evening was dragging and I knew Nikki was feeling a little fed up too. Her footsteps were slowing. Those heels really couldn't be helping either. They were ludicrously high but I had heard that females would go to extraordinary lengths to look good, or at least think that they looked good.

Eventually, after possibly 30 minutes, but what seemed like 2 hours, we trotted past a garage on a corner. Matt paused nervously and even as we turned off, he kept looking behind him over both shoulders. Nikki hadn't spotted this sudden onset of paranoia but she had obviously had enough. She made an abrupt stop and stood, hands on hips.

"Look, Matt, where we going? I mean I don't just wanna walk around all night. Are we goin back to yours?" She looked like she meant business. If Matt came out with the wrong thing now, she looked liked she would just put the whole evening down to experience and go home. She didn't look cross exactly, just a bit disappointed. I got the impression she wanted a bit of fun and for Matt to treat her like a Princess. So far he had only treated her like a dog and taken her for a walk.

Matt's suspicious behaviour increased and he snapped at her "For fuck's sake Nikki, we are almost there" and then realising what he had said he calmed down and put his arm on her shoulders. "Trust me Nikki. I'm just taking you to a mate's house and he lives just round the corner. Come on, please?"

Nikki looked begrudgingly into his eyes. His young face still had the soft corners of adolescence even thought he was approaching eighteen. His cheekbones had yet to mould his features in hard male contours. She could see no facial hair. He could have shaved really well but she guessed that the little bumfluff that did exist was easy to remove. He was attractive in an unusual way. She normally went for older, broader men. Cocksure and feisty but there was something about Matt that took her fancy. She had heard the rumours about him and Darren but all lads on the estate were up to no good at some point or another and that included her brothers and even her Dad, when he was about.

Visibly sighing and making a point of it, Nikki grabbed Matt's arm and said "Come on then but it had better be close as my feet are killing me". Looking down at the silly heels, Matt grinned and pecked her on the cheek.

"Steady tiger", she laughed. Matt pulled Adam's packet of fags out of his jacket pocket and lit two cigarettes. Passing one over to her, he stuffed me back in his shirt pocket and they two of them giggled like kids.

I felt a headache coming on. I mean I didn't want to be caught up in some voyeurism and watch these two at it all night. I also felt quite weary and unsettled. I couldn't relax as I had no idea where we were headed or what was coming next. The old days with Whin were flooding back a lot tonight. Maybe the shock of his death was only just catching up with me now.

Trying to ignore the flirtatious banter between these two fools was no easy task but no sooner as I had just relaxed than I heard Matt say "Ok we are here."

I perked up a bit thinking that at least now I could see the journey's end but all there was in front of us was a dark front door. Matt rang on the bell but instinct told me that he didn't expect anyone to answer.

Nikki shifted from foot to foot. Her disappointment was returning. She rolled her eyes and stubbed her cigarette out on the dirty path. Folding her arms under her large breasts, her body language indicated that she was really irritated now.

Matt was concentrating on getting the door open. Peering through the letterbox, he was probably hoping that a key on some string would be hanging inside. An old trick but quite dangerous these days. Maybe he was considering breaking the glass panels and hooking his hand round to the doorknob. I bet he had done that few times. Cursing to himself, he decided to scale the tall, dilapidated wooden gate next to the house. I heard him mutter something vague about that the backdoor was a bugger to shut and that most of the time it was just pushed to. He turned to Nikki and said "I can't believe he's out, he was expecting us!. I'm just gonna go round the back and see if I can get in through the garden."

Nikki tutted but I could tell she wouldn't remember the way back and had no choice but to wait. She watched Matt hoist himself over the gate and disappear into the dark passage.

I couldn't see anything and I was pretty sure Matt was blinded too. I heard him feel along the damp walls and then felt him trip over. Steadying himself, against the wall, we continued along the dank alleyway. Fortunately for us, the clouds parted slightly, enough for the moonlight to show where the back door was situated. Matt edged towards it, still nervously checking for sounds around him.

The door, just as his memory served him, was open but firmly wedged. Matt used all of his strength to heave his shoulders against it. The first two shoves did nothing but on the third push, the door gave way and Matt and I ended up on a greasy ripped lino in the kitchen. I shuddered. This place was vile but Matt was overjoyed and almost skipped down the corridor to open the front door.

Nikki also looked relieved and she entered the dark house quite willingly. In her mind anything was better than the doorstep. I think she may have changed her mind though after setting foot inside the lounge. It was filthy and I don't mean it needed a quick Hoover and a dust. I mean it was disgusting. Both Nikki and I stared around the room, taking in each revolting item. The net curtains were a very dark grey and ripped. The far wall had dark mouldy stains in the corner and the carpet looked like there were creatures burrowing around. Nikki stifled a scream and glanced around for Matt. He said nothing but Nikki just demanded another cigarette and Matt handed us over.

Nikki lit up and continued looking around the room of grime. The sofas could have been on a tip for a month, there were damp, smelly and stained. Nikki had no intention of sitting and I didn't blame her. There was an old TV, which looked in fairly good condition and apart from some cheap plastic pictures on the walls, there was nothing more to see.

I could hear Matt further down the hallway, possibly in the kitchen, getting some drinks? Then all of a sudden, it hit me. Of course! This was Adam's place. Matt had been pretty confident that Adam wasn't going to be around as seeing him slumped on the floor of the toilets, gave him plenty of time to scoot around to his gaff and check the place over. He had asked Adam for his score as well so presumably he was now searching for it.

Nikki and I scuttled along the corridor in search of Matt. I could tell she wanted to leave as much as I did. The place stank of stale booze, urine and damp. We passed the staircase on our right and a door on the left. Neither of us wanted to look upstairs, nor search another dark room so we continued until we found another door, which was wide open. Cautiously peering round the doorframe, we saw Matt's behind sticking up as he searched under a very dirty bed in the corner. "Nice arse", Nikki shouted and Matt bumped his head in shock as he automatically tried to turn around.

"Oi you, you gave us a fright!" but he was grinning. He pulled out a Somerfields carrier bag and looked expectantly inside. I wanted to go, go where I didn't know but I wanted to get out of this dump.

Without warning there was a scraping noise from the front. I could hear a key was being turned and someone was opening the door. I looked at Matt and his expression told me that he had heard the same thing. Nikki was a bit slow but Matt's frantic gesticulations made her realise what was going on.

Matt tiptoed to the door and peered round the corner, squinting in the dim light coming through the kitchen window. I couldn't see a damn thing but I was aware of movement. Matt turned and grabbed Nikki's arm and quietly pulled her out of the door and back down the hallway to the kitchen at the back of the house. I heard footsteps behind us but thankfully a whispered voice said, "You check upstairs and I'll check out down here."

At least there would be two to one initially. I was thinking the worst and way too far ahead. Positively I channelled my energy into believing that we would escape. Almost silently we crept past the bathroom. I didn't look inside but I could smell it and that was enough for me. Tiptoeing on the greasy kitchen floor, Matt jerked the kitchen door open and we slunk out into the night. Matt was keen to get as far away from the house as possible but half way up the path he remembered the wooden gate and floundered, remembering that Nikki was wearing those stupid heels. Just before he could turn to her and ask her to remove them, he heard her clacking down the passageway.

The hearts of both Matt and I sank. Surely they would hear that noise. Nikki was still oblivious and continued to click up the alley. Matt flew back to her and pulled her down to a crouching position. "SHHHHhh" he said crossly "Take those fucking shoes off". His anger had returned. Not only was it entirely possible that the Somerfields bag, still tightly held in his hand, not contain what he was after but he might also have his teeth kicked in for the pleasure of it.

Nikki suddenly grew frightened. Her boobs had got her a fair distance in life, more so than relying on her slow brain but now she felt totally out of her depth. This wasn't how she wanted to be spending her evenings. She wanted to be wined and dined and then shagged. Was that really too much to ask? Now though, she was squatting down some nasty alley, being chased by burglars and her knight in shining armour was having a go at her shoes!

Matt suddenly remembered that the kitchen was still open. I could hear him muttering whether he should chance it and return to pull it shut, thus hopefully keeping the outside safe. We could then remain here until the danger was over. The other option was to risk the wooden fence and make a run for it. The look on his face said it all. Having Nikki here was a thorn in his side and either way she could ruin him.

"Think. Think!" I could hear Matt saying as he slapped his palm to his forehead. "For fuck's sake, think Matt".

No noises were coming from inside the house and the surrounding streets were also uncommonly quiet which made the choices even more difficult. If Matt managed to secure the kitchen door, would Nikki blow our cover? Could she remain quiet and still for as long as it took? If however, we went for the gate option, was she athletic enough to hoist herself up and over with the minimum of sound?

Nikki's brain seemed to kick into life. She looked at Matt and realised that the danger they were in was very real. She looked up at the wooden gate ahead and nodded. "I can do it. Let's go"

Glad to have the decision made for him, Matt moved stealthily towards the gate. Nikki prepared to remove her shoes when Matt turned and gave a thumbs-up. From my position, it looked like Matt had found a large iron key in the lock of the gate. I heard him turn the rusty key and prayed it wasn't too loud for the intruders to hear. The key jammed half way round and Matt applied all his body weight (such as it was) to push it round with brute force. It was touch and go but finally the key gave way and the lever moved back.

Almost jumping for joy, Nikki and I followed Matt out of the alleyway and down the grassy path towards the pavement. Behind us though I heard a crunch and realised that one of the trespassers had discovered us. At this point Nikki did the sensible thing and took off those ridiculous heels and they both sped down the road. Being young they were incredibly nimble and although Nikki's breasts bounced like crazy, we still raced along the road back towards the garage.

Matt shouted to Nikki to follow him and we all entered the petrol station. It seemed the safest bet. Matt leaned over to Nikki and asked how much cash she had on her. "Just been given me wages, love so I've got a bit." She leaned in a little closer and whispered "How much do you need?"

Without replying Matt trotted up to the counter and asked if the bloke could ring a cab. Without a murmur the guy picked up the shop phone and dialled.

"What's your name and where do you want to go to?" the guy said with a fairly strong Indian accent.

"The name is Ben and I need to get back to the town centre". Matt had thought fast, clever boy. We couldn't see if anyone was watching us from outside the garage but he didn't want to run the risk of anyone following him home to his place.

I could tell Matt desperately wanted a drink or a fag or something as his uneasiness had returned. Maybe it was just the adrenaline racing through his veins. In comparison, Nikki seemed much more calm. That could be the lack of sense though.

A few minutes later a taxi pulled up onto the forecourt. The Indian man nodded to Matt and we left the safety of the shop and walked quickly to the waiting car.

In the typical manner of a cabbie, the driver began asking questions about our night almost as soon as the door was shut

"Where you two been then? Bit quiet round here for a couple of young 'uns like you init? The man droned on and on. He was trying to find out what they had been up to. I guess they did look a bit odd. Although Nikki had put her shoes back on, they both looked a little grubby and despite the cool evening air, they were sweaty.

Matt managed to talk his way out of a suspicious corner although I can't remember what it was now. I was shattered and my concentration was slacking. The fifteen minute journey was spent anxiously looking out of the windows. Neither Matt not Nikki knew what they were looking for. They didn't know who their stalkers might be, let alone what their vehicle would look like. It was human nature though, I was sure, to keep checking for danger.

The cabbie was talking continuously but the occasional verbal nod from Matt meant that his attention was away from their erratic behaviour. The non-smoking signs in the cab wound Matt up even more and the closer we drew to our destination, the more agitated he became.

We turned a corner and bright lights from a burger bar came into view. The driver looked into the rear through the mirror and asked "Where abouts do you two want dropping then?"

Matt indicated that a bit further on the left was a pub called The Kings. "Just outside that would be perfect, cheers mate"

'So,' I mused, 'back to a pub then!'

Nikki dutifully handed over the £12.50 fare and we all descended. It could have only been just before closing time and I was really hoping that this pub had a longer license or that the landlord was keen on lock-ins. I had had enough and just needed time to catch my breath.

As soon as we opened the door, a few faces turned to see who we were but when Matt entered, the faces lost interest, only to pick up again as Nikki's huge boobs walked in behind him. There was a wolf whistle from further back in the pub and I threw my eyes to heaven. 'God, how awful it must be to be a woman' I thought. 'The heels, the constant jeering, never being taken seriously,' although for Nikki that was probably a good thing! I was nervously taking in the punters in this bar. The last place had frightened me half to death and I wanted to check my surroundings thoroughly.

Matt headed straight to the counter and ordered a lager. He spun round to ask Nikki what she would like and caught her smiling at a bald bloke with a huge gold chain. Suddenly infuriated, Matt crossly whispered "Oi slag, put him down and tell me what you want to drink".

"For your information" Nikki started "that bloke is my cousin's husband, so don't you go giving me no hard time". The hard look on Nikki's face stunned Matt into silence and she trotted over to him and said, "I'll have a white wine". She softened, realising it was a combination of jealousy and stress causing the friction. "Please", she added.

Matt smiled and placed her order at the bar. Grabbing the drinks they made their way to a tatty table in the corner. I could tell he wanted to have some quite time with her and get to know each other properly. He asked Nikki for his cigarettes and he lit up immediately, relief flooding through him with his sharp intake of nicotine. I felt happy now. I was needed again and things seemed to have calmed down. I relaxed a little and let my mind drift. Matt and Nikki were talking nonsense as youths do and I rested. 'What a night!' I thought. 'There was none of this twaddle occurring when I was with Whin'. There he was again. He was never far from my mind. He had taken good care of me. All those years with one careful owner and now in the space of a few hours I had changed hands three times.

The evening progressed pleasantly. I guessed about an hour or so passed. I wasn't sure if the pub had been granted an extended license or if the landlord had chosen to make that decision himself but approaching 1am, the final bell was rung and Matt grabbed me and the remaining cigarettes and he and Nikki made their way to the door. By the looks on their faces, they had enjoyed themselves, at least the latter part of the night anyway.

"Wanna come back to mine Nik?" Matt asked cheekily. He pulled open the door and like a gentleman indicated that she was to go first.

"Yeah, ok Matt" she fluttered her eyelashes and continued "But I can't be too late, I'm on earlies tomorrow and we've got a delivery so…." she stopped as she took in the sight in front of her.

Although we were near the centre of town, the road in front of the pub was quiet and there was very little passing traffic, which is why it was strange when we all noticed our cabbie was still outside.

Ever observant, I noticed the slashed tyres first and waited for Matt to clock them too. I wasn't going to wait for Nikki or I'd have been there all night.

"Shit" exclaimed Matt swallowing hard. "Do you reckon….." his voice trailed off as he looked over at Nikki. She wasn't looking at the tyres, she seemed more occupied with what was inside the car. "Oh my God! The Somerfields bag! Shit! I left in on the back seat."

Matt bent down slightly and cupped his eyes to prevent the glare of the streetlamps. He recoiled instantly and I knew then that tonight was far from over.

"Is he..I mean is he…ok?" Nikki stammered.

"Fuck knows", said Matt anxiously "but I reckon we should get out of here. The bag's gone and he doesn't look good."

Nikki nodded slowly but just as the two of them started walking, the rest of the customers began leaving the pub. I wasn't sure if we were being watched or whether the perpetrators of this crime were linked in any way to the burglars at Adam's place but I was beginning to feel very frightened. Lord only knew what Nikki must have been thinking. There she was just expecting to taken out for a nice meal or even a relaxing drink and the events of the night were unfolding like something out of a spy film.

None of the other punters seemed to notice the cab. They were either too pissed or too wrapped in their own problems to observe anyone else. Matt decided to use the cover of other people leaving the pub and clutched Nikki's hand and led her towards the town centre. Matt looked quite nervous now. His fidgeting had stopped as soon as they had become comfortable in the pub but now it was replaced with extreme apprehension. The bright neon lights of the High Street were almost within spitting distance. Nikki was complaining about the speed. She was making it abundantly clear that she had had enough, wanted to go home and throw her bloody shoes away.

Reaching the safety of the High Street was the idea and Matt was expecting huge crowds of youths, in which he and Nikki could hide and then scurry away undetected. He was disappointed though as the road was deserted save an older couple, two coppers and a young lad on his bike, who should have been at home tucked up in his pyjamas in bed.

Glancing North and South, Matt finally decided to go home. He wanted Nikki to come with him though. He suddenly felt protective of her. If these thugs were after them, then he wanted to deal with them and not let Nikki take the punishment.

As luck would have it, Matt could see a night bus trundling up the hill and if he and Nikki ran, they could just make the bus stop in time. He couldn't quite make out the number but hoped it was the 73. But even if it wasn't, it would take him in the right direction.

He grabbed a tired and sulking Nikki by the arm and dragged her up the High Street to the bus stop. The couple he spotted earlier were waiting too and the policemen were chatting to them. I could tell that he wasn't that comfortable being surrounded by uniformed men but on this occasion, the relief was written all over his face.

As soon as they tripped up to the bus stop, Nikki took her shoes off. Blisters had appeared on both heels and were now bleeding profusely. I was shocked. Why would anyone wear something that caused so much damage? Matt, however, decided to use this to his advantage and make conversation with the policemen to keep them near, until the bus arrived. They had run faster than he had anticipated so they still had a few minutes before the bus arrived. Matt didn't want to take any chances. Launching into a discussion about the pros and cons of suitable footwear, the cops found him rather amusing. The taller man folded his arms and leaned against the metal framework of the bus stop. He seemed keen to hear Matt out. It appeared as though he was so used to dealing with the aggressive and badly behaved drunks that when he came across an entertaining character, he wanted to savour it.

The older couple, probably in their fifties, were wrapped around each other. I always find this kind of tactile behaviour so strange in older people and automatically leap to the conclusion that they are having an illicit affair or are at the start of a brand new relationship. I just find it hard to accept that long-term associations ever stay warm and loving. There may be a big possibility that I have been fundamentally affected by the way Whin lived his life. I may even have taken on board some of his theories and beliefs without realising. I never tended to be as black and white as Whin, but in hindsight, I think that Whin's personality rubbed off on me more than I appreciated.

Matt's comic act was warming up now and one of the cops had tears in his eyes. I wasn't really finding it all very funny but I guess I was tired, still frightened and totally bewildered. Even the tactile couple were laughing. Nikki seemed positively bursting with pride at Matt's ability to woo his audience, albeit tiny.

The No. 73 bus arrived and we let the others alight first. The cops saw us off with a smile and I could see the relief creep over Matt's face. Nikki headed straight for the stairs but Matt called her back. He wanted to be in full view of the rest of the passengers and have an easy escape route if required. I could almost see plans formulating in his mind.

Begrudgingly Nikki sat next to Matt downstairs about half way back. The bus swung out into the road and headed towards home. Neither of them wanted to talk and Matt put his arm round Nikki's shoulders and she nestled in to his lean, muscular body cosily.

I was using the journey to catch my breath. It was pointless trying to establish where we were going and guess what would happen next so I chose to think about Whin again.

· ·

FLASHBACK

· ·

Whin took a deep breath and looked into Tom's eyes. He had kind eyes, the type that seemed so sympathetic and understanding. Whin hoped that he could trust Tom to understand his pain and maybe even help him through it.

"Ah Tom, it's been so difficult." he said pausing briefly to take another sup of his beer. "A while back, I had heard through the grapevine that a friend of mine wasn't in too good a shape and didn't have long to live. I hadn't seen him in ages but I felt a need to visit him. We had one of those friendships where it was always good to see one another but neither of us ever planned to meet. A bit like you and I Tom." He glanced up at Tom and saw him nodding his head sagely.

"Anyhow, when I got to his place, his daughter opened the door and let me in. Instead of taking me upstairs to see him, she led me into the tiny front room and sat me down. Sitting next to me, she took my hand in hers and told me that Alan had passed away a few days ago. I had not met his daughter before and was so taken aback by the warmth that she showed to a perfect stranger, that I leaned forward and hugged her. I suppose emotionally I felt a little unstable after hearing the news that I had missed the chance of saying good bye to Alan."

Lighting up another cigarette, Whin continued, "She was great Tom. I mean she was a looker. I never asked her age, girls get so het up over things like that but I would have said about 42. She was beautiful, slim with sleek brown hair and I was smitten." Whin looked up at Alan again, wondering if he was thinking that he was a dirty old man, taking advantage of a grieving daughter. There was nothing though, on Tom's face to suggest that he thought in this way and Whin felt brave enough to carry on.

"I think I fell in love with her right there and then. I couldn't cry for Alan. Firstly I hadn't even accepted his death, it was too much of a shock and secondly my emotions were concentrated elsewhere. It's a bit of a blur, the rest of that afternoon. I know I stayed for quite a while and helped Mel write a list of people to contact. We got through a few bottles of wine. I hate the stuff but it was what Mel needed and eventually I felt more relaxed too"

Geoff came over and took the empties "Same again boys?" he asked.

Tom nodded and Whin just looked up and smiled. "I left her safe and well and I like to think she was even a bit happier. It was such a weird feeling. I had lost a good friend but I felt totally numb about it all, in fact I couldn't even focus on it. Every time I tried to think about Alan, Mel just popped up into my head. I went back the next day and just sat with her in the garden. It was late spring and although the blossom was dropping, the garden was beautiful."

Whin paused here whilst Geoff handed over two pints of beer. Both men nodded in appreciation. Silence fell as they supped. Tom's face was giving nothing away. I couldn't tell if he was intrigued or bored. He would have been great as a volunteer for the Samaritans.

Whin fiddled with the cardboard coasters and resumed "I dunno how it happened really Tom. I mean I wasn't looking for it. I wasn't even really sure I wanted to go down the whole relationship route again but that afternoon I just couldn't help myself." Again Whin looked up at Tom searching for any traces of horror but none existed. Tom seemed perfectly content to sit and listen to his friend's troubles.

"After another couple of bottles of wine, I thought that I should leave. I felt that I was invading her privacy and that she might need some alone time to grieve but the minute I started to leave, she became so upset that I did the only thing I could and hug her." Whin trailed off at this point and after a few seconds of reflection, Tom coughed and jerked Whin from his memories.

"So anyway, there I was hugging this perfect creature and I just couldn't help it, I swear. I know she was young enough to be my daughter but the longing I felt was so intense that nothing could have stopped me at that point. I kissed her and continued until she pulled away. My heart stopped when she did that and I braced myself for recriminations.

Nothing happened Tom, she smiled at me and leaned in for another kiss. From complete despair to overwhelming joy, I kissed her again and again until finally she took my hand and led me upstairs".

• •

FLASHBACK

• •

CHAPTER 5

Matt leaped up and dragged Nikki with him. They had both dozed on the bus and he had now realised that they had gone past his stop. Pushing the bell frantically, Matt scanned the road ahead for distinguishing landmarks. Thankfully they were only a couple of stops past his, so trotting back wouldn't take too long.

The driver stopped the bus and two other blokes got off at the same time. Matt used the excuse of pausing to light up a cigarette to see where the guys headed. They continued on the main road and Matt decided to lead Nikki round the back of the busy road. He knew it would cut off a few minutes although these streets would be quiet now and there would be no safety in numbers. Juggling the decision in his mind, I saw him finally take a stand and head toward a side street.

Nikki looked exhausted. The perky, flirtatious girl at the bar all those hours ago had been replaced with a rather haggard looking woman. The make up had run and the hair looked a mess. The shoes were off and staying off as far as I could tell. I thought at that point that the girl needed a long hot bath and sent straight to bed.

Walking arm in arm at a steady pace, the pair of them spent little time talking. Matt was on eggshells, nervously flitting his eyes around for the enemy. After a while they reached the bottom of Matt's road and I could hear his heart beating faster and faster. Curiously the nearer to his front door we got, the more anxious he became.

Matt drew his key from his pocket and turned through a small open gate and up a garden path. The house was similar to Verity's but a lot neater. No lights were on downstairs but the minute Matt quietly closed the door behind them, the upstairs landing flicked on and a voice whispered "That you Matt?"

Slightly embarrassed Matt whispered back "Yes mum, go back to sleep", he rolled his eyes and smirked at Nikki. I could tell she understood. She probably lived with her parents too. His mother though, was having none of it and tiptoed down the carpeted stairs

"Matt, thank the Lord. I had two guys looking for you earlier, what you been up to then?" She looked at Matt worriedly. His mother was a short woman with permed grey hair and looked like a typical grandmother. She was wearing the age-old nightdress that buttoned right up to the neck.

Her statement jolted Matt into reality and he turned to her and urgently said "What?!" He spoke louder then he meant to and his mother started to look frightened. Nikki also perked up. She had been sitting on the beige velour sofa and stood up to face Matt.

At this point, Matt's mother noticed Nikki and suddenly became aware of her appearance. Automatically she tried to smarm her unruly hair down and check the buttons at her neck. Nikki held out her hand and said "Pleased to meet you" in a telephone voice that startled both Matt and me.

"Oh mum, this is Nikki, and Nikki this is my mum, Beatrice but everyone calls her Bea".

Bea smiled at Nikki and gave her a quick glance up and down. Expertly she took in the large breasts, the lack of shoes and the state of her make up but rather than disregard her as some cheap floozie, she actually took to the girl.

"Where are my manners?" she laughed. "Can I get you some tea?"

"Mum," Matt scolded. "Its really really late and Nikki's got to get to work early tomorrow. I said she could crash here, that ok?"

Bea nodded. She turned to Nikki and said "Nice to meet you too dear" and then retired upstairs for the second time that night.

"She seems nice, Nikki said after she heard the bedroom door close. "Bet she looks after you and fusses after you!" she said teasingly. "Does she iron your pants too?" Nikki infectious laugh tickled Matt and he threw a cushion at her

"Oi you!" he laughed. "Come on, its late and you've gotta get up early." He looked uneasily at his feet and said, "Would you like to take my bed and I'll crash on the sofa?"

Nikki shook her head. Although I could see she was tired, she wanted Matt by her side tonight and gently took his hand.

Looking particularly gleeful, Matt took off his shoes and left his packet of fags and me on the coffee table before leading Nikki up the stairs.

'Well, what a relief!' I thought to myself. I really wasn't looking forward to enduring a night of screams and passionate howls and now it looked like I wouldn't have to. I looked around the room and felt at ease. The décor was similar to Whin's. It was a comfortable room, not particularly expensive but well kept and respected. The lights went out as Matt and Nikki reached the landing and I was plunged into darkness.

CHAPTER 6

I hadn't expected to sleep. I thought I would be too wired after the events of the night to crash out completely. I had imagined that I would be fidgeting all night but thankfully I was just too tired. As I awoke, I realised that it was too late in the day to be morning. It had to be lunchtime at least. I thought it strange that I hadn't woken when Nikki left for work or that Matt hadn't needed a nicotine fix before now.

Focussing on my surroundings, it dawned on me that I was not still in that comfy lounge in Matt's house. I was in a shabby site office and really straining my eyes I could even see the yellow hard hats of the employees as they walked past.

Fully awake and alert now, I did my best to listen out for sounds. I was alone in the cabin and could hear noises only from outside. Unanswered questions like "How did I get here without waking up?" seemed to be the most common and I just could not fathom who I was with now. I doubted it was Matt. As far as I could make out, he wasn't working. I don't think I ever actually found out what he did but I had certainly not heard any talk of building work.

Sighing to myself, I decided the only thing I could do without giving myself a headache, was to wait.

Almost immediately the door swung open and as a heavy set man entered, I could hear him mutter "Bastard" several times. The man came straight towards me and I guessed that he was now my new owner.

Lighting up seemed to calm the man slightly but when another man, smaller in build, entered the room, his angry demeanour returned.

"What now?" asked the smaller man in a frustrated voice. "What have I said now?" The man came up to the table and grabbed me and the fags and lit up too.

'Maybe I belonged to Mr Nice Guy then?' I wondered. 'Or maybe the Bill Sykes look-a-like! Come to think of it there is a passing resemblance to Matt. Aha! That's how I am here. Matt's dad has picked me up on his way to work!' Glad that I had the last handover dilemma sorted, I concentrated on the conversation between the two men.

"Shut it Phil. I've just about had it and I don't need the likes of you being sarky." Dragging heavily on the cigarette, the big guy wrung his hands. It didn't take a genius to see that something serious was on his mind.

This was better than those films Whin and I used to watch on a Sunday afternoon. I was suddenly enjoying this new lease of life. It was never dull, always unpredictably and strangely enough everyone seemed to respect me.

Phil sat next to the big bloke and he put his hand on his shoulder. "Look Gary mate, all I'm saying is that it's dog eat cat out there and if we can't keep the business going well, then we'll have to lay people off."

"Yeah" snarled Gary "but I bet you're safe though. I'm right aren't I?" He pointed his finger at Phil. "You make me sick. Jumped up little twat. I've been doing this job since I was a nipper, man and boy and I don't need the likes of you interfering".

"I was just trying to help you." Phil said encouragingly.

"Well I don't need no help from you so you can just fuck off," Gary shouted as he stood up and stormed out of the door.

Phil sat for a while and finished his fag. He grabbed me and the fags and wearily headed for the door.

I was stuffed in his trouser pocket as we left the port-a-cabin and I didn't see the light of day until a few hours later. Phil pulled me out just after we had climbed into his Audi, sensibly parked a distance from the site. Without a word Phil lit up and started the engine. Before pulling away, he grabbed his mobile from his suit jacket and dialled.

"Hello darling", he began in his well-educated voice "I'm just leaving now. Did you want me to pick up the wine for supper?"

I couldn't hear what was being said on the other end but I imagined it was an affirmative as Phil continued, "Okay, I'll pick up 2 bottles of the Chateau Neuf du Pape. I'll be about 45 minutes darling."

He hung up abruptly, keen to get going and threw the cigarette out of the window. Driving up to the High Street, he flicked on the radio and although I didn't recognise the station, I guessed from the sweet melodious music that we were listening to Jazz FM, that and the digital display flashing the name in orange from the dashboard console.

This was very nice. How couth! After the vigorous and rough antics of the previous few days, I just fancied some relaxation time.

By the time we reached the motorway, I felt positively invigorated. Phil plugged in his hands free kit and voice activated his mobile.

"John, it's Phil. Listen it's been quite frantic at the site and word got around about possible redundancies. Gary's taken it quite personally and stormed out after lunch. I think that perhaps you should pop in on Monday and try and pacify the chaps. Just a suggestion but if Gary gets upset then it could affect the others and I just want to try and avoid a mutiny."

He paused and listened as John replied "Ok Phil, listen I can't talk now, the wife has invited a posse of guests and I have to be wine connoisseur and make a trip to the cellar. I'll give you a buzz on Monday morning."

John hung up before Phil had a chance to respond. I could tell that his mind felt a little more settled as he turned up the jazz and tapped his hands to the rhythm on the steering wheel.

A while later we pulled up by the side of the road. I could see from my place on the front passenger seat that we were outside a rather reputable wine establishment. Phil nipped in to the shop and it wasn't long before he returned with a black cardboard wine carrier containing two bottles. He lit up another cigarette before pulling away and I studied his face whilst he drove. He was fair-haired and had pale skin. There was no sign of a five o'clock shadow and even his eyelashes and eyebrows were blond. He reminded me of a character called Ashley that I had once seen in a film that Whin and I had watched called "Gone with the Wind". He was attractive in an old-fashioned way.

A few winding turns and we were back on the motorway. Speeding along listening to the heady pre-dinner jazz, I wondered where we were headed. What type of home did Phil have? What was his wife like?

The journey took a while and I reckoned it was at least another quarter of an hour after our expected time of arrival. We scooted up a short gravelled drive and I could see high birch trees to the left of the driveway. Phil grabbed his jacket, the box of wine and double checked that I was still hiding in his pocket along with the packet of cigarettes.

The entrance was rather special. There were white columns either side of the front door and ivy had been trained to grow up and around. The large door had been painted matt black and had a matching silver knob and letterbox.

Phil squeezed his key fob over his shoulder and the shiny Audi beeped twice to indicate that the doors were locked. He marched up to the door and before he could insert his key, the door swung open and a small blonde girl threw her arms around him. "Daddy, daddy. I've missed you." The little tot could not have been much older than four years of age. She was at that lovely age where they were cheeky and adorable, all rolled in to one.

"Now Daddy, you have to come to my tea party". She grabbed his hand and led him into the house. Before Phil had a chance to sort himself out, we were guided into a side room just off the main hall. I took this to be a playroom as it was colourfully decked out and at least a dozen teddy bears were sat around a red and white checked tablecloth on the floor. "Now Daddy, come and sit next to Belinda and have a biscuit"

Phil looked bewildered. He really looked uncomfortable. He glanced at his watch. Torn between not wanting to upset his daughter and being late for tonight's events, he eventually shook his head.

"Poppet, Daddy's got to go and get ready now. Don't forget you are going to stay at Nana's house tonight so let's get your things and I can take you over". He offered his hand to the little girl and waited for her to collect Belinda and walk with him back out of the room.

After turning the lights off in the playroom and shutting the door, Phil turned to his daughter and said "Run upstairs Maria and find Mummy, there's a good girl".

Maria climbed the stairs, holding onto the banisters. Phil watched for a while and then made his way into the kitchen. I mentally sat up as we walked into a swish kitchen. It was lit by various spotlights sunk into the ceiling and a huge glass extension at the back. The units were dark and the appliances were all steel. Putting the bottle carrier on the surface nearer the enormous American fridge, Phil turned just as his wife came into the room.

"Becks, my darling. You look great." I could see from his eyes that this kind of talk was a strain and by the look of Becks, she had spent all day in the salon, having anything stripped, waxed, toned, shaped and lifted that could be. For a woman that could easily look quite horsey, without special attention, she actually looked very glamorous and even quite sexy. I suspected the boobs were fake, the hair was definitely dyed, I'd never seen that colour red naturally occur on anyone. The tan was most unquestionably a sun bed or spray and I even wondered if the lips hadn't had some collagen or botox influence. Still she looked good, it just cost an awful lot more than it would for others.

Becks trotted over in her expensive shoes and kissed Phil lightly on the cheek. "Be a darling and drop Maria off at Nana's", I have so much to do before they get here and I just cant afford to waste time now". Her voice was surprisingly nasal and with more than a hint of tetchiness, she sounded quite scary to me.

Phil started to speak and thought better of it. "Yes, yes of course darling. I'll drop her off now and then change when I get back".

I scanned Phil's face for a vague expression of annoyance but there was nothing. I would have been extremely irritated but then I didn't know the circumstances. I hoped this wasn't normal behaviour but something told me it was.

Phil casually walked up the stairs and threw his suit jacket onto the bed. He grabbed the fags and me, stuffed me into his trouser pocket and went straight into Maria's room. She was putting Belinda in to a large holdall that would be far too heavy for her to carry. Phil picked up the bag and pretended it was too heavy for him.

"Oh Maria, what have you got it in here?" Maria giggled and Phil continued "Well you must be going for at least three weeks!"

Maria's smile disappeared immediately and she looked up at Phil and said "Daddy, you wont leave me there that long will you?"

Phil looked at her like his heart would break "Of course not poppet. I promise I will collect you first thing after breakfast tomorrow morning. How's that?"

He scooped her up into his arms and carried her down the stairs. Maria clung on round his neck and showered him with kisses "Love you Daddy" she repeated over and over.

At the bottom of the stairs Becks was waiting to kiss her daughter goodbye "Be a good girl for Nana, Maria, and do as she tells you." She gave her a brief kiss on her forehead and raced up the stairs without even looking back.

Maria and Phil walked across the noble hall and out of the delightful porch. Strapping Maria into her booster seat in the back of Beck's BMW X5, Phil kissed Maria on the cheek and ruffled her hair. She smiled at him adoringly.

I am not even sure why we took the car, it was such a short journey. Five minutes later we were pulling up outside a very pretty house, surrounded by roses of all different colours.

"Thanks mum," Phil said as he handed over Maria's bag to an elderly yet very elegant and classy lady.

"Come here, you beautiful child" Phil's mother said excitedly. "Now lets wave Daddy off from the front window." Both girls kissed Phil on the cheek and they hurried inside to catch his departure from the front room. Phil beeped the horn as he drove off.

The minute we left, Phil lit up again. He seemed agitated now and nowhere near as relaxed as earlier. Mumbling to himself, words that I just couldn't make out, whilst dragging heavily on his cigarette, he drove very slowly back to the house.

The entrance looked as stylish as last time yet now Phil's manner was noticeably different. He almost dragged himself into the house. As soon as he shut the door, he sighed heavily and made his way up to the first floor. I couldn't hear Becks so I presumed she was down stairs preparing for the evening, whatever that may entail. Phil unbuttoned his shirt as he entered the en-suite and turned on the shower. I noticed from where I had been flung onto the bed, that the bathroom was black tiling with chrome devices. It was all very swish and expensive and I wondered if it was Phil who paid for this on his salary. I wasn't sure exactly what his position was but I certainly got the impression that it wasn't enough to create this lavish lifestyle.

I could hear Phil splashing around in the shower and I noticed Becks creep into the bedroom. She tutted as she saw his jacket flung onto the bed. She picked it up and spent a while searching through his pockets. Almost looking disappointed that nothing was found, she hung the jacket up in the enormous walk in wardrobe and left the room quietly.

I had quite an uncomfortable feeling about all this yet I still didn't know what to expect from tonight. If they were staying in, would they really need to send their child off for the night? If they were going out, why was Maria so concerned about the state of the house? I had no choice but to wait.

Eventually Phil emerged from the shower. I could tell he had shaved, not from the lack of stubble as there wasn't any in the first place, but because of the tell tale swatches of toilet paper plastered to his chin where he had nicked himself.

He sauntered over to the wardrobe seemingly oblivious to the fact that his jacket had gone. I was still on the bed and I did notice a glance in my direction, just to make sure I was there. Well it was probably to check that the cigarettes were still there. I was easily replaceable.

He pulled out a purple shirt, obviously designer. I think the label said Armand Bassi. His jeans said Evisu. This was all new to me. The nearest I had come to designer wear were Darren's Nikes. It was all very interesting though. He looked good. His fair complexion complemented the blue and purple of his outfit. It was however, quite different to Becks's look in comparison. She had gone for the wild sassy vixen look, as far as I could tell. I had no idea what labels she was wearing but the black dress and heels made her look incredibly powerful and to some perhaps totally desirable.

Phil grabbed me and trotted down the stairs. He made straight for the wine fridge and pulled out a bottle of Veuve Cliquot and opened it immediately. He took a glass and the bottle out through the open French windows and sat at the wooden garden table on the decked patio. The September air was warm but I could feel Autumn was just around the corner. Another couple of weeks and the leaves would turn and the inevitable blast of winter would begin. I dreaded winter. I much preferred the great outdoors. I had no problem sitting in warm cosy pubs though!

Phil downed his first glass of champagne and poured himself another. I could hear Becks tottering around inside and Phil lit a cigarette and rested his head on his hand. The minute Becks' head appeared at the door, Phil almost jumped to attention "Yes darling?" he said unconvincingly.

"Phil darling, be a dear. Can you just call the caterers to find out what time they are arriving?" As she trotted back into the kitchen she continued "Lord only know what time they'll get here".

Without stubbing his cigarette out, Phil followed Maria inside and grabbed the cordless phone. I could see him scrabbling around in a drawer, presumably for the telephone number and eventually called out "Where's the number darling?"

A muted, curt voice with a hint of annoyance replied "On the side next to the fridge". Phil picked up the brochure and brought it outside. Supping half of his glass, he dialled the number and spoke to someone at the other end

"Good evening, this is Phil Bradley. I understand we have a delivery expected this evening and wondered what time you would be dropping off the goods? " The response must have been favourable as Phil smiled and thanked the person twice.

He replaced the phone and called up to Becks that the caterer should be arriving in about 15 minutes. He returned to the garden and sat. He dragged on his fag and gulped down his second glass of champagne and was about to pour a third when the doorbell rang.

"Darling, would you get that?" came the expected enquiry and dutifully Phil got up and answered the door. I couldn't see who it was as I was a fair distance but eventually the voices drew nearer and I heard Phil ask his guests for drink preferences. When I heard more corks popping, I thought that possibly this was some kind of celebration. My world very rarely included champagne but when it did, it was to salute some form of celebration.

The doorbell rang again and this time Becks must have answered it herself. She brought another couple into the kitchen and I heard glasses chinking and laughter
growing louder. I was very intrigued now. I really wanted to know what was going on but from outside I could see nothing and hear very little. It was so frustrating. I just hoped that at some point Phil would need another cigarette and I could stow away in his pocket and watch the proceedings.

When the doorbell rang again, a few people must have turned up at the same time as almost instantly the noise from the kitchen became incredibly loud. I guessed that the caterers had also turned up as a wonderful aroma drifted out of the kitchen.

At last Phil came out onto the deck and lit up a cigarette. He was not alone though. A beautiful and curvaceous brunette followed him and took a seat. She also lit up and crossed her legs slowly as she sipped her drink.

Phil seemed mesmerised and his eyes never left her. I wondered who this lady was. Why she was here and if Becks minded that Phil appeared completely in lust with this woman. As I pondered this, I saw Phil's hand move over to the lady's leg and gently move its way up her thigh. The lady almost purred. I was transfixed. 'Blimey, this is a bit dangerous isn't it?' I thought to myself.

The lady leaned forward and kissed Phil on the cheek. I could almost see his heart palpitating. It felt like that silly film 'Lady and the Tramp' and I half expected Phil to howl at any moment!

Phil whispered, "You look ravishing Eve, absolutely edible".

At that moment Becks popped her head around the French doors and casually indicated that the food was ready. She took in Eve's body position and her outfit in seconds and smiled tersely.

Phil and Eve both stood and made their way back into the house. I could see Phil place his hand on Eve's rather sumptuous bottom and I was shocked!

Frustrated again at the lack of vision, I strained to hear what was being said. There was an awful lot of banter and small talk but eventually after a while, I sensed the atmosphere changing. The alcohol had probably kicked in now and the guests' inhibitions were undoubtedly disappearing fast.

I guessed about an hour passed when I noticed that the noisy guests had piped down. It was almost as if they had vanished. I perked up when I saw a couple heading toward me. The guy was greying but probably not as old as he looked. He was holding hands with a slim girl with short bobbed cut hair. As soon as they were outside his hands were all over her and she was laughing as he kissed her neck and unzipped her dress. Further down the garden was a large rug on the grass. Lanterns had been placed strategically around the garden and the spectacle was most impressive. I hadn't really noticed it before as my attentions had been directed in the opposite direction.

I could barely make out the couple now as they made their way to the garden boudoir but it dawned on me that this was some kind of swinger's party. No one would go to a party with their own partner and fondle in the garden, at least not at their age. The girl did look quite young admittedly but I didn't doubt for a second that they weren't husband and wife.

Lordy lordy!! This was hilarious. Now I understood why little Maria had to be accommodated elsewhere and why Phil looked so agitated earlier. It all fell into place. It was pretty obvious that Becks and Phil had little time for each other and the pretence and keeping up appearances was almost killing them but this way they could get their kicks in acceptable circumstances and I bet they even told themselves it helped their marriage and prevented Maria from growing up in a broken home.

'Different strokes' I mumbled in disbelief as I tried to avoid hearing the moans and giggles emanating from the garden. Due to nightfall my vision was impaired but I could swear I saw them fall into a hammock at the end of the lawn.

I could only imagine that Phil had eyes for Eve but I wasn't quite sure of the etiquette in these circumstances. Did Phil choose? Did Eve choose? Or were partners chosen for them somehow? I wasn't sure if the rumours of a car key lucky dip were true and unfortunately for my inquisitive mind, it didn't look as though I was going to find out.

To try and evade groaning noises, I cast my mind back to Whin, he was always a welcome distraction.

· ·

FLASHBACK

· ·

Whin looked again at Tom and I knew he was looking for approval. Poor Whin. This whole situation had devastated him. I just hoped that by telling someone and letting it all out, that he could somehow begin to cope with it and move on. Easier said than done but this was killing him.

Tom gently touched his arm. He said nothing but his intentions were clear. He wanted Whin to continue.

Whin took a long swig of his beer and scratched his forehead. "It was amazing Tom. She was beautiful and exciting. It was so unexpected that I guess it made it all the more delightful. I won't go into all the details. I don't wanna embarrass you and Mel's a lady. I don't wanna go telling on her." Whin persisted in his scratching his forehead. It was slightly raised now and red. I had noticed that whenever Whin felt stressed, he reaction was to rub his forehead. Whether it soothed him somehow, I didn't know but Tom spotted this too and softly pulled his arm away from his head.

Whin looked up. He suddenly became more conscious of his actions and picked me up and started twirling me in his fingers. I didn't mind. I was quite tactile and I enjoyed the human touch.

"In the morning, I just didn't know how to behave. Part of me wanted to run away before she awoke so that I wouldn't have to see the realisation on her face. That would have killed me Tom". Tom nodded and Whin continued, "I didn't get the chance to decide though as I then saw that she had left the bed. I couldn't hear any sounds from the bathroom so I went downstairs. I made myself decent thought Tom. I was fully expecting her to ask me to leave so I wanted to look proper for her and not disgust her."

"I saw that she was busy in the kitchen. I could and smell breakfast cooking half way down the stairs. For a split second I even thought about slipping through the front door but she heard me on the stairs and called for me to come into the kitchen."

"Ohhhh Tom. She looked even more beautiful. The sun was shining through the kitchen window and lit up her gorgeous hair. She had no make up on and the sadness in her eyes that I had seen the night before had gone. She looked young and carefree".

"Tom. She took my hand and led me to the kitchen table. As I sat she rested her hands on my shoulders and kissed the top of my head." Whin looked up at Tom and said to him "Tom. It was the kindest thing anyone has ever done to me".

Tom patted Whin's arm and nodded slowly. I could see the compassion in his eyes and knew I could trust him to hear Whin out. Whin had to get this off his chest. He had to find a shoulder to cry on. Tom seemed the best person for the job. He didn't talk much and was happy to help his friend out.

"If I only knew then Tom, what heartbreak this would all bring". At this point Whin paused for a while. I could only hope that he would have the courage to talk about it. All of it.

• •

FLASHBACK

• •

CHAPTER 7

The next thing I knew it was dawn. There was silence. I couldn't see anyone on the rug now but then it was just a tad too nippy to spend the entire night outside. To prove that, I felt a little unwell; a few aches and pains. The morning damp had made me a little stiff but nothing that a few rays wouldn't sort out.

After such fun last night, I wasn't expecting to see anyone up at such an early hour but after a few minutes, I heard footsteps in the kitchen. Craning round to see Eve slip out into the garden, I was surprised. She was wearing last night's foxy outfit so I presumed there had been no intention of a sleepover. She spotted me and the packet of fags and breathed a sigh of relief. Grabbing me and lighting up, she sat down and stared out into the beautifully coiffured garden.

She quietly puffed away and I sensed that not all was well. She didn't have that glow of someone who had shared the night with their lover. She wasn't smiling and looked, to be frank, quite haggard. She had almost finished her cigarette when I heard more noises in the kitchen.

Phil popped his head round the door and Eve smiled at him. Her face lit up. Phil looked concerned and stepped out onto the deck. He was wearing only his pants and the cool morning air was making his nipples erect. Rubbing his goose bumps he sat right next to Eve and rested his head against hers. He took in her smell and ruffled her hair.

"Trust me Eve," he said simply.

Suddenly I heard another noise and this startled both Eve and Phil. With all three of us turning to see who this intruder was into this serene scene, I was the last to see Becks storm out of the house. Wrapped in a crimson red satin dressing gown, tied at her slender waist, she looked furious.

However cross she looked though, her voice was calm when she said "I see you stayed the night Eve". Becks folded her arms and waited for a response.

Eve turned her head and looked so sad. This spiteful old witch was going to give her a bad time, we all knew it and Eve just sat there at prepared to be yelled at.

When it didn't arrive, Eve turned her head back and saw a completely different face on Becks. She was almost gloating now. It was pretty obvious that Phil and Becks' relationship was going nowhere but Becks was holding the cards and the fate of Eve lay in Becks extremely expensively manicured hands.

"Oh for God's sake Becks" Tom leaped to his feet "This was all your idea anyway" he sputtered. Propelled by years of pent up fury, he lashed out "You were the one that introduced us to this perverse life. I obviously haven't satisfied you for years so to make me a public spectacle you throw sex parties in our house. I don't know why you are happy to host swinging parties yet you have a problem if I end up with anyone. How much sense does that make?" he spat.

I was fully awake now and listening intently. Becks was still smiling knowingly. She felt safe. She believed that Phil would never leave her. He loved his swish lifestyle too much and she was certain he would never leave Maria.

Phil lit up a cigarette and sat back down next to a worried looking Eve. He stroked her hand and coolly raised his eyes to watch Becks. "I've had enough" he said. "I don't want to be in this ridiculous farce of a marriage any more".

Locking his eyes onto Becks', he continued, "You don't want me, but you don't want me to have anyone else. I cant live like that." His voice choking he continued, "I cant be what you want me to be Becks and you'll be happier without me".

Becks jaw fell. She obviously hadn't expected this. This wasn't how it was supposed to end. She was supposed to enjoy watching that silly tart, Eve, embarrass herself and leave without the man of her dreams. I could see the panic in her rise. Her mind was racing. All the 'what ifs' ran through her brain.

"What about Maria?" she gasped desperately trying to hold on to her dignity. "You can't leave her."

"You're right" said Phil "I can't leave that gorgeous girl, the one you don't give a damn about. I'll take her with me and do my utmost in court to fight you for custody"

Swallowing hard Backs composure was failing miserably. She wanted to start this conversation again but Phil was already standing up and leading Eve back into the house. Thankfully Eve had picked me up and put me in her pocket. I didn't want to be left with this cold woman.

Phil guided Eve safely to the door and asked her to wait in the car for him. He ran upstairs, presumably for some of his things. He knew they would not be in any fit state if he came back later. Eve trudged across the gravel to the Audi and opened the passenger door. She looked terrified but behind the fear was relief.

Eventually Phil came running out of the door and jumped into the driver's seat. He leaned over to Eve and kissed her fervently, much to the chagrin of the watchful Becks. Backing out of the drive he said " I hope you don't mind but I want to pick up Maria and then I guess its back to yours, if that ok? It looks like I'm homeless!"

Eve smiled and looked up at the fuming woman at the front door. Becks was keeping her temper in check for now but she had been overridden and there was no telling what she would plan.

The short journey to Phil's mother's house was silent but I could feel the exhilarating atmosphere. They were both desperate to talk, to discuss their future. The happiness that filled the car suddenly vanished the minute we reached Maria's grandmother's house. "How am I going to explain this to her?" Phil asked Eve in desperation.

"Don't worry," Eve said gently "She'll be fine".

Phil asked Eve to stay in the car and whilst he trotted up to the front door, Eve pulled me out of her pocket and lit up a cigarette. This was going to be difficult but the determination on her face showed me that she was hell bent on keeping her man, now that he had had the balls to face up to that bitch. All I kept thinking was, it will all end in tears.

A few minutes later Phil came back carrying Maria and after he strapped her into the car seat, they drove off to Eve's apartment. It wasn't far but the tension had grown and Maria sensed this and asked, "Where are we going Daddy? Why are we not going home?"

Phil looked at Maria through the rear view mirror and smiled. "It's a surprise poppet. You like surprises don't you?"

Eve looked at Phil for a while. I couldn't read her expression but when they reached the traffic lights, Eve gently guided Phil through the town's one-way systems. From their intermittent conversation, I got the impression that Phil had only visited Eve's flat once.

This all seemed rather peculiar to me. I didn't feel that they knew each other very well but it appeared to me that they were using each other. Phil was using Eve as an excuse to pluck up the courage to leave Becks. I hadn't worked out at this stage what Eve was after.

Maria was excitedly chatting to herself, the way small children do, and it wasn't until they reached Eve's apartment, that Maria took any notice of her surroundings. Phil hadn't brought any of Maria's belongings apart from the overnight bag but realising this, he just said to Eve as he slammed the boot shut, "I may have to go shopping for us. These things won't last us long!"

Eve's face was a picture. It suddenly dawned on her exactly what she had done. She was living in a two bedroom apartment that was described as 'bijou'. How on earth was she going to have room for another man and his daughter? It was obvious that Eve had not really thought this through. I don't think it occurred to her that Maria would in all seriousness be coming along too.

Fighting the urge to say something she would probably regret, Eve took Maria's hand and led them into the entrance hall. The dingy block of flats were only 4 floors high but there was a double lift. Thinking of Maria's short legs, she pressed the 'call' button and bent down to the child "See if you can guess which floor I live on?"

Maria shrugged her shoulders and judging by Phil's reaction, this behaviour was unusual. "Maria, don't be rude" Phil shouted, louder than he intended. "Eve is asking you a question".

Maria turned to Eve and apologised. "I'm sorry," she said. The look on her face, however, was not apologetic at all. Eve's initial delight faded when Maria's dislike of her became apparent.

The lift arrived and we all climbed inside. Maria didn't bother guessing which floor we would be stopping at but before Eve pressed the button, I guessed the top floor. I had an impression that we would be accommodated in a glorious penthouse flat. I was wrong. Eve pressed number 3 and we all stood in the lift, silently.

Eve led us down a dark hallway. It was dirty exactly and unkempt. It looked like it just needed a good scrub to get rid of the nasty odours and a lick of paint. In all honesty I thought the best thing was demolition!

At the end of the passage, Eve unlocked a royal blue door and we walked straight into a lounge come dining room. Directly ahead was a large picture window and Maria ran forward and looked out over the town. As we were only 3 floors up, there was nothing particular to gaze upon, except a few roofs of neighbouring flats and a glimpse of a small park.

Maria spent a while gazing out of the window and Eve showed Phil around her apartment.

"Here is the little kitchen" she informed Phil as we opened a small door to the right of the lounge. She was right. It was ridiculously small.

"Yes, I sort of remember this. And over there?" He pointed to the other side of the living space.

We moved across the dining room and facing us were four doors. The first opened up into a master bedroom, which would be just big enough for two and through the next door was a separate toilet. The bathroom was plain but it housed both a bath and a shower, always handy for children and next followed a second bedroom, which was certainly big enough for a small child. To my mind I had seen far worse cramped conditions but I had to appreciate that Eve, up until now, had enjoyed this space to herself. Phil and Maria on the other hand were used to the luxuries in life and I could understand how this could have appeared like a backward step.

I could visibly see the disappointment on Phil's face but this was momentary as he realised that this would be a temporary stop and that they would purchase a new property for the three of them.

Eve turned on the television in the lounge and found a cartoon channel. She asked Maria if she wanted anything to eat. I could see that creating a bond was difficult for her and she obviously had little or no experience with children.

Maria shrugged her shoulders and ran to Phil. She held her arms up to be cuddled. Eve, without realising, rolled her eyes but thankfully Phil didn't see. He was preoccupied with his daughter, stroking her hair and talking quietly and calmly to try and stop the steady flow of tears that had now begun to fall.

Eve strolled into the kitchen and put the kettle on. I could hear noises and soon realised she was making tea. Isn't it funny how in most situations, a cup of tea is always the answer. I say most, because I have spent most of my time in pubs and there beer or a stiff whiskey is regarded as not only the best answer, but the only answer!

Phil sat with Maria on the sofa and gently asked her "Hey poppet, what's wrong? Don't you like Scooby Doo?" He pointed to the television. Maria, however, was not interested and clung to Phil like her life depended on it.

"Now what is it?" Phil tried again. "Why are you so upset?"

Maria was still crying and Phil's shirt was soaking wet. With tears streaming down her face, she faced her father and said "Daddy, I want to go home".

To her, it was that simple. To everyone else it was a major problem. To anyone who had ever seen Phil with Maria, it was obvious that they adored each other and hated being separated. Becks was not a particularly maternal woman and Maria had acknowledged that fairly early on in her short life. She steered clear of her mother when Phil was about but now the little girl sensed tension and just wanted the security of home and familiar belongings to ease her mind. She was a very sensible girl in my opinion. The atmosphere here was so tense, I wouldn't stay if I had a choice.

Phil continued to hug Maria and rocked her backwards and forwards. Eve came back into the room with a tray. She put a chocolate milkshake with a red straw on the coffee table in front of Maria, and looked quietly confident that this would be an ice-breaker. Phil wiped Maria's eyes and showed her the milkshake. Maria glared at Eve but took a sip and returned to cuddling her father.

I wasn't sure how this was going to all pan out. I mean even Eve was looking fed up. Phil was very stressed and poor little Maria, who had no idea what was going on, was clearly upset.

Phil opened his mouth to speak to Eve but he was interrupted by his mobile phone. The star wars theme tune sounded really daft and it echoed around the lounge. Phil took it from his pocket and flipped the screen up with one hand whilst still holding on to Maria.

"Its Becks" Phil said as he glanced at Eve.

Eve shrugged and got up. She disappeared into the kitchen. I got the distinct impression that she did not want to be involved in any of it.

"Yes?" Phil asked coolly as he answered the phone.

I couldn't hear the conversation from the other end but I suspect that Becks had worked out that Phil must have collected Maria by now and I was guessing that her intention was to emotionally blackmail her daughter into coming home. As far as I could see that really wouldn't be difficult. Although it was obvious that Becks and Maria had a very distant relationship, I could see with my limited experience that she was better off at home.

Phil slammed the phone shut and looked distinctly angry. He hadn't said a word to Becks and I wasn't totally sure what he had been asked to do but he wasn't happy about it.

Eve came back into the lounge and asked for a cigarette. Phil put Maria on the sofa and left her watching cartoons whilst he took Eve's hand and led her into the kitchen. He opened the small window, which overlooked a huge tower block. He pulled two cigarettes out and lit both of them. After handing one to Eve, he stroked the side of her face and took a long drag of his fag.

"She wants me back," he said simply. "Well I'm not sure she wants me back exactly but she doesn't want me with you and ..." he trailed off. It was a complicated web of loyalties, love and lust. I wasn't sure how long this affair had been going on, not very long if Phil had only ever visited her apartment once but right at that moment Phil saw the situation for what it was. Eve was a strikingly beautiful woman and sexy beyond belief but she was wrong for him. She wasn't strong enough; there was nothing in her eyes that said she would be his backbone. Sometimes he hated Becks but my god she was powerfully strong. He needed the stability and structure that she offered.

With Maria still tearful in his arms, Phil grabbed the overnight bag and opened the front door. Eve looked on sadly and watched him leave with her arms folded. That's always a clear indicator. Body language is often overlooked but I was reading from her pose and expression, that she was very disappointed yet not altogether surprised. The disappointment didn't look like a lost love type to me though. Oh no, it looked more like the frustration of someone out to get their hands on some money. Serious money.

The minute the door closed, I realised that I was being left with Eve. I wasn't in Phil's pocket, I was here in Eve's flat. 'Oh Lord', I thought. Yet another owner, yet another life. As if sensing my confused state of mind, Eve grabbed me and lit up. Rolling me around and around in her fingers, while she smoked, she became more and more agitated.

It could only have been early afternoon but Eve headed straight for a large bottle of vodka situated on her kitchen work surface. I got the impression that this she was a frequent consumer. I think it was the clue that the bottle was in such a prime location that gave it away!

Several swigs later and I could see Eve melt a little. Her tension seemed to disappear a touch and I hoped that I would be able to find out what her problem was. The rest of the afternoon slipped away with a monotonous repeat of large vodka shots and cigarettes. Strangely the more vodka was consumed, the more restless Eve became. At first it had seemed to ease her disillusionment but numerous shots later, her demeanour had altered completely. When she began ranting, I became nervous.

Slumped on the sofa, carelessly flicking through endless channels, the totally inebriated Eve grew quite morose. I couldn't make out all the words as she was slurring quite badly now. Those I did hear however, were seriously worrying. Her mood had become so dark, I wasn't sure how this evening was going to end.

During a particularly mad rant, there was a sharp knock on the door. Instead of cursing the door or throwing objects, I was surprised to note that within seconds her façade changed from anger to utter fear.

Her eyes widened and I could hardly hear her breathe. She clutched at a cushion from the other end of the sofa and covered her mouth. Her terrified eyes were still visible over the edge of the cushion. She reminded me of a small child half watching a scary film, frightened to see what came next but overwhelmingly intrigued.

Another rap on the door shook her from her static position on the sofa and she fell onto the floor with a quiet thump. Twisting the corners of the cushion in anguish, she began rocking backwards and forwards. I am no expert in psychology but rocking is not a good sign. As far as I can tell, it actually shows severe stress levels, and psychological issues.

Yet another knock and this time, Eve tried to scramble for the bathroom door. It wasn't until recently that it dawned on me why people always seem to head for the bathroom when hiding. It's probably the only room people have that can be locked. Maybe I'm stupid I don't know but I just hadn't realised that before. Looking at Eve though and I didn't think her intellect was driving her to the bathroom, more desperate panic.

Watching her dart across the room, I wondered who on earth could be at the door and why she could be so petrified. Someone was now trying to pick the lock and after a few fumbling seconds, the lever clicked and the handle edged down.

My heart almost skipped a beat. There really was someone coming through the door. Whoever it was would soon guess that Eve was at home. The vodka bottle, tumbler and overfull ashtray was a bit of a give away. Slowly the door inched open and my first glimpsed showed a man of fairly large proportions. He looked a bit like a bouncer. He wasn't wearing the stereotypical black bomber jacket but something similar in leather. I couldn't see any facial piercing but he looked the type. He also looked like the type that you would do anything to keep in favour. In other words he looked mean. I could see why Eve would be frightened half to death. Lord only knew what she had done to this man to upset him but something had happened and I don't think he wanted to talk about it.

The man gave a furtive glance around the lounge to see what the situation was. He seemed relaxed enough to enter and close the door behind him. Poking his head around the kitchen door, he frowned. I don't think he wanted to play hide and seek. Without a word, he strode across the room and made towards the bathroom. Well he obviously knew his way around. That move made the whole thing even more fascinating.

He rattled the door handle but I think we both could have guessed that the door would have been locked from the inside. Turning slightly, he then threw his body weight onto the door. I heard a scream from inside and saw the large man smile malevolently. It took a few shoves before the door gave way. Steadying himself on the doorframe, he paused before entering.

My vision was interrupted and so I had to rely on my hearing and strained to listen to what was being said.

"What's the point of hiding?" the man asked Eve in a very sarcastic manner.

Amidst screams and what I thought were possibly thumps, I just about made out Eve saying "Sorry, sorry". I could definitely hear her crying though and my heart went out to her. Whatever she had done or said to this monster was not worth this intimidation.

"Listen, it's really simple. Just pay up and then it's sorted". The man made it perfectly clear that a sum of money was owed and he intended to get it back.

"I can't, I can't" wailed Eve from the bathroom. "I don't have it".

The next thing I knew, Eve was being dragged by her hair, into the lounge. It certainly wasn't for my benefit but I think the man felt more in control in the larger room. He pulled her to her feet and his sick smile gave me the terrors and I had no idea how Eve was feeling.

Grabbing her shoulders so roughly that huge bruises would appear the next day, he said slowly "I'm coming back tomorrow night. I will be paid". He threw her to the floor and kicked her in the stomach before leaving the apartment.

At that point I really wished I had arms so I could comfort her. I felt so useless. Lighting cigarettes wasn't really solving her problems. I was beginning to form a picture in my head. I had no idea if I was anywhere near the truth but it felt accurate to me. The disappointment written all over Eve's face as Phil left the building kept popping into my head. Something about it felt wrong. Like it didn't fit and then I twigged; she wasn't upset about the great love affair being over, she had seen him as a protector. When she realised that he was going to be totally useless to her, her attitude changed. With this in mind, my feelings towards Eve changed. I had no idea why she was indebted to this burly man but using another woman's husband to help her was wrong in my book. I still worried about her physical and emotional state though. She looked dreadful when she managed to drag herself to the sofa.

The first thing she did was grab the vodka bottle and drain the remains. This was not good. Apart from looking a mess, she seemed desperate.

After a while she summoned enough strength to stagger into the kitchen. I really hoped that she wouldn't be searching for another bottle of booze but she was looking for something. I could hear her scratching around in the cupboards and then the tap ran. Walking back into the lounge with a pint glass of water, I felt relieved. She had obviously decided to sober herself up and sort things out.

As I watched her gulp some water though, I realised that with each sip, she was popping tablets into her mouth. I couldn't see how many she was swallowing each time but I was getting nervous. After most of the water had been drunk, Eve lurched onto the sofa and buried her head in the cushion and sobbed.

Well here I was again in a ridiculous situation with absolutely no control. Lord only knows how many tablets the woman had taken and what was going to happen. I sat worrying about it for hours. The darkness seemed to go on forever and when I saw dawn break, I finally gave up and passed out with exhaustion.

CHAPTER 8

The next thing I knew was the phone buzzing. A shrill European style ring permeated the entire flat and it was constant. The person on the other end was obviously intent on contacting Eve.

I was fully awake now but Eve didn't seem to be stirring. I glanced up at the clock on the wall connected to the kitchen and it read 11:32. The phone stopped ringing and I watched Eve closely. I could have been mistaken but I was sure I could see her chest rise and fall. The relief was enormous. My sleep had even been troubled with nightmares about suicides. Although she was alive, she was not waking up and that began to panic me.

The telephone started up again and after about 5 minutes and a short break, it recommenced. This pattern went on for over an hour. I was helpless. I could only watch as this woman in front of me lay in some kind of unconscious state.

Just before 1 o'clock, I heard a dainty tapping on the door, followed by a female's voice repeating Eve's name. The knocks grew louder and louder until she finally hammered on the door. Eve still did not stir. The knocking became silent and I could only pray that the female had gone for help. The phone started again and I also became aware of a buzzing noise from the kitchen. Presumably that was her mobile.

Waiting impatiently, I grew more and more anxious. I was so sure that the outcome of this would be immense sadness and loss.

Finally after another hour I heard a loud discussion from the hallway. I couldn't even hazard a guess as to who the girl had called, but I was hoping that it would be someone with a key.

As I heard the lock turn, I thanked all my lucky stars. A middle-aged lady entered the room, closely followed by a pretty girl only just out of school. The older lady looked slightly perturbed and the girl had dread written all over her face.

They crept in the room, which was laughable since they had tried to hammer the door down earlier and they even began by whispering her name. Within seconds though they had spotted her body lying on the sofa and the girl stifled a scream whilst the older lady ran over to her and checked her over.

"Eve, Eve", the lady shouted whilst shaking her. "Katy, call 999" she said as she looked up at the girl still clasping her hands over her mouth in distress. "KATY" the lady yelled, "DO IT NOW!"

The tone of voice and the increased volume stirred Katy from her state of shock and she rummaged around in her bag and eventually pulled out a pink mobile phone covered in jewels. If I could, I would have rolled my eyes!

She fumbled with the handset and punched in the emergency number. She began stammering but managed to give out Eve's address but fell to pieces when the operator started asking further questions. Through her sobs, she answered the queries with monosyllabic responses.

The lady was kneeling on the floor stroking Eve's hair and staring at Katy but I didn't think she was seeing her. She looked a million miles away. Lost in a million and one possible scenarios as to how and why Eve was in this condition.

The minutes ticked by slowly and after what seemed like an age, a paramedic team arrived at the front door, which was still ajar. They wasted no time in attending to Eve and checking her vital signs. The female medic turned to the waiting companions and said that they needed to take her in to St Mark's as she was cataleptic.

By the looks on their faces, they had no idea what that meant but it sounded serious and they nodded glumly and waited with frightened and miserable gazes whilst the medical team fixed Eve to a stretcher and carted her out of the room.

Katy and the lady followed almost like a funeral procession but before they left, Katy ran back into the lounge and grabbed Eve's handbag along with her mobile from the bedroom, a remaining packet of cigarettes and me. I'm not quite sure why she took the fags. As far as I could remember, there was a no smoking policy in hospitals but maybe she wanted them for herself. Shock was a very strange thing. I had seen people who were fanatical about the negative effects of smoking, taking several drags upon receipt of bad news.

The older lady had parked her white Fiat Punto opposite the main doors to the apartment block and after the ambulance departed, they followed suite. The journey took a while but my vision was impaired, as I had been stuck in the boot. I took the time in the darkness to think about Whin.

• •

FLASHBACK

• •

Whin just sat without talking. Tom had decided not to remind his friend to continue. He took the time to enjoy his beer and looked around the cosy bar. There were a few regulars that he knew by sight but had never really spoken to but apart from that it was fairly quiet. Just how he liked it. He looked back at Whin and caught his eye.

"Sorry Tom," Whin muttered. "I didn't mean to drift off just then!" he gave a hollow laugh. Still a hollow laugh was better than no laugh and I took that to be a huge improvement.

"Now then, I've forgotten where I got to" Whin looked at Tom enquiringly but Tom just passively nodded.

"Arh yes. The morning after!" He smiled. It looked like he held the secrets of the universe in that smile. "God that morning I was possibly the happiest man alive". We ate breakfast in the small conservatory overlooking the garden. She made me scrambled eggs but it tasted like manna from heaven. It was the tastiest meal I have ever eaten."

Taking a sip from his pint glass, I glanced at Tom. He expression was as usual, incredibly hard to read but I thought I saw a glimmer of intrigue. Tom didn't seem a cold person but he wasn't tactile either. I was sure that once Whin's story had been told, whatever it was, Tom's heart would melt.

"I did go home. I really did. I went back when it was dark. My little house that I had felt so secure in, had felt at home in, now felt empty and cold. Even watching some documentary, that I would normally revel in, seemed boring and so I tried to sleep in my bed. Trust me Tom, until that point I had never ever suffered from insomnia".

A coughing fit paused the conversation for a while and Tom even leaned over and slapped Whin on the back. Geoff rushed over with some tap water, not the good stuff. Catching his breath eventually, Whin thanked the guys and gestured them to stop making a fuss. I knew at once that Geoff had been trying to rack his brains for a reason to trot over to the table again, to try and overhear some of the discussion. It was written all over his face how desperate he was to know what was going on. A glass of water though, was not really the answer and frustrated, Geoff retreated to the other side of the bar, accepting that he would have to wait.

After composing himself but still slightly redder in the face than normal, Whin continued.

"God that was a long night. I was so sure that after a night away from me, she would see sense. That she would see me for the old fool I really am."

Tom became slightly animated at this point and held onto Whin's arm. "Don't be silly Whin. You may be old but you're no fool." He smirked slightly and said gently "Carry on."

Whin looked slightly bemused by this and it took him a couple of seconds to collect himself " Well Tom, I did sleep at some point obviously but by the time morning came around, I was in such a state that I did a really silly thing and called Mel. I felt like such a schoolboy with his first crush. I couldn't get her out of my mind and I just needed to hear her say that she didn't want to see me again. The not knowing was killing me."

"Of course when she did answer the phone, she sounded so happy to hear from me. I even imagined her having a restless night too. I have never showered and dressed so quickly!" he joked.

Tom motioned for Geoff to bring over two more beers. Geoff, of course, leaped at the opportunity but again was disappointed when the conversation had broken off before he got to the table.

"The next two days are a blur but what a blur! The only thing that was clouding our happiness was the impending funeral." Whin let out a long sigh.

"I still feel so bad about that. I feel like I didn't give her time to grieve. When the Friday loomed, that was the day of the funeral, I left her in peace for a couple of hours before the hearse arrived. I thought that she just needed to be alone." Whin paused for a long swig of his drink.

"The service was beautiful and I was so moved. The church was packed and although I knew Alan well, I felt it wasn't my place to sit up front. I stood back during the committal and even when the Vicar invited all to Mel's for a wake, I had second thoughts about whether I should attend. I tried to catch Mel's eye to see if she wanted me there or not but she was too wrapped up in family." Whin quickly looked up at Tom and added anxiously "And too right".

Whin cast his eyes down and held his head in his palms for a while. I could tell he was resisting the urge to scratch that forehead "I did go back Tom". I knew deep down it would be better to give her some space but like an idiot Tom, I couldn't keep away. At first I tried to keep in the background but as the afternoon drew on, I had to touch her. I can admit this now but I was addicted". Whin looked rather small, fiddling with his hands nervously. I could tell he felt silly. He knew he was an old man but he had acted like a lovesick teenager.

• •

FLASHBACK

• •

CHAPTER 9

I had lost count of the time and although the drive had been fairly quick, I actually felt rather rested. I was hoisted out of the boot into the cold night air and realised that we were racing into the front doors of St Marks.

I listened as the older lady asked for information about Eve and surprisingly when the receptionist asked if she was a relation of the patient, she replied that she was her mother.

Katy on the other hand was not a relative and I could only hazard a guess that she was a colleague and must have been the one who alerted her mother when she didn't turn up for work.

We all sat patiently in the waiting room for what seemed like days but actually according to the clock above the receptionist's desk, it was actually only about an hour and a half. I loved people watching so this was quite enjoyable for me. I don't think Katy and Eve's mother were really in the mood for this sport but I studied all the individuals in minute detail. There was a rough bunch sat against the glass wall, near the entrance. They all looked inebriated and very worse for wear. My expert guess would be that they were homeless and alcoholics. They looked filthy and there were a few spare seats around them, presumably because they stank.

Across from us were a couple. I reckoned they had been together for a long time as they had started to look like each other. She looked quite odd with short mannish hair and thick round glasses. He had a very similar haircut with almost identical glasses. They reminded me of people who wear his and hers anoraks or tracksuits. Why on earth would people want to do that? I could see the female holding her wrist carefully on her lap. Mister was sitting, looking very tense with one arm round his wife staring straight ahead. It's always the quite ones that lead the most extraordinary lives so judging by the appearance of these two, the wrist could have been damaged in some wild and wacky sex game!

Next to them were a mother and son. The boy was possibly about 5 years old and looked rather hot and sweaty. I knew that kids were often seen first so I hoped that he would be going in quickly as the poor sausage really didn't look well. The mother looked close to tears and kept checking her watch, as if trying to make time pass quicker.

Eve's mother and Katy were silent and motionless. Neither of them were doing anything remotely interesting, both lost in their own thoughts, so I continued to scrutinize the remaining patients

Along the row, there was a young girl sitting alone. She was maybe eighteen at best but probably more like 16. I always enjoyed speculating and assuming a whole scenario. My guess with this little one was that she was terrified that she could be pregnant. I felt sure that her little trip to A&E was for a very quick chemical termination. I had heard that these options were quite popular, especially for the young ones.

Beside the reception desk were a mother and father cuddling a very small tot, definitely younger than 6 months. They wouldn't be here long. They would probably get priority over the small boy. A nipper of that size really should be seen immediately.

A father and two young baseball capped sons were sat near the infant. All three of them were in Nike trainers and tracksuits. Only the sons wore the obligatory caps but all of them had pierced ears with hoops. I was fascinated. I always found it hilarious when I saw people wear sportswear who were quite obviously never going to go near exercise. The young lads may have chased a football around now and then but the father's gut put pay to him doing anything but getting another round in at the pub or shuffling along to the curry house!

Whilst I was still spellbound by these males, the rowdy bunch by the window started up. One of them had fallen on the floor, probably dead drunk but it was taking 3 of the others to get him up and into the plastic chair. They were obviously having a problem with lifting him and the language that could be understood through their drunkenly slurred speech was disgusting. Most people chose to completely ignore them but a new couple entering the building, spotted the scene and instantly ran to their rescue. As soon as they had secured the man in the seat, they seemed to realise that the group were vagrants and scurried over to the other side of the waiting room. A number of the patients stifled a laugh as they watched the scene unfold.

Almost as soon as the helpful individuals sat down, the drunk collapsed on the floor again.

Disappointedly I realised that apart from the dodgy alcoholics and three chavy men, there was really no one worth examining.

A short while later Eve's mother and Katy were called by a young female Indian doctor and taken to a small room. The doctor sat them down and very carefully and calmly told them that Eve's condition was very serious. The junior doctor informed them that Eve had taken a large number of tablets with a considerable amount of alcohol. The staff members were awaiting toxicology reports to establish exactly which pills had been taken and once that was verified they could then begin treatment.

Katy asked, "why can't you just pump her stomach?" A very good point, I thought but the Indian girl, called Rupinder, replied that it was a bit too late for that, as the substances in the drugs had already found their way into Eve's bloodstream.

Eve's mother looked mortified. She sat staring at Rupinder, unable to ask any questions or answer any either. Katy wasn't faring much better but she did seem slightly more inquisitive.

"Can we see her?" Katy looked at the doctor pleadingly.

"Not yet" replied Rupinder gently. "Give us a bit longer to ascertain her prognosis".

"What shall we do? Should we wait?" Katy seemed quite anxious now and needed direction from the experts

"If you can try and find the bottle of tablets, that would really speed thing along for us". I wasn't sure if this was just to occupy the ladies or whether finding the bottle would be any good.

Katy seemed to jump into action. She pulled Eve's mother to her feet and said "Mrs Simpson, you have to drive us back to Eve's flat and I can check for any empty bottles".

Mrs Simpson became more aware of the situation and grabbed Katy's arm. "Yes Katy, come on". The pair of them trotted off through the waiting room and back into the car park.

"Please call me Elaine," said Mrs Simpson "In these circumstances I don't think we need to be so formal". She gave Katy a smile that I could tell she just didn't mean. Her eyes were dull and sad. Her mind was working over time picturing all sorts of horrific conclusions. I really felt for her. Katy looked pretty awful too. The dread and panic over the last few hours had drained her. She was surviving on adrenalin. Her usual complexion was now a drab grey and I had noticed that she had a penchant for fingernail biting.

We drove silently back to Eve's apartment and took the stairs. It was as though waiting for a lift would be a complete waste of time. Walking towards her front door though, Elaine suddenly stiffened and stopped. She held out her arm to prevent Katy going further ahead.

I was desperate to understand what the problem was, to see what had alarmed Elaine.

Katy took a sharp intake of breath and automatically her hand flew up to her mouth to avert a scream. As she stepped back and to the side of the corridor, I could see it. Eve's front door was open. Like the other two, I was trying to rack my brains and remember if we had actually closed the door when we left for the hospital. It was all a panic and I just hoped that we had forgotten as we rushed to follow the ambulance.

Elaine and Katy crept up to the door and pushed it open a little. No lights were on and from the hallway, everything looked just as we had left it. Cautiously Elaine pushed the door open a little more and slowly stepped inside. She bent down and switched on a lamp on top of the console table to the left. At first we didn't know where to look. What obvious signs would there be of an intruder? We all stood rooted to the spot trying to take in the details of the room.

Katy spotted the first abnormality and grabbed hold of Elaine's arm "There, look" she whispered. "Where's the DVD player? She did have one didn't she?"

Even I could tell that the loose wires left trailed behind the TV were where the device had been plugged in.

"Oh God!" murmured Elaine. She began shaking and turned to leave the apartment. Katy grabbed her and spun her around again.

"No you don't. We have to find those pills," she said with a lot more courage than she felt.

Katy put her handbag on the floor, crept across the lounge and quietly opened Eve's bedroom door. She peered inside. No one was there. Phew! She tiptoed down to the bathroom and again silently pushed the door back. Again no one was hiding there. Peering back over her shoulder, Katy indicated to Elaine that a quick search of the kitchen would be quite a good idea at this stage.

Before opening the second bedroom door, Katy waited for Elaine to emerge from the kitchen and with a sigh of relief she came back and gave a thumbs up to illustrate that the room was empty. Turning back she bravely decided to fling the door open and surprise any unsuspecting burglar. Yet again there was no one there.

Dispelling all their immediate concerns, Katy and Elaine summoned up the strength and speed to search the flat. Not only were they looking for the bottle of tablets but also any missing items that might confirm the place had been robbed.

From my position in Katy's bag on the floor I watched Elaine look through the trash left on the coffee table. Deep in fag butts, bottles and general toot, she grimaced as she picked up something covered in brown and sticky. Without thinking, she put it to her nose and sniffed. She smiled when she realised that it was chocolate. Spying a glass on its side, she realised that it must have tipped over and spilt its contents. "That must have been Maria's milkshake,' I thought to myself. Finding nothing relevant she tried the drawers in the console and even under the cushions on the sofa.

Feeling quite despondent, Elaine called out to Katy "You found anything?"

"No" came the hushed response "but to be honest I'm not really sure what I'm looking for."

Elaine wandered into the kitchen and I could hear a yell. "Katy! KATY!" Elaine shouted and I saw Katy run past me into the kitchen.

"What it is?" she asked and I could hear the terror in her voice.

"Look!" cried Elaine.

I was frantic to know what they had found. I could hear paper being rustled and then Elaine say "Oh Katy. I think these must be the pills"

"Come on Mrs Simpson, I mean Elaine. Let's get them back to the hospital and we can call the police on the way".

Grabbing her handbag on the way, Katy stuffed the piece of paper inside and we all raced towards the stairs.

As soon as Elaine had started the engine and pulled away, Katy dug out her mobile and dialled 999. After a few seconds waiting to connect, I heard her speaking. "Police please".

"Tell them she's in hospital and she'd never do anything silly like suicide so it's got to be him….." she rattled on.

"Shhh" warned Katy and then spoke to the police officer on the other end of the line. "Erm Hi. This is Katy McMillan. My friend was found collapsed in her home today and is in hospital". She paused and then added "Yes, that's right St Mark's". She obviously wasn't even intrigued as to how the office knew which hospital Eve was in. She continued "The doctors think that she may have overdosed so we were asked to go to her flat and try and find the tablets." Again she stopped and listened.

"Yes yes. Her name is Eve. Evelyn Simpson and I found her."

She sounded frustrated. She just wanted to get all the information out without being interrupted. "Yes I called her family and I am with her mother, Mrs Elaine Simpson right now."

Elaine tried to interject at this point but Katy kept waving at her to keep quiet.

"Yes we have both been back to Eve's place and we have found what we think are the pills so we are now on our way back to the hospital but.." again she paused and rolled her eyes.

"Look I'm just trying to tell you" she said angrily. "When we got back to the flat, we found the door open. We weren't sure if there was anyone there and we had a look round. We found a letter in the kitchen and it sounds really threatening. Now we don't know if Eve had been made to take the tablets or what." Glad that she had managed to get it out, Katy visibly relaxed and answered a litany of questions. She kept this up until she got to St Mark's and then abruptly told the officer that she had to go.

Elaine swung the car into the last remaining space in the car park and they belted into the reception area.

"Where can I find Dr Rupinder?" Katy asked slightly out of puff.

"Please be seated and I will page her" said the stern faced receptionist.

Dutifully the pair turned around and sat back in the exact spot as before. Almost instantly I heard the call for Dr Rupinder go through the tannoy system and we all sat back and waited.

After about 7 or 8 minutes, the wait was over and Dr Rupinder rushed into the waiting room and ushered the ladies back into the side room.

"We found these." Katy said as she handed over the empty pot. "They were on the kitchen surface and it was the only bottle we found". She blushed as she realised how childlike she sounded.

"Ok thanks" said the Dr. "I'll give this to my colleague and we will see what we can find out". She stood up and then said "I can let you see her now, if you like?"

Elaine rose immediately and eagerly nodded.

"Come with me" and Dr Rupinder steered them through the hospital maze.

We eventually walked into a ward with two large main patient areas and three or possibly four separate rooms. Dr Rupinder opened a door to one of the private rooms and spoke briefly to one of the attending nurses.

"They are taking some samples at the moment and of course she is still unconscious but if you can wait till they have finished I can let you have a couple of minutes with her after if that's ok?" Dr Rupinder's customer service levels were superb. Although she had an important job to do in identifying the drugs in Eve's system and determine a treatment, she knew that assisting the family where she could was just as vital.

"Of course. Of course" Elaine and Katy both said in unison. They found seats to the right of the room, sat down and began to study the leaflets pinned to the wall opposite them.

"Where's Eve's Dad? queried Katy.

Elaine brusquely turned to Eve's colleague and said "What?"

"Well, I just thought he should know what's going on?" Katy replied, sensing that she had just broached a very sensitive topic.

"Really?" snapped Elaine. "And why did you think that?"

"Look I'm sorry". Katy was trying to dig herself out of a hole and was making it worse. "I just noticed that you hadn't called him to tell him that Eve was in here and I just thought now would be a good time. I'll wait here if you want to let him know"

I could see her point and though she was just being very thoughtful, there was obviously an awful lot of history that Katy was oblivious to and continuing the conversation was quite clearly upsetting Elaine in the process.

"Katy, I think you had better quit now" Elaine responded evidently calmer that she felt. "Eve's father is a bastard and he doesn't deserve ANY information. That is all I have to say on the matter".

Elaine's body language was crystal clear. With both legs and arms folded, Katy had no choice but to do her best to change the subject.

"So." Katy began "How long has Eve had that flat?" It seemed to be quite an unobtrusive question but for some unknown reason Elaine took a particular dislike to it and almost shouted at her.

"Are you doing your best to irritate me?" Elained scowled at Katy.

'Blimey" I thought. What's the poor love done now?

"I think I'm just going to keep quiet from now on" said Katy defeatedly. "I can see that you are not in the mood to chat and I keep making things worse". She hung her head and started biting her fingernails in earnest.

"Katy, sweetheart." Elaine mellowed. "It's not you. I thought you knew," she said softly.

Katy shook her head and gazed at Elaine questioningly, still biting those very short nails.

"I thought you had known Eve for some time?" Elaine asked

"No. I have only been working with her for a couple of months. I know she is a lot older than me, well about 8 or 9 years anyway" she smirked at Elaine. "But we got on really well. We went out a couple of times and she introduced me to her friends. I had been to her place when she had a small party a couple of weekends ago. Actually" she confessed. "I thought her mates were a bit strange".

"Oh!" said Elaine looking surprised. "The girls I have met were great, very polite and friendly. In fact Eve brought a couple of them back one weekend. That was a couple of years back, mind. Lovely" she said sinking into a distant memory.

"Maybe they were Mrs Simpson" she continued "but these were all men!"

"There's nothing wrong with that these days is there? she said looking at Katy pityingly. "I mean Katy told me years ago that she hung out with a group of gay men, for heaven sake! I ask you. She told me that she always felt safe with them. That's probably why they seemed a little strange, dear. They batted for the other side." Elaine smiled to herself obviously thinking that Katy was a little foolish and very naive.

"No, Mrs Simpson" Katy replied. "Trust me, they were not gay. Not in any way, shape or form!"

Elaine looked puzzled. "Katy" she said at last "what is it you are trying to tell me?"

"I'm not trying to be funny or anything but I reckon they were paying to be her friends, if you see what I mean?" she said cautiously.

Elaine looked at Katy in total surprise. "Are you calling my daughter a hooker?" she cried.

"No, no. Oh God I'm getting this all wrong." Katy looked distraught. It was obvious she hadn't meant to upset Elaine but every time she opened her mouth, she messed up. "No listen Mrs Simpson, Elaine. I don't think she was a prostitute at all. I'm just trying to say that the men at her party a fortnight ago were all very keen on her and I think they indulged her quite a bit"

Katy looked very worried. She wished she hadn't started any of this. She carried on biting her nails and when there was silence next to her, she looked up and saw Elaine fighting back tears.

"Oh God Mrs Simpson. I'm sorry. I really didn't mean to offend you. Me and my big mouth. I have probably got the wrong end of the stick. I'm sure they were just gay and I picked up the wrong signals. I always make a fool of myself so really I'm sure it's just me making a mountain out of a molehill." Katy's attempt to backtrack was actually doing more damage than good. Elaine's eyes were welling up and Katy finally stopped talking and put her arm round the lady.

After a few minutes of muted sobs, Elaine blew her nose on an old piece of tissue from her bag. It was covered in mascara and left a small black mark on the side of her nose as she wiped it clean.

"Katy. It has just dawned on me how serious this all is". Elaine gave another blow and continued "What if she doesn't get better? What if she doesn't wake up? " She burst into tears again and Katy hugged her tighter.

"She'll be fine Mrs S. I know she will" Katy said confidently.

Dr Rupinder emerged from Eve's room and ushered them in. What a sight. There were monitors and all sorts of equipment that seemed to be plugged in to poor Eve. Katy and Elaine were visibly shocked and Elaine cried out "Oh my poor baby. Who did this to you?"

Dr Rupinder took Katy aside and asked her if she knew whether Eve had had a history of drug abuse and Katy just shrugged her shoulders. "I'm really sorry Dr but I haven't really known Eve that long. I've never seen anything that would make me suspect it though, if that helps" she added hopefully.

"Hmm… It's just that the tablets from the bottle shouldn't react with alcohol the way they have tonight, so…… I am wondering if there are other possibilities" Dr Rupinder trailed off and left Katy wondering whether her presence was still required of whether she could sit by her friend's side and console her mother.

Leaving Dr Rupinder still pondering the dilemma, Katy sat next to Elaine and held her hand. Eve was motionless as they had expected but still it was a shock to see her hooked up to so many machines. Elaine began rocking backwards and forwards and Katy took this as a bad sign. She had read somewhere once that when animals did that, they were highly distressed. Obviously she would be distressed seeing her daughter in this condition but considering they were in a hospital, there must be something the doctors could do.

Walking back up to Dr Rupinder, she tapped the girl on the shoulder. The doctor was examining a large textbook, probably to do with drugs and effects and took a couple of seconds to disengage and register that she was wanted.

"Hmmm" she said distractedly.

"Erm I just thought I'd mention it but I think the shock has finally got to Mrs Simpson and I wondered if you could give her something?"

As Dr Rupinder turned to glance at the patient's mother, Elaine suddenly fainted and slid onto the floor.

Dr Rupinder and the attending nurse both tried to pull Elaine to her feet and put her head between her legs. Katy panicked though and found a jug of water on the cubicle next to Eve's bed and threw it over Elaine.

"Arhhh" Elaine cried as she came to. "What?" She seemed quite dazed. No longer a dead weight, the doctor and her accomplice were able to sit Elaine upright and tilt her head forward.

"I'm not really sure that that helped" Dr Rupinder said disapprovingly. She took Elaine's pulse and ordered the woman to keep her head down.

Katy looked so awkward. She had upset Mrs Simpson and now she had acted childishly and had taken a reprimand from the doctor. She felt foolish and I could also see she felt out of her depth and out of place. She picked up her handbag and as she swung us over her shoulder, she interrupted Dr Rupinder and told her she was popping outside. The doctor still seemed peeved but nodded in acknowledgement and continued checking Elaine's vital signs.

We raced out of the labyrinth of corridors and after reaching the safety of the carpark, Katy grabbed Eve's half empty fag packet and lit a cigarette, inhaling deeply.

"What a day! What a fucking day!" she said to herself, aloud.

Realising that she had no transport, she grabbed her mobile and dialled a number.

"Mum!" Katy began, on the verge of tears. "I'm at St Mark's. Can you pick me up please?"

After a short break she added "No, no I'm fine. It's my mate Eve. I'll tell you all about it when you pick me up."

While Katy puffed on her cigarette, I took the opportunity to return to my favourite subject, Whin.

· ·

FLASHBACK

· ·

Whin seemed mortified at this point. He looked restless and his eyes darted all over the place. Tom took his arm and said gently "Whin, take it easy. There's no rush".

Whin gave a half smile and after a while lifted his pint and took a long hard swig of his beer.

"Well that was the beginning of the end, Tom." He said finally after wiping away a leftover trail of froth on his upper lip.

"I made a fool of myself at the wake and I embarrassed her. God I'm such an idiot" he muttered the last remark to himself as he hung his head low.

Tom didn't know whether he should console Whin at this stage. He wasn't sure if there was more to come out. Was Whin mourning the death of a friend, an end of a brief affair? I could see he thought the same as me; keep quiet and Whin will eventually spill the beans and get rid of this gloomy mood for good. We had no idea, at this stage, that it would be much more serious.

Suddenly the pub door swung open and in came four burly lads. Straight off the building site and ready for the first beer of the night. They were still wearing plaster-splattered jeans but they were reasonably clean. They had made some attempt at cleaning themselves up. I could see Geoff eyeing them up and down, making sure that they weren't bring half of the site in with them. Obviously they were an acceptable standard as I heard Geoff ask, "What'll it be boys?"

Tom and Whin had fallen silent and were both cautiously watching the young men. Maybe they were remembering being that age, full of life and plenty of energy and enthusiasm. The memories were making Whin look even more depressed and I just hoped that something would jog him into continuing with his tale.

Tom nudged Whin and said "Drink up mate and I'll get us another one in." He stood to make his way to the bar and then turned and added "then you can finish your story"

I was delighted. I truly believed that whatever it was Whin wanted to get off his chest, everything would seem better once he had. Tom appeared to be the best shoulder to cry on and I was confident his patience would hold out.

• •

FLASHBACK

• •

CHAPTER 10

Katy looked frozen. Why is it that young kids today insist on wearing very little clothing? How do they just not feel the cold? I shuddered just looking at her.

After stubbing out her third cigarette on the trot, she rummaged around in her handbag and eventually drew out some mints. I immediately came to the conclusion that Katy's mother didn't know she smoked and probably wouldn't be too happy about it. I thought I had better keep a low profile then.

We stood around for a while longer watching the ambulances arrive and the patients be dispatched. Katy was shivering now. Maybe it was the shock of the events of the day but more than likely the darn cold was actually getting to her.

Katy spotted a vehicle turning into the car park and checked her breath against her palm. Believing it to be smoke free, she waved frantically and we ran towards the blue Ford Ka.

Throwing the passenger door open, Katy's mother called out "Quickly get in." Katy jumped in slammed the door shut. She turned and before she could speak, she just wept on her mother's shoulder.

"Hey" her mum said softly "What's happened?"

Between sobs she manage to blubber a long convoluted version of the day's incidents. She had almost finished when her mother interrupted her to say "Hang on poppet, I just have to move out of the way of this sodding Volvo driver who is right up my arse". She carefully drove to the side of the car park, out of the way of incoming traffic and resumed her position as chief comforter.

From my position I was not getting a clear view but when I did glimpse Katy's mum, I gasped! For a few seconds I knew I knew the face. I just couldn't put a name to it.

'Well well' I finally thought 'What a small world'. Of course the lady in the car soothing her daughter was Fiona. Whin's neice!

Dumbfounded how I had managed to come in almost a complete circle and was nearly back where I started, I virtually jumped for joy. Perhaps there would be some sanity in my life now. I was delirious was happiness until I came down to earth with a huge bang. 'Damn'. I had just twigged that from Katy's urgent removal of cigarette smells, she wasn't going to make Fiona aware of my presence. 'Bugger!' Well this was certainly going to be interesting anyway, I though optimistically.

Katy's snivelling persisted for a while and then her crying subsided. Fiona reached into the glove compartment and snatched a couple of tissues. Dabbing her daughter's eyes, she asked gently "So what do you think happened to her then?"

Katy blew her nose and tidied up her face in the mirror. "I just don't know mum. It was so scary, especially when we had to go back to her flat". She looked across at her mother and added "At the time I didn't even think about it, but that nutter could've still been there". This revelation started up a whole new bout of crying. Fiona put her arm round her daughter and lulled her with the type of soft rocking motion, which endless mothers use to console their children.

It suddenly dawned on Fiona just how much trouble Katy could've been in. "Oh my poor baby" she said as she hugged her tighter, just thankful that she was upset but ok.

"Can I come back to yours tonight Mum?" Katy whispered.

"Oh, of course you can my darling". Fiona looked painfully worried when we eventually drove away.

The car was warm and I was tired and both Katy and I drifted off. The soft humming of the engine relaxed us enough so that sheer tiredness took over and sent us off to sleep.

I woke with a start. I was still in Katy's bag, I was sure but I could hear a very odd noise. Coming to properly and straining to see in the half light, I made out a strange shape sitting at the bottom of the stairs.

Alarmed I did my best to concentrate on the shadowy figure and make some sense of it. It made another noise and I almost laughed to myself. 'A dog!' It was only a dog barking but it just seemed so out of place that it had jolted me from my slumber.

I had no idea what time it was but looking at the pale gray light coming through the curtainless windows, I knew it was early. The dog continued barking until eventually I heard someone shout down the stairs.

"Shut up you stupid mutt". Someone in slippers was descending the stairs and the dog was excitedly bouncing around wagging his tail vigorously. I guessed it was Fiona dragging the animal back into the kitchen by his collar. I couldn't see them in the kitchen but I could hear the dog's claws on the floor tiles. Fiona was muttering away until I heard a large yelp. "Oh poor puppy" I heard her say in a soppy voice.

A light clicked on upstairs and I could hear Katy call down "Mum. You ok?"

Fiona called back up to say that George needed a cuddle and she would be up soon. I guessed George was the animal in question and presumably from his behaviour and requirements, he was still a baby and needed some reassuring human contact. I hadn't had much experience of dogs but I had seen a few. I had heard that they needed a lot of attention especially when they were young. Almost as much as a newborn baby!

With the dog now calm, Fiona tiptoed out of the kitchen and was about to climb the stairs when she stopped and turned around. She spotted Katy's bag and being a typical mother, became dubious of her daughter's antics and decided a quick peek in her handbag might be in order.

Panicking as I realised I would be spotted, I dreaded to think of the trouble I would get Katy into, just by being here. There was nothing I could do and nowhere I could hide.

Just as her hand slipped inside, I heard Katy call out "Is he ok now mum?

Fiona withdrew her hand and sighed. "He's fine now. Back to bed love." She ascended the stairs and switched off the light.

'Phew!' I thought. 'That was close'. After a few minutes, I recovered from my close shave and I settled down and started to doze.

CHAPTER 11

The next thing I knew it was broad daylight and although I was still in Katy's handbag, I knew I wasn't still in her house so with some trepidation, I took a look around. I could see the sky was a beautiful cornflower blue with a couple of wispy clouds. If we were in June or July, the day would be blisteringly hot but it was September and although the occasional Indian summer crept up on us, today wasn't going to be one of them. It felt cool. Looking around I could see trees and the dying remains of flowerbeds. 'A park' I thought, suddenly illuminated by the possibility of some fresh air.

Katy had reached a park bench and sat down, glancing at her mobile for the time. She picked up the packed of Silk Cut and lit one, distractedly. Fiddling with her fingernails whilst she exhaled, I wondered what we were doing here. I couldn't imagine Katy having a picnic by herself and the day wasn't really warm enough to sunbathe. Every few minutes Katy checked her phone for messages but as time drew on, she became more and more agitated.

I took the time to check out the surroundings and I was pleasantly surprised. It had been a long while since Whin had taken me anywhere like this and I was enjoying the moment. I wasn't particularly a rural freak but I did enjoy soaking up the green atmosphere. Our sheltered spot meant that the sun was quite warm although the air certainly held that autumnal crispness. There were very few people in the park and only two children. I spotted three dogs and a squirrel so by all accounts it was definitely a quiet day. I couldn't remember if there was a particularly important football match on but upon reflection, it certainly had that eerie calmness to it.

Suddenly Katy's mobile rang and shattered the silence. Although she was expecting the call, she still visibly jumped. She answered the phone and just simply said, "So where are you?"

I couldn't hear the other side of the conversation but it was all fairly brief. "Ok I'll see you then" was all that Katy replied and then snapped the mobile shut and threw it into her handbag. She looked a little disappointed but also very tired. It all seemed a bit secretive to me and for the life of me I just couldn't work out what was going on but the last few days had taught me to forget trying to guess the next step so I relaxed and relished the tranquillity.

We sat for a while. I took in the soft glow of the sun and Katy bit her fingernails mostly and we pondered on the events of the previous day. I briefly wondered how Eve was doing. I hoped that they had managed to find the right treatment and she was getting better. I also hoped that the thug who had frightened her half to death and pushed her into taking the damn things, was found and punished. I have always been a strong advocate of corporal punishment and although I am usually alone in that particular belief, I consider that not only is it a very good form of deterrent but it also means that the criminal is properly punished for the most serious crimes and the victim wins from the point of justice.

After an hour or so, we left the park, taking a turn to the right at the exit and past a   graveyard. Katy paused at the large iron gates. I had a sinking feeling that she fully intended to go in. It was too soon for me to think about death again. I don't think I had really come to terms with losing Whin yet and a stroll around gravestones wasn't really in my best interest. Katy, however, wasn't even aware I had interests and she took a step through the gates.

My heart sank. This was going to be tough. I prepared myself for an emotional rollercoaster and waited for the raw pain to return.

We walked along sandy paths shaded by huge leafy trees. I could tell that Katy felt as I did. We were both mesmerised by the aura of the place. Some of the gravestones were very old and a lot of the inscriptions were illegible. Years of wind and rain had swept the heartfelt messages away. Many had just a few distinguishable words but the majority of the cenotaphs were smooth. Only church records would now establish exactly who lay beneath.

It was a truly beautiful experience. We walked on and on, sometimes pausing to read the dedications. Some graves were incredibly ornate with huge stone angels protecting the dead. A lot of the monuments were small but still emotionally expressive.

We wandered for ages and as the day drew on, a strange sort of mist began to collect over the graveyard. Rather that terrify, it actually enhanced the glorious ethereal atmosphere. The mood plummeted however when we reached the children's corner. It was so depressing. Tiny graves, some marked with cherub shaped tombstones. Katy and I both read the epitaphs and I watched as a tear rolled down her cheek. I couldn't even begin to understand how the parents of some of these youngsters must have felt and the messages were difficult to read, as the raw pain was still evident. A few graves were fairly recent and some older within the last 50 years but the large majority were dated in the 19th century. The oldest I could see was a tomb dedicated to Henry Jacob Turner. I could just about make out that he passed away aged 8 years old in 1723.

We moved on and on. Towards the end of the special section, I spied a new grave. When I say new, I mean within the last decade. Flowers were still laid on the grave, albeit a few days ago but that just proved that the loss of this little one was still very much felt. Katy and I peered closer and I could see the name etched out; Charlotte Bigham. The poor little mite was only two months old.

Feeling thoroughly depressed, we walked on. Beyond the graves was a meadow style garden. I guess it was designed as a place for reflection. The tall trees hid the unsightly buildings behind and the birds certainly did their best to cover the noise of traffic in the distance. We sat on a wooden bench and gazed at the beautifully planned flowerbeds. The borders had been drafted so that the edge had a definitive boundary, full of colour, even now as Autumn was approaching. The lawn in front had been left and as a result buttercups and daisies and pretty long grasses grew in abundance.

After a moment of contemplation, Katy dug her mobile out of her bag and checked for messages. Furiously realising that her mysterious caller had not contacted her, she lit up another cigarette and nervously bit her nails.

Stubbing her butt out on the pea shingle in front of the bench, she stood up to grab her bag. I could see she felt guilty about leaving her rubbish in such a beautiful place, so she bent down and picked up her cigarette end. I was pleased she did that.

Somehow we found a shortcut to the exit and so we didn't relive the amazing aura experience. Just thinking about the graveyard seemed to make my loss easier. I felt so calm. Apart from the special place for the children, the atmosphere kind of eased your mind. I just hoped that the emotion would last.

We picked up speed when we reached the main road and as we almost ran towards the parade of shops, I wondered what was so important and why we were rushing. I could see we were passing various grocers and shoe shops but when we reached a smart contemporary style bar, we stopped abruptly and walked in. From the look on Katy's face, I could tell she recognised someone inside. However, that someone didn't share the same look of anger as Katy, more a look of shock and fear.

"Hey babe", the tall man in a tailored white shirt said as she bent forwards to nuzzle her neck.

"Get off, you bastard" Katy spat back and turned to look at the slim blonde leaning against the counter. "Who the fuck are you?"

"Nice friends you have Nick!" the blonde retorted sarcastically.

All I could think of was 'Oooh a fight!' I can unashamedly admit that I love a good fight, especially a catfight. Girls were great at fighting. The language was so much more colourful and hair was usually the main target. I am the kind that loves boxing too and I find that just watching any style of fighting just channels the aggression away and my frustration typically just melts.

Nick backed away from Katy holding his palms up as if to say 'I have done nothing wrong'. This tactic is used by both guilty and innocent parties and so is totally useless in its significance. Katy's faced had darkened. Her fury had grown to stupendous levels and I could see that any second she would blow. I knew I would pity the person that broke the dam.

Katy turned back to Nick and flashed her eyes, waiting for an explanation. Nick however, seemed reluctant to actually begin the process of justification.

"Let me get you a drink, babe." he said obviously doing his best to diffuse the situation. "Come and sit down and I'll explain why I couldn't meet you earlier". He almost pushed her back towards the entrance to a free table by the window. He called over his shoulder to the barman. "A vodka and red bull please Mick".

Although the place was fairly busy, it was surprisingly quiet. No one was looking at Katy but I imagined she felt like she was being watched. I understood how she felt. She was seething and although she wanted to scream and shout, she also wanted to retain her dignity.

I could see this fool, Nick, doing his best to rack his brain for a suitable excuse. Nick was fighting a losing battle as far as I could see and was digging himself a deeper and deeper hole.

The blonde meanwhile, was still leaning against the counter soaking in the attention of two other lads doing their best to impress. I was saddened to see how fickle these idiots were being. Katy was visibly upset by the disloyal and lecherous attitude of her boyfriend and the object of his desire wasn't even spending a second defending her actions or worrying about the outcome before moving onto the next fool. There was a name for people like her.

Katy seemed to have calmed a little. Nick had done well by removing Katy from the scene of the crime. She still looked incredibly angry though and if Nick wanted to be forgiven I could see him having to do an awful lot before her trust could be rebuilt. Personally I would have advised her to dump him. Who needed to worry about fidelity, especially after the day she had had yesterday?

"Look!" Nick said wearily. "I just came for a beer with Craig and Jimmy", he nodded towards the bar and I presumed he meant the men fawning over the snooty blonde.

Katy looked blankly ahead. It was clear she had had enough and I felt she had been in this position many times before. What was it with these men? Katy seemed to be an attractive and sensible girl. Why on earth would Nick fall for such a nasty bit of work as the slut propping up the counter? Hormones I guessed.

"Honest Katy", Nick said stepping up his excuses as he noticed Katy's total lack of interest and belief in his story. "I'm sure I told you we were going to meet for a beer after the match this morning!"

I liked his style. He was turning the blame on Katy. She should have remembered the conversation they'd apparently had. Katy turned slowly to look Nick in the eye.

"Nick, I don't believe you. I don't trust you and I have had enough. I can't go on feeling like this and I'm just tired of it all. You obviously want to be free so I'm letting you go". She was incredibly calm and I felt that the time spent in the graveyard possibly had something to do with it.

She stood up to go and as she tried to walk away, Nick grabbed her arm and said "But Katy, I love you". He sounded quite genuine and totally astonished. He must have believed that she would forgive him yet again and he could continue. I had a distinct feeling that no other woman had ever spoken to him like that before. I thought for a moment that Katy would reconsider but true to her word she shook off his hand and replied "But I don't love you" before serenely walking out of the door. I was very proud of her but I could tell that she wasn't as detached as she appeared. I was desperate to turn around and see the look on the blonde's face but Katy had more dignity that that and strode through the exit and off down the pavement without so much as a hesitation.

Katy made it to the next corner and once out of view from the pedestrians of the High Street, she lost control and broke down. Sinking to her knees, she sobbed and sobbed. I was having a kind of déjà vu. It seemed that everyone I had been with since Whin was in some form of emotional turmoil. I had never seen so many tears.

After a while, Katy picked herself up, checked her make up in her compact mirror and blew her nose. Her eyes looked a little puffy but aside from that she could get away with just having a bit of a cold. I had noticed that in women. They would have a mini breakdown and then spend forever making sure the world didn't know they were upset.

We walked on and ended up back outside a terraced townhouse 3 stories high. Katy opened the wrought iron gate and trotted up the steps. She hadn't got a key so I was presuming this wasn't her own place. She pushed the doorbell a few times and anxiously waited for the door to open. A Filipino woman answered, Katy smiled and the lady let her in.

"Thanks Andrea" Katy said as she closed the door behind her. Andrea walked through a door at the rear of the house and a couple of seconds later I heard the familiar whir of a vacuum cleaner.

'Aha, the cleaner' I deducted. I looked around, desperately trying to fathom who owned the property. The artefacts and décor were not giving any clues however. Katy marched up the stairs and into a small room that was probably used as a part time office but doubled up as a den. It looked like somewhere to go for peace and quiet. Katy sat on the low leather sofa against the wall. She kicked off her shoes and curled her legs underneath her. She flicked open the window behind her and reached into her bag for her cigarettes. She lit one and kept me in her hand. I felt like a source of comfort for her but admittedly that feeling was a little tenuous.

An Applemac iBook sat on the coffee table in front of her and she leaned forwards and opened it up. The battery looked almost full and so she dragged in onto her lap.

I had had a little experience with computers. Not through Whin. Bless him. I don't think he would even know how to switch one on but through various conversations in the past I had picked up some knowledge. It was limited, I recognised that but the intrigue was so immense that I leapt for joy when Katy opened up her laptop. This would be great opportunity to learn more at close hand. I decided to watch like a hawk and follow exactly what Katy was doing.

At first she checked her emails and mucked around with various sites that had been forwarded by friends. She grew bored with this after a while and she then clicked on a website that shocked me.

I couldn't read the web address but the images were horrendous. There were pictures of females so thin that their stomachs were concave and many looked like they didn't have the energy to stand by themselves. I was horrified but as I watched I realised that Katy must know this website well as she navigated her way through the menu expertly.

Katy was definitely slim but not what I would call a Kate Moss type but studying her frame now I could see that she had broad shoulders and could carry a lot more weight without even being considered chubby. In fact the more I looked at her, the more I understood how she came across as a 'normal' teenager. Her fashion sense meant that she wore several layers of clothing but cleverly this also disguised her diminishing figure. Thinking about it, I hadn't actually seen Katy eat for the entire duration of our time together. I had seen her sipping drinks and of course smoking but other than that, nothing had passed her lips.

Agog, I read through the articles on the website and I was fascinated to see how girls all over the world sent in blog style information about how to lose weight and how to conceal their loss. I had no idea that girls and some boys felt this way. It was not something that I had ever really come into contact with. It hadn't even occurred to me that people would suffer in this abnormal behaviour.

Katy read through some of the pages with sheer concentration. She was taking every morsel of information, ironically with hungry attention. Focussed totally on the techniques used by her peers to hide their actions, she seemed almost to be making notes in her mind.

I was so upset by some of the messages I read. One girl from Budapest called Ilona was celebrating that she had reached 3 and a half stone. She was 18 and although she was over the moon at the level of her weight loss, she did feel she could lose more but was terrified that pretty soon she would be sectioned. Her hospital visits were a regular occurrence but the little tricks she had up her sleeve to outwit the doctors were being discovered. She talked of how she had made a hole in soles of her shoes and filled them with stones. She even drank more water than her body could handle just before the weigh-in sessions, which resulted in her passing out on one occasion. The list was endless when it came to way to fool the medical team but it sounded like Ilona was running out of ideas.

I felt so sad. Ilona looked such a beautiful girl. Her photo showed a before and after picture. The before was possibly when she was 10 or 11 and showed her rosy healthy cheeks, blue sparkling eyes and gorgeous long blonde wavy hair. The after photo was awful. I could barely look at it. I had guessed she had sent in the photos with pride but all I could see of the teenager was a hollow, gaunt even haunted look. Her sunken eyes looked dead and her once beautiful hair was now short and dry. I could have cried for her.

Katy however, was almost looking jealousy at Ilona and I could only pray that she would not be following her example. Today's calamity with Nick certainly would not have improved her confidence and I had a sneaking suspicion that in Katy's case, this would be the root of the problem. Yesterday's events would also have had a negative effect on the poor girl so no wonder she was seeking solace from people who claimed to support her and be her friend.

A tap on the door and Katy lifted her head. Andrea peered round the door and shook her keys.

"Ok Andrea, see you soon. Thanks" Katy called as Andrea disappeared.
Katy and I were alone now and I was feeling quite nervous. I had seen an awful lot of upset in the last few days and I really didn't want to see anymore. To my relief however, we spent the rest of the afternoon snuggling up in the den, smoking and occasionally skyping a friend called Joe90. Actually some of the conversations with Joe90 were very amusing. He, and I could only presume it was a 'he', was doing his utmost to bring a smile to Katy's face but there was possibly an overuse of emoticons. He must have been fully aware of the ongoing frustrations with Nick and although he was being fairly supportive, he was mostly telling her what a plonker Nick was and how she was better off without him.

Admittedly I was struggling with some of the abbreviations and vowelless words but I could just about make sense of most of it. From what I could tell, this Joe90 seemed a decent bloke. He was witty and made fun of himself which, was always a good sign in my book. I like people who don't take themselves too seriously.

As the evening approached, I heard the door slam downstairs and a few seconds later there was a call up the stairs

"Katy." A slight pause and then "KATY, you in?"

Katy jumped to her feet and ran to the door. "Here mum" she yelled and a while later, Fiona appeared at the door. Aha, so that's where we were. It looked different from last night.

"Hello you. You ok?" she asked as she embraced her daughter.

Katy suddenly burst into tears. She had obviously been bottling up her emotions all afternoon and her mother's gentle question had broken the dam.

"That two timing bastard" she began. "I caught him this morning with some blonde slut". She broke off at this and sobbed in earnest.

"What?" Fiona asked. "Nick?" She sounded astonished so I could only guess that Katy hadn't been particularly forthcoming with his previous antics.

"Yes Nick" Katy almost shouted back. "He is the biggest bastard I have ever met", she said, sounding quite childlike.

"Oh poppet" Fiona sighed, her maternal instincts on full power. She grabbed Katy and squeezed her tightly. "Don't worry my darling. He is not worth it. They never are," she added cynically.

Fiona said nothing. She looked like she was enjoying a rare tactile moment with her mother. The hurt and disappointment were still etched on her young pretty face but I think this time with her mum was exactly what she needed. She looked too young to be living on her own, without the support of family. From what I could gather she had moved out of home some time ago and she had been fending for herself for a couple of years. Nothing had been mentioned of her father and I wondered if he had been one of the random guys that Bert and Dan had alluded to back at the funeral. I did remember hearing that she had spent time with several men on a short time basis. I could only think that perhaps Katy was the result of a rather short-lived affair.

What had happened, Eve's attempted suicide and Nick's infidelity, was drawing her closer to her mum. This was obviously the catalyst they needed to strengthen their bond.

Katy and Fiona trotted off down the stairs with talk of Ben and Jerry's ice cream. Jealously I watched them disappear, arm in arm, through the open door and descend the beige carpeted stairs towards the kitchen.

The room was quiet now and I took the opportunity to reflect. I couldn't believe that just a short time ago I was living a carefree life with Whin and how the last few days had totally upended my existence. I wondered how Verity was coping without Reg. Was she regretting her decision? Were Darren and David behaving themselves like they promised? I had liked Verity. She was a woman of her word. She didn't cheat, lie and steal her way through life. She was a grafter. All the cards had been stacked against her but she didn't give up. I just hoped that the nonsense she had had to go through with Reg would teach her boys a thing or too about honesty and respect. In an ideal world their lesson would be learned and there would be no more brush-ups with the law or dicey dealings with the seedy drug world. Thinking about drugs, I pondered on the fate of that addict Adam, slumped in the toilet of that God forsaken pub. Was he ok? Had the guys who were after him, got him in the end?

Matt and Nikki had experienced a shaky start to their relationship but I hoped that they were enjoying each other's company now and were relaxing a little. Hopefully that frightening incident in Adam's house had taught Matt a thing or too about what was important in life. It was doubtful that he would totally avoid the drug underworld but I could only remain confident that it would at least be a turn off for Nikki and if she meant anything to Matt, he would be reluctant to put her in danger again.

My mind then turned to Matt's dad Gary. I really was optimistic that he would be able to secure his job and keep his colleagues in work too. It was so disheartening to see a man try his hardest to hold onto his job and his dignity and fail. Phil really hadn't been the best man to get through to Gary. I hadn't realised it at the time but in hindsight I could now see that his focus was solely concentrated on the desperate state of his marriage. John sounded promising but time would tell. Could Gary trust the managers? Could he put his all into doing the best job ever whilst unresolved issues hung over him?

Meanwhile poor little rich girl Maria was living through the hell of parents on the brink of a separation. Sometimes I hear people talk of remaining together for the sake of the children and other times I hear that parting was the best option so that youngsters would not have to wade through the tense atmosphere. I was undecided. I guessed it depended on circumstances. Whichever route the mother and father chose, unhappy parents meant unhappy children. Admittedly Maria came across as a spoilt child but I could see underneath she was a sweet girl and very much closer to her daddy.

I hadn't liked Becks from the second I had entered her home. I thought she was a manipulative bitch. Her loathing of her husband was so apparent, it was pitiful. In these circumstances it was blatantly obvious that these two should divorce as quickly as possible and make the remainder of Maria's childhood a happy one. I wasn't quite sure what she had wanted to achieve by introducing swingers into the family home and I wasn't really certain what she had intended by allowing Phil to sleep with other women and then give him hell. The whole scenario was all so perverse.

Eve was another mixed up girl. Her desperation nearly resulted in the unfeasible and unsustainable grouping of her, Phil and Maria in a grubby two bedroom apartment. I could only imagine that she had branched out into swinging from escort work as an attempt to find a provider. Someone who could dig her out of her enormous financial hole and fend off the gruff intruder that had almost terrified her to death. Perhaps the pill popping was a huge cry for help. With Elaine by her side, perhaps Eve would get the help she so obviously needed. Elaine seemed like a very capable woman. Her fainting trick towards the end of our time together didn't appear to be a regular occurrence with this lady and certainly did not fit the description I would give.

I wasn't sure what to make of Katy. As far as I could see she was an ungainly thing, awkward in her approach and quite clumsy in her methods. I could see her vulnerability quite clearly and put it down to her having to grow in terms of responsibility rather than tact.

Here I was though, back with Fiona, the closest link to Whin in quite a while. I really hoped that she would give me some background on her uncle. I suppose I had secretly wished that she had spotted me and noticed that I had been Whin's partner for such a long time. I confess that I had only met Fiona a couple of times and a lighter is hardly a remarkable or unique object. Only Bert and Dan had recognised me but then again they had spent many hours in my company so I would have been most offended if they hadn't recollected me.

If only Fiona could pass me back to Dan, back where I belonged, I could resume my fact-finding mission and relax in the security of a normal but quiet life. I knew my journey back to civilisation would be arduous. I also knew that my link to Whin was so tenuous that it could be broken at any minute. There was nothing I could do apart from accept my fate and enjoy the ride.

I had a headache now and decide to sleep it off. Katy and Fiona would be gone for a while, bonding over their ice cream. I didn't want to think about Whin right now. I was feeling emotional. Maybe the rollercoaster of events from the past few days was catching up with me. I drifted off into a comfortable snooze.

BANG. I was awake. It had only felt like 15 minutes since I dozed off but it was night and the lights on the landing were off. Nervously I tried to listen for any other noises in the house but there was silence until… BANG. That noise again.

BANG! BANG! There didn't appear to be any sequence or reason to the noise and I couldn't for the life of me, work out what it was.

The light on the landing went on and I saw Fiona shuffle past in a very bedraggled dressing gown. A trip to M&S was definitely on the cards for her.

I saw her disappear down the stairs and open the front door. I strained to hear any conversation that might be taking place to explain the noise but all I could hear was Fiona muttering out loud. The front door was wide open and I could hear the wind howling.

Eventually Fiona came back into the house. I heard her rustle about and go back through the front door. I was very intrigued by this point and even though Katy hadn't woken, there was no way I would be able to get to sleep until that awful banging noise had ceased.

BANG! BANG! BANG! There it was again. It dawned on me. It was only a fence or something in the wind. The past few days had obviously affected me more than I had realised. With a huge sigh of relief I dozed until I heard Fiona locking the door and I fell into a deep sleep.

CHAPTER 12

When I awoke, I felt troubled. Sometimes I get that feeling of impending doom. I can't quite explain it but I'm usually right. I can never predict what exactly it is, or how I can prevent it but sometimes it can last for weeks. With the loss of my best friend and the intense journey I had undertaken since Whin's death, I couldn't really imagine things getting worse but as the morning drew on, the sensation lingered. I had enough on my plate without trying to establish what this new problem was so with a concerted effort, I pushed the qualms to the back of my mind and concentrated on getting back to Dan. How I was going to orchestrate that I had no idea. What could I do? If strength of mind had any power, I would be back tomorrow but life doesn't work like that and I just had to accept the journey, wherever it took me.

The house was still quiet and so I took the opportunity to think about Whin…

• •

FLASHBACK

• •

Tom returned from the bar with a pint in each hand and two bags of roasted peanuts hanging from his mouth. Slapping the beers on the small table, he handed Whin a bag of nuts, after wiping off his saliva, on the back of his jeans. "Get them down you mate" said Tom in a whimsical tone. I guessed he was trying to lighten the situation but looking at Whin's face, the sentiment fell on deaf ears.

The builders at the bar were relaxing now and looking forward to a night out. With work finished, their first drinks had been downed. They hadn't even touched the sides. All of them were already on the second round and I could see that they fully intended to purchase many more rounds before the night was out. Their physical job was clearly demanding but I wasn't really sure how tucking away ten pints was going to help them the next day. Mind you it was Friday and I guessed that they had no intention of doing much the following day.

Whin looked away from the boys and studied his new pint. He carefully opened his bag of nuts and slowly popped a handful into his mouth. I could see that he was really only going through the motions and his taste buds weren't even involved. Tom was waiting patiently for Whin to begin again. I think he was feeling quite anxious at this point. He recognised that Whin had suffered some form of personal trauma and no doubt the full story would emerge. He also accepted that Whin would probably need some form of consoling or advice and this was what was worrying him.

"Would you like to see a picture?" Whin asked suddenly.

"Yeah" Tom said simply.

Whin drew out his wallet and pulled a passport size photo from the back sleeve. He gazed at it for a moment and then passed if over to Tom. A puzzled look flitted across Tom's face but he didn't respond. I wondered what it was he had seen.

"I loved her Tom. I loved her so much. I'm not a romantic fool and I have never believed in love at first sight but there was just an enormous amount of chemistry between us. I watched some documentary once about male and females being attracted to each other by smell, like we were still animals. Sounds funny doesn't it?" Whin rambled. He laughed to himself and continued. "I don't like to think that we are just animals Tom. It all feels a bit stupid but I just explain it any other way."

Whin paused again and finished up the packed of peanuts with his glassy expression still intact. He sipped his beer and jolted out of his trance.

"Anyway Tom. About three or four weeks after the funeral I had a phone call from Mel. Well, I was shocked. I had spent a month grieving not only my friend but a woman who wanted nothing more to do with me."

"What happened at the wake Whin? Tom asked. "You didn't tell me what happened at the wake."

"Nothing really Tom" replied Whin. "I had a few too many whiskies and I couldn't leave her alone. I embarrassed her and myself although I couldn't give two monkeys about that." Whin took a deep breath and leaned forward slightly. "I would stand behind her whilst she was listening to condolences from various gifts and my hands were involuntarily touching her."

Leaning even further forward he continued. "You have to understand Tom, I was slightly insane at the time. The loss of my friend and the addictive desire to be constantly close to Mel combined with copious measurements of alcohol took me beyond logical behaviour. The lunacy I encountered was beyond my control. I had to be near her." Whin's face had a look of desperation on it. He was determined for Tom to understand and appreciate his foolish behaviour.

Tom calmly took Whin's arm and said "Hey listen, it's happened to us all. Tell me what happened".

Whin seemed to take some comfort from Tom and with more vigour he carried on"

• •

FLASHBACK

• •

CHAPTER 13

It was broad daylight now and I was hoping that Fiona and Katy would be getting up so that I would have some focus to my day, some entertainment to mask the insecurity I felt deep down.

I looked around the room, desperate to take my mind off things and noticed that the laptop had not been fully closed. Strangely even after an entire night of non-utilisation, it was still showing the anorexia and bulimia website. I didn't know why the screen saver was not functioning but at least it gave me an opportunity read up a little more on this debilitating illness.

For more than an hour I read personal stories from girls around the world. I also read with sadness a blog from a boy called Wenton in the US. Apart from weight concerns, I think there were some even more serious underlying issues. The boy was only 14 but knew already that he preferred men. He had no interest in girls and although he had tried kissing one, just to join in with his peers, it felt wrong and disgusting to him. What made matters even more worrying was that I felt he also had body dismorphia. He hadn't said as much but reading between the lines I could tell his future lay in sex reassignment. It was clear that he saw himself as female and he slightly alluded to admitting he tried on makeup and women's clothes.

Although my heart went out to the poor confused boy, I was also very perplexed myself. Here was a poor lad who would be subjected to ridicule possibly for his entire life. If he went ahead with a full sex change, he would never procreate and finding an understanding partner is hard for relatively stable heterosexuals but for an individual with these difficulties, the future looked so bleak. I couldn't even begin to imagine having to deal with weight issues as well although upon reflection I supposed that the bulimia stemmed from his unhappiness.

Mentally I shook my head and continued with the plight of the other youngsters on the website. There were messages from children all over the world. They really were a shining example of a global community but sadly for the wrong reasons. The main thread of their communication was to impart knowledge on new tricks and ways to outsmart the system. They helped each other starve themselves to death. My heart sank to remember that Katy was avidly scanning through the suggestions.

Feeling thoroughly depressed, I turned away and tried to put the images of painfully thin children out of my mind. It was no easy task but luckily I heard noises on the next floor and realised that Katy and her mother were finally getting up.

A blurred vision of Katy rushing past the open door to the study made me wonder where she was going in a hurry but as the blurry figure of Fiona hurried past, I could only imagine they were playing a game or racing to the shower.

After a while of just listening to Fiona and Katy laughing and generally making a lot of noise downstairs, Katy ran into the den and grabbed her handbag. We dashed down the stairs and into a large open plan dining and kitchen area. It was very plush. Not quite as expensive as Phil and Becks' place but still impressive. Fiona was grilling bagels and turned to ask Katy how many she would like and whether she would prefer Philadelphia or just butter.

"No thanks mum, I've got to go. She wrapped a glittery tassled scarf round her neck and was about to leave when her mum reached for her arm and stopped her.

"Katy, you haven't had breakfast. Come on have a bagel and a coffee with me. I've got to pop to Cherry's in a bit so I can give you a lift."

Katy looked torn. To keep refusing food in front of you mother is never a good idea. They have this ability to work out exactly what you are doing whether you are 3 years old or 41! I could see the cogs of Katy's brain turning, trying to recall the recommendations from her fellow starvers for advice in this particular situation.

"Ok mum. I'll have a small coffee and a bagel but only if you have Philadelphia Light."

Fiona smiled and looked as though she was pleased with the response. Her suspicions appeared to be unfounded. Turning back to her open paper on the granite work surface next to the six slice toaster and resumed reading.

Katy fumbled around in the fridge and brought out a tub of cream cheese. I knew exactly what was going through her mind. This morning I had read some of the tips to avoid detection. By far the most popular was eating the food in front of the mistrustful adults and forcing yourself to vomit it all up at the nearest opportunity available. I suppose I could see the benefit of this. Tasting the food is the part we all enjoy so by ridding the body of the food before it has a chance to be absorbed, means it is a win-win situation. Unfortunately though the consequences were dire and after looking at some of the snaps of the malnourished sufferers had only made me want to consume an entire chocolate cake, if only that were possible.

Fiona folded up the paper, removed the bagels and took the tub of Philadelphia from Katy. Slathering on heaps of cream cheese on to the bagels, I was sure I could see Katy wince. The last bagel in two halves was still bare and Katy reached over and offered to finish up whilst Fiona made the coffee.

Fiona may have been still asleep for all the notice she took and didn't seem at all suspicious. She picked up two mugs out of the dishwasher and added a couple of spoonfuls of coffee in each of the cups. As she poured the hot water she said distractedly "Can't remember how you take your coffee. You want milk and sugar?"

"Neither" replied Katy a bit too quickly for my liking. "I like my coffee like I like my men" she added, trying to bring humour into the moment.

It was totally lost on Fiona. To be honest she looked like she had been up boozing all night. Her eyes were red and swollen and her hair was definitely not having a good
day. I remembered the banging noise last night that I had put down to a loose fence panel being blown about in the wind. Surely a few minutes in the middle of the night to do some urgent temporary repair work wouldn't make her look so rough?

I watched Katy smear the smallest amount of Philadelphia on her bagel and take both plates to the kitchen table. She was clever I'll give her that. She hid one slice of bagel behind her coffee mug and tilted the other slice towards her so that even if Fiona suddenly came to she wouldn't notice the miniscule covering. They made small talk over breakfast and I felt as though an ice wall had melted between them. Katy calling Fiona from the hospital and asking for her assistance must have been a pretty rare phenomenon and had broken through a barrier that I could sense. I had no idea, of course, why this barrier had been erected in the first place nor why Katy had been reluctant in the past to rely on her mother. I had an inkling that the truth lay with the errant father but getting more information on that matter would take a lot more probing and I wasn't entirely sure how I could do that.

With the bagels consumed and the coffee mugs empty, Fiona darted up the stairs to wash and dress. Already clad, Katy put the breakfast things in the seldom used sink and made her way to the downstairs bathroom. I did my best to listen out for any telltale wretching sounds but alas the walls must have been too thick. Either that or Katy was managing to bring up her bagel in silence.

I became worried at this point. It would be so painful to see Katy denying herself to death. Not being able to do anything to help her was going to be pretty impossible to cope with. Everyone I had met since Whin's funeral was suffering. Was this journey supposed to teach me something?

Eventually Fiona came down to the kitchen and after a few minutes of searching for car keys and cursing, we made our way outside. I had forgotten about the previous night's proceedings and walking out of the front door gave me quite a shock. Quickly remembering the banging and Fiona's disappearance outside, I had expected to see a badly nailed fence, repaired enough just to stop the noise but I was wrong.

From what I could make out, there were shards of plastic scattered across the path to the pavement. They resembled the black dustbins and I could only assume that the banging was from someone bashing the bins against the brick wall of the house. Katy stopped dead in her tracks and looked horrified.

"Mum, what on earth…" she stopped and raised her hand to her mouth.

"Don't worry petal. It's all under control." Fiona said a lot more confidently than she appeared.

"But Mum. I mean what is going on?" Katy turned to her mother and continued "Don't tell me its that bloody family down the road still"

"Maybe" said Fiona looking embarrassed.

"Oh my God! Is that still going on?" Katy raised her eyes to heaven and as she did so she froze. "MUM!" she shouted. "I don't believe it. You've got security cameras up there!"

Fiona tried to drag Katy down the path to the car parked in the road but Katy wasn't budging.

"Jesus Mum." exclaimed Katy. "I think we had better go back inside and you had better tell me what's been going on."

"I haven't got time now. I told you. I'm off to meet Cherry. We're off to have a half day spa treatment and then pizza up at Ask." I could see what she was doing. She was talking in a musical tone trying to deflect from the real issue, which was that she was suffering the effects of a retard family, attacking her home and making her life a misery. Luckily though, Katy was on the ball this morning and wasn't taking no for an answer.

"Right then. What's Cherry's number? I'm going to call her and rearrange your massage. I think this is a bit more important."

Katy grabbed her mum's hand and gently steered her back into the house. Fiona slumped on one of the chairs in the kitchen and sunk her head into her hands. Katy put the kettle on and rifled through her mother's bag for her mobile. Whilst the kettle was boiling she scrolled through her contacts list and found Cherry's number.

"Hi Cherry?" Katy asked when someone answered the phone. "It's Katy. Listen Mum and I have got a couple of urgent things we need to sort out. Is there any chance you could cancel the spa?"

She paused for a while, presumably whilst Cherry spoke and then continued "Ok thanks Cherry. Take care. I'll get mum to call you later". She hung up and carried on making tea.

Katy sat at the table next to her mum and opened her handbag. She brought out her fags and offered one to her mum. Fiona looked shocked.

"I didn't know you smoked," she said taken aback.

"There are a lot of things you don't know" she said curtly "but right now we have other things to talk about."

Fiona took a cigarette and Katy lit it and then lit her own. Puffing away they sat in silence for a while, just smoking and sipping their hot tea. Katy fixed her eyes on Fiona and asked "So. What happened? I thought those bastards got an ASBO and that was the end."

Fiona threw her head back and exhaled her smoke. "Yeah. The Symons got the ABSO but it didn't stop. It did calm down but about a month after they just started up again. It wasn't just me this time either. They have been hassling Mrs Collins next door. I thought the best way to deal with it was to install cameras and catch them red handed."

Fiona finished her cigarette and stubbed it out in the pretty yellow Spanish ashtray.

"Go on" urged Katy.

"Well the problem was they saw the bloke that put the cameras up and the minute he left they threw eggs and stuff at it. I was at work but Mrs Collins rang me."

"So how long ago was that then?" asked Katy looking extremely concerned.

"Erm I think it was early August." Fiona stated.

"How much footage have you got?" Katy asked.

"Not enough" Fiona looked up at her daughter. "I didn't always put the tapes in."

"Mum!" Katy wailed. "What's the point of paying for all that equipment and taking the stick for having the bloody things in the first place if you don't use it?" Katy looked quite angry now and lit another cigarette. Fiona looked at her but decided not to mention her chain smoking.

"I know, I know. I have had such a lot on at work and there has been one thing after another and to be honest I sometimes forgot." She looked down at her hands and began crying. "I'm sorry Katy. I have been such a shitty mother to you". She collapsed her head onto the table and carried on crying.

"Hey. Hey. What's brought this on?" Katy looked totally bewildered. "We were talking about the cameras and the sodding Symons Mum." She said trying to make light of the situation.

Fiona didn't reply and remained face down on the table. Katy inched her chair nearer and rubbed her back. She softened her voice and said "Mum you have been great. It wasn't your fault dad left us and I think you have coped better than I would have done."

"But I was never there for you when you needed me" came the muffled response.

"Yes but you were out working. You were bringing in a salary for us to live on. What else could you have done?" Katy asked.

Fiona sniffed and raised her head. "I don't deserve you," she whispered, stroking her daughter's hair.

"Yes you do and you and I are going to sort out this camera mess. Now. Where are the tapes?"

Fiona led her up the stairs into the den and opened a small dark wooden cabinet. Inside were plenty of tapes still in their wrappers but two were lying on the top with the word 'Symons' written on the spine. She opened up the recording device and gave another to Katy.

"That's all there is I'm afraid poppet" she said as she removed a tissue from her pockets and dabbed her eyes and blew her nose.

"Well three is better than nothing so lets go watch them and see what we have." Katy was very much taking control of the situation and I could see that this was exactly what Fiona needed. She might be a successful businesswoman but in her own home so had lost the strength she needed to tackle obstacles of this nature.

They sat down in the den and popped the first tape into the ancient VCR. Katy picked up the remote and fast-forwarded the boring parts. There was about 3 hours on the tape so I knew it was going to take some time.

Katy paused the tape about 10 minutes into the tape and pointed out a hooded figure creeping around in the front garden. "Look" shouted Katy. "There is some proof that those bastards have been hanging around".

"It's not quite as simple as that darling" Fiona said sadly. "I can't prove who that is as his face is totally hidden. They might be bastards Katy, but they are not totally moronic. More's the pity." She added.

"Ok well let's keep going. They are bound to trip up at some point," Katy said enthusiastically.

We sat through the first tape and about half way through the second tape when Fiona sat up and asked Katy to rewind slowly. I hadn't seen anything but then I was almost comatose with boredom. Don't get me wrong. I knew that this had to be done and if I were human I would be doing exactly the same thing but it was mind numbingly tedious.

Rewinding the tape, we all peered at the screen and scrutinised the figure hovering outside the front door. A lad had appeared and seemed to be checking around him to make sure all was quiet. He threw a couple of stones at the camera. One missed and the other just knocked the casing slightly. He was kicking the drainpipe underneath the camera presumably to test whether it would take his weight as he then grabbed it with both hands and started to shimmy up it. Even from this angle, we couldn't see his face. He was wearing a baseball cap with a hoody over the top. Suddenly a car drove past and the headlights managed to catch the brat's face and illuminated it perfectly. The fool jumped down. He realised he had been caught and his first thought was to run away.

"Got him," Katy yelled. "See mum. That must be enough to show that he is still up to no good"

Fiona smiled brightly and nodded. "Yes. That's great but we need more". She took the remote control from her daughter's palm and carried on watching the recording.

The excitement soon gave way to sheer repetitiveness and I could feel myself falling asleep. I couldn't keep awake and even though I noticed a few more yelps of joy due to possible sightings of the Symons boy and identification, I couldn't help but pass out.

It can't have been a long nap as the girls were still in the den, flicking through the tapes but they seemed to be wrapping it all up now. I was rather pleased that I had timed it so well.

"Mum, I really do have to go now" said Katy standing up and smoothing her jeans down. "I'm glad we got this sorted and I want you to promise me that you will go and see the police tomorrow. You can't let this scum get away with this"

Fiona stood up too and gave her daughter a huge hug. "I love you," she whispered in Katy's ear.

"I love you too mum and I promise I'll be back next weekend." She gave her mother a kiss on the cheek and added "Thanks".

"What for? It should be me thanking you. You have sorted me out not the other way round." She stroked Katy's hair and said, "You are amazing".

"Right I'm definitely off now or you'll make me cry".

Fiona waited whilst Katy grabbed her bag from the spare room and then we all went down the stairs together. "Oh. Shall I still give you a lift?" Fiona asked?

"No mum. I'm fine. I need the exercise and I want you to stay safely indoors". The girls hugged again and said their goodbyes.

Katy and I walked along the road and as we followed the curve of the pavement, we slowed down when we approached no 27. I was guessing that this was the home of the delinquent Symons family. Katy glared at the cheap brick home, complete with nasty lace net curtains and three fishing gnomes on the front lawn. The funny part was there was no pond, well possibly there was but the ridiculously high grass and rubbish strewn all over hid any inkling that the gnomes were dangling their rods into water.

We moved on and after about 20 minutes we reached a narrow road with small terraced houses. Katy opened the gate of a sweet house with a blue front door. She called out as she entered "James. JAMES. You in?"

There was no reply so Katy trotted up the stairs and went straight into her bedroom. It was more girly than I had imagined. I hadn't really thought of Katy as a typical teenage girl. She was far too mature to have dolls on her bed but there were two beige teddy bears propped up against her pillow, both of which looked very well loved. I supposed they had been childhood comforters and it was an endearing touch to see that this girl who came across as so overly confident, actually needed a soother.

Katy sat down and placed a large mirror and a sack of make up on the bed next to her. For the next 30 minutes she applied layer after layer of foundation, mascara and blusher. When she finally rolled a lip gloss over her mouth and blew a kiss into the mirror, I was secretly impressed with the result. She looked a lot older, possibly a woman in her mid twenties and if she found an outfit to compliment her face, she would look stunning.

James must have returned home as he knocked on the door and came in without permission holding a mug of tea.

"You're a star," she said holding out her hands.

"You ok?" James asked timidly. "I haven't seen you for a couple of days and I was wondering what you had got up to". He appeared to be fairly blasé but although he put on a good act, I could see that he had been very worried.

"I'm fine," Katy said without looking up. "You coming out tonight?" she asked

"Oh I don't know" James said and then in an excited voice added "I didn't sleep much last night". I huge grin on his face showed that he had got lucky. "Oh Katy he's gorgeous. He works for BA as cabin crew on their longhaul flights from Heathrow. I suppose I won't see much of him but he is so lovely".

James had a dreamy expression all over his face and it took Katy a while of shaking his arm to snap him out of it. "So where did you meet him?" she asked whilst applying yet another layer of lip gloss.

"My friend Gregor was celebrating a birthday. He wouldn't tell us which one" James smirked. "And he suggested the Black Cap in Camden. I hadn't been there before but my God there were some gorgeous boys in there."

"Oh James" said Katy. "Don't tell me he is a pup?" She looked at him chastisingly.

"Oh God no!" said James over emphasising. "He is older than me!"

Katy swallowed the dregs of her tea and scratched around in her pine wardrobe. James continued to sit on her bed, reliving the antics of the previous night presumably.

Katy threw a black dress onto her bed and then began to undress. She was totally unfazed by James's presence. She was down to her bra and knickers when I thought any minute now one of them will realise and die of embarrassment. I was wrong. Katy fully stripped, sprayed herself all over with Dove deodorant and then put on fresh underwear without either of them batting an eyelid. I had heard that it was very common for women to have gay best friends. Someone they could confide in and trust implicitly. It looked like I had just met Katy's.

The doorbell rang and James jumped up nervously. "What if it is him?"

"Well answer it and found out." Katy laughed as she pushed James out of the room. She put on her dress and wrapped it around. She stood in front of the mirror and checked herself from all angles. The dress looked great but Katy wasn't totally happy. She scratched around in the wardrobe some more and pulled out a pair of Esprit jeans. She put these on under the dress and added a pair of beautiful black heels. I knew what she was doing. The dress showed up her skinny legs too much and wearing the jeans not only gave her some more confidence but also bulked her up a little so that spotting her real size was more difficult.

James burst into her room and threw himself onto the bed. He looked thoroughly depressed. "I promised myself I wouldn't get my hopes up. He's probably not even in the country. He's probably dying to call me but he is on the way to Sydney or something".

"I take it that it wasn't him at the door then" Katy said as she tried to find a jacket to go with her outfit.

"No. It wasn't him. It was some meathead from the gas company wanting to read the meter"

"Never mind" said Katy with a sympathetic tone. "He'll call. Have a little faith. Now are you coming out or not?" She grabbed a long black cardigan with a fur collar. I thought it looked quite a strange combination but who was I to discuss fashion?

"Oh go on then," James stated as he swept out of the room with excessive camp vigour. "Give me half a mo to look gorgeous," he called over his shoulder as he headed to his room.

I could see the attraction of being a fag hag and cohabitating with a homosexual gentleman. They could be a protector if required. The very presence of a male would automatically deter some unwelcome company. They could compare boyfriends and be totally supportive and understanding in a way that most heterosexual men would find problematic. The more I looked at their set up, the more I realised how much fun it would be.

Katy was downstairs by the time James had completed his make over. Previously he had been wearing baggy lounge pants and a long sleeved t-shirt but now miraculously he was dressed in a very tight white shirt and low slung trousers. The overall effect was quite dazzling and if I had been a homosexual man, I think I would have found him most alluring.

"Come on Queeny" Katy joked. "You driving or shall we take the bus and drink ourselves silly?"

"Oh the latter my dear child" James said linking arms like something out of the Wizard of Oz and led her to the front door.

As we walked towards the bus stop it suddenly dawned on me that I had been led away from Fiona and my link to Whin. I just hoped that I remained with Katy until we visited her mother again. Perhaps then I could make my way back to Dan. I had no idea if this possibility was viable but it was the only hope I felt I had.

It must have been around 9:30 and it was quite chilly. No rain but there was more than just a nip in the air. Katy wrapped her cardigan tighter around her. If we had to wait long for the bus she was going to feel the cold. James on the other hand wore a big leather jacket with a fleecy lining. Again I wasn't sure of the mixture of winter outer garments and decidedly summer garb underneath but again I really wasn't the best individual to give advice on the matter, not owning a stitch of clothing myself!

As we approached the bus stop I could see a group of youths hanging around. That either meant that a bus was due any minute or it was where the local youngsters liked to hang out. I could never see the point of just sitting around in the cold but then I had never been a teenager with lots of energy and nowhere to go!

Sure enough a bus crept round the corner and trundled its way toward the crowd. Katy and James readied themselves and produced their Oyster cards ready to flash at the machine inside. The others however, just became louder and even started shouting at the unusually dressed couple. James looked like he was used to the attention and nonchalantly boarded the bus. Katy looked irritated and flashed a glare at an older boy who was definitely the ringleader. Rather than keep quiet, he upped his obscenities and the younger kids followed his lead and joined in. Fortunately the bus driver closed the doors rapidly and drove off. I was quite perturbed by this outrageous attack. There just seemed to be no respect these days.

Katy and James headed towards the back of the bus and sat in front of an old lady. She looked ancient but I think she was possibly younger than she appeared. James pulled out his mobile and began furiously texting. Katy just looked out of the window. I was mesmerised by the old lady. Her short white hair was slightly curly, possibly the remains of a perm but her hair was so thin that I could see her pink scalp quite clearly. I could also see what looked like a large wart protruding from the back of her head and as the bus shuddered, the growth swayed as well. I was disgusted but captivated. I couldn't stop looking at it. What was it? Why had she done nothing about it? I was assuming of course, that she was compus mentus but when I overheard her muttering to herself and saw her scratching away at something under her coat, I realised that the poor woman was a loon. Not very PC these days admittedly but she was a loon nonetheless.

The bus journey took a while and I made a conscious effort not to look at the old dear and concentrated on the view out of the murky windows. It was dark now and quite difficult to take in the sights but the neon lights grew more abundant and I had a feeling that we were headed toward the centre of town.

About 10 minutes later, James stood up and pressed the large red button. He grinned at Katy and said, "Come on love".

Katy rolled her eyes and replied, "I thought you were all cut up about lover boy?" She joked.

James stuck out his tongue playfully and pulled her off the stationary bus. We ran across a busy road dodging the traffic and walked down a side street. There were few street lamps and I was beginning to feel uneasy but Katy and James were chattering away about some bloke called Rex and I had no option but to wait and see where we were headed. It didn't take long until we reached a tatty black wooden door. A huge guy was on the pavement talking loudly into his mobile. James and Katy ducked out of his way and pushed the door open. We walked into a shabby corridor and down a dirty flight of stairs. I could see fag butts all over the floor but the noise was incredible. The music got louder as we descended the stairs and pushed open another grungy door. It was so dark inside. It took a while for my vision to correct itself. James and Katy headed straight for the bar and ordered two pints of snakebite. I had no idea what that concoction was but it sounded revolting. They sipped their drinks and looked around the room. In the distance I could see a stage. It was unlit but I presumed that we had come to hear a band. James obviously recognised someone and shouted something over the heads of the other patrons. Katy kept an eye out. Something told me she was wondering if Nick would show up. Her eyes darted around the club and content that he wasn't there, she dragged me out of her bag and lit a cigarette. She offered one to James and he took one eagerly.

Although I felt I was constantly on tenterhooks wondering where every second would lead me, I think deep down I was enjoying the ride. Life with Whin had been safe and secure but predictable and dare I admit it, dull. Don't get me wrong, I would have chosen Whin over anyone else but after years of unsurprising events, I was experiencing another side to life.

Katy and James were on their second pints when the house music stopped and a loud booming voice echoed through the club

"Here is a very rare treat. Please welcome the one and only The Faithful". The applause was tremendous and Katy and James looked at one another excitedly. They jostled their way nearer to the stage and I saw four lanky guys walking onto the stage. The wolf-whistles behind me were deafening and couldn't hear what the lead singer was trying to say. Neither could anyone else for that matter and after a few attempts to shout at the crowd, someone from the back realised that the microphone wasn't switched on. A crew member jumped up on the stage and fiddled about with the mic and miraculously the thing began to work. A guy at the back settled down behind his drum kit, another picked up his bass and the final man strummed his electric guitar. With another roar of applause the lead singer launched into song. He was also playing an electric guitar and although it was loud, I found myself enjoying it.

A few songs later and the group announced they were having a beer and would be back later. They jumped off the stage and headed toward the bar. The house music was turned up again and the crowd carried on talking and drinking and waited for their return. As the lead singer passed Katy, she grabbed his arm and shouted, "I'll get this".

The man recognised Katy and pecked her on the cheek. His forehead was dripping with sweat but Katy didn't notice. He followed her to the bar with James close behind and she yelled at the barman for three snakebites.

"You're looking good, girl" the man said mischievously. I watched him checking her out. His eyes followed her body and he winked.

"Stop it Rex, you cheeky boy" said Katy but secretly loving the flattery.

James asked Katy for a cigarette and she offered one to Rex as well. The three of them stood next to the packed bar for quite a while, catching up. When Katy explained that she had caught Nick with some blonde tart, both men stared at her.

"Oh sorry James. I hadn't had a chance to tell you. Yeah that bastard. I always knew he couldn't be trusted but hey" she said lifting up her pint "I'm free and single and loving it!"

I knew that wasn't really how she was feeling and that the alcohol was feeding her courage but it was one way to deal with it.

Rex increased his attentions when he heard that piece of information and began seriously flirting with Katy. She was lapping it up but James looked a little put out to be a gooseberry so soon into the evening. Just as Rex tried to move in for a kiss, one of the band members grabbed Rex's arm and pulled him off in the direction of the stage

"Rex. Get with it you perve." He laughed and Rex turned back to Katy.

"Wait for me" he said desperately waiting for her to agree.

She shrugged. Good girl. She was going to play hard to get. James looked a little more pleased that he had Katy back and they made their way to the front again.

Another 4 or 5 songs were played and Katy and James were positively bouncing about. The alcohol had obviously kicked in and they were loving it. I was feeling a little nauseous at that stage and just wanted to go home. It seemed that luxury would be a while off though.

The band played their last number and left the stage to a frenzied audience. The house music didn't start up immediately and most of the mob was waiting for an encore. As soon as the lights on the stage went out though, people gave up and carried on drinking again.

I wondered what Katy was planning to do. Was she going to do as Rex asked and wait for him? Or was she going to leave with James? James was thinking the same thing and bellowed in her ear

"What's next sexy?"

"What do you fancy?" she asked encouragingly.

I really hoped he wasn't going to suggest some gay bar. I wasn't sure I was ready to witness the type of places he hung out.

"Come on. Drink up. I need to eat" James shouted back.

That was a relief. At least a café or restaurant would be a lot quieter. I saw Katy's expression falter. Oh dear. That was probably the last thing Katy wanted to hear but she can't have been that keen to hang about as she downed the remainder of her pint and nodded.

They made their way back to the entrance and Katy looked around. She stopped as she noticed Nick leaning against the back wall. He had spotted her too and nodded in acknowledgement.

"Hurry up James. I need to get out of here". She pushed James out into the corridor and immediately the decibels lessened. I tried to see if Nick was with anyone but it was impossible.

"What's wrong poppet?" James asked as he saw her sad face.

"I just saw Nick". Katy said with a sigh.

"Come on then. Lets go to Crushhh. We can get cocktails there and a side order. You can drown your sorrows and I can stuff my face and we'll both be happy." He clapped his hands, happy to have found a solution. James must have been aware of Katy's problem with food but

I wondered if he had ever tried to help or whether he just accepted her as she was, like she did with him.

They had just opened the door onto the street when a yell behind them stopped them in their tracks.

"Wait up."

Katy turned round and saw Rex racing towards them.

"Sorry Rex. I saw Nick and I just want to get out of here".

Rex nodded and looked at James.

"We're off to Crushhh if you fancy it?" James said with a slight look of disappointment.

"Ok" said Rex. "I'll meet you there. I've just got to pack my stuff up". He pecked Katy on the cheek and dashed back into the club.

Once on the pavement Katy took James's arm and said "Sorry. I can tell you don't approve".

"Nonsense" James said as he plastered a grin over his face. "A girl needs what a girl needs". They laughed and drunkenly made their way across the dark road towards the main street.

It was a short trip and I was pleased to find that Crushhh was just a late opening diner. Not particularly civilised but it was better than some of the establishments I had frequented recently.

Katy plonked herself down on a maroon velour booth seat and James handed her a menu. Katy ordered a screaming orgasm and didn't even blush! James, it seemed, was starving and chose a huge burger with fries and onion rings.

They were half way through their orders when Rex and a lanky guy rocked into the bar. James made a slight groan and I saw Katy kick his shin. "Behave," she said.

They men marched over to the table and Rex immediately slipped onto the bench next to Katy.

"I'm James" James announced quite comically I thought, as there seemed to be a dollop of ketchup on his chin.

"All right mate" came the response and in this light I thought he might have been the drummer.

I relaxed and enjoyed the peace. James and the drummer bantered their way through a conversation and Rex plied Katy with more drinks. I knew what he was up to and just hoped that James would protect her. I liked what I saw of Rex but I thought he was moving a little too quickly. This would be a rebound relationship for Katy and it just didn't feel right.

The four of them carried on boozing, eating and smoking and generally have a good time. Katy was enjoying herself. She needed that after the nasty few days she had had. She looked wasted though and I was wondering how this night would end. I really hoped that Rex would come to his senses and behave like a gentleman. I couldn't stand the thought of him taking advantage of her.

Although I was worried, I was exhausted. I was comfortable in here and just wanted to snooze. It was warm and relative to the club, it was quiet.

CHAPTER 14

I woke up with a start. I didn't recognise my surroundings and I wasn't definitely not still in the bar. Looking around I wasn't acquainted with my environs and I had a nasty feeling I had been switched again. A groan from the corner of the room alarmed me. It was still dark and I couldn't make out what or who had made the noise. I suspected it was human though. There was another moan and the rustling of material.

The curtains were thrown back and full sunlight burst into the room. Well I must have slept longer than I imagined. The blackout drapes must have confused me. With bright daylight flooding through the bedroom, I was able to make out who I was with. To my relief I saw Katy still out cold in bed. Rex was standing stark naked in front of the window, stretching and scratching. It was quite a revolting sight actually so I averted my eyes. Looking around the room, it was apparent that I was not in Katy's bedroom but by a process of elimination, I decided it must be Rex's room.

Rex staggered back to the bed and slid under the covers next to Katy. My heart sank. I could see that Katy was also unclothed and could only assume that Rex's longings had overtaken his consideration for her and he had had his wicked way.

Rex started whispering in Katy's ear but as he received no response he increased the volume and ran his hand up and down her thigh. Still nothing. Looking a little worried Rex shook her and screeched her name.

Katy opened her eyes and looked startled. She took a minute of two to figure out where she was. She sat up suddenly and then held her forehead as it appeared to be pounding. She sank back on to the mattress and groaned.

"Come on you. Fancy a fry up?" Rex seemed very eager to get up and out.

Katy shook her head and groaned again. "Go away. I'm ill." she croaked. She pulled a pillow over her head to block out the streaming sunlight and turned towards the wall in a vain attempt to sleep. Rex was having none of it and leapt on her and tried tickling her into submission. Katy was quite a mild person but this attack, albeit friendly brought out a side I had only glimpsed with the Nick incident. Now she was angry. Her hangover most likely being the cause of her ill temper but Rex was going to have to take the brunt of it. I felt quite pleased. If he had used her last night then this was his comeuppance

She slapped him and screamed like a banshee. Looking at her behaviour maybe she was just venting all the frustration and grief she had experienced in the last few days. Rex was slow to duck and took the full force of a good right-hander. He looked dazed and as he brought his hand up to his bleeding lip, she punched him straight between the eyes. Rex fell backwards, luckily onto the mattress but as far as I could tell he was out cold.

At first Katy ignored him and tried to curl back under the duvet. I presume she thought he was pretending and just being annoying. A few seconds later though, when it dawned on her that he hadn't moved, she crept up to him and shook him gently.

"Rex", she whispered. As she did so, he stirred.

"OWW" he sat up and rubbed his forehead. "What was that for?"

"Sorry. Sorry." Katy looked really remorseful and hung her head. She was kneeling on the bed and with one hand she took Rex's arm.

He brushed her off and got up to look at the state of his face in the mirror.

"Jesus Katy. What the fuck was that about?" He looked really angry and after inspecting his split lip and a red mark on his forehead he turned to her and said.

"I think you should go".

Katy stood up and I saw her thin body. Her skinny legs and almost non-existent breasts made her look more pre-pubescent rather than a grown woman. It really saddened me to think she was even trying to make herself look even slimmer. She grabbed her clothes and dressed quickly. Rex turned back to the mirror and re-examined his wounds.

She grabbed her things and walked towards the door. As she exited she turned around and murmured another apology. It wasn't until I heard the front door slam that I realised I was still on the bedside table. 'Damn'. Yet again I had lost the link to Whin and was on my way travelling further away from him and Dan.

Rex disappeared down the stairs and I could hear him talking to someone. As I couldn't hear another voice I could only suppose that he had made a call. The conversation continued and although I tried to eavesdrop, Rex must have made his way towards the back of the house until eventually I couldn't hear him at all.

Sitting there alone, I had no option but to ponder. Rather than sulk about my situation, I decided to make the most of this opportunity and think about my favourite person, Whin.

• •

FLASHBACK

• •

"At first I just hung about. I watched her from afar and then as she mingled I followed her from room to room, even into the garden.

I probably looked a right fool. Anyway I could sense that Mel had noticed my stalking and after a while she was getting the hump." Whin paused to take a long swig of his beer.

"I couldn't stop though Tom. I wanted to know whom she was talking to and what she was talking about. The jealously that flowed through me was extreme. I felt powerless."

Tom was looking more and more disturbed. We both knew that there was going to be a climax to this story and the more Whin continued, the more concerned we became. This didn't have the sound of just another brief affair, which had fizzled out. There was more to this.

"So when the people started leaving, I started getting closer. At first I just touched Mel's arm whenever I had a chance. Then I gave her a hug. I suppose I just looked like a friend supporting another during her hour of need but Mel knew what I was up to and I suppose deep down so did I. I wanted people to know. I wanted to get caught and have no choice but to come clean. Jesus Tom. I wanted the whole world to know. I was totally in love with this woman and I would have sung it from the rooftops, if I could."

Whin took a break. Tom's expression was growing more dismayed by the minute. I don't think Whin was aware. He looked absorbed in this historical event and carried on.

"Mel tried to get me to leave her alone. She pleaded with me to leave. I know she was worried that I was becoming unpredictable and just wanted to avoid any humiliation and shame. Tom. I wasn't listening. I wanted to convince her that her father's funeral would be the perfect place to announce our union." Whin lowered his head. "Obviously in hindsight I can see what drivel I was talking but at the time I thought it made perfect sense. One by one the relatives and other friends, all of whom I had never met, noticed the fracas and quite plainly made their disgust apparent. They all ended up leaving and Mel was mortified."

Geoff collected the glasses on the table, emptied the ashtray and removed the peanut bags. Again he had chosen a time when nothing was being said and once more missed the chance to overhear the conversation. A quick glance at Tom though and he scuttled away. Tom's face was a picture. Body language is so interesting. I can't remember the exact figure but apparently verbal dialogue is only about 30% of human communication. I find that fact fascinating. Looking at Tom's expression, though, and I understood exactly how he was feeling. He looked concerned and troubled by Whin's revelations. Not the information he had received so far. It was the story he had yet to tell that was worrying him.

"She was furious with me Tom" Whin continued, totally oblivious to Tom's reluctance to move on. "She threw a fit. Tom. She went mad. The minute the last guest had left, she screamed, thumped and slapped me until I had to leave. I just couldn't make her see sense. I only wanted to cuddle her in my arms and tell her I loved her but she wasn't having any of it." Whin was slurring slightly. The beer had finally reached his veins and rather than become maudlin with the sad news he was carrying, he became agitated and fractious.

"I just don't get women Tom. Tell me what I did that was so wrong." Thankfully Tom appreciated that this was a rhetorical question and made no move to answer it although I don't think Whin would have noticed if he did. He was still going.

"Anyway she kicked me out and I didn't get a chance to speak to her until about a week later. I tried calling and I popped round a few times, nothing. I send 3 different bouquets of flowers and you know what? She refused to accept the delivery from Interflora!? I have never heard of that before. Have you?" Whin looked across at Tom who was mid way though sipping his pint and realised that this time Whin was looking for affirmation.

"Erh no Whin. No. Never." Believing that he had got his point across he carried on drinking.

"Well I got angry too Tom". At this point Tom froze. Was he about to hear something nasty? Something that he really shouldn't hear?" Again the body language was speaking volumes. He looked terrified.

"I had hardly slept for the past week. I was drinking heavily just to forget and my love and jealousy grew and grew out of all proportion. I knew that I was mess. I just didn't know how to fix it."

The builders in the bar were getting quite rowdy and the noise level was increasing every minute. Soon Whin would have to be shouting out his problems, just to be heard.

"So about 8 or 9 days after the wake, I got a call from Mel. It was like I had given up hope and then all of a sudden there she was. I remember it was a Monday afternoon. Maybe about 4ish. I had been drinking a lot that weekend and I had a hair of the dog on Monday morning. Just to set me right Tom. You know how it is?" He looked at Tom quizzically trying to get his old mate to agree.

Tom being slightly more sober than Whin and certainly more alert than his friend, answered quickly "Erh yes Whin".

Encouraged by his friend's corroboration, Whin carried on. "Well Tom I was gobsmacked. I literally couldn't think of anything to say and twittered away like a fool. She could tell I was still drunk Tom. I just knew. I tried my damnedness to appear straight but I could tell by her tone that she wasn't taken in."

Whin must have been at least on his second pack of cigarettes by now. My fluid was running low and I hoped that he had equipped himself with a refuelling kit.

"So she started talking Tom. I remember she started off calmly and grew more and more irate. She told me that I had thoroughly embarrassed her and she had had to fend off all sorts of awkward and upsetting questions from members of her family. She told me there and then Tom that it was over." Whin looked close to tears and realizing that his eyes were dangerously near to filling up, he paused and downed most of the pint in front of him. Tom looked over at the bar and managed to catch Geoff's attention. He nodded and Geoff nodded back. Once more body language had the required effect and he was understood without the need for words.

"I can't even begin to tell you how I felt after that conversation. I didn't get much of a chance to talk. I suppose even if she had given me the option, I still wouldn't have known what to say." Whin looked quite worse for wear now and his speech was slurring. Fortunately Tom was looking almost as bad and as such understood exactly what Whin was talking about.

• •
FLASHBACK
• •

CHAPTER 15

Rex had been gone some time but I was suddenly stirred from my thoughts of Whin when he stumbled back into the bedroom. For someone who was quite slim, he was incredibly clumsy. He could have just been hungover and out of kilter but I thought it probably his natural demeanour.

I didn't realise he was still on his phone until after opening his wardrobe door, he suddenly repeated "Yeah," several times. He then sat on the bed and looked like he was listening intently.

"Look man. I had no idea ok? I'll be down later. If I have fucked this up then I'll sort it out. Give me an hour." After waiting to hear what his phone buddy said, he continued. "Yeah. It's cool. I'll meet you there and we'll sort it out."

He snapped the mobile shut and groaned out loud. He looked around the room and spotted me and a packet of B&H. He grabbed us and lit up. He threw himself back onto the bed and blew a plume of smoke up in the air towards the ceiling. He was holding me in his hand and it was very sweaty. I really didn't like it.

We were lying on the bed and Rex was enjoying his nicotine fix when I heard the door slam. Rex shot up and pulled on a pair of pants, lying on the floor by the side of his bed.

"Shit shit" I could hear him mutter and he stubbed out the cigarette a bit too quickly and left it smouldering. He opened the window and tried to fan out the smell. He threw me back onto the bedside table and ran down the stairs. I could hear him though. I could hear his laboured breathing.

"Mum?" He shouted quite nervously.

There were more voices but I couldn't distinguish the words, mores the pity. I sat waiting for something to be resolved and for Rex to collect me but the morning wore on. I presumed it was morning as I could see broad daylight but the blackout curtains had affected my clock and it could quite easily have been afternoon.

A while later Rex returned and pulled on some jeans, trainers and a black 'Cure' T-shirt. He grabbed a jacket and threw the cigarettes and me, into his pocket. 'At last" I thought. I really did want to get out of this place.

We casually trotted down the stairs and as Rex was just about to open the front door, a lady walked out of the room opposite and nonchalantly asked where he was going.

"Mum. I'm really late. I'll talk to you later." He tried to open the door but his mum stepped up closer.

"Rex. I don't know what's the matter with you. You knew I was coming back today and the house is disgusting. You have obviously only just woken up and it is after lunch. I asked you to collect the car for me but I can't see it outside so you must have forgotten that too. " She then nodded to the kitchen, further up the hallway and added "I can see that there is nothing in the fridge so what you did with the money I gave you, Lord knows".

She looked angry in a sort of expectant way. Like leaving her teenage son was always going to end in disaster but relieved that the house hadn't burnt down, he hadn't got himself arrested and that there wasn't a posse of naked women strewn around the house.

"Mum. Leave it. I'll be back later and I'll cook you a nice meal." He smirked and gave his mother a quick peck on the cheek. We left quite abruptly after that. Rex obviously didn't want to give his mum any more opportunity to detain him.

As we walked down the path, I noticed that the cul de sac we were in was really rather pleasant. It was leafy and spacious and each house had a driveway and nicely appointed front lawns. Admittedly Rex's lawn looked a little worse for wear but nothing a good mow wouldn't sort out.

As we strolled towards the road, several messages bleeped through on Rex's mobile but he was either deep in thought or snubbing the caller. After maybe a dozen texts buzzed through, Rex pulled out his phone and switched it off.

Mobile phones fascinated me. They were such a superb invention. People could be reached at any time in pretty much any place, in the western world of course, and yet if they chose tranquillity, a quick switch and they could be left alone. Fantastic!

Rex pulled out a set of keys from his pocket and we approached a rough looking Volvo. The car had definitely seen better days but I realised that Rex was a struggling teenage musician. To be honest it was a wonder he had a set of wheels at all.

He threw himself into the drivers seat and started up the engine. I looked around and as one might have expected it was a bomb site. The well of the passenger seat was full of debris, mostly burger wraps and empty fag packets. There were a few cans of beer and by the odour emanating from the floor, the cans had leaked the remnants over the nasty carpet. Rex wound down his window. It wasn't really warm enough but the smell had obviously driven him to it.

We screeched out of the cul de sac and speedily weaved our way through the twists and turns or the town's roads. Rex kept banging a small box on the dashboard and after eventually it lurched into life, I realised it was a radio. I had expected something a little more modern, maybe like attaching his MP3 player but then I remembered he had sort of been in a rush to leave the house so maybe all his teen paraphernalia was at home.

The DJ was laughing at some joke he had just made and then introduced some bands I had never heard of. The car sped through the town and lurched towards the more affluent area of the business district. We reversed into a space opposite a park, which looked like no mean feat. It was packed with cars so luck was on Rex's side now. He slammed the door but didn't bother to lock it. I agreed with him. Even joyriders would avoid this heap!

He lit up as we crossed the busy road and hung around a tall building mainly made of darkened glass whilst he finished his cigarette. He looked nervous and a little shifty. I had no idea where we were headed but Rex was anxious. Just as he stubbed out his fag with the sole of his trainer, another lad about Rex's age loped up to the building. He was sporting a ridiculous haircut. Well I thought of it as ridiculous but I guess in his circle it was deemed cool. It was jet black, so obviously dyed as his pale eyebrows looked almost white in comparison. It was cut so that one side was longer than the other and gelled so that it swept to one side. I recognised him as the guitarist from last night although he looked a touch worse for wear today.

"You just got here" the youth asked Rex.

"Yeah" Rex blew a plume of smoke into the air and opened the large glass door. "Dunno who else is here yet". Rex added as they headed to the lift.

The youth pressed the 'call' button and once inside pressed number 9. Upwards we went with both Rex and the youth remaining silent but both positively uneasy. The lift pinged as it reached the designated floor and both boys stepped out.

The floor was all open plan and very modern in its design and layout. Huge white leather and chrome sofas sat opposite the life entrance but the lads trotted past these and around the corner. From the full length windows, I could see the most amazing view. The whole of the city was stretched before us and I could have spent hours taking in the sights but Rex flung himself onto another huge leather couch by a brick wall and so my vista was obscured.

"Ah boys. You have arrived." A tall man with a greying goatee beard appeared before the two guys and checked his watch. He looked the epitome of cool wearing a jacket with a crisp white t shirt underneath and a really good pair of jeans. I have heard so many times that you just cannot go wrong with a good, expensive pair of jeans. Admittedly, this tip was always regaled by women but now I had first hand experience of their wisdom. Rex and his partner looked slightly in awe of this man and sat up straight immediately.

"Are we still waiting for the others or have you two decided to come alone?" The man asked with a pleasant if formidable manner.

"Ermm" Rex started and then coughed. "I think Tony and Al are on their way". He looked across at his friend for affirmation. "You spoke to them, didn't you Jez?"

Jez looked like a rabbit in headlights and stared blankly at the man. Rex nudged him and repeated "You spoke to Al and Tony, didn't you?"

Jez nodded and finally found his tongue. "Erhhh yeah. They're definitely coming but the traffic's bad".

Rex rolled his eyes. I understood what he meant. It was a pretty stupid thing to say. Both boys lowered their eyes to the floor, not really sure how else to continue.

"Ok. No problem but we do need to crack on so how about we get started and the lads can join us when they get here?" It was a question but not one that Rex and Jez could have refused. It was quite clear that this gentleman was fully at ease with his position and very confident that he was in control.

Jez and Rex followed him across the wooden floor scattered with enormous cow hides. In the corner was an office made with frosted glass. The man opened the door and held it open for the two boys to enter. He then gesticulated for them to sit on yet another leather sofa and sat behind a glass desk. These guys must have had a cow and glass fetish and some seriously strong links with South America!

"Now we have had the contracts drawn up and they are ready to sign." The man pushed them across the table towards Jez and Rex and folded his arms.

The two boys glanced at one another and Rex said "Well, if its ok with you Mr Butler, then I'd like to ask if we can wait for the others".

Mr Butler smiled but it didn't quite reach his eyes. I reckoned he was a nice enough fellow as long as things were going his way. The minute someone else was in control, he would make a fierce enemy. The boys acknowledged this and were understandably nervous and nowhere like the arrogant chaps they had been the night before.

"Please boys. Call me Brian. If you guys want to wait, that's fine with me." He didn't look fine and he sat staring at them with his elbows on the tabled and tapping his fingers together. "I'll get some drinks. Coffee? Coke? Something stronger?" He looked at them expectantly.

"I I I'll have a coke" stammered Jez.

"Erm. Black coffee please. No sugar" Rex said assertively.

The boys sat in the office quietly whilst Brian tapped a contraption on his desk and spoke into a speaker, " Two black coffees and a coke please Mel"

My ears pricked up. Was this Whin's Mel? Surely not.

"Excuse me boys. I'll be back in a minute". He sauntered out of the room. My guess was that he just didn't want to make small talk with the youths until their partners and agent arrived on the scene.

Rex and Jez looked at each other and Rex exhaled deeply "Thank fuck for that. I totally forgot about today. What a nob! How could I forget the most important day of our lives?"

"I wouldn't worry" Jez was trying to pacify him as Rex looked really gutted by his failure. "I forgot too and so did the others. It was only when Billy reminded me earlier on the phone that I remembered."

"Of course he should fucking remember. He's our fucking agent and is going to cut a stupid percentage of our earnings" Rex shouted back.

Jez sat back in the chair and tried to look unaffected by his outburst. Clearly he wasn't cut out as an actor as both Rex and I spotted him smarting from the eruption.

"Look mat,e" Rex said in a softer tone "I just meant that Bill should have called us earlier or reminded us sooner. We've been waiting for this meeting for weeks." Rex stopped and started picking at the skin around his fingers.

"Yeah I know" Jez replied. "I can't believe he's not here either. He's fucking useless".

"Yeah well let's just get this deal signed and we'll go searching for a better agent. How's that?" Rex asked conspiratorially.

"Sounds good to me" Jez smiled back and stood up. He paced the room for a bit and then said excitedly "They're here".

Rex jumped to his feet and both boys peered through the frosted glass. They could make out the figures but couldn't identify faces so they pushed open the door and both grinned as Al and Tony headed towards them. Tony, the bass player, was presenting a rather impressive black eye and scratched cheek whilst Al, the drummer who had been drinking with us at Crushhh, was wearing very dark glasses and didn't seem anywhere near to being ready to remove them. Behind them, bringing up the rear was another lanky guy, only this time he was probably in his late thirties and balding. He had thick, round pebble glasses and looked quite odd.

"About bloody time" Rex called out jokingly.

"Fuck off," Tony replied.

"Shhh," Al gesticulated with his fingers for the pair of them to pipe down.

Brian appeared at this point and motioned for the three men to enter his office. No sooner had Brian sat down than a female entered the room.

'Oh my god', I thought as I realised the woman in front of me was indeed Whin's lady friend Mel.

I couldn't really concentrate on the proceedings between the agent and the record producer as I was taking in Mel's appearance. She looked a lot older. It had been several years since I last saw her but she had aged considerably. I wasn't surprised to be honest. In fact I was impressed that she was even behaving normally, under the circumstances.

She handed out the drinks and took more orders from the new arrivals. I was relieved that none of the lads gave Mel a hard time or made wise cracks. They were polite and respectful. Maybe her body language gave away tips on how intolerant she was with insolence.

She left the office just as Bill was standing up. "Come on guys" he said with rather a strong Australian accent. I had only ever heard the Aussie drawl on 'Neighbours' but I liked it. It sounded like an interesting drawl, not like the American twang, which just made them all sound simple.

"You need to autograph this contract," he continued and he gestured for the lads to come forward and sign the deal.

I could see several large platinum disks in frames on the wall but other than that, there was no association that I could see that would link this office to the music world. I hadn't seen a name and had no idea who these people were. Spending the little time I had with Mr Butler, I would have employed the best solicitor available just to scour the contract for any dubious clauses. I didn't trust him and he reminded me of the snake in 'The Jungle Book'.

Both Mr Brian Butler and Billy were grinning which made me suspect that these lads had no idea what was in store. I also thought that there was probably a tiny passage in this agreement, which would ensure the older gentlemen benefited greatly. The poor lads were so eager to be signed up that they weren't even conscious they were being shafted.

One by one the four boys took turns and signed their names on the sheet of paper of Mr Butler's desk. They were barely holding the excitement in. I think they thought that immediately they would become an overnight success and revel in their millions.

After the completion of the contracts, Brian and Billy had a quick word outside the office. The guys huddled together, not wanting to be overheard. They all sounded so childish

"Bloody hell Rex. Why didn't you warn me?" Al joked. "I was with you all night".

"Not ALL night" Rex responded winking at his friend.

"You dirty bugger" Al looked at Rex jealously. He wasn't a stunner but I would have thought he would have found it fairly easy to entice the opposite sex.

Jez coughed loudly and leant in to whisper, "Can you believe it?" he said. He still had that 'rabbit in headlights' look on his face. He just looked totally astounded at his luck.

Rex crossed his legs nonchalantly and threw his arms up behind his neck. "Nah. We deserve it," he said cockily. "We're bloody brilliant and this lot are lucky to have us".

The others nodded but not quite as convinced about their status as Rex.

Brian and Billy were opening the door and we could all hear the remnants of their conversation.

"Wednesday would be good," Billy confirmed enthusiastically.

"Ok" said Brian "I'll book them in".

All four faces glanced up at Brian, wanting to know what was occurring on Wednesday but Billy just waved their concerns aside and quickly ended the meeting.

"Right then lads. I think I should be treating you to some very expensive fizzy stuff." he said beaming. "And I don't mean coca cola," he laughed but no one else did.

The boys looked at him like he was a complete fool, but they did as they were told and left the office after shaking Brian's hand in turn.

Once outside, the bright sunshine had gone and it was replaced with a dark grey clouds. I had a feeling a large thunderstorm was on its way. Rex started walking towards his car but Billy stopped him by shouting "You can't drive that if we are heading up town!"

"Sod off Billy" Rex shouted back over his shoulder. He looked like a man on a mission. "Text me where you're going and I'll meet you there. I need a shower".

I could hear the others hanging outside the enormous glass building waiting expectantly for a cab.

Rex started up the old Volvo and we cruised back to the cul de sac. This time it was a gentle sail rather than a high-speed hovercraft. When we pulled up to the two storey detached property, I saw a Mercedes in the driveway. Admittedly it was an old style 190 but it looked good and was well loved.

Rex clocked the car at the same time and slammed his fist onto the steering wheel. "Damn" he muttered but we jumped out of the car and straight up to the house.

"Mum?" Rex called out as soon as he turned the key in the lock. "Mum? You in?"

There was no response but as we walked into the rather lovely kitchen, I could see Rex's mother in the garden with an older gentleman. Rex watched the two of them for a minute. It looked like he was either plucking up the courage to go outside or biting his lip to remain polite.

"Mum. There you are," he said eventually as he sauntered through the French doors into the tidy garden. "Oh hi Jim" he added pretending to have only just noticed him.

"Well hello young Rex," Jim said rather haughtily and took his hands out of his pocket to shake the teenager's hand.

I think Rex spotted this out of the corner of his eye and made a move before Jim had a chance to speak. It had the desired effect and made Jim look awkward.

"Sorry I'm so late back. I've got some great news but before that let me take you to collect your car". He ushered his mother into the house so quickly, it almost looked urgent.

"Sorry Jim" Rex yelled back without even turning around "I promised Mum I would help her pick up the car. Can you let yourself out?"

The reply fell on deaf ears as Rex had already taken his mum's hand and was opening the front door. I could hear though and Jim just garbled something about that was why he was round in the first place.

It was very apparent to me and to everyone else that Rex had no time for Jim. Whether it was just the idea of an older man slathering over his mum or whether something had occurred previously, I had no idea but Rex remained polite, which was interesting and didn't say anything bad to his mother either.

The journey in the car was brief but too long for a walk to collect a car. Neither talked in the car but the atmosphere wasn't tense. Rex hummed to himself and I just realised that again I had been taken a step away from Mel. She would not have noticed me I was sure. She had only seen me a few times and those occasions were either far too passionate or too miserable to be concerned with a small inanimate object like myself.

Things were getting strange. Well I suppose things were getting stranger. It was interesting nonetheless that all these random characters were inextricably linked. I felt like I was travelling in a figure of 8. All handovers seemed to lead away from Whin but strangely all had an odd habit of leading back to him.

About 20 minutes later we pulled up at a garage and Rex's mother jumped out. "You don't have to wait for me darling" she said keen to get rid of him. "I can just see you back at the house".

"It's ok Mum. I'll wait. Just in case it's not ready or something". Rex looked determined so his mother shut the door and trotted up to the reception area at the bar of the showroom.

Rex watched his mum make her way into the building and then relaxed in the car. He pulled his mobile out of his pocket and texted a message through incredibly quickly. He sent two or three more and then rested his head back against the rest and chilled out. Today had been quite stressful. I wasn't sure how he was feeling with regards to the Katy situation. She had behaved appallingly but then he had plied her with copious glasses of alcohol last night so he was partly to blame. I wonder if he would forgive her or was it more a case of he got what he wanted and he was on to the next. I had seen many sides to Rex but I believed that the most predominant was Mr Arrogant. I had like Rex at the beginning but now my opinion was changing. I wasn't really sure what to expect with him. He was very unpredictable.

A couple of texts beeped back on his phone but he didn't reach for his phone. He opened his eyes every few seconds to check the progress of his mother's enquiry.

A while later Rex's mum tottered down the path to her son's waiting car. She wasn't smiling so I presumed Rex had been correct in his fears.

"Bloody hell" Rex's mum fumed as she opened the passenger door and sat down. On the journey here she had been quite reluctant to sit on the soiled seats and wasn't really sure where to put her feet, there was so much rubbish but now she was beyond caring. She was angry.

Rex sat up and started the engine. A small suited man with a monk style haircut walked briskly out of the building and tried to catch her eye. He was waving a piece of paper and almost broke into a run, so determined was he to grab his customer.

"Mrs Halliday. Mrs Halliday please wait." Rex was about to drive off when his mother put her hand on the gear stick and asked her son to hang on.

"Mrs Halliday. Thank you." The little man actually sounded out of breath as he drew up to the side of the car. He looked at the heap of a car before him and he was so disgusted with it, he pretended it didn't even exist.

"What is it?" Mrs Halliday replied as she wound down the filthy window.

"I am so sorry for the mix up. Look! I have just checked my records and I can absolutely promise you that your vehicle will be ready to collect tomorrow afternoon". The little man seemed so pleased with himself. As he waited for Mrs Halliday's reaction he drew a handkerchief from his pocket and dabbed his sweaty brow.

"Well Mr Dunn" Mrs Halliday had a look of superiority as she continued "It had better be here tomorrow by 3pm or your life won't be worth living." She looked straight ahead and said calmly "Drive Rex, drive".

Mr Dunn was still mopping the sweat from his chubby face. He didn't look like he knew what had hit him. It was obvious that most of his clientele were polite and respectful. Mrs Halliday was a completely different kettle of fish. She had been a delight to serve but now, when a mistake had been made, her fury had really rattled him.

Still staring after her, Mrs Halliday looked in the wing mirror at the salesman and laughed. "What a creep".

Rex drove slowly back to the house. My guess was that he was trying to make sure Jim had left. We weren't driving down the same roads so I thought Rex had probably taken a circuitous route. Mrs Halliday seemed totally oblivious to this and was still fuming about the mistake of her car delivery date.

As soon as we reached the cul de sac, I could see the old Merc 190 still parked outside Rex's house. Rex sighed deeply but again his mother was unaware of his reluctance to converse with Jim and jumped out of the car the second Rex stopped. I could see a figure in the Merc and presumed it was the suspect. Mrs Halliday flirted outrageously and I could see the disgust on Rex's face. He parked the car, switched the engine off but before he disembarked he checked through the texts he had received on his mobile.

"Oh for fuck's sake" he growled. Immediately he dialled a number and waited for the person to pick up the call. "What is your problem?" Rex snarled. "Haven't you given me enough grief?"

Rex listened for a while before losing his patience and snapped the phone shut. "What a prick" he muttered and grudgingly stepped out of the car and headed towards the front door. His mother and Jim were already inside and had quite thoughtfully left the front door wide open for him. Slamming it shut behind him, Rex marched straight into the kitchen and grabbed a carton of orange juice from the fridge and glugged it down.

"Rex!" came a yell from his mother in the garden "For God's sake, use a glass".

"Bloody eyes in the back of her head, that one" Rex mumbled to himself. He made his way to the French windows and leaned out into the garden.

"Mum. Can I have a word please?" He glanced at Jim who was making himself at home, quite nicely, relaxing on a wooden garden chair.

Mrs Halliday tutted and got up. She made her way over to Rex and pushed him into the house. "Look Rex. I know you don't like Jim but he makes me happy and I think you should just grow up a bit". She had gone bright red and looked like she had plenty more to say to her teenage son.

"Whoa Mum. Calm down. I just wanted to tell you that Dad texted me earlier and he wants to pop over". Rex looked at his mum, waiting for a reaction. His mother though, just burst into tears. It obviously wasn't what Rex was expecting and for a second he froze.

"Now Mum. Hang on. Don't cry." I could tell Rex wasn't really a natural when it came to empathy and understanding. He could be cocky and egotistical and I had yet to see a concerted effort to be sympathetic.

He hugged her and she continued sobbing on his shoulder. Rex looked over at the French windows and could see Jim patiently waiting for his younger companion to return. His awkwardness had vanished and he looked rather too comfortable for Rex's liking.

"Mum" he interrupted her crying and said "Look can I just ask Jim to leave us. It'll be easier for us if he's not here when Dad arrives."

Mrs Halliday was caught in a weak moment and nodded. Rex handed her a piece of kitchen towel and headed out into the garden. He approached Jim and rather than utilise this time to offend the older man, he hid his repugnance and kept his dignity and just plainly asked him to leave. He told him there were family issues that needed to be resolved. Again the awkwardness returned as a direct response to the proximity of Rex. He was frightened of him. I suppose he had good reason. Rex was tall, not particularly manly but still young enough to defend his mother in any way possible without considering the consequences.

Jim stood up, straightened his jacket and bade Rex farewell. Rex followed him in through the French doors and watched as he searched downstairs for his friend. Mrs Halliday must have disappeared upstairs and realising that, Jim stood at the bottom and called up.

"Bye Helen. I'll give you a call tomorrow. I hope everything's ok." Jim unwillingly opened the front door and with a cursory peek back at Rex, he shut the door behind him.

Rex leaned against the hall wall for a moment. He had both his hands in his pockets and seemed a million miles away. He sighed heavily and then he trotted up the stairs to see his mother.

"Mum? You Ok?" Rex called out as we reached landing. Helen hadn't replied but she was still crying and as Rex tracked down the source of the sobs to his mother's bedroom, he knocked briefly. Without waiting for permission, he pushed the door open and sat on the divan next to his mum.

"Oh Rex. I'm sorry". She blew her nose and carried on "I really thought that I had got over your dad but when you mentioned him popping round, I just fell apart." She blew her nose again and checked the mascara damage through her hand mirror.

"Mum. It's ok. It can take ages to get over these things. I'm sorry too." I must admit he had improved his compassion style. He gave his mum a hug.

"So". She blew her nose again. "What else did that father of yours say?" She looked nervously into Rex's eyes.

"Nothing really. He just said that he wanted to pop round this afternoon. I didn't tell him he could or he couldn't and for all he knows we might not even be in." He held her hands. "We could always pretend not to be here. Or we could go out?" He looked eager to please but Helen just looked sad and a little worried.

"No Rex. I don't blame you if you want to go but I feel I should stay".

"But Mum. He always calls the shots. Stand up to him for once." The patience was wearing thin and I could sense the irritation in Rex's voice.

"NO." She said loudly. So loudly that it Rex retreated a little.

"Ok Ok. Whatever you want". He put his hands up in mock surrender. "I'll be here too. I'm not about to let you face him alone."

Helen looked thoroughly relieved and kissed her son on the cheek. She got up and walked towards another door, which I presumed was her en-suite. "Just got to sort myself out".

Rex walked down the stairs and went straight out into the garden. He lit up a cigarette and sat in the garden chair with his feet up on the wooden table, blowing smoke rings into the air. He pulled his phone out of his pocket and scrolled through his contacts. I could see on the screen the name flashed up as Jez.

"You ok mate?" said Rex as soon as Jez answered the phone. I couldn't hear what was being said the other end but after a pause Rex continued.

"Listen. I don't know if I can make it out tonight. Long story but its all gone tits up and I need to sort some shit out. Where you headed anyway?"

Again I had no idea what Jez was saying but Rex was nodding, which was odd seeing as Jez wouldn't be able to see him.

"Cheers mate. I'll buzz you later when I know what's occurring. Laters".

Helen came out into the garden. I wasn't sure why everyone was spending time out here. It was decidedly cold and an angry cloud hung overhead. I felt that Helen didn't approve of smoking and certainly wouldn't have allowed it in her home, hence the hastily action this morning when she returned home.

"What do you think your dad wants to talk about?" Helen asked warily.

"No idea mum but it's bound to be a load of bollocks."

"REX!" Helen looked alarmed.

"Sorry mum but it's true. I don't believe a word he says and neither should you."

As Helen sat at the slatted wooden table, I heard a screech of car tyres outside. Rex rolled his eyes and Helen laughed. It was nice to see her face light up a little. She had looked so dour. The grim face returned instantly though when she realised that she now had to face her ex-husband.

"I'll get it" Helen said as she rose.

"No. I'll go." Rex said incredibly forcefully.

Rex stood up and stubbed out his cigarette in a small dainty ashtray. He headed inside and took two deep breaths before opening the front door. In front of us stood a man I thought I recognised but I couldn't quite put my finger on it.

The minute I realised who this person was, I was terrified. Of course I had seen him before. I had seen him at Eve's flat the night she was beaten senseless by a thug. And that thug was standing right in front of us now.

"Dad". Rex looked nonchalant as he looked at his father. I could hear his heart thumping though and knew he wasn't feeling anywhere near as brave as he appeared.

Rex did not automatically open the door to his father. He didn't want him to think he had a guaranteed right to step into the house.

The thug looked at Rex and smirked. "All right son? Your mother in?" He sounded exactly the same although the tone was more upbeat that the last time I had hear him speak.

"She might be. What do you want dad?" Rex was playing it cool and I could see his confidence growing as his father's smirk evaporated. I think he took that as a sign of fear that perhaps he shouldn't mess about with his son but unfortunately once a thug, always a thug.

Rex flinched as his father shot forward. The recoil was the weakness and reaction he was looking for and he grabbed his son round the neck with both hands. Rex suddenly went weak at the knees and I heard his heart thump even louder and faster than before.

"Don't play games with me Rex" his father spat in his face. "I'm fucking warning you." He was a nasty vicious bully and it didn't even faze him that his son was petrified.

"Is she in, or isn't she?" He continued.

Before Rex had a chance to gurgle the truth, Helen appeared behind her son and calmly asked the thug to let go.

Rex's hands flew straight to his bruised windpipe the second his father released his grip.

"Jesus Max". Helen uttered as she saw the red welts round her son's neck. "What do you want?" She sounded thoroughly pissed off and enraged with this man.

"Arhh the lovely Helen". Max threw his arms up in mock delight. "What an honour!". He was a really smarmy man. I hadn't liked him at Eve's and this wasn't improving my opinion. He was bald although, from the faint stubble marks, I got the impression that this guise was chosen, possibly speeded up by a receding hairline. His eyes were small and to be honest the overall impression was not beauty but I could identify with a certain vibe that would possibly excite the ladies. He looked like a player and not someone to be trusted at all.

"Can I not come in?" Max asked sarcastically as he pushed the front door wider. "What about a nice beer Helen? You must have some in the fridge." He pushed his way forwards and Rex stepped back. Max shut the door and I wondered how this afternoon was going to end.

Rex's courage grew, spurred on by the realisation that he would have to protect his mother. I could feel hatred pouring from every pore in Rex's body but his pulse had slowed.

Helen walked into the lounge and Max followed. Rex stood at the doorway and leaned against the door jamb. Max threw himself on to the brown leather sofa and Helen just stood behind the matching armchair holding onto the back.

"What do you want, Max?" she asked firmly.

Max just smiled and looked around the place. "Changed a bit since I was last here. These new?" He asked pulling at the seams of the sofa.

"Max!" Helen was losing patience or perhaps just her nerve. "What do you want?" Her voice was heavier.

"Oh Helen. Can't an old friend pop by for a chat?" He leered at her. He was clever. His words were not threatening but his demeanour was and so was his intention.

"Max. I'm not in the mood." Helen moved to the front of the armchair and placed herself directly in front of her ex-husband. "Now. Tell me what you want or I will call the police."

I was very impressed with her resolve. She looked determined not to be intimidated by this animal but I wondered what had happened before. What had caused the marriage breakdown? Had violence been a factor?

Rex was still leaning against the door but I could sense he was ready for action if needed. He was confident that his presence would be enough to deter his father from trying anything on.

Max must have realised that by bringing Rex into the conversation, he might have a chance of being heard.

"Rex, my lad. What you up to these days?" It was clear that this man didn't have the first idea of what Rex was up to. He was his father yet didn't even know about his son's budding music career. It was shameful. Absent fathers were getting such bad press and it was men like this creature in front of us, which gave them all a dreadful name. It made me sick.

"What do you want dad?" Rex just glared and stood with his arms folded. A fool could have read the body language in that stance. I could only watch as a woman and her child repelled the man they both loathed.

"Rex! Rex. Such hostility!" Max was trying to lighten the situation but his attempt to throttle the boy had damaged his prospects and eventually it dawned on him that he was getting nowhere fast.

"I came to tell you that my solicitor has been in touch. I was going to get him to contact you but I thought I would take the opportunity to visiting my family." He was making an effort to be serious in a non-threatening way but after years of bullying and aggression, it was impossible to lose the intimidation tactic.

"It seems that now Rex is a big boy now and isn't attending school anymore, I get to stop paying maintenance and I get my house back". I wasn't sure all of that was strictly true but I had heard about financial allowances being allowed to cease if the child in question was eighteen or over and not in education. One of the terms of the divorce and settlement was obviously that he could make Helen sell the house and claim his rightful share.

A flicker of relief crossed Helen's face and she looked across at Rex. "Great Max. That's good news. I'll get on to the Estate Agent in the morning and we'll go ahead." She finished her sentence and made it quite clear that she had no more to say on the matter.

Max looked round at Rex and said "You going to help your mum pay the bills then son?" The sarcasm in his tone was cutting. He clearly found the idea preposterous.

"Yes." Rex said simply. I liked the way he stood up to him. He wasn't sinking to Max's level.

Max wasn't stupid and realised that his little game hadn't really worked so he nodded his head slowly and stood up.

Rex walked ahead and opened up the front door ready for his father's departure. Neither Helen or Rex uttered a word and in unison they watched Max like a hawk until he stepped out of the door.

The second they were able, they closed the door and hugged each other. Curious to know what Max was doing they crept back into the lounge and watched him climb into his BMW X5 and drive off. They both sighed deeply and hugged again.

Rex went outside and lit a cigarette. I wasn't sure if Helen would react but I think in these circumstances, the boy was entitled. He had protected his mother and shown his ability to confront harassment in a non-violent manner. I would think Helen would be delighted at this outcome and comforted in the knowledge that her son had not inherited his father's aggressive tendencies.

Rex flipped open his mobile and dialled a number. He blew smoke rings into the air whilst waiting for the other person to answer. I guessed the service had clicked over to voicemail as Rex left a brief message.

"Just me. Ermm listen not too sure I'm gonna be able to make tonight. Loads of shit going down at the moment. If I can get away I'll give you a buzz. Text me where you are and I'll call later."

Rex snapped his phone shut and closed his eyes momentarily. He looked thoroughly washed out. The day had started with a girl, he quite clearly fancied a great deal, attacking him, nearly losing his record contract to dealing with a dirty old man letching after his mother and culminating in being physically assaulted by his father. Considering the day hadn't yet finished, if I were Rex, I would stay firmly indoors and make sure that nothing else occurred. I wasn't a teenager though desperate to celebrate the good fortune of hitting the big time and getting a record contract under my belt.

Helen appeared in the garden carrying two bottles of larger. "Thought you might need this" she said softly as she handed him a bottle of Stella Artois.

"Cheers Mum" Rex smiled at his mother and waited for her to sit next to him. "Listen about Jim" he started and then paused for a second, trying to assemble the words so that he didn't sound too critical of her choice of companion. "It's not that I don't like him. It's just that I don't think he's right for you." The advice sounded very grown up and I think Helen was shocked that not only had Rex broached the subject but had expressed an opinion on the man.

"I know'. She hung her head and carried on. "Oh I know Rex. I think I was just enjoying the attention and the compliments. I don't even fancy him!" She made a funny face, mimicking being sick.

Rex laughed and I saw beyond the youth with attitude and the cockiness. I actually saw a brave and intelligent man that had had to deal with some serious issues in his short life. His mother had done a good job especially considering the conditions.

The rest of the evening drifted along. There were short bursts of conversation, but it seemed they were actually very happy and relaxed in each other's company and didn't feel the need to fill it with needless babble. They didn't mention Max and his news and quite honestly I didn't see the need either. It looked like they had been given a reprieve from a death sentence and talking about it might change the outcome.

It must have been approaching 10pm when both of them decided to head indoors. Rex had been smoking almost incessantly and Helen had not uttered a word of chastisement.

"Come on babe" she grabbed her son's arm and enticed him back into the warm house.

"Mum" Rex began. "I have some news for you" Rex and his mother were now standing in the kitchen carrying a few empty bottles of beer. As Helen busied herself by putting the bottles in the recycling bag Rex continued. "I went to see a company today with Al and Tony and Jez."

He looked up at his mum who had now stopped what she was doing and was listening intently.

"We just signed a 3 year record contract". He was beaming as if admitting his victory for the first time.

"What?" His mum looked elated. "Oh my God Rex. That's fantastic! How on earth did you keep all this quiet?"

Rex shrugged but was grinning like a buffoon. "Dunno mum. I just didn't want to tempt fate". He spilled out all the lead up to the signing including the near miss he had had earlier when they had nearly overlooked the appointment.

I began fading away at this point. I was tired and the ups and downs of the day had worn me out. As Helen and Rex shared a bonding session in the cosiness and warmth of the lounge, I drifted off to sleep.

· ·

A DREAM

I dreamed I was moving really quickly, like through sand. Then I was up in the air, looking down at the sand. The image flicked to a close up of the sand and I couldn't see the object moving but I sensed its direction. Another image appeared. It was the same sand but this time the object was moving in the opposite direction. Each time the image altered, I became aware of the impending doom and realised that eventually these two objects would collide and it would all end in disaster.

· ·

Normally I awoke feeling refreshed but this time, I felt like I had been run over by a truck. I had an overwhelming sense of imminent tragedy. I just couldn't shake the feeling. I had no idea what the dream meant and unlike most dreams, which tend to fade during the day, this seemed to be etched in my memory.

The day had begun but there was no sign of Helen and Rex. After the events of yesterday, they both certainly deserved a lie in.

Desperate to rid myself of this anxiety, I turned my mind to Whin.

• •

FLASHBACK

• •

Both the men looked a state. They appeared haggard and extremely drunk. Their ability to remain sober had suddenly evaporated and I was finding it difficult to interpret their slurred ramblings.

"I loved her Tom." Whin's eyes had welled up and this time he wasn't holding his emotions in check.

Whin's tears rolled down his cheek and even when one of the builders noticed this old man crying and nudged his colleague, Whin didn't notice.

"I must have spent weeks getting over her. For something that was so short lived, it was incredible how painful it was. " Whin suddenly wiped his eyes with his sleeve. If he was embarrassed by his lack of manliness, he didn't look it.

"I reckon I did some serious damage to my liver!" He was trying to lighten the mood by joking about the mess he found himself in. "I went through a few bottles of whiskey I can tell you." He chuckled to himself.

"What happened?" Tom was anxious to hear the rest of the story.

"Well after a few months, the pain felt less raw and I kind of realised my drinking was a major problem. I wasn't an alcoholic" he said defensively "but I appreciated that if I was going to live a while then I was going to have to slow down. It took a while Tom and it wasn't easy. Being sober was tough but my blitz spirit shone through!"

I suddenly became confused. If all this upset had occurred some time ago and the affair was over, why was Whin still in so much pain? If he had reduced his drinking and was coping with the separation with Mel, why now was he feeling such immense sorrow?

"About six months later, I was having a drink with an old mate of mine when I saw a relative of Mel's in the pub. I could tell they didn't recognise me. I suppose I had let myself go a little Tom. I mean I had sort of giving up on shaving and I wasn't quite so interested in my appearance. Don't get me wrong, I still bathed." He sounded like he felt he had to justify his actions. Tom just nodded sombrely.

"This relative, I dunno an aunt or something, was obviously having lunch with one of her cronies and she was talking about Mel. Well, she didn't actually say her name but it didn't take much for me to work out who she was referring to. I had to eavesdrop Tom. I couldn't resist it. Just hearing about her made my pulse race. I was addicted to that woman. Even after a few months of detox and rehab recovering from the Mel drug, it only took an instant to become hooked again."

Geoff arrived with the beers and picked up on the last few words. From his expression, it looked as though he had got hold of the wrong end of the stick. He looked at Tom alarmed but Tom just shook his head and Geoff walked away, totally bemused.

• •

FLASHBACK

• •

CHAPTER 16

I was jolted awake by a rapping on the door. It wasn't a hammering or a gentile knock, it was a matter of fact rap. It was as though the person at the door felt he had every right to enter.

Nervously I waited to see if the noise had woken Helen and Rex and within a few minute Helen stomped down the stairs. She was an attractive woman but this morning she did look a little rough. The hair, which I had only seen in a neat style, was wild. Mascara ran down one cheek and I would lay money that there were black marks on her pillow. She looked pale and blotchy but she wasn't fully awake to realise her appearance was less than flattering.

She swore as she stubbed her toe on the wall by the front door. Cursing aloud she opened the door and suddenly wrapped her dressing gown tighter around her slim body.

"Blimey Jim. You're up early aren't you?" Clearly having no idea of the time.

Jim almost barged his way through the front door and began rubbing his hands gleefully. "You lot had breakfast yet?" I could tell he was really hoping the answer would be 'no', so that he could tuck his feet under the kitchen table and feast at their expense.

"What?" Helen looked really puzzled. Food was not really up there on the list at the moment and it was more than apparent that all she had in mind was at least another couple of hours sleep time.

"No, Jim." She looked cross that she had been awoken because someone else's stomach was growling and after her chat with Rex last night, she seemed to have come to her senses and realised that the dirty old man needed to be told to leave her be.

Jim wasn't a particularly bright button from what I could see and he wasn't picking up on the body language, the tone of Helen's voice or in fact the words she was using.

"Great!" he looked at Helen expectantly and said, "Shall I lay the table?"

Helen looked incredulous but glimpse of a very foul mood on the horizon flittered across her pretty face.

"Jim. I'm sorry but Rex and I are unwell and we need to recover in bed, so I would like to ask you to leave now and I'm sure I can give you a call when we are up and about."

I was very observant and I knew that Helen had no intention on calling this man again but Jim just wasn't really getting the picture. "But Helen, you poor darling. You really must eat. 'Feed a cold, starve a fever'", he looked pleased with himself as if this old anecdote was exactly what Helen needed to hear to be convinced to fry him up something delicious.

Helen's temper was rising and her fury was quite evident but she remained calm and concise "Jim. I'm asking you to leave now". She sounded very firm but I wasn't sure that it was getting through to Jim.

He stood for a moment, again looking increasingly ill at ease but although he was silent, I just knew he was racking his brains to stay just a while longer in Helen's presence.

Helen just stood still holding the door handle in her right hand. Her face spoke a thousand words and eventually Jim got the message. He realised he was endangering his chances for the future by pressing the issue now. He walked towards the door and attempted to kiss Helen on the lips but she moved her head and he lurched forward nearly head butting the door.

"I hope you feel better and please call me if there is anything I can do." It all sounded very hurried and desperate and I could tell he was kicking himself for acting so nervously.

Helen shut the door the second his feet left the carpet and she stomped back up the stairs and I heard a bedroom door slam. I was pleased that this man, who reminded me of a weasel, was history. I always associate humans with specific species of animal, bird or reptile. It astounds me that no one ever seems to comment on it. I suppose the most common is a pigeon. A large hooked nose and eyes slightly too close together are incredibly prevalent. I saw someone once at a party who looked so much like a mouse that I almost expected her to squeak! It's not necessarily an insult, I mean some animals are beautiful. I remember a teacher once, in a pub somewhere. Whin wasn't with her but she was sat at a table next to us and I couldn't help but eavesdrop when she was chatting to her colleagues. The second I had spotted her, she had reminded me of a tadpole but when I overheard that she was a biology tutor, I nearly laughed out loud. I have heard a saying that many owners take after their pets and begin to resemble each other but I thought this was hilarious!

Deep in thought about Jim and his weaselness, I didn't notice Rex tiptoe down the stairs until he reached the bottom. He grabbed me, the fags, put his wallet and keys in his pocket, and the minute we silently left the house, he pulled out his mobile and began dialling.

"Yeah I know mate. But I just reckoned you'd still be up from last night!" Rex laughed and listened to his friend and cackled whilst I presumed his pal recounted the events of the previous night.

"No!" Rex looked seriously impressed. "You dirty bastard! Three!!" Rex carried on laughing and he settled himself into his rusty old Volvo.

Rex started up the car and drove a little way from the house. He didn't want to disturb his mum with the noise of the engine. Such a thoughtful boy! He carried on listening to one of the band members and caught up on some of the highlights of last night.

Although Rex was laughing and asking for more details, I could see that he felt utterly gutted that he had missed such an important key night in the history of the band. I felt for him but I also knew that given the option again, he would choose protecting his mother every time.

"Ok mate, listen you sleep well. Kick those bints out now and get some shut-eye! Call me later". Rex's fingers typed out a speedy text and then he snapped his phone shut. I had noticed that this was a trait with him. He didn't bother with his seat belt, which I found very stupid, and we sped off.

Of course I had no idea where we were going as usual and although I knew it couldn't be that early, it seemed very premature for a youth of Rex's age to be heading out. Didn't young people sleep all day and stay up partying all night?

A couple of minutes later, Rex's phone beeped and I guessed a text had come through. We were approaching a set of traffic lights, which were still green but Rex slowed down so that they would turn red and he would have a chance to read his message.

"Sweet" Rex smiled as he flipped the phone shut and he revved up ready to speed off once the lights changed.

We were heading towards an area I had visited before. The countless homes I had stopped at, just in the last few days, were all tangled up, and I just couldn't remember whose home it was until I saw a little terraced house with a blue front door. Katy! Good. I liked her, even if her outburst was totally unprovoked and a bit outlandish. She not only had a few issues but had had a particularly stressful few days so I think losing the plot, albeit knocking your bed partner out cold, was fairly understandable.

Rex parked the Volvo half on the road and half on the pavement. I didn't think it was because he was precious about the heap, more about being conscious that it would give more space for other cars to pass. He really was so thoughtful.

Rex slammed the door and walked down the short path to the blue front door. We stood for a second. I suppose Rex was maybe summing up courage, or words of apology, or maybe even patience so that next time she flipped, he would be ready and not behave so insensitively. He rang the bell and we waited.

I heard a thudding, like someone running down the stairs and sure enough James opened the door breathlessly.

"Oh Rex!" He didn't look too happy at the visitor at his door but I guessed that he was entertaining upstairs as even an unwelcome guest couldn't quite put out the fire in his eyes.

"Katy's out the back. Go through. Sorry I'm busy" He winked and flamboyantly sashayed up the stairs.

I could tell that Rex didn't have an issue with homosexual men but it was pretty obvious that he hadn't spent an awful lot of time with them. He was staring, open mouthed, at the camp character disappearing out of view on to the landing.

He closed the door behind him and timidly walked through the open plan lounge and dining area. Before entering the kitchen, he politely knocked on the wall so as not to frighten Katy but there was still no one around. He spotted an open door leading onto a courtyard style garden and popped his head round the corner.

Katy was sitting on a short brick wall, smoking a cigarette. It was dry but not warm, certainly not warm enough for a short sleeved t-shirt and as we approached her, I could see the goosebumps on her arms. The number of butts in the ashtray told me that she must have been sitting here for some time.

"Hey" Rex was behaving cautiously. Not because he thought he was in danger of being attacked again but I think he wanted to show her he could be sensitive.

Although Rex spoke quietly, Katy nearly jumped out of her skin.

"Blimey Rex. I didn't expect you round so quickly.

"Well, to tell you the truth, I was on my way round anyway." He looked at his feet. "I wanted to apologise for asking you to leave so abruptly yesterday. It was very rude of me". I couldn't quite believe how chameleon-like this boy could be. One minute he was acting like a diva, in the recording studio office, the next he is a rock god inebriating a haunted young girl to satisfy his own urges, then the softer side of him protecting his mother and missing out on a wild night that most men his age would have given all their teeth for and now he was acting sweet and loveable and begging for forgiveness. How many personas did this guy have?

"Oh". I don't think Katy knew what to say. She was probably embarrassed by her action and I could tell she felt slightly awkward, the way people do after they have had sex for the first time and haven't had a chance to bond afterwards.

"Listen. I wanted to know if you fancied lunch?" Again I was liking this grown up Rex, the one who wanted to behave like a gentleman.

Katy's eyes widened. He was turning into Mr Right just before her eyes. Instantly though, I could see the panic rise. Going out to eat with someone means that you actually have to consume some food but the minute she said 'yes', I knew she had decided to try some of the advice from that website. I just wondered what ghastly plan she had up her sleeve.

"Ok. Well it's nearly 2pm now so if you are ready, lets go and catch something before they all close".

"Right. Erm ok. Give me two seconds. She tugged at some very tatty grey leggings and said "I couldn't possibly wear these out, so I just need to pop upstairs". She fled indoors and Rex looked around the small garden. On all four sides were the brick walls of houses but it was incredibly quiet. I couldn't hear any birds singing but there were very little in the way of foliage for them to be tempted to visit. Rex lit up and sat down on the wall Katy had just vacated.

He brought out his mobile and for a few seconds, flipped it open and shut continually. Eventually, after I was getting quite fed up with the repetition he suddenly stopped and punched in some numbers. He hung on impatiently and left a message.

"Pete. Its Rex. Listen I think we need to talk. I'm busy now but if you're free tonight, let's meet up."

The message had an urgency behind the words. He was trying to be casual over something, which was far from relaxed. I was intrigued. I hadn't heard this Peter being mentioned before and wondered whether it had anything to do with the band and their new signing. Actually it sounded more like it had a connection to his father.

Katy floated into the garden, wearing a black wrap around dress and some green wedge heels. She had wound her hair into a chignon and looked incredibly classy. Rex's expression was of pure delight and I had to agree, she looked beautiful.

Rex wolf whistled and I saw the blush rise in Katy's cheeks. Rex led her through the house and out of the front door. Katy paused and shouted up the stairs

"James. I'm off now. See you later."

There was no sound from upstairs but I guessed James was a little too busy to answer. I'm sure he had his hands full, so to speak!

This new side of Rex was growing more and more prominent and as he opened the passenger door for his lady companion, I mentally nodded approval. He was treating her properly and she deserved it.

The conversation was a little stilted in the car. I suppose it would be difficult to know where to take up again after a steamy night of passion and then a huge row the next morning. They were taking things slowly and I thought they were making the right decision. Katy was glowing. After the last few terrible days, she had quite clearly made a mental choice to blot out her lying, cheating ex-boyfriend and Eve's serious hospital condition. Talking of which, I wished I could ask Katy what the latest news was. I really hoped Eve was ok. She had behaved appallingly but then desperate people do tend to take drastic actions.

Rex was driving out into the countryside. Well possibly not countryside exactly. There were not miles of rolling hills sweeping across the horizon but there were trees and a couple of fields and to the left of the main road was a huge wood. In fact the longer we drove on, the more I was convinced it was a forest. Rex knew where he was going and after a few turns, we pulled into a pub. This was no inner city public house, this was a carvery with a serene garden in front and some impressive vehicles in the carpark. This was the kind of couth establishment I had taken to believe I was in tune with. The ambience was comfortable and friendly yet decked out with impeccable taste.

Rex and Katy ordered drinks at the bar and I even noticed that Rex asked the barman for an orange and lemonade. My opinion of him was growing by the second. Of course all this could be an act. I had seen him at work in Crushhh when he had purposefully insisted Katy drink far more than she was capable solely to have his wicked way so if he could stoop that low then I guess he was a competent con artist. Still his behaviour over the last 24 hours had been remarkable so I had to give him the benefit of the doubt.

As soon as the pair sat down, their conversation altered. Gone was the humorous banter and now in its place was a sense of mutual lust. At last some romance was being injected into this relationship and I for one just hoped that it blossomed fully.

We were sitting by a window overlooking the back of the pub gardens. The building itself was fairly old, in fact I would go so far as to suggest it was Georgian in origin. I don't profess to be a connoisseur of architecture but I do know what I like and I really liked this property. Through the pretty windows I could see the gardens, which were flanked on 2 opposite sides by box hedge about 7 feet high and on the remaining far side was a beautiful old stone wall. In one corner was a space dedicated to children and I spotted a slide, some swings and just about made out a roundabout. I liked the fact that they had made provisions for families. So many places these days don't cater for people with children and taking them out proves to be so stressful when there are no facilities available to the parents. The rest of the garden was mostly laid to lawn with table benches dotted around. As this was September and no hope of an Indian summer, the garden was empty and even the parasols had been removed until next year.

I looked around the place and decided that Whin would have liked it here too. He was a man who liked simple pleasures in life but I had definitely felt a sense of pride too. I thought of him as a bit of a chameleon, someone who could change depending on the surroundings. There were many people I had met who had this ability and I think it was a very undervalued. The people with this unusual talent were normally top raconteurs, presenters and generally people with a knack of tuning in to others.

Rex surprised me by leaning over to Katy and kissing her gently on the cheek. I had been deep in thought but now my attentions were drawn back to the couple in front of me.

"What was that for?" Katy smiled as she spoke so we both knew she was more than happy at his tactile performance.

"Nothing" Rex smiled back "Just felt like it". They were sitting next to each other on a window seat and Rex took Katy's hand.

"I'm sorry about yesterday" she spoke without looking at him.

"Hey" Rex squeezed her hand tightly. I could tell because his knuckles went white. "I don't want to talk about yesterday. Well actually I do but not about that."

She looked up and we were both curious. "Oh?"

"Yes well I had a bit of good news yesterday and I wanted to share it with you." He was beaming and I think for the first time since the signing, it had dawned on him what this miraculous event would mean.

"Yes?" Katy was sitting up straight now and was listening intently.

"After you left." He looked up at Katy who blushed slightly. "Yes well anyway after you left I got a call reminding me of an appointment that had been booked for weeks. Typically though, I had forgotten and going out with you to Crushhh after the gig and getting mashed didn't really help me remember. Anyway the appointment was with Brian Butler." He paused and wondered whether Katy would know the name and deduce the nature of the meeting.

"Brian Butler" Katy frowned. "I'm sure I have heard of him. Hang on was it anything to do with the gig?"

"Well in a way, indirectly I suppose. He is THE signings manager for a record label worth a mint. Can you believe what a dork I had been and nearly fucked up my chance by forgetting something so important?"

They both laughed and then Katy put her hand on his knee and said "Come on. Tell me"

"I had just hung up from Jez and was getting my head together when mum walked in. It's a long story, which I won't bore you with now but I was delayed slightly. Still I was still the first there!" He looked proud that he was the earliest of the late arrivals!

"Go on" Katy was beside herself with excitement.

"Well when the others turned up along with our numpty of an agent, basically we all signed the contract. To be honest I don't really know the ins and outs of it all but I think it is a 5 record deal but initially it is for 3 months just to see how it works out so that should send the money our way!" If he was worried about the legalities of the royalties, he wasn't showing it. He was bright lad but he was also a master of disguising his true feelings so who knew what was going on in that head of his.

Katy screamed and looked like she was going to burst. "Oh my God! That's so fantastic," She opened her bag and pulled out her pink and green Mary Quant style purse. "I'm going to get the champers in"

Just as she stood, Rex pulled her back down. "Not now thanks babe. Maybe later. I'm driving and I want to save a special celebration when just the two of us can enjoy it, if you know what I mean?" He winked and Katy blushed again.

"Oh Ok," She looked a little put out but she could see he made sense.

A waiter came over and took their lunch order. Rex needed feeding up and I was glad his long lanky body was going to get some steak and chips. Katy on the other hand took a century to decide. I could see the cogs turning. She was weighing up all the fat contents, carb levels etc and finding it difficult to know which one to choose.

"If you don't hurry up, I'll choose for you!" Rex was trying to make light of the situation, which was in danger of becoming quite intense.

Spurred on by Rex's threat, Katy quickly asked for omelette, chips and salad. It was an interesting choice. Eggs are full of protein and are always listed on diet sheets although I was sure they were quite high in cholesterol. I'm not sure that Katy was really considering the health aspect of slimming down so egg seemed like a perfect solution. Add to that the salad and a portion of chips, that we both knew were never going anywhere near her mouth, the order seemed perfectly normal.

Rex looked slightly sceptical but his cynicism didn't last long. Katy resumed her pre-champagne offer refusal and was almost bouncing on the seat.

"I'm so excited for you Rex. I think the band is fantastic and you are so talented". She realised that she was pandering to him and stopped abruptly, pretending to need a slug of her drink.

This time Rex blushed. "Cheers babe" he clinked his orange and lemonade glass with her vodka and coke tumbler.

They chatted on and on, mostly about the first time they had met and who they were still in contact with from the old days. That amused me. I mean the old days could have only been 2 or 3 years ago but they were making it sound like decades.

"How's Jez doing? I haven't spoken to him in years." Katy listened as Rex explained how he had gone out to celebrate the deal last night and had pulled three young ladies.

Katy's eyebrows nearly shot through the roof. She quickly swallowed her mouthful of vodka and spluttered "What?! You are kidding me? Three? What a dirty boy!"

"That was pretty much my reaction." Rex laughed but when Katy questioned why he hadn't attended the big night out, his expression changed.

"It doesn't matter. I'm sure there will be many opportunities to go out in style and get mashed." He smiled at Katy but the smile just didn't quite meet his eyes and both Katy and I knew he was incredibly disappointed he had missed such a significant party.

"Rex," Katy had softened her voice. "Why didn't you go then?" It seemed a simple question but Rex didn't really look like he wanted to go into the finite details of his traumatic childhood and the fact that he chose to protect his mother from his bastard of a father. I agreed with him in the sense that such a heavy conversation so early on in their relationship, might bring things down a little. I disagreed with him though, that Katy wasn't the one to share such trust issues with. In my mind she was the perfect person to support him and help him deal with emotional matters.

Katy inched closer and she waited for a response. She held his hand again and looked at him impatiently.

"Katy. Do you mind if we don't talk about it right now?" I was glad that he hadn't brushed the topic completely under the carpet and I think he made the right decision to discuss it at a later stage. Katy looked concerned for a brief moment and then decided not to dwell on it and recommenced her playful demeanour.

The food arrived and as such was a blessing. It provided a perfect and smooth transition to a different subject. I decided to watch Katy like a hawk and just see which meal-rejecting plan she had concocted for today. The longer I stared, the more I realised that all her forkfuls were going directly into her mouth, were being chewed and swallowed. I was looking out for the cheap stunts she was supposed to be pulling like pushing the food around to make it look like she was eating and hiding things under lettuce leaved and cutlery. I was positively impressed. So far so good. It seemed Rex's company was keeping her mind off the idea of starving herself. His keen interest in consuming everything on his plat was possibly rubbing off on her. I was beginning to relax and by the time she pushed her knife and fork together, she had eaten most of her meal. A small pile of chips lay abandoned but as she had eaten the majority of her portion, I was ecstatic. In my naive mind, I really thought that a cure could be so simple.

A while after the plates had been cleared, puddings refused and coffees ordered, Katy excused herself. At the time I thought nothing of it. I was familiar with the irritating functions of humans and knew that they had to relieve themselves several times a day. It was only when she returned that I noticed a change. I don't think Rex was aware but then men don't tend to be quite as observant. Her eyes were a little watery but the biggest give away were the redness around her fingernails. I hadn't really noticed her hands before but by trying to cover them up, ironically she was actually bringing attention to them. Apart from the redness, the skin had peeled back and the nails themselves looked very dry and brittle. I couldn't quite make sense of it but I could tell by her conduct that something was awry.

Like a flash, I remembered Ilona. She was the Hungarian girl on that odd website. She had offered all sorts of tips on how to beat detection. I had thought at the time that little tricks were silly when it would be quite plain to see that a stick thin person had lost weight. Amongst her arsenal of tools, she used to make herself sick. When all other options and excuses had failed, she resorted to eating the food, thus avoiding suspicion and then after leaving an acceptable interval, she trotted of to the bathroom where she expertly stuck her fingers down her throat and bringing up all the food she had consumed before it had had a chance to infiltrate her system. The telltale sign of this ritual was the damage that the stomach acid did to the skin. I had had the time to thoroughly read up on Ilona's story. I don't think Katy had been interested in side effects and by looking at the sorry state of her hands, she had quite clearly not taken time to read the whole article.

Rex welcomed her back without any inkling and after a while Katy grew confident that she had got away with it. I was very unhappy with her. I wished her mother had noticed the poor girl's attitude to food and her tiny frame but with her own problems to solve, I suppose it can be very easy to miss even the largest signs.

They sipped their coffees and Katy snuggled up to Rex. They looked so good together and I was praying that now they had had an opportunity to relax and just enjoy each other's company, things would improve for them.

Rex' phone rang and before he answered it, he apologised to Katy. He looked at the incoming number, which had flashed up on his mobile and answered it cautiously. In hindsight it must have been to prevent Katy getting any ideas of what he was planning. He left the table to continue the conversation out of earshot of Katy. I was still in Rex's pocket. I hadn't been used as this was a non-smoking pub and the numerous notices all around the place made it quite clear that ignorance would not be tolerated.

"Thanks for calling me back Pete." Rex was talking in hushed tones even though he was standing in a far corner of the pub.

"I needed some assistance from you please." He nodded, which amused me as this Pete wouldn't be able to see him.

"Yeah, yeah. I can pay. Listen I cant talk now but are you free later?"

There was a fairly long pause whilst I presumed Pete was running through his social calendar.

"Ok. I'll meet you there at 9."

Rex snapped the phone shut and walked swiftly back to Katy. He held her hand and said. "This has been great. I've really enjoyed it. Thank you for giving me another chance."

"Nonsense!" She almost snorted. "Its me who should be thanking you. I'm surprised you haven't still got a headache"

"Well I do feel a little dizzy" Rex pretended to faint. "No I'm fine. It was my own fault for attacking you after plying you with so much drink!"

I was glad he had brought that up. It was good to hear that he was being honest about his attempt to seduce Katy. Admittedly it had worked but it was still morally wrong.

"Listen poppet. I'm going to have to shoot off now. I can drop you back but I've gotta go see a man about a dog!" He made a silly face and Katy grinned at him.

"Ok but only if I get to take you for a meal in return and pick up the bill".

"Shit!! The bill!" Rex looked horrified that he had nearly walked out without paying.

He motioned for a redundant waiter hovering by the bar to bring over the bill. He pulled a couple of twenties out of his scruffy wallet and placed them on the silver dish the minute the waiter brought it over.

"Come on then babe. Let's get you home". They walked arm in arm towards the door. I smiled at them disappearing in the direction of the car park and once again found myself disbelieving that I had been left behind.

Rex had taken me out of his pocket when he needed notes from his wallet and in his haste to depart had totally forgotten to put me back.

Disappointed and rejected, I wondered who on earth was going to pick me up this time. I couldn't see how I was going to mend the broken link now between Whin and me.

The waiter cleared the table and popped me on his tray and I was carried out into the kitchen. The waiter was dark, maybe Italian and dressed in a simple black shirt and trousers. His black wavy hair was smarmed old-fashionedly to one side but the overall effect was quite striking.

The kitchen wasn't as bustling as I imagined but then again the lunchtime diners had long since departed. I had expected the chefs to be prepping for the evening reservations but apart from a young lad in checked trousers washing the dishes in a large butler style sink, there was no one about. The kitchen was gleaming so I knew I was in good hands. Here were people dedicated to perfection. I just wondered how I fitted into that picture.

The waiter didn't speak to the boy but he placed the crockery on the side and clapped him on the back. The glasses he took back to the bar and put them in the large dishwasher behind the counter. I was still on the tray but the minute the dishwasher door was shut, the waiter picked me up and placed me at the back, under the optics.

Lord only knew how long I was going to sit here but it was quite a good vantage point. The waiter disappeared and I sat waiting for my next adventure. To while away some of the time, I drifted back to Whin.

• •

FLASHBACK

• •

Tom jeered Whin on and I think by the look on his face, he was torn between wanting to speed up the process of what he thought was going to be some type of confession and leaving Whin to let it out in his own time.

Geoff was peering inquisitively from behind the bar. He had removed the tray from the washer and was putting the clean glasses back on the racks. I could tell he was desperate to pull Tom aside and find out what was going on. Whilst I was concentrating on Geoff, Tom stood up. He wobbled slightly but controlled his balance before saying

"Whin mate. I've gotta go."

Whin looked distraught. "But Tom I haven't finished"

"I'm only going for a pee Whin. Give me a minute and I'll be back"

Whin nodded and stuck his head down and stared into his pint. The conversation was slightly slurred but I was very impressed that I was making sense of it. All that practice in the past had stood me in good stead.

Tom was gone for a while. I guessed he had quite a few pints to expel. When Whin still hadn't returned after 15 minutes, Whin began to fidget. He called Geoff over and said in a whisper

"I think Tom's fallen in!" Whin giggled but Geoff looked concerned and trotted of to the Gents to check. I saw him disappear but after just a second Geoff ran back out and went straight to the phone at the back of the counter.

Whin had been watching the door and his amusement at the thought of Tom stuck in the toilet evaporated when he saw the look on Geoff's face. He lurched to his feet and tottered over to the counter. I could see from the table that Geoff was still talking on the phone and Whin's ability to balance himself was diminishing by the second. He swayed and missed the bar and most unfortunately fell into one of the builders.

Whin lost control of his legs completely and fell flat on the floor. Geoff still hadn't noticed but the builder whose face had turned to thunder when he realised he was now wearing his pint, actually softened when he saw the mess Whin was in. He urged his mates to drag Whin to his feet and hauled him back to his seat. They propped him up on the chair and left him slumped on the table.

Geoff had put down the receiver now and was about to go back and check on Tom when he noticed Whin collapsed in the corner. As she rushed over, one of the builders stopped and informed him that he had just fallen on the floor. Poor Geoff looked even more worried. He came over and checked Whin was all right. Satisfied that he was ok and still breathing, he raced back into the Gents.

I was very concerned about Whin, not just his present state though. I knew tomorrow was going to be messy but he would be fine after a nice long sleep and a big feed when he woke up. The part I was fretting over was this unfinished tale of a lost love. I had a horrible sinking feeling that the worst was yet to come. Whatever Tom's condition in the toilet, there was no chance of finishing this conversation tonight, and I was desperate to know what happened.

After a few minutes of snoring from Whin, two paramedics rushed through the door and headed straight for the bar. Geoff appeared out of the toilets and gestured for the men to hurry.

• •

FLASHBACK

• •

CHAPTER 17

I was roused from my memories by a lot of noise coming from the reception area. Suddenly the doors burst open and a large lady with an enormous bust and a bunch of helium balloons entered followed by a posse of giggling women.

The large lady threw her handbag onto the counter and shouted "Service!" very loudly. The waiter re-appeared and although I saw him grimace, as he turned the corner into the bar, he put on a very convincing fake smile. He asked the gaggle of females for their orders and his sexy Italian accent was an instant hit.

Smiling, flirting and tittering like schoolgirls, they all shouted at my waiter friend at the same time. Rather than become irritated by their impatience, he gave them a sexy smirk and at once they became like putty in his hands.

I had gathered from the large balloons that this evening was some kind of celebration and I could only presume that the lardy girl was the one rejoicing. The balloons had no message so the party could have been in aid of all sorts; hen night, big birthday, work leaving do. Hazzarding a guess, I reckoned tonight was a divorce party. This well-built lass looked a little long in the tooth to be so fervently commemorating a forth coming wedding plus I was sure I could almost see the pain still buried under the hype.

The waiter, whose name I discovered was Carlo, unsurprisingly, appeared to be thoroughly enjoying his playful evening with these ladies all vying for his attention. I was watching from behind the bar so I could see the keen faces waiting in line to be served. I could also see Carlo's expression when he turned to fill a glass from the optics. He was loving it. And why not? At a guess, I would imagine he was about 30. He was still trim and handsome in a cliché type of way. The girls here tonight were under no illusion; marriage was for suckers. Only one thing was on their minds tonight and that was to have fun and that meant finding a man. Being the only clientele so far, Carlo was the only male in the bar and thus receiving all the attention but I was sure that pretty soon some more men would arrive and redress the gender balance.

The party was in full swing now that all the girls seemed to be on their third or fourth beverage. A steady trickle of customers were arriving and joining in the festivities. My large friend was sat over in the corner, fairly near to where Rex and Katy had had lunch. She was talking animatedly but from here I couldn't see who she was with and had no idea what the conversation was about.

A group of four young men arrived at the bar. I could smell the aftershave and it was incredibly potent. Rather than join forces and wear the same brand, they were all outdoing each other and the end result was a cacophony of musky smells which, to be honest wasn't really working. Doubtless to say by the time these guys plucked up enough courage to link up with these very feisty females, I was sure the aroma issue would be the least important issue.

The boys were ordering pints of Fosters and kept looking over at the girls who were dancing about and giggling. The blokes looked nervous. I had heard that women in a group can be quite terrifying and I could see fear written over all four faces.

Receiving their drinks, they stood around for a bit supping their beers, trying to make rather silly small talk. One lad brought out a packet of fags. He only offered the pack to one friend so I presumed that the other two didn't smoke. The friend took a cigarette and waited for a light. The first fellow patted his pockets down and shrugged. He came forward to the counter and asked Carlo for a box of matches.

Carlo shook his head and said "We don't provide matches here " he paused. "But hang on. Someone left this lighter earlier so you can have that". He handed me over to the young man and I was used immediately used and stuck in a shirt pocket.

It was a good view and I immediately felt part of the gang. I could see the girls mocking the boys but it was too early for them to have the courage to join them. I reckoned it would be at least another two pints before they relaxed enough to have some fun.

"Hey Mick!" The tallest of the bunch was looking at my new owner. "What happened last week then? Spill the beans!"

Mick just rolled his eyes and smirked. He looked thoroughly embarrassed and gulped down a good quarter of his pint.

"Come on" Another guy was speaking now. The other smoker. He was the tubbiest of them all. I think if I were a human female, I would have possibly liked him. I didn't know the man but from a simple beauty aspect, he was the better looking of all. He was broad with a darker, more olive skin than the others and had short jet black hair. He was dressed in beige moleskin trousers and a white shirt with the sleeves rolled up just below the elbow. Although he was speaking in a very English accent, I thought that maybe his parents had originated from the Mediterranean. He looked a little lighter than Carlo but I wouldn't be able to bet on his nationality.

Mick coughed and said "Calm down you lot. I was an idiot ok?" He put his hands up as if in surrender. "You all know what happened so leave off." He jokey nature was masking an annoyance that they were bringing up such a delicate matter. I would have left it there but either these men were fools and had no idea when to quit or they were blind to his underlying fury.

The tall one wouldn't leave it off and carried on teasing him. "Aww Mick. We upsetting you?" He put on a silly voice as though talking to a baby. "I don't think Ryan here has heard it." Ryan was my tubby boy and the tall one slapped him jovially on the back.

"Shut up Syd?" Ryan was sticking up for Mick. I was glad to see that this man had moral integrity and wasn't behaving in a moronic fashion.

"Keep your knickers on" shouted the tall guy and I recognised his type. He was brash, rude and ridiculed others to lift up his own sorry self. A big time bully but just by his reaction to Ryan standing up to him, I could tell that he would probably dissolve into tears if he was faced with a really nasty character.

The quiet one of the group began a new conversation and the tension slipped away. The talk soon turned to girls as the brash guy Syd was starting to eye up the drunken hopefuls still dancing about. From what I could make out, both Ryan and Mick both had long-term girlfriends although Ryan's partner seemed to live some way off and their long distance relationship was suffering.

Syd was making snide remarks about females in general. He was being cocky but also blatantly jealous. He wasn't a stunner. In fact not only was he very average but so far his personality had turned him into a very ugly man indeed. He was trying to impress someone by insinuating that all women were loose and in doing so was just making himself look a total plonker.

Ryan and Mick had moved slightly towards the bar so as to use the ashtray. I could hear Mick talking about a girl called Stacey. I imagined that this was his lover. From the discussion so far, Mick was apparently still reeling from his proposal to Stacey. I deduced that this was the embarrassing event to which Syd was referring. On hearing this, my low esteem for Syd sank even further. What a cruel, vindictive man to joke about such a humiliation.

"Listen mate" Ryan stubbed out his butt and blew smoke in the air "Just give it time. You know she loves you but she is young. There's no rush". Ryan was being sympathetic but also offering his friend a get out clause of embarrassment by placing the blame on Stacey's age, or rather her youth.

"Cheers Ryan. I must admit I was gutted but I suppose looking at it, she only 22 and just finished Uni." He pulled out his wallet and ordered another round of lagers.

"The only reason I asked her is because I have this feeling that she is going to take some time out and go travelling and she would leave me. Stupidly I thought that if we got engaged at best she would stay behind but at worst she would be faithful to me and then come home early cos she missed me." He looked back at Ryan, who was downing the dregs of his beer, and laughed sadly.

Ryan slapped him on the back and just said "I'm off again in a couple of days, so how about you have a bit of break and come with me. I can take you about for free but you'll have to pay for food and of course you'll have to stump up for the flights."

"Is Macey not meeting you?" Mick looked shocked.

"I dunno mate". Ryan's cheerless face spoke volumes. "I have being trying to get hold of her for the past week and she's not returning any of my calls. I'm going to fly out a day early and try and catch up with her but I don't even know if she is in **Buenos Aires** but I really do need to see her before I leave."

"Where's the tour to this time?" Mick looked really interested in Ryan's offer but was also worried about the apparent breakdown in his friend's relationship.

"I think I'm meeting the group in Rio and then we are flying up to Foz de Igacu and travelling around Paraguay and then travelling back overland through Argentina back to Buenos Aires. You should come. It's one of the best trips man. Igacu is just awesome".

Ryan cheered up a little and I could only imagine that his forthcoming jaunt to South America was doing it. The guys picked up the new drinks and walked back over to Syd and the other man.

"Now drink up," said Mick. "We are gonna have a good night but not if you too are going to drink like pansies!"

Syd laughed and grabbed his pint and swigged more than half his pint in one go. After wiping his dripping mouth, he burped loudly and it looked like the boys night out had well and truly begun.

I was tiring now. I wasn't really into this scene. It was actually very difficult for me to watch the things these people were doing in order to get attention and the nonsense they were speaking in order to keep the interest going. I zoned out for a bit and let them all get on with it. The boy and girls joining forces was the limit and I pondered about my previous fellow companions and wondered if their lives had improved.

Eve was still a worry to me. Even if she did survive the overdose, would she try again once she got home or would her mother take control and sort her out? I could only hope. I even thought about Becks and her dopey husband Phil. Would they ever sort out their failing marriage? That poor little girl Maria deserved a whole lot better. She was running the risk of becoming a spoilt brat and all the fights and tension she had experienced was likely to affect her future prospects at settling down happily.

I hoped Reg saw himself for what he really was, a wife beater and kept away from Verity for good. She was a good, decent, hardworking woman and was worthy of a much better man. I really hoped she would find him; a man that her sons could respect and take guidance from but more importantly who would offer her support, love and protection.

Mel suddenly sprang to mind. How weird that I saw her working with Brian Butler. I had had no idea that she worked in the music industry. Not that I really knew much about her at all but it was strange how people linked to Whin, kept popping up. It almost felt like fate. Maybe Whin, was directing this seemingly haphazard journey and just maybe it was all planned. I didn't know what I believed about deep meaningful philosophical uncertainties like; life after death or the meaning of our existence.

I hadn't really met Mel many times but I had paid close attention to her on the occasions we had convened. She was an extremely likeable character but she had an overwhelming sense of sadness consuming her entire persona. It was hardly surprising but such a shame. I am quite a believer that you make your own luck and Mel came across as a pessimistic soul, probably supposing that if you accept the worst case scenario, you can't ever be disappointed. I wholeheartedly disagreed with this opinion. In my view, you can create positive events just by total belief that they will succeed. Mel had never really focussed on the future though and I wasn't really sure if she was ready to acknowledge the past and move on. I didn't hold up much hope with therapists for the two main reasons that I only think the individual can help themselves and only when that individual is ready.

The last time I had seen Mel was about six months after Whin's drunken night with Tom. I was never sure if the encounter had meet engineered or just plain coincidence. We had trundled into a smart coffee shop on one of the main drags. It was small but stylish. Outside the pavement was particularly narrow so it almost felt as though the buses, cabs and cars were about to join us. We had sat at a bench overlooking the busy street and a curly haired waitress took Whin's order of toasted bagel and a black coffee.

We had only been sitting for a few minutes when Mel strolled in. They locked eyes immediately and Mel came straight to the bench. She sat down and removed her red raincoat without speaking. I remember looking at Whin's face and feeling pity for the man. His expression was one of unrequited love, the oldest condition in the book. He eyed Mel without speaking but when the waitress appeared with his order he just said "Same again please love".

Mel sat next to him and stared out of the window until her order arrived. The silence wasn't exactly uncomfortable but it was so apparent that these two had unfinished business to discuss and neither of them knew just how to begin.

"Do you want some sugar?" Whin passed the ceramic bowl full of sugar packets, over to Mel.

She smiled hollowly and took a Demerara pack and emptied the contents into her coffee cup. Neither of them ate their bagels but sipped on the coffees almost in unison.

"Whin, I, I" Mel started but just didn't know how to continue.

Whin just gently patted her hand and whispered. "You don't need to explain anything to me. I understand". His weak smile must have given Mel the courage she needed to finish her sentence.

"I'm going away." She looked relieved that she had managed to get it out.

Whin looked up at her. "Where?"

"I have a friend in Greece, one of the islands. He runs a bar and has offered me a job".

Whin looked astounded. "You are moving out to Greece?" He looked more than gutted. It was as though his heart had been ripped out too. I guessed he couldn't say anymore.

"Before you ask, yes he is just a friend, in fact he is as camp as a row of tents, so don't go thinking the worst of me."

Whin didn't look at her but tightened his grip around her hand. I could tell he was fighting back tears and needed to control his emotions.

"I just need to get away Whin. Everything is just a reminder. I have asked for some unpaid leave, a bit of a sabbatical form work, and I want to go and not think about it all for a few months."

Mel stopped and resuming sipping her coffee. She had explained where she was going and why and felt no need to expand on it. The pair of them sat in silence, their food getting colder by the minute.

Eventually the waitress collected their cups and asked if they wanted anything else. I saw her looking at the uneaten bagels but she didn't mention anything and took an order for two more coffees.

I wasn't quite sure how this encounter would end. Whin looked devastated that Mel was leaving him and Mel just couldn't cope with being around for another second. If Whin had volunteered to travel with her, would she have agreed? He didn't ask and she didn't suggest it so the idea was left unsaid.

Mel drank her second coffee quickly. She had had enough. Whin was making the situation far worse, in her eyes and she made it quite clear as she stood up that she would be leaving in a few days but he was not to contact her.

After she left, I saw a single tear roll down Whin's cheek. I had never seen a man looking so lost. The last few months had taken their toll on him but this appeared to be the ultimate kick in the teeth. I could tell that Whin would not have thought about skipping the country to dodge his depression, he was not that sort of a man. He wasn't a runner, he was a stayer.

I can remember the rest of that day was so bleak and miserable. We went straight home and Whin sat in front of the TV for hours. He wasn't watching any of the programmes but it was background noise and it gave me something to watch.

I must have been pondering for quite a while because I suddenly came to as Mick and Ryan were leaving. I couldn't see Syd and the quieter one so I could only presume they had got lucky with one of the rowdy ladies.

We made out way outside and stood just under the canopy whilst the rain poured down in front of us. Both boys lit up cigarettes and smoked waiting for their cab.

"So listen. Are you interested in coming away with me?" Ryan obviously wanted to ensure that Mick was serious.

"I'm gonna be there with bells on mate". Mick grinned. "Just let me know all the details about visa requirements, money and flights and stuff." He looked sad and added "I'll sell the ring tomorrow, that should pay for the trip."

Ryan slapped him on the back and just said "You are gonna have the trip of a lifetime mate, leave it to me."

The cab arrived and after a journey back past the forest, we dropped Ryan off outside a nice cottage style house in a leafy road. The area looked affable but not too pricey. Whatever he did exactly for this tour firm, it was paying enough.

The cab drove on to Mick's house and at first I couldn't see where we were. Mick had been muttering under his breath "Shit, shit, shit."

Once the taxi driver had put the interior light on, he turned to Mick and said "Everything ok mate?" He nodded towards several houses on the right of the road.

"Bloody typical" Mick snorted. "Yet another power cut. Bastards! It's the fifth time this month and it's only ever the 6 of us. The other houses never get affected. I reckon they've got it in for us."

"You gonna be warm enough?" The driver asked Mick. I was touched about his thoughtfulness. "Do you need me to take you some place else?" Then I realised he just wanted to capitalise on some more fare.

"No mate. you're all right." Mick handed him some cash and slammed the door. It was raining heavily and Mick was getting soaked as we ran up to the front door. He rummaged around in his pocket for his keys, cursing under his breath that she should have got them out earlier in the cab.

By the time we got in, the lights were flickering on again. I could hear all sorts of things beeping and presumed that due to the power cut pre-set clocks and timers had been tuned back to zero and all needed resetting.

Mick threw his wet jacket on the newel post at the bottom of a very narrow, steep staircase. I could see him trotting into the kitchen and heard him yawn loudly and then run the tap. He walked past me with a glass of water and headed up to bed. I was relieved. I was very tired and although the jacket was damp, I had to get some sleep.

CHAPTER 18

Bright and early I heard Mick thunder down the stairs. Things had stopped beeping but from the comments Mick was muttering under his breath, he had forgotten to sort out his alarm and was late for something. I never knew which day of the week it was as they all seemed the same to me but judging by Mick's attire, it was a weekday. His shirt was crumpled but luckily his jacket and tie covered most of it and he looked fairly presentable.

It had stopped raining but it was cold and misty. It was the kind of morning where you really wanted to ring your boss and ask for a duvet day. Going out didn't really seem like a pleasant option but I guess Mick had his reasons for racing out the door. We ran down a pleasant road towards a main street and stood waiting for a bus. Fortunately the rush hour had departed so Mick and I could take cover under the small awning of the bus shelter. I imagined that on a day like this, the people would have been shoving and jostling to take refuge. One other person was waiting for the bus and she was perched on the slender red plastic bench patiently watching out for the bus.

Mick seemed impatient, possibly because he was late for an appointment but I suspected there was something else on his mind too. He was pacing around the small shelter and after irritating the lady on the seat, he took notice and leaned against the see through glass wall. Most of the shelter walls I have seen have either been covered in graffiti or smashed. This one looked in good condition. There were no grey lumps of chewing gum stuck to them, nor was the floor awash with crisp packets and other debris. I was impressed. Mick pulled out his mobile and rapidly sent someone a text. He clutched his phone and eagerly awaited a response but before a message came through, the bus was spotted and both Mick and the lady got ready to board.

Mick ran up the stairs and sat near the front. There was an awful lot of condensation so the view was obscured. Some of the earlier occupants had written obscene language on the windows and I was horrified at the vulgarity. I watched Mick fidget. He wasn't allowed to smoke on the bus and he obviously desperately needed a nicotine fix.

We trundled along for about 20 minutes and Mick jumped up and almost flew down the metal staircase. I had no idea how he could tell where we were as the steamed up windows made it almost impossible to judge our location.

The rain had started up again and a cold wind accompanied it. The day was grim and getting worse. Mick ran along the pavement and skipped inside a huge revolving door. The reception area was grand. It wasn't enormous but the glass and steel roof was possible a few floors high and a beautiful mobile suspended from the ceiling. It looked like steel raindrops, quite apt really for today's weather. The shiny surface caught the spotlights and it lit up an otherwise gloomy morning.

Mick didn't race towards the fancy lifts of the right but up a wide marble staircase to the back of reception area. Maybe he didn't like lifts and suffered a little from claustrophobia. Maybe the lifts were unreliable and he knew it would take him far less time to bolt up the stairs but when he opened a glass door on the next floor, I realised you would have to be pretty lazy to take the elevator up one level!

Mick sprinted into an office in the far corner and without knocking surprised an older gentleman. "I am so sorry" Mick grabbed a blue chair on wheels and dragged it closer to him bosses desk. "I had another power cut last night and the alarm was affected."

Mick's cheeks were flushed and as I looked at the other man's face, I realised I knew him! It was Phil!

"Mick! This is the third time this month that you have missed the weekly meetings." He didn't look cross. In fact to be honest he looked amused that this young man was finding arriving at work so difficult. Maybe it reminded him of his own tardiness as a youth.

"Mr Bradley. I mean Phil. I will make up the hours I promise." He looked pleadingly into Phil's eyes and the man just relented.

"Ok listen Mick. I have some really important clients coming this afternoon. We won a bid for a large hospital down on the South coast. The CEO is coming in to start off discussions so I need your assistance please." Even I could tell, without any knowledge of the building trade, that Phil didn't need Mick's help, but he wanted to earn his trust and making him feel important was going to be the ticket.

"Absolutely. Let me get you a coffee and you can brief me." Mick was doing his utmost to appease him boss and it seemed like it was working.

I spent the next few hours trying to follow what the two men were discussing. It was all above my head and whilst I can usually keep up with most topics of conversation, this was making me giddy. I gave up and thought that the best solution would be to think about my dear departed friend.

• •

FLASHBACK

• •

Whin was still slumped on the table when the paramedics led a very worse for wear looking Tom out to the ambulance. I could see he had a red blanket around his shoulders and a bandage around his head. I could only imagine that he had slipped or passed out in the toilet and fallen on something hard.

Tom was awake but looked very drunk. He was going to have a serious headache in the morning.

Geoff came over and started shaking Whin. He looked relieved that Tom had been taken care of and now just had to sort out poor Whin. He dragged him to his feet and shouted to Pam for help. We had never stayed the night at the pub but I had heard that on frequent occasions, one of the spare bedrooms on the first floor would be leased out and occupied by intoxicated friends. It looked like this was where we were staying tonight. I was pleased. Whin was in no fit state to get home and would not be capable of looking after himself either.

Pam and Geoff hauled Whin up a flight and a half of stairs and down a short narrow corridor. I hadn't thought the pub was that old but judging by the rickety staircase and sloping floors, the place could be at least a couple of hundred years old. Pam opened the door of a room at the end of the hallway and in we stepped. It was like travelling back in time. The seventies décor was still in mint condition. I suspected it was original and due to the very nature of its status as 'spare room', it wasn't used much and therefore the walls and the contents were still as good as new. The single bed was covered in a pink piped velour throw and the orange and brown flowery wallpaper clashed hideously. The curtains were frilly and lacy around the edges and a completely different hue to the bedspread, giving the overall impression of a garish nightmare. Thankfully the inhabitants were normally too inebriated to care. Whin was almost comatose and the sooner they removed his shoes and shut the door, the better. He needed to sleep it off.

I could hear Pam questioning Geoff as they tiptoed back down the landing. "What happened then?"

"I dunno" Geoff sounded peeved that he hadn't actually discovered the root of the problem. I couldn't hear any more as they disappeared down the stairs.

Whin was snoring heavily so I knew that would be it until the late hours of tomorrow morning. I settled down to sleep and hoped his snoring wouldn't keep me awake.

• •

FLASHBACK

• •

CHAPTER 19

Phil and Mick were still poring over plans, which I could only assume had something to do with the hospital build people coming later on.

Phil stood up and looked over at Mick. "Fancy a fag?" Mick nodded and they grabbed their jackets and we made out way back down to the reception area. It had stopped raining and the gusty wind had died down but it was still cold. The two men stood outside puffing away moving from one leg to another to keep warm.

"Bloody unfair, if you ask me," Phil mumbled as he drew a long drag of his B&H. "Why can't we have a little room at the back of the building where we can smoke? I remember the good old days when you could smoke at your desk".

"Oh really," Mick looked shocked. "You don't look that old."

"Oi, you cheeky wotsit." Phil cuffed his young apprentice round the ear and laughed. "Now listen. The guys that are coming in later are a bit ferocious so don't give then any cause for action"

"Why, what do you mean?" Phil suddenly looked nervous. He was racing ahead with his boss and he was dealing with issues that he had barely covered during his day release college studies.

Phil laughed and just said "Leave it to me. Don't speak to them apart from 'Hello' and 'Goodbye'."

Mick looked away. This guy was helping him out and he didn't even acknowledge his assistance. What a complete lack of manners. Mick looked terrified and unsure of himself. "Phil?"

Phil was stubbing out his butt. "Yes?"

"Well, I mean. Why are you doing so much for me?" It was a good question. Admittedly I had leapt ahead and considered the lad rude for not thanking Phil for his advice when really Mick was just pondering on why this man should be spending so much time on him.

"Come on lad." He pushed open the enormous door and gestured for Mick to enter. "We've a bit more to go through before our guests arrive."

Mick flicked his smouldering cigarette high into the air and I watched it, with satisfaction, fall into a puddle in the gutter and extinguish itself immediately. He walked through the door and followed his leader back up to the office.

The next two hours passed uneventfully. I was bored but I couldn't think about Whin or the others so I just sat and watched the master and his trainee perfect documentation for the meeting that afternoon.

At about 1:30, a smartly dressed female interrupted them and reminded them that some gentlemen had arrived for a meeting. Phil put his suit jacket back on and ran his fingers through his hair. I guessed this was some kind of preparation ritual that helped him focus on the project in hand.

"Thank Alicia. Can you send them in? Oh and if you can take some coffee orders too, please, that would be great."

She beamed at him, clearly not having a problem with waiting on men and serving them their afternoon beverages. "Sure Phil". She caught his eyes for a little longer than was necessary. Not another one! This guy was desperate. I mean she was sexy and pretty but in all fairness

Eve had been gone a matter of days and here he was reacting to a flirtatious brunette. Shame on him!

Two tall, grey haired men were ushered through the wooden door into the glass office. "Please gentlemen, come in. I would like to introduce you to Mick, who will be assisting me today." Phil turned to Mick and said, "These distinguished gentlemen are Frances Thatchman and Neil McTabbit. Mick shook hands with both men and then hastily retreated to the other side of the large pine desk.

Phil did most of the talking although Frances and Neil questioned him alternately, almost like firing cannons at him. Phil was undeterred by their brutal style of inquiries and seemed to me, to be in total control. I could see Mick looking askance at the behaviour before his eyes. I could read his confusion. 'Where was the mutual respect and trust?' 'Why do these men look so dour?' I could see his point. Financial gain is usually the key point to business transactions but I do think it is important that you enjoy whom you work with. It makes the job so much easier. It looked like Phil was going to have his work cut out with this mean couple though.

I lost interest pretty quickly and daydreamed until I heard one of them mention lunch. At least there would be a change of scene and hopefully a change in topic. I'm sure listening to the planning stage of a new building is fascinating but when you have no idea what the jargon meant, it could quite easily have been Japanese.

All four men trotted down to the reception area and turned left at the exit. Another sharp left and across the road was an Indian restaurant. I loved the smells from a curry kitchen. We were seated by the window and I took the time to look around at the traditional red flock wallpaper and glitzy ceiling lights, whilst the men ordered their lunch.

Both Phil and Mick lit up whilst the sour faced men looked on. I had yet to see either of them break into a smile and just thought how sad their lives must be if they have to constantly wear a grim mask. When the drinks arrived however, both Francis and Neil became quite animated. They talked more and without a sharp tone. Mick just looked lost. He was totally out of his depth. If Phil had included him in this meeting from hell, then it was probably to teach him a lesson. Just because his day release work was going well, it didn't mean he knew the first thing about the building industry. Mick stayed out of the conversation. I could tell he was an intelligent boy and knew when to shut up. He watched the three older men bond over their chicken Madras and Bombay potatoes.

Lunchtime dragged on and both Mick and I were thoroughly bored. I could see Mick's eyes glazing over. Phil noticed and brought the meeting to an abrupt conclusion.

"So gentlemen. I trust I have dispelled any fears you may have had." He stood up and is to reiterate that the discussion was over. "And please call me if you have any further queries.

Mick stood and shook hands with the men, who had resumed their miserable expression. Phil saw them to the door and then went to pay the bill at the counter, which was situated at the far end of the restaurant.

Mick sat down again and lit another cigarette. He still had half a Kingfisher beer left and wasn't going to be parted from it. Phil returned and sat next to him.

"Bloody hell Phil." Mick looked thoroughly depressed. "Those two were bastards. How did you stop yourself punching them?"

Phil laughed and said "Now I asked for assistance today because I wanted you to see that if you are not prepared, you will get eaten alive."

"I thought there would be a lesson in this for me somewhere". Mick looked up at Phil glumly.

"Well. You have to learn to put your heart and soul into this. A half hearted attempt and strolling in late frequently and you are just not going to cut the mustard."

"Ok. Ok. Lesson learned." Mick managed a thin smile. He knocked back the rest of his beer and followed Phil to the door.

The afternoon passed slowly but towards the end of the working day, Mick received a text message. I only heard it bleep so I was unsure as to the content.

Mick logged onto the Internet and began hunting for flights to South America. He eventually came across a website, which specialised in booking late departures. He filled in the enquiry form and sent it off. He filled out a leave form and took it into Phil's office. I presumed Phil needed to sign it before Personnel stored it for prosperity.

Phil was on a call when Mick knocked but he gestured for him to sit down. I watched Phil. The worry and tension I had seen etched all over his face had gone. I didn't think he had resolved his marital problems that quickly so he either convincingly turned off when he was at work, or he had finally done something about that old witch and moved on. To be honest I didn't think he had the balls.

Phil slammed down the phone and ran his fingers through his hair. "Yes Mick. It had better be quick."

Mick suddenly looked nervous. "Erm. I know this is really cheeky and everything, especially after my lesson today."

"Yes yes. What is it?" Phil was getting impatient.

"Well you see the thing is, my mate has invited me to go with him. Well he is this tour leader and well I've had such a shitty month and it would be really great."

Phil looked at Mick totally non-plussed. "What are you drivelling on about?"

"Can I have some leave, starting the day after tomorrow please?"

"Well why didn't you say so?" Phil looked amused. "Actually it's not a bad idea. Take some time off and whilst you're away think about how much you really want this job". He signed the form and continued. "When you get back, you and I can have a little chat about your future."

"Cheers Phil". Mick looked really relieved. He grabbed the form and we walked off. After several glass corridors later, we came across a door marked 'Human Resources'. The lady sitting at the first desk we saw, looked rather formidable.

She looked up but didn't smile and waited for Mick to speak.

"Erm. I've got to hand this in". He looked really nervous.

The lady read through the form and removed her black-framed glasses. "You have to give at least seven days notice for leave." She didn't say any more and I could see Mick's cheeks getting more and more pink by the second.

"Look. It's a bit of an emergency and Phil Bradley has signed it so if he is ok with it…" He left the sentence unfinished. I think she grasped what he was getting at. She tutted and threw the form onto a pile next to her.

Mick and I left rather rapidly. We didn't go back to his desk but rather made our way back to the impressive entrance and headed home.

I hadn't seen much of Mick's place last night. Due to my exhaustion, the power cut and the swift departure that morning, I just hadn't had a chance. The journey on the bus had been uneventful and although the rain had held off again for our short walk to the house, it was really cold. There was no hanging about and even Mick didn't want to stop, even to light up a cigarette.

We swung into his front garden and swiftly opened the front door. I remembered the narrow stairs but that was about all I could make out from last night. Once Mick had switched on the spotlights in the ceiling, I was able to take in the décor. For a single man, the place looked decidedly un-batchelorly. Not that there were vases of flowers dotted around the place but I guessed that his ex girlfriend cum fiancé-refusee had assisted in putting the place together. The furniture didn't look expensive but it was all clean and neat.

It was almost open plan and we made our way into the kitchen at the back of the house. I reckon about 90% of houses are built with the lounge of the front, near the front door, and the kitchen at the back. I guess it was just a recipe that worked in the building industry. It was a shame I couldn't speak, I could have chatted to Mick about it. I'm sure he learnt all about that sort of thing at his day-release college.

The kitchen was a dark red with black and chrome units and handles. It felt warm and cosy even though the heating was not on. Mick realised this at the same time and groaned. He left me on the work surface and trotted off, presumably to check the timer switch and do his best to get the radiators up and working.

After last night, I would be surprised if Mick wanted to venture out again so I was looking forward to a cosy night in.

Mick finally got the heating working and came down stairs in a hooded top and tracksuit bottoms. I gathered he had had a shower. Seeing him in this attire confirmed my hopes that we would be staying in. Mick pottered around in the kitchen and although I couldn't really see what he was doing, I could make out he was boiling some pasta. I tutted silently as I watched him pour the contents of a jar of sauce over the tagliatelle.

The evening passed slowly and I felt relaxed and at peace. The house was cosy and warm by the time dinner was finished. Mick relaxed on the sofa and flicked through the numerous channels on Sky Plus. I felt dizzy just looking at the long list of programmes. Freezing the football highlights when Mick went to the bathroom and then rewinding and fast forwarding them when he returned, totally astounded me. My head was buzzing with questions about how this could all possibly work.

Mick received a couple of phone calls throughout the course of the evening and I presumed the first one was from Ryan, enquiring whether his offer would be taken. After a brief chat, Mick said he'd call tomorrow with flight details. He mentioned that he hadn't had a chance to take the ring in to the jewellers and sell it but would do so the following day. I began to wonder if he would take me. How exciting! Whin had never travelled abroad. We had seen a fair bit of England though and in particular, Cornwall. South America, though, that was a completely different continent. I had no idea what to expect. The night passed with Mick falling asleep on the sofa and me worrying about the forthcoming trip.

I had dozed off when Mick came too. It must have been the early hours and without a word, he slumped off up the narrow stairs and I heard his collapse into bed. I drifted off again.

CHAPTER 20

When I woke up, it was broad daylight. There was no sound in the house so I really hoped that Mick hadn't overslept again. I didn't think that would have gone down well with Phil, especially after yesterday's lesson and his leave booked. I couldn't see a clock on the wall. After a while I spotted a digital readout on the DVD recorder and could just about make out that it said 11:23. Blimey he was really late!

I carried on musing about out holiday until after another glimpse at the DVD machine, I realised that another hour had elapsed. Not only that but no phone call had come through to jolt Mick awake so I could only fathom that he had rushed off to work without taking me. I wasn't upset. The frosty attitude from the CEO and his partner had left me cold and I wasn't keen to repeat that experience. Besides being here at home was far cosier. Looking outside I could see that the mist was still hanging around and the day looked damp and unwelcoming. I was more than happy to relax here and I decided to take the opportunity to think about my dear, departed friend.

• •

FLASHBACK

• •

It was actually Pam who woke us up the following morning. She had brought in a steaming mug of tea for the rather dishevelled looked Whin. She had to shake his shoulders to rouse him but once he had opened his eyes, he looked very apologetic.

"Oh Pam!" He was rubbing his eyes. "Why am I in here? What did I do?" He looked like he was dreading the response.

Pam just smiled gently and sat on the edge of the bed. "Hey poppet. You had a bad day yesterday. You and Tom just sunk too many beers and you both just passed out."

"Where's Tom" Whin looked like memories of parts of the night were returning.

"Well. You were lucky. You passed out on the table and didn't do yourself any mischief but poor Tom, he had collapsed in the Gents!" She stifled a laugh. "I'm sorry. I shouldn't laugh." She noticed the concern on Whin's face." Hey don't worry. He's fine. The ambulance took him away to check him over as he had bumped his head but we had a call this morning and he is back home and he's just suffering with a bit of a headache. He asked after you."

Whin smiled thinly and sipped his tea. I had heard about the miraculous properties of tea and right in front of me, I could visibly see Whin improving. His washed out face became brighter and his eyes lost their 'dead fish' look.

"Now. How do you fancy a bacon sarnie?" Pam's eyes twinkled. She had such a natural maternal instinct.

Whin sighed. "Pam that would be great."

"Ok well here is a towel and a clear pair of pants. Go and wash yourself and I'll get the bacon on." She stood up and just before she slipped out the door, I saw her turn and look at Whin. The pity was so intense I nearly cried. Fortunately Whin was unaware and he began dragging himself out of bed.

He disappeared and I presumed he had found the bathroom and managed to sluice himself down a bit. The stench of stale alcohol was quite overwhelming and I hoped that someone would open the window soon.

Whin returned and looked much better. It's amazing what a shower can do. Not that I have ever had the pleasure, but I have marvelled at the noticeable effects. He pulled the covers back over the mattress, which was sweet but I strongly suspected that Pam would be up later to strip the bed.

We headed down the stairs and I could smell the wafts of bacon rising up to meet us. Whin quickened his pace and we arrived in the bar just as Pam brought a plate with two doorstep sandwiches and placed it on the counter.

"Get that down you." She turned and shouted "Geoff, come and take Whin's order"

Geoff appeared but looked very sheepish. I bet he still wanted to know what the two men had discussed last night but now he felt awkward about asking.

"Morning." Geoff looked ill at ease but offered his a pint.

Whin shook his head quite violently and said "God no Geoff. Can I have a strong black coffee with 3 sugars please?" Whin looked almost desperate and his plea helped Geoff slip back into normal conversation.

"Coming right up mate." Geoff looked pleased and busied himself with the prepared filter coffee packs.

Whin and I made our way slowly to a table. Not the same one as last night. Even Whin realised that would make him feel worse. I could see the sun was shining outside but I knew Whin would want to stay indoors. He was just about coping with his delicate head but strong sunlight would probably finish him off.

Geoff brought the coffee over and noticed that Whin hadn't touched his bacon buttie. "You ok?"

"Yeah Geoff. I'm fine." He looked anything but fine. . The sparkle in his eyes brought on by a hot cup of tea this morning had vanished by the time he had reached the bottom of the stairs. The deep sadness had returned and I can't imagine that the hangover was helping. "Cheers" he said as he took the steaming coffee.

Geoff sat down. He had spent ages pussyfooting around his old mate and now he had found the courage to confront the issues that were bothering Whin so much. "Listen mate. I don't know when Tom is going to be back on the scene again but if there's something bothering you, you know you can come to me."

Whin looked embarrassed. As a rule, men don't really do the crying on shoulders thing, that particular pursuit is taken up by women far more readily and effectively. On average males just don't have that same ability open their heart and soul to another human being, especially a man. They think it makes them look weak and incapable.

"Cheers Geoff." Whin still looked mortified but he nodded. "I'm not sure I am capable right now but thanks for the offer."

Geoff stood up and looked Whin in the eye. I could tell he was proud of himself. He had offered his help and now the ball was firmly back in Whin's court. He looked to me to be the sort of character that needed to know where he was and what's expected. I couldn't see him as a leader, more of a sheep. If he had orders, he would follow them implicitly but left to make decisions or intercept a situation and he floundered. Pam was obviously the backbone of the relationship. She wore the trousers and everyone was happy with that arrangement.

Whin looked dreadful. I could almost hear the hammering in his head and combined with the pain in his heart, he looked utterly defeated. I watched him as he slowly munched his way through Pam's generous portion of bacon sandwich. The bacon must have been cold even before he had started but the hot coffee was doing the trick. With every sip, I could see a little tension lifting.

The day drew on and a few clients frequented the pub but it was a quiet shift and I could see that Geoff was doing his best to keep an eye on his old pal. Whin didn't move on to the hard stuff after the food and coffee had done its best to restore him. He had another coffee and just sat at his table filling in a crossword from a paper someone had left behind. He was quiet and even when Geoff trotted over a couple of times, he just nodded his head in response to questions.

Just as Whin had decided to move on and go home, Tom came staggering into the bar. He had a large bandage round his head and looked a little worse for wear but he was obviously keen to see Whin. He rushed over "You ok mate?"

Whin's mood lightened a little. "Yes Tom. I'm ok. How are you feeling? That looks like a nasty bump."

It was Tom's turn to look humiliated. He looked down at his feet whilst still unconsciously touching his bruised skull. "I'm fine. I'm fine. Sorry about that. I kinda ran out of you!"

"Hey listen. I must've crashed before you because I only have a hazy recollection of you going to the bog! I woke up here this morning!"

Tom looked less embarrassed and motioned for Whin to sit down.

"Well actually I'm off to get some late lunch. Come with me, my shout."

Tom looked surprised. "Yeah ok. Where you headed? Oh but I'll pay my own way"

"Well there's the Turkish restaurant round the corner, or the Chinese buffet or Aunt Flo's café. Take you pick and yes it's my shout. I insist."

Tom rolled his eyes and said "Ok what about the Chinese?"

"Done!" Whin smiled and marched up to the bar to tell Geoff that he was on his way and to thank him for his hospitality.

The two men didn't speak until they arrived at Zen Palace. The pretty waitress showed them to a small table in the middle of the restaurant and took their drinks orders. As she left she informed them, in a very heavy accent, to go to the buffet whenever they were ready.

The two friends waited for their drinks to arrive and laughed when glasses of orange juice with ice was served up.

"We're getting old Whin. We can't hack it anymore." Tom sunk half of his juice before Whin had even touched his.

"A bit dehydrated Tom?" Whin joked back.

I couldn't hear the conversation whilst they loaded their ornate plates high with spring rolls, chicken chow mein and Singapore noodles. They carried on with chitchat for most of the meal and it wasn't until after their third trip to the buffet counter, that the talk from last night was resumed.

"Thanks for listening last night Tom. I really appreciate it. I'm not sure I made total sense but I just needed to get it off my chest."

Tom looked up. "Whin. I know there's more and if you need to unload the rest of it, it's ok." He looked quite solemn.

• •

FLASHBACK

• •

CHAPTER 21

The front door slammed and roused me from my daydreaming. Mick raced up the stairs and I could hear bangs and thumps for the room above. I could only assume that he was in his bedroom and packing his case in readiness for tomorrow. Not having been with him at work, I had no idea if the tickets had been sorted, money collected etc but by the speed at which Mick was throwing his case around, I'd say it was all arranged and an early morning flight had been booked.

I suddenly became nervous. I had never left the country and I just didn't know what to expect. What if Mick lost me over there and I spent my life in South America? I would never be able to get back to Dan and learn about Whin.

Excitement took over from the anxiety and I was imagining evening drinks on a hot balmy night, the hacienda stretched in front and a beautiful sunset fading away on the horizon. I was thinking about all the new and wonderful sights and then Mick stomped downstairs and loudly rummaged through the drawers of a bureau underneath the stairway. His phone started ringing and he picked it up still anxiously searching for something in the desk.

"Yes?" He sounded really impatient and cross.

He stopped searching and stood upright. "What's wrong?" His worry had changed direction and his concern was now focussed on the caller.

"Do you want me to come over?" There was a very short break between each exclamation from Mick so I assumed that the caller was in trouble.

Mick's voice softened. "Look I don't mind."

Another pause and he continued, "Yes, yes. Ok, well look, call me if you change your mind." He hung up and looked rather reluctant at ending the call. He sat on the arm of the sofa and stared into space. He spotted me, and the packet of B&H, lying on the coffee table and lit up quickly. As he exhaled the smoke, he was muttering under his breath. 'I just don't know.' He kept repeating this over and over and by the time he had finished his cigarette, it had become a mantra.

Mick picked up his phone again and pushed buttons. It looked like he had sent a text and sure enough the mobile beeped a couple of seconds after he threw it back onto the coffee table. He lit up another cigarette and was deep in thought when the Bond theme tune started up.

Mick grabbed the phone and just said "What?"

He rubbed his forehead with his right hand and calmed down a little. "Yeah yeah. Sorry mate. I've just had a call from Stacey and she's been caught speeding. I just feel I should be with her."

The caller must have given Mick a bit of a talking to as I could see the colour flood his cheeks. Mick was listening and his face became darker and darker. "I know," he kept repeating, probably not even loud enough to be heard at the other end of the line.

Eventually the speaker calmed down and Mick tried to explain his actions "I only wanted to see if she was ok. She seemed really upset on the phone. Yes, I know. I know. Look I'd better go. If I've gotta be at yours by 5am then I need to get myself sorted out and I'm still trying to find my passport."

I could hear Ryan shouting and although I couldn't make out the words, I could make a wild guess at their content.

"Calm down Ryan. I know it's here, I just need to find which drawer it's in, that's all."

Mick started laughing and added "See you tomorrow, with my passport." He looked happier now and I could see that Ryan was a good influence on Mick and a true friend. The other men he had been partying with the other night seemed hopeless. Rather than help him through the traumatic break-up with his girlfriend, they ended up taking the mickey.

The evening was spent hunting high and low for the passport and eventually finding it in a small rucksack tucked down buy the side of the sofa. Mick ordered a pizza and whilst he waited for it to be delivered, he spent the half hour in the bathroom. I could hear the running water and as the doorbell rang, I noticed his clean-shaven chin as he raced down the stairs to answer the door. Lord knows what else he had been up to in there but I could smell the cloud of aromas, which wafted down behind him and I nearly choked.

Mick settled down on the sofa and munched away at his large pizza and guzzled two cans of Guinness. We were watching a moronic programme called 'Big Brother' although admittedly it was strangely compelling. Before he passed out on the settee again, he packed me away in the reclaimed black rucksack and although it was pitch black, after a while the comforting snores lulled me to sleep.

I must have slept all the way to Ryan's place and on the journey to the airport as the first thing I remember was the noise at the check-in counter. From my pocket, I could just about see Mick and Ryan collecting their boarding passes and moving off. We headed through security checks and made our way up to the bar overlooking Duty Free. There was still a smoking section to the rear of the bar and after Ryan brought back two pints of lager, Mick removed me from his rucksack and both boys had a pre-flight cigarette.

I wasn't sure exactly what their conversation was about but I though that it possibly had something to do with Stacey's phone call last night.

"Yeah I agree mate. She shouldn't have come to me but she did and it just left me wondering if she really wanted it to be over."

Ryan was sipping his pint but he nearly spat it out when he heard that comment. "What! Are you kidding? Listen, she very publicly humiliated you and threw the ring at you. She now gets done for drink driving or whatever it was and expects for you to have a shoulder to cry on. I think she's bloody lucky you picked up the phone and didn't slam it down when you heard her voice. You don't owe her anything ok!" Ryan had finished his speech and decided it was time to consume some alcohol so he literally poured half the beer down his throat.

Mick was still staring blankly at Ryan but eventually he started nodding his head slowly and came to. "Yeah you're right. I don't wanna talk about her anymore. Tell me more about the trip. Oh and what's happened about Macey? Have you managed to get through to her?"

Ryan wiped his frothy mouth and shook his head. "No mate. I haven't but I did manage to get through to her sister and she just said she was away."

"Hey listen. I'm really sorry. Maybe there's just some stuff she needs to sort through and she'll be in touch when she's worked it out." Mick obviously couldn't really think of anything else to say and looked worried that he might something to make the situation worse. He understood how Ryan was feeling and he felt the best thing was to change the subject. "So listen what's the full itinerary then?"

Ryan looked pleased for a diversion and animatedly talked Mick through the various highlights of the trip. "Hey listen you just gotta check out Foz d'Igacu man. It's awesome. I mean it. I think the best side is the Brazilian side and you take these boats out to a kind of jetty and it's just so cool."

"I must admit I've never even heard of it."

"That's the weird thing. Victoria Falls and Niagara get all the attention and yet this one is definitely the most impressive. I also want to take you over to the Argentinian side too. There's this beautiful walk alongside the waterfall and it's got to be seen."

Ryan looked so mesmerised in the beauty of his subject and Mick was utterly captivated by Ryan's ability to bring the place to life.

They boys chatted on and on about various things to do and see in South America and after a few beers and cigarettes, a call on the tannoy system announced that their flight was now boarding. Mick stood up and excitedly gathered his belongings. Ryan grabbed his holdall and the smoking paraphernalia. As we sauntered down the open stairs, I could hear Mick talking nineteen to the dozen. Abruptly Ryan stopped and starred straight down. Coming up to him was an absolute stunner of a woman. She had bra-strap length jet black hair, chocolate eyes and a deep brown tan. At first the woman didn't notice the man in front of her but as she looked up to ask him to move aside, she took a sharp intake of breath.

"Ryan" she said in an alarmed but very sexy Spanish accent.

"Macey! What the hell are you doing here? I have been trying to get hold of you for nearly a fortnight. Even your sister wouldn't give me information other than you had gone away." Ryan looked angry now. I could see relief on his face that she was alive and hadn't been run over by a coach but now the fury was seeping in.

"Oh God Ryan. I need to talk to you." She carried on up the stairs to the bar. Ryan didn't think twice and followed her up. I had no idea where Mick was or even if he was aware that Macey had just turned up. I couldn't see him but I was sure the minute he couldn't see Ryan, he would make his way back up to the bar.

"Macey. I have been worried sick. Where the hell have you been? And why didn't you answer my calls?" His questions were coming thick and fast, leaving Macey no time to explain. She ordered a two double vodkas and a pint. She downed one of the shots before they made their way to a table.

She looked at her watch and looked panicked. "Ryan. I need a cigarette." He handed one over to her and she lit up and blew a huge plume of smoke upwards. Her lipstick was dark and she looked deeply perplexed.

"Look I'm sorry ok? There has been loads going on and I had to fly out to Rome for a few days." It didn't look like she was going to give Ryan any further explanation although he continued sitting there waiting for enlightenment.

"What do you mean you had to go to Rome for a few days? Why?" Ryan wasn't giving up and I was behind him all the way. Maybe she did have her personal reasons for travelling halfway across the world without informing her partner but all the possibilities I could come up with were all incredibly shady.

"Look I can't really go into it now." She checked her watch again and drained the second double vodka. As she stood up she took three last puffs of her cigarette and then stubbed it out in the large green ashtray. "I have a plane to catch. I really have to go. Can I meet up with you in Buenos Aires?"

Ryan was still sitting down and he watched as Macey re-adjusted her sunglasses and scurry off down the stairs. He took a large gulp of beer and left the remains on the table along with the empty cigarette packed and me!

I could only watch from a distance as Ryan hurtled down the stairs, his eyes darting across the packed concourse searching desperately for Mick. I began to panic. Here I was left alone in an airport. Lord only knew who would pick me up now. I was dying to know why Macey was having secret meetings in Rome and then more covert appointments elsewhere.

I would just have to sit and wait for the next passerby to collect me and just hope that I would make my way back to Whin's family and friends.

I waited about an hour and then a hairy man with two teenage daughters sat at the table and gave me a shock. I had been deep in thought. Mostly about how disappointed I was that I missed a chance to see the world.

"Mica. Go and get your old dad a packet of dry roasted nuts. There's a love." He dug around in the pockets of his enormous trousers and pulled out a handful of change. Passing it over to the older of the two girls, she tutted and went to the bar.

The younger girl looked at her father and shook her head. "Dad you know you're not supposed to eat crap like that."

"Abbey!" Her father looked embarrassed and pushed his index finger against his lips. "Shhhh."

"Dad. I'm not three. You have been warned to cut down on fatty foods and packets of nuts are not good." Abbey seemed a sensible girl. Just on the cusp of puberty, I'd say that she was about 13. She sat next to him and linked arms. "I'm just worried. I don't want to lose you aswell".

Mica returned with two packets of crisps and a bag of nuts. She offered her sister a pack of Cheese and Onion flavoured Walker crisps but Abbey shook her head.

Mica sat down opposite her father and I could see immediately that she had inherited her dad's frame. She was broad and if she wasn't careful the small soft rolls of puppy fat would get bigger and bigger.

Abbey reached into her black record bag, covered in skulls, and brought out an MP3 player. She plugged it into her ears and sat staring out at the crowds.

Mica and the hairy man were facing each other devouring the savoury snacks. There was silence but it was comfortable and peaceful. I could tell that these two were very similar and not just their love of cuisine. Whilst they ate, I had a chance to observe the three of them. From what I had gathered so far, maybe the girls' mother was deceased or had run away. Their father was morbidly obese and needed to go on a strict diet to save his life, something he was not even considering doing, if watching him pour the last remains into his mouth, was anything to go by. It didn't look good for these youngsters.

The hairy man wiped his powdery fingers over his large trousers and left a few grease marks trailing down his thighs. I was revolted by this gesture of bad taste. I could see him eyeing me up and itching to touch me but neither of the girls had noticed his interest.

After a few minutes, the fat man leaned forward and began casually playing with me. He was rolling me between his fingers like Whin used to. It brought back so many happy memories.

Suddenly Abbey spotted me in his chubby hands and yanked the earphones out and screamed "Dad! No!"

The fat man looked shocked by Abbey's outburst and almost dropped me. Mica looked over nonchalantly and without even pausing, looked away again.

"Dad. Don't even think about it." Abbey's face was almost scarlet. The poor child looked utterly furious.

"What?" Her father was desperately trying to look innocent and I could see a complete role reversal here. It was entertaining and sad at the same time. "I just found it here on the table. It's not mine or anything." He was blushing but it was quite difficult to spot underneath all his facial hair.

Abbey suddenly became agitated and turned to her family. "I think that was the last call for our flight. She grabbed her black bag and stood up. "Come on. We've got to go." She looked impatient. She rolled her eyes and started heading towards the stairs. Fat man and his younger daughter followed suite and I was left alone again.

Over the next few hours, I was visited by a couple of lanky youths, talking non-stop about some bands they were off to see. I could hear them talking about festivals but it was all gibberish to me. They could have been talking in a foreign language for all the sense I made out of it. They were followed by an elderly couple who said almost nothing to each other and whose body language was so out of kilter, I wouldn't have been surprised if today was their first meeting. Either that or that had been together for years and had just grown so far apart that neither of them even registered each other. That was particularly sad.

A couple of families joined the table and the noise was incredibly. One child screamed continuously and I could feel a headache brewing. Fortunately they didn't stay long. The minute they realised this was a smoking area, they left. The other family were quieter but again had had no idea they were seated in the smoking section.

There was a long pause and the only visitor I had for about an hour was the bar man collecting the glasses and running a dirty smelly cloth over the surface of the dark brown wooden table.

It must have been about lunchtime and I wondered how Ryan and Mick were getting on. I presumed they had met up and I could just imagine Mick trying to give some advice back to his friend.

Two large bikers sat at the table with pints of what looked like snakebite. I could tell from their drawl they were American. Most of what they talked about didn't make sense either but I was fascinated. I have heard so many stories over the years about the Hell's Angels and how they kidnapped women and kept them barefoot and pregnant so they couldn't return home. I would have loved to have been able to ask these men about the reality of these legends. They moved on but not until they had sunk about four pints each.

I was getting quite fed up. The traffic of people was interesting in a voyeurism sort of way but I wanted to be picked up and taken home. I was becoming maudlin when I heard laughter coming up the metal staircase. I could just about see the heads of four people. When they reached the top of the stairs, they were all in uniform and I guessed they were cabin crew. I prayed as hard as I could that they would take my table. I watched them all giggle at the bar and then collect their drinks. My prayers had been answered and a pretty brunette led the others to my table. The two lads were as camp as a row of tents and would have given James a run for his money. I had the impression though that they were laying on the attitude a little for display purposes. This was either to outdo the other or to impress the girls with their bitchy manner. Nevertheless it was very entertaining and I was enjoying eavesdropping on such a lively bunch.

"Now look I really need to remove my trousers and have a thorough hose down so drink up and we can decide where the night will take us." The taller of the men downed his alcopop and stood up. "Now who wants to lead me into temptation?" The girls laughed loudly at his outlandish comments and actions and both gulped down their drinks. The three of them headed back towards the stairs and the second man picked me up. He was about to put me back down again but changed his mind and stuffed me in his pocket. I was so relieved. If these guys were drinking, then it meant they had just come off duty and were heading home. Although I had previously been upset about not seeing the world, I had now come to the conclusion that the nearer I was to Whin, the better.

We all jumped into a banged up old white Ford Fiesta and one of the girls drove us back to a house overlooking a tired looking park. I didn't recognise the area but at least I wasn't lost somewhere deep in South America.

The two boys scrambled up the stairs and I presumed they were racing to the shower. As I headed up in a pocket, I could just about see the female driver escort the other girl into the kitchen. I assumed she didn't live here and judging from her slightly nervous disposition, I guessed she was new on the job and had only just met her colleagues.

"You bastard" my current owner shouted as he heard the water in the bathroom. He had barely taken off his jacket, let alone stripped. He rummaged through a very tidy wardrobe and settled on a black opaque shirt and black trousers. It looked a bit "Saturday Night Fever' to me but then this young fashion sense totally confused me.

I was put on the bedside table whilst my owner slipped off his trousers and hung them up. He discarded his shirt and underpants and sat on his bed waiting for a shout to indicate it was his turn in the shower. I took the opportunity to look around the room and studied the strange arty pictures on the wall. I couldn't make them out. I had really not had the occasion to discover art. I could appreciate a nice painting but abstract art was a whole foreign entity to me. I didn't understand it and I couldn't really see the point. I put it down to ignorance. I was frustrated. If I could talk, I'm sure my friend would have been able to explain, if only I could ask.

Eventually the bedroom door burst open and a wet man grinned and said "All yours boyo."

"There had better be some hot water left, you tart, or there'll be trouble." It didn't sound like a real threat, more of a playful banter.

"Calm down Andrew." The wet man dodged out of the way as a pair of used underpants flew across the room. "Help help! I'm being attacked by Andrew's knickers."

"Oh shut up you Ian, you pansy" and with that Andrew leapt off the bed and minced into the bathroom.

I waited for his return and sat pondering about what the night would bring. I was beginning to feel quite lonely. All these incredibly experiences were one thing but I had no one to share my stories with. I couldn't communicate and had no control over my destiny. To some that would be their idea of hell but it was the simple fact that no one else was aware of my very existence that I found the more difficult. With Whin, it had never really been an issue. We did things together and although we never spoke, I felt part of his life. Since his death I had been plunged into utter chaos and I suppose the insecurity of it all was wearing me down.

Andrew came back into the room and as he rubbed himself down and moisturised every inch of his well toned body, I marvelled at his physique. I wondered if he worked out much. With a chest and arms like he had, I guessed he would have to. He also looked rather tanned. Perhaps a little too brown. I wasn't sure if it was due to a sunbed or fake spray on tan.

Ian suddenly burst into the room again. I detected very little privacy in this house. Maybe Ian and Andrew had once been an item and so therefore were fully aware of how the other looked naked.

"What are you wearing?" Ian looked worried. He looked at the shirt and trousers, already laid out and folded his arms. "You cheeky minx! When did you go shopping in Prada?"

Ian looked unfazed. "Oh I was on a night stop in Milan last week. Isn't it beautiful?" He proudly smoothed down the collars and then stepped into the well-made trousers.

"You bitch! I am pea green. Go on. Tell me the bad news. How much?"

"Ooh you know I never kiss and tell! Oh listen go on. I have a couple of tops that I think you will like, hanging up. If you ruin them though…" He drew a line under his throat to indicate that the punishment would be death.

Ian jumped up and down with excitement and rushed to the wardrobe. "Oh the choice!" He sounded like he was in heaven. Even though the repartee flowed easily, I could definitely recognise that these two men had entirely different personalities. Andrew seemed to put on a risqué mask but underneath was a sensible chap and highly organised. Ian appeared to be a flipperty gibbert and scamper about like a large gay dog. He came across as loyal but totally disorganised and lived a shambolic life taking undue risks. I suppose opposites attract but it was a strange friendship.

The two lads made final adjustments and descended the stairs almost like they were waiting for a fanfare. I couldn't see the girls so I could only presume they were still dressing.

Ian scampered to the fridge and pulled out two bottles of a Vodka based drink. Handing one over to his friend, he pleaded, "Have you got any smokes my good man?"

Andrew pulled a half empty packet of Silk Cut out of his superbly fitted trousers passed one over to his mate. "That has to be about 7 packets you owe me now"

"All right. Keep your highlights on. I'm rostered for Dubai on Tuesday so I'll bring you a packet of 200. Will that keep you happy?"

"Well it will, if you remember. If I had a man for every time you promised to bring back some duty free, I'd be dead!"

They both laughed at that comment and during their hilarity, the girls entered the kitchen. "So what are you poofs laughing at then?"

"Tish! That's not very PC. You on rag week?" Ian joked.

"Sorry PC? I thought there was an outright ban in this house. Aren't Cheryl and I allowed a drink then? Seeing as I paid for them."

Andrew dutifully pulled out two more alcopops and handed them over. Cheryl looked very uncomfortable and wasn't quite sure how to join in other than to giggle at each and every comment. Ian was clearly finding it annoying and rolled his eyes.

"So where we heading then?" Tish looked at Andrew. "Have you boys not yet decided?"

Andrew shrugged and Ian piped up "Well there's always Kenzi's or how about we start off at Crushhh and take it from there?" I leapt at this comment.

"You tart!" Andrew cried out. "You just want to see if that Rex is there!" Actually I could see the hurt behind the fake smile and twigged. Andrew was in love with Ian but it looked like a one-way street.

"Well he might be!" Ian looked slightly cheesed off that his plan had been so transparent.

"Is that the guy from The Faithful?" Cheryl had finally found her entrance into the conversation.

"Yes that hunk of manhood is the lead singer." Ian slightly flushed.

"Oh yeah. I know him. My cousin's in the band too!" Cheryl looked so pleased with herself.

Ian nearly knocked her down as he leapt across the kitchen and started interrogating her. From an irritation, she had now climbed the ladder to idol in seconds.

"Really?!" Ian sounded breathless. "What's your cousin's name?"

"Erm Anthony. Well Tony really but most people call him animal! He used to love that character in the Muppet Show when he was little and then he grew up to be a drummer !" She was rambling but I could tell she was making the most of her chance to be liked by the flat mates. "I can give him a call and see where they're headed tonight, if you like?"

Ian nearly fainted with the prospect of partying with his idol. I looked at Andrew who was busy concentrating on a mask of nonchalance but it was slipping. I could almost envisage the night ahead. Andrew would drink too much and when he spied Rex and Ian in a conjoined state, he would explode. The only thing was, as far as I knew Rex wasn't bi-sexual and he certainly wasn't gay as he had been incredibly keen to bed Katy. Someone was going to be very disappointed.

"Would you?" Ian almost whispered. He was ringing his hands, praying for success.

Cheryl dug around in her leather bag for her mobile and scrolled through her contacts list and found her cousin's number. She dialled and looked edgy as she waited for the phone to be answered.

Ian was practically holding his breath and Tish had raided the fridge again and brought out another four bottles of Orange Vodka drinks.

"Tony? It's me. Listen I can't really chat right now but I just wanted to know…are you and the boys out tonight?" She waited as Tony responded.

"Great ok. What time are you heading there?" She gave a thumbs up. Tish rolled her eyes. Andrew grimaced and Ian nearly passed out.

"Ok. See you later." She snapped her phone shut and looked triumphantly at her new found friends.

I was rather gobsmacked. Here I was back in the loop again. It was a tenuous link, granted, but I just couldn't believe how so many people were all inter-connected. Mulling it all over, I couldn't really see any rhyme and reason to it. There was no pattern that jumped out at me, anyway. I was pleased that my journey was heading back the way I came but I wasn't holding out too much hope. This had happened on numerous occasions and it felt like the nearer I got, the further I swung away. Look how nearly I travelled to the other side of the world? I could only wait and see how this evening would all pan out.

Ian rushed upstairs again, presumably to rethink his outfit. He wanted to look irresistible. Even If I had been able to talk, I wouldn't have had the heart to tell him his hopes would be dashed. As he bounded up the staircase, I could only think how Ian and Andrew would make a lovely couple, as long as Ian could open his eyes and see that his soul mate was on his doorstep, literally.

Ian was bellowing down the stairs and Andrew was forced to go up and answer him. The girls were downing their drinks and pinched Andrew's Silk Cuts whilst he wasn't looking.

"I didn't know you knew Rex?" Tish looked suspiciously at her colleague.

"Well I don't know him exactly but Tony has introduced me a few times. He seems a really nice guy." She looked so happy that she had managed to find a way in to the gang.

"I am really surprised."

"What that I know someone famous?" Cheryl sounded a little hurt.

"No. No. That Rex is gay. I wouldn't have said so but then I don't have a gaydar."

"I.I.I don't know if he is gay or not. I have never seen him with anyone, boys or girls. Maybe he swings both ways." Cheryl sounded hopeful but looked devastated. She realised that if Ian was knocked back by Rex, she would bear the brunt of it and that would be it, her acceptance into the group would be well and truly denied.

"Oh dear. Let's just hope that he likes our Ian, otherwise there will be tears before bedtime." Tish hadn't fully realised the importance of the situation and carried on applying lipgloss in a rather gaudy shade of red. Her idea of evening wear was an interesting choice. She had donned a pair of painted DM's, black leggings and a very short denim skirt. Her black shirt was tight and only just skimped over her breasts. She had looked so smart when I first saw her in the airport terminal. She had looked the epitome of an air hostesses. Now she looked like a tramp with attitude and I just couldn't figure out for the life of me why she would be happy with such a transformation. Cheryl's outfit, on the other hand, didn't look that different to her uniform. She had mumsy shoes on, actually they could still have been her crew shoes. Her hair was still neatly plastered up in a chignon and her tight black skirt was so long to be tarty and too short to be fashionable. Her loose blouse made her look like a lawyer. It was rather amusing to see such a varied wardrobe in people all destined to frequent the same drinking establishment.

Ian bounded down the stairs and Andrew trailed behind. "So. Anyway I didn't even ask. Where will he be? I mean where are we going?"

"Right well Tony said that they were going to meet up in Crushhh but he didn't know what time but they were then going to head to this club called Twenty- Five about 12ish. I think I know where it is. I know it's behind Green Street but if Tony's not in Crushhh, then I'll call him later for directions"

"Right." Ian looked sick with excitement. "Come on then guys. It's nearly 10 now and we want to get the best seats in the house, don't we?" He linked arms with Cheryl and we left.

Walking down the road with Andrew, Tish whispered "I don't even know if this Rex is gay. What does your gaydar say?"

"Mine hasn't worked for ages. No seriously" He added as he spotted Tish's smiling face.

"You guys all have gaydar. You must be able to tell which way he swings."

"Tish my darling. Trust me. I would love to be able to pick up on these things but the truth is, I am always getting it wrong. I even tried it on with this beautiful blond boy I met in a gay club. I thought if he was in a gay club then he must be gay. Wrong! He was just there with his brother who had just come out and wanted a little bit of moral support!" He laughed. "I ask you! I mean he was probably the only straight guy in the joint!"

Tish laughed and then her voice softened. "You'll find someone right for you".

"But it wont be the same." Andrew looked so depressed.

"No. It will be better." Tish was trying to cheer him up but it wasn't really working. "I know how much you love him but unrequited love is not the way forward."

Andrew and Tish both lit up cigarettes and then we had to run to catch up with the new two best friends.

I recognised Crushhh the minute we turned the corner. It had that square red and gold sign sticking out above the door. The large floor to ceiling windows revealed a packed bar. Well actually it was the fact that the windows had steamed up that made me guess that much. As soon as we entered, I was struck by how different it felt tonight.

The previous time I had visited with Rex and Katy, it was very subdued, non-eventful music, neither too loud nor too offensive. Tonight I felt somewhere quite foreign. For a start the bar was packed with young men. I suspected that the majority were homosexual and all eyes seemed to be on Andrew. It was too dark to tell if he was blushing but I don't think he was feeling too comfortable with the attention. Ian noticed though and I saw a flicker of jealousy. Ian and Cheryl scanned the room expertly. I could see Ian almost leaping up and down with pure hope. After a minute or two, both realised that none of the band had arrived yet. The night was young though so they made their way to the counter and ordered a round of drinks.

Andrew and Tish hung around by the wall. They had found a shelf, which looked perfect for holding their drinks, ashtrays, cigarettes etc. Neither spoke but they appeared to be comfortable in silence.

From my position on the shelf, I had a fantastic view of the bar and the various goings on. I spotted several pretty boys giving Andrew the eye and after each occasion, Tish nudged Andrew in a supportive manner. "Go on." She was hoping that Andrew would have some fun with one or two of the willing participants and try and forget Ian.

Andrew was struggling with this. He knew it was probably the right thing to do. We have all heard the expression 'the best way to get over a man, is to get under another' but I could just tell that his heart wasn't in it.

Cheryl and Ian returned with a tray laden with drinks. "Blimey Ian. How many people are in this round?" She grabbed a bottle of beer and started glugging immediately.

"Right well I just thought that if we got in a couple of rounds now, that saves queuing back up again for a bit." Ian looked smugly at Tish.

"Yeah and you just thought that by standing here and not at the bar on numerous occasions that you wont have to miss Rex." Tish laughed back at him.

"Ooh you're a cruel woman Letisha Henry but I still love you." He sent air kisses and started handing out the drinks.

The evening wore on. I thought I would have enjoyed being back. I had had fun the last time albeit exhausted. This time however, it was loud, sweaty and I felt positively on display, so I had no idea how Andrew was feeling. The glances were increasing and one incredibly camp chap came up for a brief chat. I couldn't really hear their conversation but I managed to catch the last part. Andrew had quite politely said that he was seeing someone else and the other man became quite upset by this remark.

"What a tease. Why look me up and down if you're not interested?" He flounced off with Andrew still trying to explain and apologise for something even I knew he hadn't done.

Andrew's confidence decreased after that and I could see him almost squirming each time another man looked in his direction. In the end he turned sideways on and leaned against the shelf. Tish had been unaware until this point just how much attention Andrew was receiving. Rather than egg him on any further, she realised that it was upsetting him.

Ian was getting more and more drunk but also more and more excited. He seemed to be convinced that tonight was the night that he and Rex would meet and it would be a joining of souls. No one had the courage to tell him that the chances were Rex was probably straight. Ian was on such a high that he was missing all the fuss with his flat mate.

About an hour later, Tony walked in and spotted Cheryl by the wall. He bounded over and gave his cousin a huge hug. "Good to see you babe. So how come you're down here tonight?"

Cheryl was turned away from me so I couldn't hear what she said to Tony but at one point she turned around and introduced her cousin to the rest of the gang.

"So listen, how's the job? Copped off with any captains yet!?" He sniggered.

Cheryl was still turned away so I missed her recount of the highlights of being a cabin crew member. She talked for quite a while and I was doing my best to read the expression on Tony's face. Unfortunately he was giving nothing away.

Tony broke off to head to the bar but promised Cheryl he'd be back after he'd had a quick word with a mate who was working behind the counter.

Ian nearly leaped down Cheryl's throat. "And??? What did he say? Did you put in a good word? When's he due down here?" He checked his watch and looked very flushed. I wasn't sure if it was the prospect of meeting Rex, the alcohol or the heat. It was probably a combination of all three.

"Whoa steady tiger." Cheryl looked alarmed. There seemed to be a hell of a lot riding on Rex's availability and interest in Ian. I could see the pressure mounting. "I haven't had a chance yet. He's just gone to the bar so I'll speak to him when he gets back." She looked him up and down and added, "What if he's not out tonight?"

Ian looked devastated. "What do you mean, not out tonight? Did Tony say something?"

I could almost hear Cheryl's brain moaning 'Oh shit, what the fuck have I started?' "No Ian," her temper was failing and she sounded almost cross. "I said I haven't spoken to Tony yet but you know, there's no guarantee he'll be here, or that he'll fancy you or that he is even gay"

She'd said it. She had planted the seed of doubt into Ian's head and left it to grow. Ian said nothing in response and just looked away. I instinctively knew that his mind was reeling. Andrew and Tish were oblivious to this ruckus and were talking quite intimately. I strained to hear their conversation above the din of the house music.

"I know but you have to let go Andrew. He's not worth it. How long are you going to wait for him?" Tish was obviously trying to talk Andrew out of giving up life to wait for Ian. It was clear that Ian thought of Andrew as a flat mate, gay buddy and that was it. I could sense no lust or true sense of love. Poor Andrew. He seemed such a loving, loyal person. In fact just the kind of partner Ian needed. A touch of security goes a long way.

"Oh Tish. I'm not sure I can give up on him. We've been living together for almost six years and at the beginning we had so much fun, you know?" He looked up at Tish making sure she was listening. "We had a bit of a thing going on and it was just perfect. Before you moved in, we had another poof living with us. He was a Brazilian guy, Marcus, but he was so aggressive that after about 6 months, we had to get rid of him. He attacked Ian in the kitchen once."

Tish stopped drinking and took Andrew's arm. "Shit, what happened? I heard he was violent."

"Yeah well I don't know why I never told you about this. I came home and walked into the kitchen. I found Ian against the fridge with his trousers round his ankles. He looked terrified. Marcus was behind him and had his arm round his throat. I just went nuts. I hit Marcus and I hit him hard. Poor Ian was in such a state. I think it was that moment that I fell in love with him."

"Jesus" Tish looked shocked. "What happened then?"

"Well luckily I got there just in time. I frogmarched a bleeding Marcus out of the house and threw his stuff out."

"No I mean, with Ian"

"Oh well I sat him down and just held him until he stopped shaking. He pretends that he is street-wise and knows how to handle himself but he is so soft and childlike really. It's all a mask. I think that incident made him realise just how vulnerable he was and he hated it. For ages after that, he wouldn't really go out and if he did, I had to be there, escorting him. " Andrew smiled at Tish. "I didn't mind. It was a pleasure to have him on my arm. I loved him. It was as simple as that. I wanted to protect him."

"Tish gave Andrew a big hug and lit up a couple of cigarettes and passed one over. "You are too nice for your own good, you know that?"

"You'd do the same. If you met the right one for you, you'd go to the ends of the earth for them, wouldn't you?"

"Yes Andrew I probably would. But listen, why does he not show you any respect? After you saved him and then helped him back into the real world, why does he run rings around you?"

"Well I think he resented my strength and the fact that I had seen him so helpless. He changed a lot after that. He became even more cocky. It was almost like he wanted to get himself into a dangerous position like that again. I don't know. I just don't understand him. I suppose that's why I find it even harder to walk away. He needs looking after."

Andrew downed his beer and Tish looked at him, obviously not having a clue how to help.

Ian suddenly rushed up and said, "Oh my God, He's here."

Tish rolled her eyes and led Andrew to the bar. "Come on let's avoid this embarrassing situation and get us some drinks."

Cheryl looked so relieved. The first hurdle had been crossed, now he just had to fancy Ian and she'd be the Queen Bee.

Tony made his way back and intercepted Rex on the way in. I had no idea what they were talking about. It could have been the band, contract issues or finite details about the party with a bang that Rex had missed a few nights before. Eventually Tony brought Rex over to meet his cousin.

"Hiya" Cheryl shook Rex's hand. "We have met before but it was at a party somewhere and I think we were both pissed."

Rex smiled but looked impatient to get to the bar. Cheryl noticed his eagerness to leave and quickly added "Oh erm, this is Ian. He's one of my colleagues at the airline."

Rex nodded at Ian and Ian almost swooned. He steadied himself and stuck out his hand. "Pleased to meet you. Can I get you a drink? I'm just off to the bar."

Rex looked delighted. There was a huge crowd at the bar and he would find it tedious waiting for service, so rather this queer little bloke than him. His thoughts were etched all over his face. Rex's order for a beer almost signified an acceptance into his bed as far as Ian was concerned and he literally floated to the bar.

Cheryl and her cousin chatted with Rex for a while but they were a little too far away for me to hear. The noise in the bar had increased. It wasn't just the music but the rowdiness had increased, probably caused by the consumption of alcohol.

I couldn't see Andrew and Tish but I presumed they were still queuing. I watched Rex to see if I could work out what was going on, by body language alone. It was difficult and I could see that Rex was anxious. He was continuing the discussion but his eyes flitted all over the room. It was quite apparent that he was looking for someone.

Ian came back with drinks and stood trying to join in the banter a little too enthusiastically for Rex's liking.

Tish and Andrew were still nowhere to be seen but I assumed that they were still queuing.

Ian was quite clearly getting on Rex's nerves and at one point he even leaned in and told him to calm down. I could see Ian becoming even more excited at this point and just knew it was all going to end in tears. Cheryl had also sensed the tension and was doing her best to disrupt any possible flare up. The only person who couldn't see Ian's excessive behaviour was Ian. This was going to be nasty.

Suddenly Rex smiled and moved towards the door. Katy! That was a good sign. They were still together. She looked good and her floral dress over jeans gave the effect of a curvaceous body. I admired her tenacious hold on looking good whilst her body wasted away. Although Rex was undoubtedly overjoyed at Katy's arrival, Ian was not. At first I could see he was trying to establish exactly who she was. After a moment though, it was quite clear. Rex was all over her. In fact it was so extreme that even Tony looked embarrassed. Cheryl looked horrified. Her plan had backfired in such a way, she was going to be completely ostracised now.

Ian however was keeping a straight face. His manner revealed no sign of the turmoil he must have been experiencing inside. His excitability had calmed down and he held his composure so well, I was amazed at his acting skills.

I could see Tish and Andrew making their way back, not from the counter but from the other side of the bar. A rather dashing young man accompanied Andrew. He had streaked blond hair, tanned face and an exquisite smile. I was temporarily mesmerised.

Andrew tapped Ian on the shoulder and said, "Guess who I have just seen?"

Ian tried to play along but I could tell he was finding this masking business rather tricky. "Don't know Andrew and I don't care."

Andrew ignored his friend's sulky attitude and carried on "Look! It's Graham!"

"Oh right," Ian barely looked up when Graham stepped in front of him and leaned forwards for a hug.

"Don't be such a sour puss!" Graham was trying to make light of an awkward moment but Ian wasn't really helping.

Rex moved away to a quieter part of the bar with Katy and I could see Ian peering over every now and again. Watching his idol stroking his girlfriend's hair must have been hard but to give him credit, he didn't turn on his heel and walk out. He didn't collapse in a corner and sob. He held his head up high and decided to get pissed.

Cheryl and Tony were chatting and laughing hysterically. She had obviously realised that she couldn't make the situation any better and had given up completely.

Tish had disappeared. Maybe she had found someone to chat up. Andrew and Graham was getting very friendly. Their body language was screaming 'LUST'. They were only just about keeping their hands off each other.

I watched the proceedings and enjoyed the pantomime unfolding. It was such a farce that I could have predicted each and every step to come.

Eventually Andrew and Graham decided to head home. I was forgotten, as usual. These days, people just don't care. They live a jettison lifestyle. Throwing things away is second nature. I was discarded and felt quite bitter about it.

Ian slumped against the wall and lit up a cigarette. His mask was slipping and he was thoroughly dejected. Tish came back with a ring of white powder round her left nostril. I was disappointed in her. Then again, I wasn't a single young woman with a demanding job and a couple of love lost flat mates, so who was I to criticise and judge?

"Where's Andrew gone?" She looked at Ian.

Ian shrugged and took a long drag on his cigarette. "Don't know. I think he might have left with that Graham." He looked totally disinterested.

"Good" Tish smiled. "Then hopefully he'll have a bloody good fuck and forget all about you." She stubbed her finger on his chest.

"What do you mean, forget about me?" Ian looked thoroughly confused.

"What do you think I mean, you tease?" Her words were jovial but the tone wasn't. She thought it was high time that this man knew the chaos he had caused.

"You are a prick tease Ian. You have known for years that Andrew was in love with you and you have wrapped him round your little finger. I'm really disgusted with you." The words matched the tone now and Ian's face looked quite troubled.

"Tish. What do you mean? Andrew's not in love with me. We're just good mates that's all." He didn't look convinced and neither was Tish.

"You bastard Ian. Well I hope he's getting laid right now and loving it." She picked up her drink and headed over to Cheryl and Tony.

Ian looked even more upset. I could see the cogs in his mind, slowly taking everything in and piecing it all together. Maybe deep down, unsubconsciously, he had known that Andrew had been waiting for him, had loved him from afar but then again, he hadn't really thought of Andrew as anything other than a mate.

Rather abruptly he collected his belonging, including me and ran out of the bar. I was pleased that this time I had been remembered although it was possibly only because he had remembered the half pack of cigarettes and I had been balanced on top of it.

It was freezing when we got outside. The sudden change in temperature didn't seem to faze Ian and he rushed up to the main road and hailed a taxi, which just happened to be speeding past.

He shouted the address at the driver and held on tightly to the door handle. I could tell he was desperate for a cigarette but there were 3 large no smoking signs up, so it was pretty clear that the driver was adverse to it.

It didn't take long and Ian stuffed some notes and coins into the driver's outstretched hand before racing up the garden path and knocking brutally on the door.

"Open up, I know you're there." Ian shouted through the letterbox. "Come on I'm freezing out here."

I couldn't hear anything and I was beginning to believe that Ian had reached home before them. The other possibility was that Andrew had gone to Graham's place. If that was the case, poor old Ian would be waiting a while. It was doubtful that Tish would have an early night. With the amount of drugs she had snorted up her nose, she would be partying for quite some time yet.

Realising his attempts to disturb the romantic duo, Ian slumped to the floor and rested against the front door. He lit up a cigarette and put his head in his hands. I could feel a 'woe is me' moment coming on. This guy was incredible. He was possibly the most shallow person I had ever met. I had yet to see any effort to think about anyone other than himself. I wondered how he was feeling right now. What was it that was making him so unhappy? Was it that Rex had turned out to be completely straight and not interested in him in the slightest? His fantasy meeting had come to reality and then humiliated him publicly. Or was it the fact that Andrew was supposed to be the fool trailing after him but now he was off having fun with Graham?

I could only hope that this would prove to be a turning point for Ian, that his awareness for other people's feelings would grow and that he would consider his actions before proceeding. It was a tall order and not likely to happen overnight, if ever but I could wish.

We sat for quite a while, getting colder and colder. In hindsight it might have been quicker and easier to go back to the bar and borrow Tish's keys. Eventually after we were both freezing and aching, two figures appeared at the front gate.

Ian jumped to his feet and threw his arms around the taller of the two. "Thank fuck you're back. I was beginning to think hypothermia had set in." He then thumbed the figure and added, "And why didn't you tell me you were leaving?"

Andrew stepped into the light and I could see the smile slowly vanish. "Ian. What on earth are you doing on the front step? Where are your keys?"

Ian shrugged and looked close to tears. Graham looked uncomfortable and shifted from leg to leg. "I forgot." His voice was so small, like a child. "Where have you been? I've been sitting here for ages."

"Sorry!" Andrew sounded a little harsh. Was he finally fed up with Ian and his whining? "I didn't know I had to report back." It was a sharp comment and both Ian and Graham looked startled. This wasn't the Andrew they knew and loved.

"Well it would have been nice for you to tell me you were going off, especially with him." Ian had decided to take the bitchy road and poor Graham was plunged right in the middle of the argument.

"Why do I have to tell you anything? The last thing I knew, you were drooling over Rex. Would you have come to find me to tell me you had pulled? No Ian. You would have gone off and I would have been the one left worrying. Anyway where is Rex?"

"None of your business." Ian spat the words out. His humiliation was complete now. Not only would Andrew be mocking him but Graham could take the opportunity too. How had the evening gone so wrong? It had all started so promisingly.

Andrew rolled his eyes, pushed past his pathetic little friend and stuck the door key in the hole. "For God's sake let's just get inside shall we? Graham you must be freezing."

"Why are you worried about him? It's been me sitting here waiting for hours in the cold." I had hoped that Ian would become a more caring person but my hopes were diminishing abruptly.

Once inside the house, Andrew sent Graham upstairs to have a hot soak in the bath with a promise that he would join him soon. I could barely watch the thunderous look on Ian's face.

"You bastard! Why are you sleeping with him when it is me you love?"

"Oh! So you are aware of my feeling then? You have known that I existed and that I loved you?" Andrew looked really angry and if Ian's expression was anything to go by, this was unheard of.

"Well yes, no. I mean no. I didn't really think about you that way. Tish. She and I had a little argument."

"Oh you're doing well tonight then aren't you?" Andrew folded his arms. I had a feeling this was more to keep a check on them than express closed body language.

"I know. I know. She told me that you had been in love with me all this time. Andrew. I didn't think." His voice had grown softer and he was trying to move closer.

"No. You never do, do you?" Aware that Ian was moving towards him, Andrew backed off a little, hoping that this would make Ian realise he didn't want to be touched.

"I just meant that I thought of you as my best friend. I didn't know you had stronger feelings for me and I am really sorry that I upset you in anyway."

"My God. What's come over you? Not Rex, that's for sure!" Attempting humour at this point was a dangerous tactic. Ian could easily have flipped, presuming his apology and effort to be considerate was being taken as a joke. Luckily Ian saw the funny side and laughed.

"Oh Andrew. What a night? That Rex. Well it's over before it started. He's straight and to make things worse even if he was gay, I don't think I'd have been his type." From Andrew's expression, it was unusual for Ian to be so open and frank.

"Hey come on. There are loads prawns in the paella. You'll be fine. Just put it all down to a crap night and in the morning, it'll be forgotten." He stood up and made his way towards the stairs.

"Where are you going?"

"Well I can't very well leave poor old Graham on his own, can I?" Thinking it was safe to leave, Andrew climbed the steps.

"Has nothing I have just said to you, sunk in?" He bellowed the words and both Andrew and I nearly jumped out of our skins.

"Well what are you saying to me Ian? That Rex does girls, not boys and so because you are cheesed off about that, you want me to kick out that gorgeous hunk of manhood upstairs and take you to bed instead? Is that it?" Andrew's cheeks had turned a very deep red and his neck showed signs of a stress rash too.

I was very interested to see how Ian could retaliate. I mean everything Andrew said was true. "Leave me alone," was all he could manage. He was defeated and I was disappointed in him. I thought he had more balls than that.

Andrew shook his head slowly and carried on up the stairs. He had a beautiful man waiting for him and he wasn't going to waste it.

Ian kicked off his boots and curled up on the sofa. He started crying but I felt no sympathy for the man. His utter selfishness and blinkered vision had caused this upset, nothing else.

The sobs died down and after a while I realised he was asleep. At this point I realised how tired I was too and I drifted off. My mind was racing with all the new things I had seen and heard. Hopefully more dreams weren't on the way.

CHAPTER 22

A slam of the front door stirred me from my deep sleep. It took a while for me to adjust. I saw Tish stomp into the lounge and tut at the still sleeping Ian. Tish looked worse for wear and when she reached for a cigarette, I could see her fingers were a deep yellow from the nicotine stains. She stank of booze, smoke and something else, which I couldn't quite put my finger on.

I couldn't see a clock but I guessed it was nearly lunchtime. Tish tottered into the kitchen and started banging about. I just couldn't imagine her as cabin crew. She was possible the most ungainly woman I had ever met. She wanted food. That much was clear to everyone in the house. Ian stirred and groaned. Clasping his head he staggered in the kitchen and I could hear some abusive bantering although from my place on the lamp table, I couldn't make out the words.

Andrew tore down the stairs wrapped in a flimsy towelling gown and joined them in the kitchen. I could hear the kettle boiling and the toaster pinging and all three of them fighting for the last dregs of orange juice.

Graham crept down the stairs. He was more sedately dressed in his white shirt from the night before and a crisp pair of pants. If I wasn't mistaken, those were clean on. Had he know he was going to pull? Full marks for organisation but a little too cocky for my liking. Rather than join the brawl, he nipped back up the stairs for the remainder of his clothes and tiptoed out of the front door. He pulled it to, behind him and no one was the wiser. I thought he came across as a coward but I had been far too judgemental over the last few days so decided to wait and see what transpired.

The eating and chatting in the kitchen went on and on and I wasn't really sure if this was playful or serious. Considering some people had very little sleep and some made free use of as many drugs as they could lay their hands on, and some were suffering from morbid embarrassment, I was surprised that the three of them were so loud.

Eventually the three of them moved back out into the lounge and I could finally hear their discussion.

"If you want but I need to get a couple of hours kip beforehand. Wake me up about five and I'll think about it." Andrew sounded quite jolly. Last night must have been quite successful, although his beam would be on the other side of his face once he realised his love had upped and left the building.

"Me too but I'm not sure two hours is going to be enough. Wake me when you go and I'll see what I feel like. I'm on standby tomorrow but I just know I'll get called." Tish looked awful. From where she was standing, I could get a real eyeful. Her makeup had slid down her face and her pale skin reflected how tired she felt. The girl needed a hell of a lot more than a couple of hours. She needed a couple of days to get rid of those eyebags and a full on detox.

"Please yourself but premiere tickets do not grow on trees and I just know that once I broadcast them, I'll be inundated." I wasn't sure if Ian was purposefully in denial about last night or whether they had already discussed this matter and agreed to forget it and move on. It sounded odd to me but I hardly knew these people.

A minute after Andrew bounded up the stairs, I heard a shout and feet clambering across the landing. Andrew rushed down the stairs and frantically looked all over the small downstairs area. It was pointless really, as one look from the bottom of the stairs would have told Andrew that Graham had done a runner, without so much as a by-your-leave.

Poor Andrew. He looked wounded. I could have cried. His happy-go-lucky attitude had vanished completely and he looked on the edge of despair.

"Why?" he asked out loud when Tish came running down.

"Has he gone?" she said, a little naively.

Andrew couldn't answer but nodded slowly. Ian walked slowly down the steps and although his expression was deep empathy for his friend, I just knew that under that thin veneer of sadness was a face of joy, delighting that he had his shadow returned to him.

"What a fucking bastard," Tish said as she looked at Ian.

"Don't look at me. I could have told him that last night." Andrew stomped up the stairs and we all heard his bedroom door slam.

"He's a bit touchy," Ian was being a real pain.

"I'm not surprised. That Graham has left without saying goodbye. Not only is that very rude but downright selfish." Tish was on a roll. "Jesus, you gay blokes are all the same. Where's the loyalty and sense of commitment. You all go around humping like a pack of wild dogs and wonder why the more sensitive ones get upset."

"If you put it like that." Ian actually looked embarrassed.

"Yes! I do put it like that. Now how about you go upstairs and comfort your friend." Tish looked like she wasn't going to take no for an answer so Ian sheepishly walked up the stairs and knocked on Andrew's door.

I couldn't hear how Andrew responded but the door was opened and shut again. I presumed he had let him in, as there was silence.

Tish reached across and lit up a cigarette. She still looked like she needed a good rest but I thought that now she lost her temper, adrenaline would still be whizzing through her body and sleep would be unlikely. She slid onto the sofa and picked up the remote control. She flicked through the channels and became entranced by a re-run of 'Porridge'. She chained smoked about three more cigarettes and just before the end of the programme, we both heard noises from upstairs.

Tish was just as curious as I was and she pressed the mute button to enable us to hear exactly what was going on. By the sounds of it, they were still in Andrew's room and Ian's voice echoed through the house. They were laughing! Tish looked relieved and turned the volume up and continued watching Ronnie Barker.

I tried to tune in but I was worried about Andrew. He was such a sweet man. He didn't deserve to be treated the way he was. I just hoped that Ian was cheering him up and not laughing at him.

Tish and I wasted a few hours watching old British comedy shows and I was just beginning to drift off when I heard the two boys coming down the stairs. They had dolled themselves up and prodded Tish who was snoring on the sofa.

"Come on sleeping beauty. You coming to the premiere or what?"

"What!" She sounded half asleep and really not in the right frame of mind to be tarting herself up to watch a new film.

"Suit yourself then. I might drop your ticket in to Simon's. He'll appreciate it.." Ian's bitchy attitude had returned but this time Andrew looked on, lovingly.

"Looks like you two have sorted out your differences then." Tish was waking up and her observant skills were returning.

"Oh yes. You could say that!" Ian joked as Andrew watched him dewy-eyed.

Tish turned over on the sofa and pulled the cushion over her head. She was exhausted and I sensed a flicker of annoyance that she had been disturbed. "Go on then, if you're going. I need to sleep. I'm on standby tomorrow, I told you."

Ian pulled a face and Andrew laughed. "Come on sexy" he said as he pulled Andrew to his feet. "Let's go meet some stars."

I could hear the boys giggling as they left the house and then….silence. Tish resumed her position on the settee and we both promptly fell asleep.

I vaguely heard the front door bang but I was so weary I thought nothing of it. As I drifted back to sleep, I was aware that the boys had returned home and the smell of alcohol was overpowering. They tiptoed past us and up the stairs. I only heard one door slam and realised just as I passed out, that they were now a couple.

CHAPTER 23

I woke up as I was being thrown into Tish's bag. I was nestling between a rather filthy looking makeup bag and a bunch of keys. We raced out of the door and into the car parked outside. I couldn't see Tish fully but she looked good in her uniform. Gone was the grungy look and here in front of me with a woman looking very slick.

The car was a mess and I hated to think when it had last been cleaned but it started, so that was the main thing. The journey to work was tedious. The traffic was atrocious and the language spilling from Tish's mouth was even worse. The steady rain wasn't helping anyone's mood and I wondered what would happen if Tish did get called to fly. Would I be travelling too? Where would I end up? I felt excited but also very nervous.

After what seemed like an age, Tish parked in the staff carpark and we went straight to the crew offices. I couldn't really see much and everything was slightly muffled but after clocking in, we sat in a small common room surrounded by other similarly dressed young people. A handsome young man approached Tish and said "Hello gorgeous. Did you hear about Gav?"

They both grabbed a coffee and sat at a tall table with stools. "No? Why? What happened?"

"He's been suspended. I can't believe it. He had been out clubbing and was still pissed when he came on duty. I think he'd forgotten he was flying. Well old Saunders came down on him really badly. I know he has been looking for a way to get rid of him." The good looking man paused and sipped his hot latte.

"That bastard. He wants to sack everyone he can't screw." Tish may have looked prim and proper in her attire but she made no bones with opinions.

"Too right. Anyway he's called the union in. Not really sure how they can help but it's his last hope so he's got to give it a go. Poor Gav. I feel so sorry for him."

"Yeah" Tish screwed up her face. "But he's always pissed. Everyone knows about his drink problem. It was going to happen sooner or later."

"Oh come on. Who bloody hasn't got a drink problem in this place? At least he's not a smackhead." The man looked slightly put out.

"Ok fair enough." I was impressed that Tish backed down. "So what did you get up to last night then? You look a bit worse for wear!" She didn't mince her words but I actually respected her for that.

The man blushed and in a softer voice said. "Oh I met this gorgeous man last night and I only got about an hours sleep!"

"Pete. You are so bad. What about poor Jon? He doesn't deserve you."

"Why thank you!" Pete beamed at Tish.

"No. I don't mean that in a nice way. You are so mean to that man and he adores you. I'd never treat anyone the way you treat Jon."

I could see Tish's point. Apart from the little amount of time I spent with James, the only homosexuals I had only really met were Ian, Andrew and Graham and they were all as promiscuous as each other. It all sounded very confusing, tiring but above all heart-breaking.

"Jon is away at the moment so Lord only know what he's been up to." Pete swigged the remains of his latte and said "Oh shit. I've got to go. Laters." He blew her a kiss and sprinted across the room to a small door leading into the terminal building.

Tish rolled her eyes and carried on sipping her coffee. She grabbed a paper from the table next to her and began scrolling through all the main news. I couldn't see the name but I recognised it was a tabloid. I had no idea what the headlines were but it was probably all nonsense. My life was far more interesting that any magazine or newspaper.

It was a non smoking room so I sat in Tish's bag for ages and dozed until I heard her chatting to a blonde girl. She had a slight Liverpudlian accent and chatted non-stop. I could tell by Tish's sighs that she was fed up listening to this girl droning on. I was feeling a bit like that too. This girl hardly paused for breath.

Eventually Tish excused herself and moved outside for a crafty cigarette. I took in my surroundings, which to be honest were quite dull. The rain had stopped but it was overcast and cold. Tish wasn't wearing a coat but she had pulled a thick green scarf round her neck. We stood for a while. She puffed away and I began to plane spot. I tried to guess the carrier by the design on the tail fin. I was no expert and before my trip to the airport with Mick and Ryan, I had never had first hand experience of planes, not that I have boarded one, even now and because of this I wasn't doing too well.

A brunette girl trotted round the corner and waved to Tish. Tish waved back and walked up to her. "My God Claire, I haven't seen you in ages. Our rosters must have been totally out of sync for about 6 months. How are you?"

They kissed each other's cheeks and I suddenly recognised Geoff and Pam's daughter! Blimey, this really was a small world. I had no idea she was even working, let alone as cabin crew.

"Tish!" Claire lit up a cigarette and blew smoke up into the air before standing close to Tish for warmth. "Fuck me, it's cold! Anyway yeah I'm good, how are you?"

"Yeah. Not bad. You flying today?"

"No, I'm on standby. You?"

"Me too. So come on, what's the goss? Have you heard about Gav?"

Claire nodded and then shook her head. "Bound to happen sooner or later, the guy's a nutter!"

Tish nodded in agreement. "That's exactly what I said to Pete but he got all arsey."

They both laughed at what she had said. "Tish, can I ponce another fag? I need to pick up some duty free. I so am low on supplies."

Tish offered up her packet and Claire took one and lit up. "So hows the love life? You seeing anyone or are you living a delicious life of freedom?"

"Yeah I wish!" Tish nearly choked on her smoke. "The nearest thing I get to sex these days is listening to those poofs I live with!"

"You still there? I would have thought they would have driven you mad. Andrew's lovely but that Ian gets on my tits!"

"Yeah I'm still there but only because I just can't be arsed to move out. Where are you now? Still at home?" Tish lit another cigarette and threw her empty packet on the floor. I tutted to myself. I hated litter louts. What a selfish way to live. To think that other people would automatically pick up the rubbish left behind. My opinion of Tish had diminished and I looked at her ashamedly. I always promised myself that I would never utter the immortal words 'the youth of today' in a derogative manner but I only just bit my lip on this occasion, I was so cross.

"I'm still at the pub with mum and dad. Mum's cool but Dad's just so over protective. Even if I am on overnights, he expects me to call. It's ridiculous. Anyone would think I was 9 not 19!" Claire was ranting but I understood her point. She was an adult, responsible for her actions, holding down a job but I guess staying at home was not always the easy option.

"Hey maybe we should get a flat together?" Tish suggested. "It's gotta be better than living with those two!"

"Thanks!" Claire looked slightly offended.

"No. I meant that as a joke! Seriously though, if you've had enough of your folks, then maybe we should think about it."

"Yeah ok. I'll work out my budget and see what I can afford. Not much from the pittance they pay us here though!"

"I know. Still it beats working in an office and at least we get to top up our tan every now and again! Talking of which, you're looking mighty good. Where have you been?"

I suddenly wondered if Tish was a lesbian. I had never met one before and so had no real idea of what to expect. I was sure that the stereotypical shaved head and piercings with heavy boots was quite rare. Tish was an attractive girl. A little on the plain side but when she was scrubbed up, she looked almost beautiful. I had been disappointed in her clubbing attire though and wondered why she had chosen to dress down on a night out.

I suppose the notion of Tish fancying woman came into my head because I felt the chemistry in the air when the two girls were talking. Funny thing, chemistry. Supposedly whether of not humans fancy each other all boils down to smell! I wasn't sure if Claire was aware and from what I had seen in the pub all that time ago, she had seemed rather keen on the boys, rather than females but then I have been wrong on many occasions. Tish gave me the impression though that she was rather taken with young Claire. I just hoped that we weren't going to have a repeat of the Ian and Rex situation.

The girls stubbed out their last cigarettes and waited inside for a call. It was a lot warmer and as I was placed back in Tish's bag, I could see and hear a lot less. I could only make out one word in three and I got bored trying to piece together the conversation. They were giggling a lot and I wondered if Tish was flirting.

A couple of hours went by and then I was dragged out of the bag and into the cold air. This time I was with Claire on my own. She had borrowed Tish's green scarf and I noticed her sniffing it several times. It had started raining again. Not heavily like earlier but a steady drizzle.

She had her phone glued to her ear and was listening intently to a voice at the other end whilst she inhaled the smoke.

"But I didn't do it on purpose." She sounded almost close to tears. "You have to believe me. I didn't plan it." I was very intrigued. What on earth was she referring to?

"I promise I will think about it but tell me you believe me." There was a short pause and then she said, "Because I need to hear that you believe me"

After another short pause, she cut the caller off and ground the cigarette butt out with such venom that I was beginning to worry.

Claire walked back into the restroom but Tish was nowhere to be seen. Perhaps her call had come through and she was now making her way to the aircraft for a debriefing session.

Claire sat back down at the table and held her head in her hands. She looked frazzled. Earlier she had looked radiant but that vibrancy had disappeared now. It was incredible the effect that stress could have on the human body. She picked up her mobile again and began franticly typing out texts. By the sounds of it there were several messages going through and the sent signal kept beeping every few minutes.

The room had emptied slightly. There were a couple of guys in one corner whispering and laughing. Another older lady was on her own and flicking through a wedding magazine. I could make out the white gowns but couldn't see the name. There was some traffic through the room but other than that, it was fairly quiet.

I was very curious to know what was going on with Claire. Her demeanour this morning showed no indication of impending doom and so I could only think that the phone call had been her first knowledge of this terrible situation. Or maybe it was just a reality wake-up call and something she didn't want to acknowledge was being thrust in front of her. Why she was so insistent that the caller believer she was innocent, I couldn't imagine.

It was as though all of a sudden, Claire made a decision. She picked up her belongings and trotted up to a blue door with a name badge affirming that 'Ms Eliza Gerrard' resided in this office. Claire knocked swiftly and entered barely waiting for the response.

Ms Gerrard was on the telephone and looked up inquisitively at her visitor. She motioned for Claire to sit and then ended her call. She swung around on her chair and clasped her expensively manicured hands together.

"So Claire. What can I do for you?" There was definitely a slight twang but I needed to hear more to identify its origin.

"Sorry Ms Gerrard. I am on standby today but I have just received some bad new, erm of a personal nature and I just wondered if I could be taken off the standby roster for today please?"

Eliza's facial expression had not altered and I could tell outright sympathy was not her style yet I could feel the rippling waves of curiosity under her cool exterior. This was a lady that could not be brow beaten, would not break under any form of interrogation and believed that weak women let the female gender down. She was terrifying.

"Well let's see Claire. How many days have you taken off in the last 12 months, other than leave?" She spoke slowly and it seemed to intensify each word. I still couldn't really make out the nationality of her inflection.

"Oh erm. I have only been with the company for just over 8 months but in that time I had a week off to visit my cousin in Tenerife. She's a holiday rep!" Claire's excess information was not really helping her request and I hoped she would realise that Eliza only wanted a concise reply.

"Anyway I had a weekend in Bruges and I have booked two week in Jamaica for next February. Apart from that though…..no I haven't had any sick leave."

Eliza raised her eyebrows in a positive manner. "That's good to hear Claire. What sort of personal problem is it? Is there anything either I or the company can do to assist?" Her tactic to empathise and draw out information was clever but it wasn't going to work. I could tell Claire had something serious on her mind and she wasn't about to tell her boss.

"Erm well no it is sort of personal but apart from today, it really shouldn't affect my work schedule again." Claire was getting the hang of this now. She understood that she mustn't give this woman any ammunition and short specific answers were the only thing that would work.

"Right ok. Let's see." Ms Gerrard peered at her computer screen and began tapping away at a keyboard. "The roster says that we have 3 on standby today. You, Letisha Henry and Briony McLoughlin."

"Yes I have seen Tish but she has already been called onto the Athens flights. I don't know where Bri is though." Claire sounded like she felt she was losing her battle and instead of holding her confidence, she was justifying and explaining. A bad move.

"Well, I think on this occasion Claire, we can grant permission to leave, however I will need this conversation to be held on file that I offered you assistance and you refused and stated, I quote "apart from today, it really shouldn't affect my work schedule again.""

Claire looked worried. I had an inkling that the predicament she was in, possibly wouldn't be able to be sorted by tomorrow.

"Erm yes Ms Gerrard. That's right. Does that mean I can go now?" Claire looked desperate.

Eliza nodded and held up an open palm, as if to signify her ability to leave at her will. I thought perhaps the accent was a mix of Southern Irish and South African. The soft lilt combined the two subtle dialects maybe of Cork and East London on the Garden Route. An unusual combination but the fact that this lady had spent a long time in the UK, the definitive source was only a guess. I had learned so much from the documentaries I had watched with Whin. I do remember a series of programmes about South Africa. It was mainly about the apartheid years but it also highlighted the changes since that had been abolished. It was a very moving history.

Claire literally flew out of the room. She clocked out and raced out to the staff car park. Her black ford KA was packed the opposite end of the car park. I presumed that was possibly due to her being one of the last in.

Throwing all her stuff onto the back seat, Claire grabbed her mobile and dialled a number. I could see her pacing around the car but unfortunately I couldn't hear a thing. She spoke for quite a while and I could see her becoming more and more anxious and upset. She jumped into the driver's seat and flung the car into gear. She lurched out onto a main road, totally oblivious to oncoming traffic. She had forgotten to fasten her seatbelt and I just prayed that her erratic driving wouldn't end in disaster.

We drove for about an hour. I was beginning to tire. There is only so long that adrenaline can keep racing. We then started approaching an area that was becoming increasingly familiar. My heart leapt for joy. I wanted to scream. I was following the road back down to the Cock Inn. I just could not believe it. What were the chances of that? I had hoped, from the second I recognised Claire, that somehow she would perform a miracle and take me back to Whin's old haunt but I scarcely believed it could happen. I was so delighted that I hardly remembered parking and running into the pub.

Geoff was serving two builders and he was laughing about something as he handed over two pints of lager. I just couldn't believe my luck. It almost felt like home. My odd journey had not really taught me anything about Whin but my God, I had learned some facts about life and some of the people that had strange connections to my dear departed friend.

Claire ran into the bar and as soon as Geoff saw her, he broke off and made his way towards us. His face looked like thunder. "What on earth….." He started but before he could finish, Pam darted out and dragged the poor girl upstairs.

"I am so disappointed in you." Pam was almost in tears. We were standing in the lounge area of the private rooms upstairs and Pam was holding on to Claire's shoulders.

I was becoming alarmed. What could have possibly happened? I could see Claire's face. Just by being at home and facing their wrath almost relieved her stress. As if the guilty secret had been removed from her shoulders and she could breathe again.

"Mum. I am so sorry. I really didn't mean it to happen. I just don't know what to say." She burst into tears and the two women ended up hugging each other tightly. It was such a touching moment but I couldn't really understand what the root of the problem was.

The embrace lasted a good ten minutes and by the time they separated, Claire had stopped crying and was dabbing her eyes with a mangy piece of old tissue. She looked a state and her mascara had run down her cheeks. Strangely, her eyebrows had turned red and swollen. Overall her appearance was quite grotesque but as she sat with her mum on the sofa, he face calmed down and the constant dabbing of the tissue removed the worst of the make-up stains.

"So?" Pam volunteered to tackle the problem head on.

Claire just shrugged.

"Well you have to make a decision. What do you want to do about it?" Pam had calmed down now and had put her practical hat firmly on her head.

Whatever the dilemma was, Claire looked like she was less accepting of it and denial seemed to be her idea of a solution. Claire just stared at the rather hideous carpet. Admittedly it was vile enough to stun you into silence but Claire should have been used to it, considering this was her family home.

"I don't know mum. I just don't know." She began crying again and her eyebrows turned red and swelled up again. I was mesmerised by this. I had never seen this effect before. The tears had re-dampened the mascara and black streaks were forming on her blotchy cheeks. Some women look beautiful when they cry. Some look frail and men have an urge to protect and comfort them but in Claire's case, I think it was only the true love of a mother that was preventing Pam from running from the room.

I heard footsteps up the stairs. I could only presume that Geoff's curiosity had got the better of him. The minute I saw his face, I knew that the quiet chat between mother and daughter was over. Geoff looked furious. His face was almost crimson and I suddenly worried that a heart attack might be on the cards. I wasn't sure what he was going to do but the look on his face gave me the impression that Claire was about to take the full brunt of it.

Before Geoff had a chance to speak, Claire stood up and whispered. "Daddy. I'm so sorry." It did the trick and his anger subsided in seconds and by the time he walked over to his little girl, he normal pallor had returned and his arms outstretched ready to hold his baby tightly.

His kissed her on the forehead and rocked her to and fro. I could still hear Claire muffled voice, apologising.

Pam had become tearful at Geoff's visual display at emotion and it looked like the whole crying game was going to start up again.

"Listen sweetheart, whatever decision you make, we will be here right beside you." His normally gruff voice had softened considerably and I could almost hear the pain in his voice.

"Look I just don't know. I only found out last night and when I told Darren, I'm not sure that he is that happy." My mind was reeling? Surely she wasn't referring to Verity's son? Was the world really that small? "Well I didn't exactly tell him, I posted a note through his letterbox on the way to work and I just received a call before I left the airport." She stopped talking at this point and Geoff and Pam looked at each other, clearly neither of them knowing what to say.

"I have the feeling that he won't be sticking around." More tears formed in her eyes and gently fell down her face. I sensed the anguish of making such an important decision alone along with the pain of Darren's betrayal.

I had guessed before Geoff entered the room that the poor child was pregnant and although not too young to cope, would still struggle financially and emotionally, especially as a single mother. I couldn't imagine the pain of having to make such a difficult choice. Presumably this morning, her radiance had emanated from hope that Darren would leap for joy at the news and would promise to look after her. The second she received his phone call, her realisation that he was furious about it suddenly made a good situation, bad.

Geoff kissed Claire's head again and left the room, advising the girls that he had to get back to the bar. Pam nodded and sat next to her daughter. She put her arm around her and kept on repeating "It'll be fine."

Eventually Pam stood up. "Come on poppet, let me run you a hot bath and you can relax whilst I make you some lunch." She took Claire's hand and led her out of the room.

I sat pondering on the scene I had just witnessed. It was quite frightening really. I mean the precarious balance of the human race. There was quite possibly the next Prime Minister inside Claire but due to Darren's upset at the news, that new person would perhaps not even get the chance to exist.

I believe termination is for the female to decide. A man should have his views heard but ultimately the final choice has to be made by the woman. Her body is host for nine months. She is the one that has to experience excruciating pain upon delivery and for her the umbilical cord is never really cut. Sometimes, in certain circumstances, the best way forward is to allow the foetus to be removed but I was quite sure that no decision like that could ever be taken lightly.

I really wasn't sure how this state of affairs would materialise but I hoped that Darren would have a change of heart and at least offer support to this poor confused woman.

A while later, Pam came back into the lounge and threw herself onto the couch. She looked shattered. Not knowing how to comfort her daughter and unable to make the decision herself, she knew all she could do was be there for Claire and pick up the pieces. She spotted a packet of cigarettes in Claire's handbag and pulled them out. I hadn't taken Pam for a smoker but as I have said before, stress and unusual positions can turn the most devout to alcohol, drugs and cigarettes. She rummaged around for a lighter and pulled me out. A brief flicker of recognition ran through her eyes and my swift leap of joy was immediately quashed as she lit up and threw me back into the bag.

So Pam wasn't going to rescue me and pass me back to Dan. I felt so depressed. My utter delight at returning to my spiritual home had been short lived. Not only was I was so close but I felt so hurt that I wasn't recognised fully. I was nothing to these people yet I had known them for years. All I could imagine now was that I would be taken away and this would be my only trip back. I was so upset that at that point I didn't care.

I ignored all noises from the flat and concentrated on my own pain. Whin's face came into my mind and I took the opportunity of thinking back to our first day…

• •

FLASHBACK

• •

"Yes Tom, you are quite right. There is more. A lot more." He shoved a large forkful of food into his mouth and continued, "You sure you want to hear?"

"Yes Whin. Of course I want to hear it. Trust me you'll feel so much better when you get it all off your chest."

Whin smiled. "I doubt it Tom but thanks for your support. Well erm I'm not really sure where I got to last night?"

"Arh yes well the last bit I remember was about you having lunch and seeing some old aunt or someone. Is that right?"

Whin nodded. "Yes yes. I was out with a mate having a drink. I would like to point out that it wasn't even a beer. I think it was coffee or something but the point is I had done so well that when I heard what she said, it cut through me like a knife. I hadn't even consumed a single pint to soften the blow."

"Go on Whin." Tom looked quite eager now to get to the crunch. The tale had been brewing for so long now that he just wanted to hear the end.

"Well as I said, I was only eavesdropping and at this stage I had no idea of what I was about to hear."

"Yes yes Whin. What did you hear?" Tom's impatience was infectious and I was desperate to know too.

"Well the old lady was talking about Mel. It took me a while but it was pretty obvious. She said that she was over the moon. It wasn't every day such a wonderfully exciting event took place." Whin looked up at Tom and with moist eyes he added. "She said that Mel had just given birth to a baby girl."

Well I'm not sure about Tom but I hadn't been expecting that. Tom looked equally shocked and couldn't even find words to express his surprise.

Whin cast his eyes down and carried on. "Yes well you can imagine how I felt can't you? I had reached this ripe old age without parenting any children and then I find out that the love of my life has not only given birth to my daughter but neglected to tell me about it. Tom, I was gutted."

Tom still looked stunned and he knew he had to somehow comfort his friend but just didn't have the first idea what to say. He grabbed his arm. I think Whin knew what he was trying to say and a sad smile crept over his lips.

"Hey big guy, it's ok. You know as soon as I stopped shaking, I made a beeline for Mel's place. It seemed wrong to just turn up unannounced but I was so desperate to see for myself. Had the old bat in the bat got it wrong? Had I overheard a conversation about someone else entirely? I had to know Tom and by not warning her of my arrival, I thought that the shock would prevent further deceit."

Tom tapped Whin's arm, urging him to go on. "My legs were like jelly Tom. I could hardly walk. I felt sick. I couldn't breathe. I felt as thought my heart would fail but I carried on and I knocked on that door loudly. I saw a flicker of a net curtain upstairs but I couldn't be seen under the porch. I had parked the car a little way down the road purposely so that my presence wouldn't be given away until the door opened."

"Mel didn't come to the door. I guessed it was her mother or an aunt, although she wasn't the same one who had spilt the beans in the bar. She must have met me at Al's funeral but maybe I looked different. She smiled at me and invited me inside. Tom I swear my beating heart was like thunder. I was sure the lady could hear it. If she did she didn't say anything."

Tom finally found his voice, "Whin, my God. I can only imagine how you must have felt. I just never knew." It was a start. It wasn't a speech to be proud of but Whin understood. He looked at Tom and carried on.

"The lady called up the stairs and told Mel she had a visitor. Mel bounded down the stairs but the second she saw me, she stopped. She asked her aunt to check on the baby and she took hold of my arm and dragged me into the dining room."

"What on earth are you doing here?" She was so angry.

"She spat at me Tom! I mean here I was the victim in all this mess and she is annoyed with me? Tom I swear till my dying day, I'll never understand women."

"I don't think we are supposed to mate. Maybe that's the whole point. So what happened then? Did you get to see your child?" I could tell Tom was bursting with intrigue.

"Hang on, hang on. I'll get to that bit. Anyway Mel started having a go at me and shouting at me to leave and not to come back. I just asked her straight out, you know if the child was mine. Do you know what Tom? She couldn't even look me in the eye." Whin paused to let the waitress remove the empty plates. She took orders for coffee and left them alone.

"And?" Tom's eyes were huge and it was as though he was holding his breath until the truth came out.

"She didn't say anything Tom. She just nodded. I mean what kind of a person does that? Anyway I was calm, really calm. I just asked some questions about her, you know like how old she was, what her name was, basic stuff that a father should know. She had calmed down by that point and just gave the answers I needed to hear. Until that is, I started asking to see her. Can you believe it, she was going to start fighting?"

"You're joking?" Tom looked almost as angry as Whin.

"No! I'm not! She said that she didn't see why I had to get involved! I ask you. Of course I replied that I wanted to get involved. She was my flesh and blood and I wanted to meet her."

"Blimey Whin. What a nightmare."

"You're not wrong Tom. I remained composed but even thinking about it makes my blood boil. Anyway after a few minutes it was obvious we weren't getting anywhere. I stood up and told her that I would contact my solicitor. The second I mentioned getting legal representation, her attitude changed completely. She started crying, trying to soften me up and then just pretended that her hormones were still all up in the air. I didn't believe a word of it Tom. Still it worked and she went upstairs and brought down the most beautiful baby you have ever seen. I was worried about picking her up in case my clothes or hands weren't clean enough but my heart nearly exploded Tom. I was so happy that I cried."

I looked at Tom and could see that tears were welling up in his eyes. What a softie! Mind you I was feeling quite emotional myself. Whin's eyes twinkled as he described how she smelled, how her gorgeous black eyelashes looked so perfect against her soft white skin. He explained how she fell asleep in his arms because she knew he was her daddy. The two men almost fell to pieces, I'd never seen such sentiment from men.

"By the time I left Tom, I was hooked. I had weaned myself off the Mel drug, only to be completely addicted to the Cerys drug."

"Cerys?" Tom looked confused.

"Yes. Cerys. That's what Mel had named her. It wasn't a name I had particularly liked before. Actually I'm not even sure I had heard it before but now I think it's the most beautiful name I have ever heard.

"So listen, what happened after that then? Did Mel let you see her again?" Tom looked quite worried.

"Oh Tom. What happened after that was something I didn't expect. In fact I still don't think I can believe it."

• •

FLASHBACK

• •

CHAPTER 24

I came to as Claire shuffled into the lounge in an enormous towelling dressing gown. I could only think it belonged to Geoff but I could see that it was offering the kind of security that Claire needed right now. She curled up on the sofa next to her mum and laid her head on Pam's shoulder. It was a lovely sight. No words were spoken. No words were needed. Both women were lost in a confused world of their own and needed time to work things through.

Geoff popped his head up a couple of hours later and he had obviously decided not to get involved in the decision-making. His attitude was that it would be better to carry on as normal and see what panned out. I liked his head in the sand approach and thought that as a father in his position, it possibly wasn't a bad choice.

Geoff whittered on about some funny story an old boy in the pub had told him. When he repeated it, neither of the girls laughed. Pam pulled a funny face and Claire smiled politely, not wishing to upset her father twice in one day. I could see Geoff felt awkward and he disappeared again, probably intending to stay away for the entire evening. I didn't blame him. Claire needed to hear her father say that he would support her but she needed her mum more.

Claire flicked on the television and watched some ridiculous programme about a fat man in Mexico. The man had issues and without some serious attention to diets, exercise and extensive surgery, this man was going to die. It was exactly the kind on nonsense Claire needed to watch. Not only did it take her mind off the impending decision but it also made her see how little her problem was in comparison to someone else's. I hoped that watching this man's courage would incite her to consider keeping the baby.

Pam was not the type to collapse on a sofa in front of a television but at that moment, I don't think she was capable of doing anything else. So the three of us sat and watched mind numbingly boring television.

I was beginning to tire and almost as soon as I closed my eyes, I was woken by an almighty noise from the bar. It grew louder and louder and then I realised that was because it was coming nearer. It sounded like fighting. I couldn't make out words, there were more grunts and shouts than actual conversation from the men. Geoff appeared first and tried to barricade the door but he was an older man and no match for a strong young man like Darren.

Claire screamed as both men tumbled into the lounge. Pam jumped up and started kicking Darren. As the two men rolled over and twisted and turned, she sometimes kicked the wrong man and kept apologising. From a distance, this would have been hysterical but I knew what was a stake here – a baby's life.

Darren's strength won through and as he straddled Geoff and pinned him to the hideous carpet, Darren just screamed. "For fuck's sake you prick, let me just talk to her." Pam wasn't sure of the best course of action. Now Darren had control over Geoff, kicking the youth possibly wasn't the right approach.

"Get off him Darren." Claire suddenly found her voice and her nerve and stood up to this bully. "I said get off him."

Darren climbed off and Geoff rolled over. He wasn't seriously hurt but his pride had been ripped apart. He couldn't protect his daughter from this monster. His age was his weakness and he looked utterly defeated. Pam helped him up and then Claire turned to the pair of them and said softly.

"Can I just have a moment alone with him please?"

Her parents dutifully left and although they said nothing, they gave the young man a glare of hatred.

Finally I got a good look at the infamous Darren but when I saw his face, I was relieved to see that he wasn't Verity's son. Agreed, the last few weeks of my life had been coincidences after coincidences but I had hoped that Verity had pulled her family together and now I could go on believing that.

"Babe. I'm so pleased that you gave me another chance."

Before the youth had a chance to continue, Claire slapped him round the face. He looked shocked and his initial reaction was to punch her right back but thankfully he had enough sense to know that wasn't the best way. I watched his clenched fist shake by his side.

"What the fucks that for?" He rubbed his cheek and stared at her. He was angry but he was keeping his temping in check.

"You arsehole. I left you that letter this morning because I thought you loved me and because I thought we could bring this baby up together as a family but after that torrent of abuse you hurled down the phone earlier, I know there's no love at all. It takes two to make a baby and it wasn't all my fault." She looked really angry and defiant. Her pretty brown eyes looked dark and menacing now.

"Look babe." I was impressed that this fool was keeping calm, although I could tell any minute now, he was going to explode. I just hoped that Geoff had some lads ready to sort him out. "I do love you. The baby was a shock, that's all. Hey listen if you want to keep the child then I'll be with you every step of the way."

For a second, a glimmer of hope sparkled in Claire's eyes but she realised that this was a pipe dream and that this guy wasn't ever going to support her and love her like she needed. I agreed with her. This was a boy, not a man. He hadn't had the courage to deal with the fear of an unwanted pregnancy and at the first sight of trouble he had given her an earful. He wasn't what she needed.

"Get out." GET OUT." She yelled at him and he flinched. She pointed to the door and shouted again, "GET OUT YOU PIG."

Although the idiot in front of me was just a boy, he wasn't entirely stupid. He recognised defeat and mentally he weighed up his options. Downstairs were a bunch of rowdy men who would easily take the side of the landlord, just for the price of a pint. His fingers were still itching to give this female the punishment she deserved but only his sweaty hands were giving away this secret. His face looked honest and upset and I could tell that Claire had nearly fallen for his charm. I wasn't sure exactly what had been said on the phone that morning but the lad had done enough damage to hang himself.

He slunk out of the lounge and I heard him trotted down to the bar area. There was a muffled exchange of words and then thundering footsteps toward the upstairs flat.

"You ok?" Geoff looked out of breath and anxious but seeing Claire in one piece, he sighed deeply.

"Yes Dad I'm fine. Thank you." She gave him a hug and I could just about hear he whisper "I love you daddy" as his bear hug nearly swallowed her.

Pam rushed in and just said, "what happened?"

"Nothing mum. It's over with Darren and I have made my decision. I am going to keep the baby, that's if you don't mind helping me out?" She smiled thinly at them, desperately hoping they would approve.

"Oh baby." Geoff hugged her even tighter. "Of course we'll be here for you."

"Yes sweetheart. There's plenty of room for a little one here and you didn't do so badly growing up in a pub, did you?" Her mother looked as pleased as punch.

I was over the moon. A new little human being was granted the right to live, not that Darren had really helped the process.

Geoff beamed as he returned to the bar and Pam and Claire snuggled up on the sofa. The day had been exhausting enough without further heavy discussions so the brief sentences between soaps only covered light topics such as names, gender, colour schemes and the fact that the spare room used for housing drunken customers would now have to reserved as a nursery.

I was so happy. Calmness resumed and the chaos of the last few days disintegrated. I felt so relaxed and a little light-headed. I realised that my fuel level was low and hoped that someone spotted this before it ran out all together.

I decided to sleep and make the most of the peaceful evening.

CHAPTER 25

When I woke up, it was morning and Claire was nowhere to be seen. Pam was plumping up the cushions on the sofa. Claire must have gone off to work. Her bag had gone.

Pam spotted me on the coffee table and she picked me up along with the empty packet of cigarettes and a dirty ashtray. She gave the table a quick wipe and took the handful down stairs to the bar. I was propped up at the back of the counter. From this position I could see the entire pub. It was great. I could watch all the regulars and just maybe overhear some more information about Whin.

It was still early as the pub wasn't yet open. I could hear Geoff bottling up a bit further along and decided to take the opportunity of travelling back in time to that conversation between Whin and Tom.

• •

FLASHBACK

• •

Tom looked totally captivated. At the beginning, he had wearily listened to Whin's sorry love affair but how the tables had turned. Tom was champing at the bit, to get the full story out of his friend.

"Come on Whin. What happened?"

"Ok Tom." Whin looked up and thanked the waitress as she delivered two mugs of coffee. "Well I started ringing up every day, asking about Cerys and demanding to know when my next visit was allowed. Mel was being cautious. I can see now that she might have even been suffering from the baby blues, like she said but she started making it more and more difficult. I would pop round and either no one would be in or no one would open the door. Sometimes for days on end my calls would go unanswered. When she did pick up she would claim she had been staying with friends or family. It was getting to a point that I would be lucky to see her once a fortnight. For a man completely addicted to his newborn daughter, it was torture. I wanted to become the sort of father I had seen on TV. The kind that is modern thinking, you know changing nappies, giving baths and reading stories, that sort of thing. I was being denied Tom and I was so angry."

"So what did you do about it?" Tom hadn't even touched his coffee. He was too caught up in the tale.

"Well I did go and chat with my solicitor in the end. I didn't want to make things difficult but I had no idea what my rights were and what I could about them. I was desperate Tom." It was almost as if Whin needed Tom to have the same opinion.

"Totally Whin. I would have done the same thing." Spurred on by Tom's assurance he carried on.

"Well the solicitor gave me some advice. I was entitled to see my daughter and if Mel was unwilling then the case could be taken to the family courts where the magistrate would decide. I couldn't imagine for one minute that Mel would let things go that far. I asked my solicitor to write her a letter. I was hoping that the threat would be enough for her to compromise."

"I waited a month Tom. Can you imagine being separated from your own child for a month? It was horrendous. I was so tempted to just block out the pain with several bottles of whiskey but I just couldn't take the risk. All I could think of was Mel using my drink problem against me. I tell you what Tom, my view of her was getting dimmer by the day."

Both men sipped their coffees although they must have been quite cold by now. The weighty conversation was taking its toll and both Whin and Tom looked shattered. Although I guess the previous night could have had something to do with that.

"Anyway by the end of the month and two official letters later, Mel calls me to say I can see Cerys and would I help pay for a cot. Well Tom. I took my chance. I said that I would only give her some financial support, if I could see my daughter. That's fair isn't it?"

Tom nodded and kept staring at Whin, waiting for the next instalment. Whin shook his head and said, "What is the world coming to when you have to blackmail the mother of your child into permitting visitations? I ask you."

"What did you she say Whin?"

"Well Thomas, my old friend, at first she agreed. The next day I went round with a bundle of notes for some baby equipment and I cuddled Ceryl for hours. Well actually it was about an hour because then Mel said she had to go out. I offered to babysit but of course I wasn't allowed. I didn't mind at that point Tom. I'd spent some time with my beautiful girl and I was floating on air as I walked down her garden path."

"So it all worked out?" Tom looked hopeful.

"Oh no Tom. It was all a ruse to get some money. How low is that?"

• •

FLASHBACK

• •

CHAPTER 26

I must have been daydreaming when the door were opened because when I came to, I noticed that the bar already had five customers, most of whom were half way through their first drinks.

I looked around to see if I knew anyone but at this time of day, it was too early for any of Whin's old mates to meet up. I enjoyed listening to the banter of the clientele though. It took me back. It felt great to be close to Whin again. I could see him at the bar on a stool, supping his pint and smoking like a trooper. I could almost hear him too, discussing the old days to anyone who would listen. He never talked about Mel or Cerys though. Apart from that conversation with Tom, they were never mentioned. Maybe Mel's betrayal had pushed him over the edge and he missed Cerys too much.

The day drew on and more and more customers entered the Cock Inn. I could tell lunchtime was on us as the food orders mounted up and Geoff had to shout up at Pam to get a move on. I knew they had a young lad helping in the kitchen. I had seen him in his whites and checked trousers. He looked the part and maybe by believing he was working in a top class restaurant somehow transformed his dishes. It worked though. The Cock Inn had a reputation for being a gastro pub and as the prices weren't too high, people flocked in for a taste of their steak and kidney pudding or fisherman's pie. The trouble was there was no specific dining area and if punters just drinking took up tables, neither Pam not Geoff could do anything about it. No free tables meant turning away hungry mouths. I wondered why they hadn't done something about this before. To the side of the pub was a huge car park. They could easily build a conservatory to be used solely as a dining area. Maybe the cost was worrying Geoff. I wished I could tell him what a golden opportunity he was missing.

The lunchtime crowd disappeared and the graveyard shift began. Most pubs have a dip in the numbers after lunch and before work ends but not the Cock Inn. There were a particular bunch of old codgers that turned up most afternoons from around 3pm onwards. This was the moment I had been waiting for. I just sat and waited and prayed that someone from Whin's past would remember me and save the day.

At about 4:30, I still hadn't seen anyone I recognised. I was focussing so much that I missed a conversation Geoff had with a customer. Before I knew it, Geoff had picked me up and handed me over to a guy in a pale blue t-shirt. I wanted to scream. This was so unfair. I was so close, it hurt.

There was nothing I could do. The guy lit his cigar and I sat on the counter. The view wasn't as good but hope grew again when I realised that by being nearer to the public, I would be more easily spotted and identified.

The graveyard shift came and went and I saw no one I knew. About 7pm, the man with the blue t-shirt picked me up and stuffed me in his pocket along with a wallet and a bunch of keys. I didn't really get a good look at the man's face but I sensed he was older than he looked. His attempt to stay looking sprightly didn't just end with bright clothing, he had taken time out to dye his greying hair and I thought that possibly a few sun beds might have been on the shopping list. He looked strange actually. It wasn't just the 'mutton dressed as lamb', which so many older women adopt. In fact it actually made him look gay. I sensed that he was straight and the wedding band on his left hand was indeed the real McCoy and not a token of a civil partnership.

My heart sank as we left the pub. I felt in my heart that I wouldn't be coming back. Neither Pam nor Geoff remembered me. I saw no one during the graveyard shift that would have been close to Whin and my last chance to be reunited with Dan was over.

I could see very little but I could just about make out the route the man was taking. We were walking out of the car park and along the main road. As I watched the shop windows go past, I drifted back to Tom and Whin.

• •

FLASHBACK

• •

"So, did you take her to court?" I was just as keen to hear how Whin dealt with this double betrayal.

"Funny you should say that Tom. I went straight to the solicitor's office the next morning. I think he liked me and although he didn't come right out and say it, he hinted at the fact he had maintenance and contact issues. He told me that we needed to proceed. The only way to get Mel to see sense was to go to a court of law. I was really frightened Tom. I wasn't sure how she was going to react to this."

Whin stuck his hand in the air and motioned for the waitress to return. He ordered another two coffees. Neither Whin not Tom had drunk much from the first cups, maybe they were just a little too cold.

"Yes but Whin. She should just have let you see her and then she wouldn't have had to go to court. Why is that so difficult to understand?" Tom looked angry that this woman had given Whin such a hard time for trying to be a good father.

"I know that and you know that but Mel was going through something. I don't know what she was thinking. Maybe Al dying had affected her more that I realised and with Ceryl being born and all the baby blues, it just tipped her over the edge."

"I think you are giving her far too much benefit of the doubt. I bet you, if it had been the other way round, she'd have dragged you to court the minute she could."

"Now now Tom. Not all women are like Mel. You've got to remember this was all out of character for her. Well maybe the Mel I had got to know was the pretend one. Oh I don't know anymore."

"So go on then. Did you get to court? What happened? Did they give you visiting rights?"

"Slow down old boy." Whin chuckled but then his face became grave. "Yes I took the decision that if I wanted to see Cerys and have a proper relationship with her, I was going to have to force the issue. The solicitor did what Solicitors do and arranged a date with the court. It took ages though and meanwhile I was out of my mind. All I could think of was Cerys. Her smell, her little fingers clenched round mine, the way her eyes looked like my mother's. Oh Tom. I almost went crazy."

The coffee arrived and this time both men paused to add sugar and stir their mugs. They each took a sip and Tom waited for Whin to continue.

"Eventually the day arrived. I hadn't slept for two nights and I looked rough so I decided to dress in a suit. I've only got one now, just for funerals and things but I thought it would make me look more serious. I wanted to be taken seriously. You see Tom one of the reasons I was so restless was that I could imagine the magistrates laughing at me, you know about my age. Let's face it, I looked more like a grandfather or even a great grandfather!"

"Oh stop it Whin. You're not that old. In fact I'm older than you and I'm only just a grandfather!"

Whin smiled but it didn't reach his eyes. I had a feeling that the worse of the story was about to revealed. "Well I got to the court about an hour earlier than asked but I was so nervous that I just pounded the pavement in front. I knew how many steps there were between each of those huge sycamores. I sat on the wooden bench in front of that contemporary statue and I even bought a coffee from the vending machine but it was just so vile, I had to throw it away."

"Did she agree in the end? Did she see the light?"

"No Tom. She didn't. In fact she didn't even turn up."

• •

FLASHBACK

• •

CHAPTER 27

Whilst I had been taking a trip down memory lane, Mr Blue Shirt had taken a trip up to the cemetery. My suspicious nature woke me up and I watched his journey very carefully. He seemed to know where he was going. It didn't appear to be an amble. He was taking very determined steps to a specific destination.

I recognised this path. A bit further along on the left was Whin's grave. I struggled to catch the man's face. Maybe I did know him. I caught his profile and desperately tried to imagine his hair being flecked with grey or even white. The harsh black dye he had used not only looked a fake colour but to me it didn't even look like real hair. It could quite easily be mistaken for a wig. Besides he had dyed his ears by mistake and the colourant had stained the top ridges and make him resemble a gorilla.

If I hadn't been so excited, so curious and hopeful, I would have found the whole matter utterly hilarious but right now I had to concentrate. What could I do to bring Whin's grave to attention? I sighed deeply. Nothing.

We were approaching the grave now and I was concentrating on his plot so much, I didn't notice two hooded youths leaning against a tree opposite.

"Oi poof." I heard one of them shout. The other one laughed and they both started yelling obscenities at my new owner. I knew he looked a little too effeminate and these boys had picked up on it. The fact he had his yellow jumper tied round his neck and a small dyed moustache just didn't really help his cause. Not that I have anything against homosexuals. I have met some great characters in the past and have often felt frustrated that I couldn't have a proper friendship with them. I just happen to think life isn't about your sexual preferences and standing out in a crowd is fine if you have the confidence to take the comments. If you can't handle the attention, then it's probably best not to be too conspicuous. Human nature dictates that there are some rotten apples amongst you and bullying is inevitable. Knowing this and taunting the bullies is plain stupid, as far as I can tell.

My friend tried to ignore the jibes and even carried on mincing down the gravelled path. We were nearly opposite Whin's grave and all I could do was watch the events occur, powerless to stop them.

A can half full of lager flew threw the air. I had spotted it but poor old Mr Blue Shirt was concentrating on moving away from these louts as quickly as possible. The consequence of that was that he didn't see the object until it struck him on the side of his head. He was lucky, a couple more inches to the right and he would have been killed outright. Maybe in retrospect that would have been easier. The lads laughed to see this older man stumble. Mr Blue Shirt automatically threw his hand up to his head to check the damage. When he brought his hand down, it was covered in blood. I felt quite woozy at this point. I'm no good with blood. Silly really as I love boxing and don't mind watching a fight but this was different. Mr Blue Shirt was no match for these two hooligans. I was horrified at their behaviour. What kind of parents brought up children to disrespect others so violently?

Poor Mr Blue Shirt looked terrified. His path was now blocked. One boy stood in front and obstructed the way ahead whilst the other lad stood behind him. I could only imagine what would happen next. Here we were in a deserted cemetery with two adolescents intent on causing havoc and one man who was slightly too camp for their liking. Whichever I looked at it, it was going to end in disaster.

Mr Blue Shirt held up his arms in surrender. "Please. Please leave me alone. I have ten pounds which you can take but I don't have anything else."

"Shut it faggot" They both shouted out at the same time. "We don't want your stinking money."

Mr Blue Shirt ignored them and reached for his wallet in the back pocket of his beige chino style trousers. He was being clever. He removed the cards and threw the wallet a fair distance from him. I knew what he intended. I have heard many times that one tip when you find yourself in a mugging situation is to throw the money away from you. Whilst the thief goes after the cash, you have an opportunity to run away. On this occasion it wasn't going to work. Not only were the boys totally disinterested in his wallet, but even if one picked it up, the other lad was still very much keeping an eye on his prey.

Realising that he was trapped Mr Blue Shirt staggered back on the path but he lost his footing and fell against a headstone. I couldn't read the inscription but I knew it wasn't Whin's. It was too soon for the headstone to be in place. Strange how the mind works really. I should have been concentrating on the fate of this poor man yet all that came to the fore, was whether of not Mr Blue Shirt was desecrating Whin's grave.

The taller of the two boys, dressed in a blue Nike hooded top turned to his partner in crime and asked "So what now Sy?"

"Shut up you prick" came the terse reply. "Do you want this dickhead to know our names?"

"If you leave me alone, I swear that I won't tell a soul. Please leave me alone. Please" I felt sorry for Mr Blue Shirt. He was snivelling now, which is never a good look for a man. He was on his hands and knees. The blood was still oozing from the wound on his head and his arms and face were smeared with mud.

The shorter, more aggressive boy suddenly lurched forward and kicked my friend. "Fucking shut up you ponce." The boy was angry and I kept feeling that this resentment had nothing to do with Mr Blue Shirt. It felt as though there was something much deeper that was unresolved and still caused him serious anguish. I could only hazard a guess and suppose that in his past, he had been abused by an older gentleman, possibly one that looked quite similar to my friend. It would explain his severe dislike of homosexuals and this man in particular.

Mr Blue Shirt groaned as the troubled boy kicked him again and again. The first attack had been aimed at his face. He had caught him on the forehead and I wondered if something had broken as I heard a cracking noise. The second kick was directed further down and connected with Mr Blue Shirt's chest. This winded him and I heard the air escape from his lungs.

The taller lad was standing, doing nothing. His face was a picture and looked totally horrified. Jeering and making fun was one thing but serious assault had not been on the cards and even though the shorter boy called for his assistance a couple of times, he was very reluctant to have anything to do with it.

Sy stood back and looked at the mess he had created. Mr Blue Shirt looked like he needed serious medical attention. I could see he was still breathing but it was laboured and I suddenly wondered if this man suffered with a dodgy heart. The pain and stress that these two yobs were causing would easily be enough to bring on a stroke or a heart attack, especially if he was frail.

Sy looked like he had no intention of giving up yet. His eyes looked cold and determined. There was still work to be done but thankfully the older boy had decided that enough was enough and pushed the little thug back to other side of the path. Shorty struggled but although he was the one with the serious temper, the taller boy had more strength and managed to hold him back.

Mr Blue Shirt seemed to come too and realised that this was possibly his only opportunity to escape. He dragged himself onto his feet, using the headstone as support. One eye was cut badly and he was desperately trying to wipe the blood from his other eye to ensure he had enough vision to make a clear getaway.

Shorty spotted his victim getting up and with one final surge of power, he broke free and ran over to my friend. With a powerful punch he swung round and thumped Mr Blue Shirt on his bad side and my friend flew back and hit the headstone with a sickening crunch. The impact jolted me from his pocket and I flew through the air before landing on soft grass. It was a soft landing and fortunately for me, there was no damage. I was low on fluid but apart from that, I was fine.

I could see my friend slumped on the ground and had a horrible sneaking feeling that he had just taken his last breath. The two boys suddenly realised that they had gone too far and with a panic, sprinted off down the cemetery path, back the way we had come.

I wondered how long it would be before Mr Blue Shirt was discovered. It could be hours, in fact it could even be tomorrow.

There was nothing I could do. I was pretty sure he was a goner. The last few minutes had been terrifying and I wanted to catch my breath. As I lay on the grass, I looked around me. In front was the very still body of Mr Blue Shirt. To my left was a grave. I couldn't quite read the words on the tombstone but a pretty bouquet of white lilies lay on the grassy mound.

To my right was a hole. The gravediggers had prepared this for an upcoming funeral and I thought to myself how ironic if Mr Blue Shirt had fallen back into this grave. The mourners would have had quite a shock.

I struggled to see what was behind me but with a sudden realisation, it dawned on me that I was sat on Whin's grave. I was in shock for a few minutes and couldn't concentrate. For all this time I had wanted to get back to my dear old friend and now here I was, on his grave. Joy tinged with extreme sadness overcame me and I sobbed and sobbed. My fluid was dangerously low but I didn't care. As far as I was concerned, my journey had ended.

As I lay on the grass, I thought back to the last conversation with Tom.

• •

FLASHBACK

• •

"You're kidding me?" Tom looked astounded that someone could flout the law so brazenly.

"Oh I wish I was Tom, I wish I was." Whin hung his head and I noticed that tears had welled up in his eyes. By reliving this trauma, his emotions had got the better of him.

"Hey mate. You'll get it sorted. She can't just do that. You have rights." Tom held his arm.

Whin snivelled for a bit and a few of the other customers had noticed Whin's eruption of tears and had turned to look at him. Whin was oblivious but Tom was feeling a little uncomfortable. I could tell he wanted to protect his friend and had to bite his lip to stop himself shouting out and telling these nosy bastards to mind their own business.

"Tom." Whin had found his voice again. "It's over mate."

"Hey don't give up. Let me help you. I'm sure we can find a better lawyer who is more experienced in these matters." Tom looked desperate to assist.

Whin just shook his head. "You don't understand."

Tom became quite agitated and blurted out. "Listen I'm not going to stand by and let this woman take you for a ride. You can't give up and I won't let you." The determination on Tom's face was a far cry from the weary listener who had first sat down with Whin.

Whin looked up at Tom. His eyes were red and his face was wet. He looked totally unashamed of his state in such a public place. "Tom. Listen to me. It's over because Cerys is dead."

Both Tom and I were shocked into silence. I wanted to cry. The poor man. That's why his grief had been so raw. I just didn't know how Tom was going to react or how on earth he would even begin comforting him.

Tom just stared. He was unable to speak. I could tell he just hadn't been expecting that. All his anger had dissipated and I could tell he was on the brink of tears.

Whin began speaking but I could tell there was a huge lump in his throat and his voice sounded slightly distorted. "The lawyer took me to one side and told me that earlier that morning, Mel had been on her way to take Cerys to her aunt's, or something, for her to babysit whilst she came to court. She was up on that big roundabout when a lorry hit Mel's car side on and Cerys was killed instantly."

Whin paused to compose himself and Tom grabbed both his arms. "What about Mel?" It was about all he could mutter.

Whin shook his head. "She's fine. Well she broke her nose and has severe whiplash but she's ok."

"Oh my God Whin." Tom was totally unprepared for this and had no idea how to help.

"I just can't help thinking that it is all my fault. If I hadn't pushed her into court proceedings and just let matters run their course, maybe she would have grown to trust me with Cerys and my beautiful baby girl would still be here."

Whin broke down at this point. It was true what Tom and Geoff had said yesterday. He had needed to get it off his chest but at the time neither of them had had any concept of just how painful his tale would be. Tom had no idea what to do but he called the waitress over and asked for the bill.

"Hey listen. You are not to blame. You had nothing to do with it." Both Tom and I were suddenly worried. Guilt was always a normal part of the death of a loved one but Whin seemed to believe he was seriously to blame.

As Tom threw £20 on the table he took Whin's arm and guided him outside. He was aware that the gaze of the other clientele was growing by the minute and like all rubber-neckers, they were dying to know what the upset was all about.

Whin and Tom walked slowly out of the door and along the pavement. We turned a corner and there was the park I had visited on my first day with Whin. We made our way over to a bench and Tom let Whin sit and sob. He knew it had to be done.

Mourning is a strange process and it affects different people in different ways and at different times. Now Whin had finally got the entire story off his chest, he could begin the grieving process. It would take years to heal, if ever, but each day would make the pain become slightly easier to cope with.

• •

FLASHBACK

• •

Thinking about Whin's sad tale reminded me of how much I missed him. I couldn't even begin to imagine the pain he had encountered and I knew that he had never really recovered. Here he was though, below me and I could only hope that he was now with his beautiful Cerys again.

About The Authors

Anna Hyndman-Lahna lives in Essex with her husband Damey, three daughters and Beryl the cat. Figure of 8 was based on idea by Graeme Milne.

"Writing this book was an utter joy. Telling the tale of Whin and his faithful companion was a smooth ride and thoroughly enjoyable. The story only took six months to complete but a few years to get to the publishers! Over a few drinks in a familiar drinking establishment in the West End of London, Graeme announced the core idea for the book and asked me to then create the story and write the book for him. On the odd occasion, when suffering from writers block, I turned to Graeme and my husband for inspiration and received huge encouragement and support. I enjoyed the process so much, I may just have to write another!!"

Graeme Milne lives in Surrey with his wife Lucy and two boys.

"The storyline for this book has bounced around my head for quite a few years. My wife has often heard the idea for the book chatted about at parties and in bars and thought it was as pipedream. One of those conversations was with Anna, and finally I had my co-author. This is one of many ideas and we all wonder which one will make it on to the page next."